Speak to Her Kindly

A Novel of the Anabaptists

Jonathan Rainbow

Third Edition, 2010

Preface to the Reader

In historical fiction, to which *genre* this novel belongs, a fictional story is imbedded in true historical events. There are, in other words, some things that really happened and some things that didn't. Usually the things that really happened "feel" like history, and the author's fictional tale "feels" more imaginative, more contrived, more fantastic or preposterous. But in this novel it's the other way around: the most unbelievable events, persons, and details are the things that are true. And I feel some obligation to assure readers that the Münster story as I tell it is historical, even to its most incredible details.

Paulus, Marga, Onkel Langshammer, and the Montau community are my creations, though refugee settlements like Montau did exist in Moravia in the 1530s, and Anabaptists did in fact take the commands of Christ literally and suffer the brutal afflictions which I describe. Anabaptists were scattered by persecution across central Europe, so there is nothing inherently unlikely about Paulus' and Marga's long, inexorable journey west, or back to Moravia again. A few of the Münster characters – Julius Fettbauch, Arndt Manns, Ari, the woodcarrier – are mine, but the public figures – Matthys, Bockelson, Knipperdolling, Rothmann, the Krechtings, and so forth – are historical. The prince-bishop Franz von Waldeck and his captains – historical. The military events, their dates, their results – historical. Heinrich Gresbeck, the cabinetmaker who showed von Waldeck the way into the city, later wrote one of the two eyewitness accounts of the story. The religious ravings, the trances of Bockelson, the theocratic punishments, the communism, the polygamy, the promises of cobblestones turning to bread, the dinner table with pegs and holes – historical. Bockelson really had sixteen wives; I've added Marga to their number. The starvation, the games and diversions, the final bloodbath, and the executions of Bockelson and his henchmen all happened as I describe them. The three bodies were hung in iron cages from St. Lambert's Church and remained there until the 1880s; the cages are still there as a tourist attraction, and some of the weapons and artifacts of Bockelson's kingdom are on display near a tourist desk. In the minds of many Germans, the name "Anabaptist" is still synonymous with violent fanaticism, communism, and polygamy, so powerful is the impress of the Münster event.

In short, the most fantastic sounding things in this novel are true. So, while Paulus and Marga did not exist, the fiery cauldron of tribulation through which their marriage and love proceed in my story did exist, and it is at least possible that some real believers, if they were not spiritually and physically consumed by the red frenzy of Jan Bockelson's kingdom, if by the grace of God they made it through the purging with their faith still whole, learned – like Paulus and Marga – to speak to each other more kindly.

Jonathan Rainbow
Visalia, California

CHAPTER 1: CHAOS

April-October, 1529. Paris to Moravia.

Paulus Ketterling watched a man burn to death, and it seemed to Paulus that the wretched man's smoke and cries ascended to an empty heaven.

The executioner was lighting fire to the tinder when Paulus came to the Place Maubert on the way back to his room. Paulus stood with the gawking, gaping crowd, transfixed, and watched. The cone-shaped, yellow paper hat on the man's head – with its single word *Heretic* – was the first thing to ignite. Then the man's shirt. Then the man's life went up in a glowing column of heat and pain and dancing, quivering air.

Feeling suddenly empty himself, Paulus stopped studying and attended no more lectures. He wandered the noisy, dirty alleys of Paris's Latin Quarter at night, brooding and uneasy, and slept by day. Then came the inevitable summons. In a single afternoon of April 1529, Paulus threw away his education at the University of Paris, and with it his future as a man of power and prestige in the church.

He stood before the rector of the College des Lombards, a soft-spoken but dogmatic Dominican monk. The rector sat behind a table piled with manuscripts. They spoke in Latin.

"What is your problem, my son?" asked the rector in his best confessorial tone, without looking up. "It is reported that you no longer attend lectures."

"I can't continue here," said Paulus. Now the rector's eyes rolled up.

"You are almost finished with your course of study. I have already sent letters of introduction to the bishop of Bamberg on your behalf. Your career, your family's history and reputation, so much to think of. And the church needs dependable leaders now, as never before, with the Lutheran heresy."

"I have considered these things," said Paulus.

"Then I counsel you to stay, and finish." For the rector, this was the last word. He began to turn his attention back to his manuscript.

"I can't."

The rector frowned at the insubordination. "Why?"

"The God of this place, the God of the lectures, the God of Paris, your God – this God is not one I can serve or love anymore." Paulus had considered this statement carefully.

The rector squinted. "This is the God of the Holy Catholic Church you are talking about, my son. He is the only true God. To deny him is to invite damnation."

"The damnation is already here," said Paulus coldly. Then he began to speak straight from his insides, and there was a hard edge of anger in his voice. "The poor man who died at the stake last month found his hell right here, didn't he. That was your God's work. You were there, blessing his torture. You and most of the faculty. Your God was silent in heaven while the man screamed out his life."

The rector was a man of iron self control; he chose not to be provoked by a student. "This is a very serious situation," he said quietly. "Your father must be informed."

The rector placed Paulus in custody in the abbey and sent

off a courier to Paulus' father, the Count von Malbeck. Three weeks later the courier returned with two of the count's own knights. An arrangement was negotiated. The rector would allow Paulus to withdraw from the university; all records of his matriculation there would be erased; and, out of consideration for the long service of the Ketterling family to the Pope and the Holy Catholic Church, the rector would not bring charges of heresy against this youngest Ketterling son. It would be as if his three and a half years at the University of Paris had never happened. The count's knights escorted Paulus back to Malbeck in Württemberg. Paulus had avoided lethal danger by a hair; others, less important, less connected, were being burned to death in Paris for departures from the Catholic faith. Paulus had seen it happen.

At Malbeck, Paulus and his father were alone together in the ancestral castle. Paulus' mother was dead and his older brother Franz was off soldiering in Italy. The count was enraged that Paulus had disgraced the family and wasted his chance at a life in the church. They argued several times. Their violent words flew past each other like errant projectiles.

Late one night Paulus walked away from Malbeck, going east. He had no money. He had no destination. He had lost his future and his home and his father and his God.

He moved among the placeless people now, people who did not belong to a city, or an estate, or a monastery, but who lived along the rutted roads of Germany: thieves, cutthroats, lapsed monks, idiots, runaway serfs, magicians, gypsies, peddlers, jugglers, acrobats, lunatics, bigamists, debtors, minstrels and atheists. He begged for food, in villages and at monasteries, and when he grew weary of begging he began to steal. Dogs chased him, and wandering, bloodthirsty soldiers shot at him, and peasants cursed him. He spent a night in a town square with his head in a pillory and a sign saying *Vagrant* hung from his neck. The whole world seemed to Paulus like a belligerent, snarling beast.

Through the summer, Paulus followed the Danube river eastward to Vienna, and there he turned north through the valley of the Morava river into the region of Moravia. Castles of German warlords sat on high places, watching for the Turks from the east. He skirted the city of Olmütz. Then he left the cultivated river valley and climbed into the foothills of the Carpathian mountains. Autumn was here, and winter was coming with its prospect for Paulus of death by freezing in the desolate hills. But the desolation had its own beauty to Paulus, for in it he was beyond the cities and the villages and the organized world with its Catholic God. Beyond the snarling.

Several days after passing Olmütz, and well into the hills, Paulus came upon a strange thing. He stood for a long time and simply gazed. He was looking at a large section of cleared forest and in the clearing a complex of neat, geometric buildings made of logs. The building nearest him was a large shed with a single-pitched roof, surrounded by a jumble of carts, barrels, planks, and crates. Farthest from him was another large building with shuttered windows and a wide stick-and-wattle chimney that sent up a slender spire of smoke. These two buildings formed the ends of the settlement. Connecting them were two long rows of small apartments, each with its own chimney. All doors opened toward a central, grassy area, like a city square, laced with footpaths.

The whole place seemed contrived, artificial, and alien. No dirty, cobbled, narrow streets. No dogs or beggars. No church building with tower and bell; no pillory for public humiliations, or gibbet for executions.

Paulus observed this strange place on a warm, gusty October afternoon. A rain storm was coming from the west, with clouds piling up in the sky behind a quickening breeze. In the settlement, as Paulus watched it from the edge of the forest, people moved quickly to prepare for rain. Voices filled the air. A man was on all fours on the shed with a hammer in hand, shouting now and then to someone inside, checking the building for leaks in the roof. Several women with shocks of mown wheat in their arms hurried back from the field. Men on the far side of the clearing drove a few sheep into a pen made of split rails, screaming and switching at the animals. Others carried wheeled plows, carts, bags, ropes, and other implements into the shed. They yelled and laughed and gesticulated.

Paulus was hungry. He sat cross-legged on a sheepskin that he carried with him as blanket, pillow, and haversack, and he watched the storm approach and the people scurry to the shelter of the large building on the far end.

He waited, impassive, patient as an animal, while the wind gusted about him and the rain burst upon him in warm, drenching drops.

Then, in the rain, in the twilight, Paulus crept across the open field, past a manure heap, past the pen where the sheep watched him dumbly and their heads turned in unison to follow him, and he came to the storage shed.

Inside the building he could see nothing. It smelled of organic things – grass, wheat, chaff, manure. He felt his way along the wall with his hands, finding scythes, rakes, and pitchforks. He bumped into a handcart filled with new hay. Eventually he found what he was really looking for, a pile of threshed wheat in the back corner of the shed. It would feed him for many days; he would boil it in the small iron pot he carried on his belt until it was swollen and soft, and it would fill his stomach wonderfully, and with roasted lamb it would be a feast. He could almost taste it. He took off his sheepskin, laid it dry side up on the ground, and piled grain onto it with his hands until it would hold no more; then he picked it up by its corners, slung it over his back, and turned to find his way out the door.

A flash of torchlight in the doorway. Two men, large bodies in jerking light and shadow. Paulus shrank back against the wall, trying to make himself invisible among the sacks and tools.

"Dry wood, dry wood," said one man. "You'd think Krem

could have taken some from the woodpile before the storm."

"He was patching the roof here," said the other.

"Oh," said the first with a grunt and bent over, searching among the barrels and bags and piles for a few pieces of dry wood while the other held the torch for him.

"Here we are." He gathered up an armload of sticks until it reached his chin. "This should keep the soup warm."

"And Katrina happy," said the other.

They turned to leave, then stopped in the doorway.

"Is everything dry? Onkel told us to check." He held the torch as high as he could and they scanned the contents of the shed and the roof above. Just a moment of silence, just one more moment of invisibility, and the men would be gone, and Paulus would be on his way. He pressed himself further back into the darkness. But one corner of the sheepskin slipped from his grasp and the grain slid with an audible hiss to the ground behind him. He felt it piling up against his leg. The eyes of the two men went immediately toward the source of the sound. They saw him.

I'm a dead man.

Here he was, with no escape. They would surely beat him to death; it was all a thief could expect. They were large, strong men and he was taking their food. The man with the torch swallowed hard and tried not to show his own fear. Woodcarrier broke the silence.

"Come with us to supper. There is no reason for you to steal here."

There were no compartments in Paulus' mind to receive words like this. They came from another world into his world. He stood uncomprehending, unresponding. Woodcarrier spoke again, kindly.

"Come, friend, eat with us. There is plenty and it's almost ready on the table." He waited for an answer but Paulus gave none. "Claus, tell the women to set another place."

Claus left, breathing easier. Paulus dropped his

sheepskin in the corner and came to the side of woodcarrier. Together they went through the dribbling rain the length of the settlement toward the building with the large smoking chimney.

CHAPTER 2: ORDER
October, 1529. Moravia.

Paulus stepped into a spacious room filled with the buzz of many voices and the orange light of oil lamps and the smell of bread. The walls were made of logs, and the floor was hard beaten earth covered with straw. Long trestle tables in rows filled the room; the men sat on one side and the women and children on the other. The sound of conversation fell away when the people saw Paulus, and as woodcarrier led him past the women and children they stared up at him with open, curious faces, like the sheep in the pen. Woodcarrier reached a table of men and stopped, stole a quick glance at Paulus and `then spoke.

"Onkel, this friend is hungry and we have invited him to eat with us."

The man called Onkel turned from his meal with a full mouth and took Paulus in with a steady, inquisitive gaze while he chewed. Onkel was a man in his fifties, with a broad, red face, full lips, and a large, pock-marked nose. His eyes were a watery pale blue and he squinted them as he tried to focus on Paulus. His thin blonde hair was brushed straight back over a large dome of forehead. He chewed his food without hurry and swallowed it bit by bit.

"Where did he come from? Did he fall from the sky?" said Onkel, and laughed.

"We found him in the shed," replied the woodcarrier. Everyone in the room was listening now. A subtle contraction of Onkel's eyes told Paulus that Onkel understood what had happened. He knew that Paulus was a thief. *Now the judgment, now they kill me.* But Onkel said:

"It's good you found our shed. To get out of the storm. Good, good idea." Onkel was chewing, speaking, and smiling at the same time. A fragment of food flew from his mouth. Then he lifted a large hand, and extended an index finger, and commanded: "Get the man a blanket!"

Paulus suddenly felt ashamed. He was dirty and wet and uncivilized, a scarcely human creature from the forest. The people around him were simple and clean, and they were living as humans ought to live, eating together in an ordered arrangement and talking with each other. And he was a thief, and they were treating him kindly even though they knew he was a thief.

"What is your name?" asked Onkel.

"Paulus Ketterling."

Onkel turned to the other people with a public gesture and announced: "Brothers, brothers! We have here one Paulus Ketterling, whom we welcome in the name of Christ to our table." There were many smiles. Onkel's big face had a grin that sparkled from the eyes.

"Come then, sit," he said loudly. "Please, brothers, make room for Herr Ketterling here, next to me." The benches at the table shuffled and banged and an empty place appeared beside Onkel. Paulus stepped over the bench and sat. His sitting made a wet squishing noise.

The women brought Paulus blackbread and watery, salty soup. Paulus ate fast, and when he was almost finished there was suddenly more on the table before him. He kept his eyes on his food. Onkel leaned over.

"My name is Heinrich Langshammer. The people here call me Onkel."

The people around him were mostly young, and as they ate and talked Paulus studied their faces and listened to the relaxed energy of their conversations. They seemed peaceful but somehow sad. There were smiles but not much laughter. There was love and familiarity; Paulus could see it in the way they looked at each other when they listened.

As the eating wound down, the strong drone of conversation diminished to a purr. Onkel sat with his eyes shut. Suddenly he stood and began singing a hymn in German in a strong, even tenor voice. The others in the room joined him after two or three words. And Paulus was engulfed in a music from outside his world. It was a strange sensation; Paulus was used to the singing of trained choirs, and the sound of Latin words ringing bell-like off stone and stained glass, and the glint of marble and gold and silver and the glow of glorious vestments, all sensory simulations of heaven. This was ordinary, common, earthy. The people sang loudly with their unpolished rough-hewn voices, the way people sing songs of harvest and love and homeland and war, with passion and joy, and in words which meant something not only to God but to them. A rolling, warm tide of sound filled the room. Paulus knew that this was a religious event, but what he felt intensely was the humanness of it and his own humanity, for the first time in months.

After finishing the hymn, the people began rearranging the room, stacking tables along the sides and placing the benches in rows near one end of the room where one table was left standing. They took the oil lamps off the tables and hung them on hooks in the walls. Onkel went to the table at the front, sat down behind it, set a leather bound Bible down on it with a thud, and began to study it. As the various tasks were completed, men and women took their places on the benches, men on one side and women on the other. Paulus sat on the back bench of the male side with the blanket he had been given still around his shoulders.

Onkel Langshammer prayed, and then he preached, still sitting, in German. It was about suffering, and following Christ, and carrying a cross. Again, a strange sensation, like a piece of the world turned inside out. These people were obviously not Catholics. They were worshiping their God with nothing but a wooden building and a Bible. All around them were cathedrals and bishoprics and monasteries and the whole hoary paraphernalia of a thousand years of Roman Catholic civilization, and these thirty or forty people were acting as if none of that mattered. The German of Onkel's sermon and their songs was the same German they spoke to their children. The benches they sat on to worship were the benches they sat on to eat. It seemed to Paulus like the partition between the spiritual world and the natural world did not exist here.

They believed that God was among them, speaking to them in German, through an old man with mud on his boots. This felt preposterous to Paulus until the image of another man of God, the rector of his college at his table stacked with books, presented itself to his imagination.

Onkel finished, and they stood, and they all said the *Our Father* together, in German. It sounded new to Paulus. He had never heard it recited in anything but Latin.

The meeting ended as suddenly as it had begun, and the people stirred and separated; husbands and wives found each other and gathered up their children and went to their little cabins by the light of lanterns. Paulus lingered. Woodcarrier said good-night to him as he went out. Finally, only Onkel and Paulus were left; Onkel took the last lamp and Paulus stood and followed him to the open door.

The storm had passed off completely to the east and had left the night in the grip of wintry, rain-washed air, with the promise of frost in the morning. Patches of cloud still hung in the sky as dark, shapeless blots against the stars. The couples went across the clearing with their lights jiggling in the dark. Onkel closed the door.

"Thank you. For your kindness." Paulus meant this from his heart. "It's been a long time since anyone spoke to me kindly."

"You are welcome, very welcome, friend Paulus Ketterling. What we have is simply what God gives us. We don't cling to it tightly, as the world does. Stay with us . . . a night . . . a week. Forever." He paused. "I should tell you that you are in some danger here. If they come to arrest us, they will assume that you are one of us, and you'll have to talk a lot to persuade them otherwise. But as far as we are concerned, you are welcome. Understand?"

Paulus nodded yes and managed a smile.

"I think I must go," said Paulus.

"Where does your journey take you?"

"Back to the forest. Silesia, perhaps. I have never been to Silesia."

"Back to the forest, on such a night? It's too cold!" Onkel rubbed his arms together. "Why must you go back there? Pardon my interest, it's none of my affair, I know, but I'm an old man. We're nosy."

"I don't belong anywhere, not here anyway," said Paulus. "I don't really know where I belong, or where I'm going to stop. But thank you. And thank the others also, the women who cooked, and Claus and . . ."

"Peter."

"Peter. Thank Claus and Peter. I thought they were going to beat me to death. I've never been treated that way before."

"I will thank them for you. That treatment, it is the way of Christ." As Onkel said it, Paulus turned to go. He hoped in his heart that Onkel would reach for him, enfold him in his arms, make him stay. But without Onkel's intervention, the present momentum of Paulus' life would take him back into the forest. Perhaps he would lurk about the place for a few days and watch it from a distance, like the stray cat fed by a kind hand. Onkel let him go, and said, when Paulus was a few steps away:

"Remember, you are welcome here."

Paulus reached the end of the settlement, where he had first entered it. He passed by the shed, where the light had flashed and the wheat had dropped. He stopped just beyond it and watched Onkel Langshammer move to his own house and disappear into it; with a deliberate mental act he noted which door it was, and in that exact moment knew he would go back. He loitered in the wet, brown and beaten meadow grass and considered his next few hours: to be buried in frost and fog, to find a cave, or a crevice, or a couple of fallen logs, and to sleep, damp and alone, a forest creature. A few people in the settlement were making fires and smoke wafted toward Paulus. Onkel's people were getting into beds in warm houses.

It dawned on him that he still had nothing to eat for the next day. The shed was there, full of food, untended, but completely inaccessible to him now. A strange way to cure a man of thievery: give him what he came for.

You are welcome. But was the old man just being polite? And the group was overtly, drastically heretical. But what did that matter to Paulus? *Just one night and then I'll move on toward Silesia.*

He turned just as he reached the edge of the forest. It was a decisive turn, as it had to be. He went back across the cleared field and straight to Onkel's door.

He knocked gently, and Onkel's voice came from within: "Paulus?"

"Yes, it's me."

"Ach, marvelous, you've come back! I'm glad," Onkel said as he opened the door and extended his hand. Paulus took it. The hand was smooth and meaty and the grip was firm.

"Come in, come in. Put your shoes there by the fire, next to mine, they'll be dry by morning." The little compartment had a table in one corner and a chimney and hearth against its back wall, where the single-pitched roof was highest. The dark matted straw on the ground had not been replaced for some time. The fire burned briskly. Against the two side walls were two beds, and a pile of half worked boards lay in a jumbled heap in the middle of the room along with an adze and a saw.

"Now here, you see, there is a bed for you. Two beds in every house. But I have no wife, so there is always room here. When someone comes through Montau, he stays with me." He was going on, as old people do, expressing his happiness with an excess of talk. He felt the bed with his hands to make sure it was ready to be slept in. "Perhaps a little dust, but you don't mind, I'm sure. Might as well be slept in, no?"

Paulus hardly remembered how to get into a real bed. Onkel stood to one side.

"There! Go ahead, son, fall in. You're tired."

Paulus undressed and slid into the bed. It was a simple peasant bed with a straw-sack mattress and several blankets that smelled of lanolin. He stretched his full length; he could feel the nakedness of his skin against the cool wool; he could sleep the whole night through; he would be warm and dry. Onkel put three more logs on the fire and rubbed his big hands together in a happy way and got into his bed. In seconds the fire caught the tiny sap beads on the bark of the wood, and they fried with hisses.

"What are you thinking?" Onkel asked.

"That this is a strange place."

"So it is, if what is around us is normal. If love and peace are strange."

"Oh, they are."

There was a long silence while the fire crackled.

"Who are you?" said Paulus.

"The world calls us Anabaptists these days, among other

things."

Anabaptists. People who refuse to baptize infants. People destructive of the social order. Paulus had heard the term used at the University of Paris, but its connotations in that context bore no resemblance to what he had seen here.

"I am the bishop, the pastor of this congregation," Onkel went on. "Freely elected by the people, freely elected. I have no power over them except the power of the word."

"But you are not from Moravia."

"Ah, you can hear the Swiss! And I can hear the Stuttgart – am I right? – in your speech."

"Near Stuttgart, yes. Malbeck."

There was a long silence, the kind that men feel no need to fill with talk. Puffing, cracking, consuming little sounds came from the fire.

Onkel finally said: "It's a beautiful country that the Lord has exiled us to. Wait until morning, and you will see what I mean. The pine trees up on the hillsides look blue in the morning light. Blue! And you can see it directly out this window. Often I lie here alone and watch."

Alone. He had said that he had no wife.

"Is it against your beliefs to marry? Like the Catholic clergy?" asked Paulus.

"I was a priest in the pope's church, before I believed in Christ. But now my celibacy is voluntary."

"Many priests are marrying these days." Everyone knew that Luther had married a nun, and Paulus was used to the coarse jokes that were made on that subject at the University of Paris.

"I have wanted to be married, God knows how I have wanted to be married," said Onkel, and it was as if Paulus were not in the room. "I watch the people go to their homes together, as tonight I did, and I think how it must be for a man to touch his wife. To nestle into his bed at night next to a woman. One of God's truly good gifts, I think . . . a man and a woman . . .

warm in bed."

"But still, you choose not to marry," prodded Paulus.

"My life is forfeit, you must understand that. My life is on loan. There is not a day goes by when they could not come and take me away. And then, what would become of a wife, or children? I am a marked man. They know my name from Zürich to Prague, and probably in Olmütz as well. And I will not run from them any farther than this." He pointed from his bed to the ground beside it. "There are other bishops like me, men in Switzerland and the Tyrol and Austria, most of them married men. Most of them die, suddenly, horribly. And when that happens they leave widows and fatherless children. Oh, my heart aches for them! I am certainly going to die for my faith, and when I die, I will leave no one bereft." There was a time of silence. Then Onkel said, "Paulus Ketterling, I'm so glad you came back. I really am glad. We will be good friends, and talk. But in the morning. Sleep well."

Paulus heard the old man turn over in the bed, clear the mucous from his nose with a snort, cough, and begin to snore.

The man cared for him with a caring that was more than simple hospitality to a needy stranger. It felt like the old man was reaching for him, and he seemed, in his reaching, almost as alone as Paulus. Paulus lay on his back, and he felt the warmth of his own body begin to suffuse the bed above him and underneath him. Random shots of light from the fire played on the ceiling. Softly, again and again, he hummed a phrase from the hymn which had stuck in his mind.

Paulus was in the mental twilight between waking and sleeping when he sensed that someone was near him. He opened his eyes. Onkel Langshammer stood over him, looking down at him. It was too dark, and Onkel's eyesight too poor, for Onkel to know that Paulus was returning his gaze while Onkel bent forward a bit, closer to Paulus' face, and peered into it. *What is he searching for in my face?* Onkel then went to the fire and added two logs and stood in front of the fire until it quickened and the light in the room increased. Then Onkel came back to Paulus. Now Paulus closed his eyes as Onkel leaned over him. Paulus could feel the old man's face near his, and could hear the breath passing in and out of Onkel's nose. Then Onkel turned away and went back to the fire, and Paulus heard him whisper:

"Oh Lord, have you given me back my son?"

CHAPTER 3: PEACE
October-November, 1529. Moravia.

Paulus intended to leave the next day. But, like the stray cat, he had allowed himself to be touched, and could not leave. There was simply too much pleasure in staying. There was a bed, and there were hot meals, and there was a man who treated Paulus well.

Onkel walked with Paulus around the settlement, and into the forests that surrounded it, and introduced Paulus to the people as they encountered them. None of them seemed to be wild-eyed insurrectionists. True, their children were unbaptized, but Onkel's people were not tearing anything apart. They were building.

They called their place Montau. In bits and pieces, as Onkel offered them, Paulus learned their story. They came from a Swiss village near Zürich called St. Matthew, which they had left to escape the persecution of the Zürich religious reformer Ulrich Zwingli, and they had come to Moravia because it was well known that the feudal barons here were tolerant and independent.

Onkel's band found their asylum, beginning in 1527, on

the lands of Otto von Abersicht, an aging feudal lord in a dilapidated castle.

"He is a good man, in his own way," said Onkel about von Abersicht. "A ferocious warrior in his youth, it is said, but mellowed and humbled by age."

Von Abersicht let them clear land and farm it, and he took a portion of their crop. As they cleared land, they built their settlement with the logs, and as they had more logs than they could use, they renovated a water driven sawmill on a creek that fed into the Plava river and began manufacturing fine straight planks, which they sold – usually through middlemen – at the confluence of the Plava and the Morava.

They rarely saw other people. Local traffic hugged the Morava river and its adjacent fields and villages. When a few of the Anabaptists went to Olmütz to trade, they were not recognized. None of the merchants who purchased von Abersicht's planks had any idea that they had been manufactured by outlawed heretics.

IN MONTAU, ABLE-BODIED people worked, so they gave Paulus a job: he would gather firewood. They gave him a mule and the sled and an axe, and they sent him into the woods. And Paulus, the son of a noble family, worked for the first time in his life. For a couple of days he was not very productive, but soon he became the master of his mule and his axe, and the woodpile in the open square began to grow. He found himself gazing at his woodpile, thinking to himself that it was the first valuable thing he had ever done in his life.

They all worked in Montau, but there were no personal possessions. Onkel had mentioned this doctrine before, but Paulus did not comprehend it until, one evening, the worship service after supper took a different turn.

"Tilman is to stand before the church," said Onkel, at the place in the service where he usually preached. Eyes turned toward Tilman, and Tilman shot a frightened glance at his wife on the women's side.

"Tilman is to stand before the church," said Onkel again, more loudly. Tilman rose and came to the front. He was a small man, dwarfed by Onkel Langshammer.

"Brother," said Onkel, "you have been caught in a sin, and it is our duty as your brothers to help you repent. Brothers, you know that Tilman was sent to town last week to sell a load of boards. He brought back the payment, but he kept part of it for himself."

Tilman's face was getting red and his eyes moist. His wife was weeping. Onkel continued.

"Brother, you may keep this money if you wish. We will not take it from you. But if you keep this money, you may not keep us. You must leave. You must make a choice, right now."

Tilman wept and confessed his sin and handed over to Onkel a handful of coins in a bag, and there was a spontaneous chorus of prayers and thanksgiving. Some of the men came to the front and shook Tilman's hand and put their hands on his shoulders and said things like *praise God* and *welcome back* and *the Lord is merciful.* Paulus was astonished.

"Whose money is it?" Paulus asked that night, when he and Onkel were alone.

"The money belongs to the whole church," said Onkel.

"And the land, and the buildings . . ."

"Everything. Everything except the wives, " chuckled Onkel.

"Why?"

"Because Christ and the apostles teach it," was Onkel's simple reply. "The wood you cut, Paulus, it is not yours. It belongs to anyone who is cold."

ONKEL BAPTIZED A woman who had come recently from Austria. They stood outside on a warm afternoon in November. Claus held a bucket of water with a ladle near Onkel.

"Gretel Schirmer, child of the world," said Onkel with a

huge smile on his face, "do you now renounce the world with all of its evil and its power?"

"Yes, I renounce it." Gretel's eyes were closed and her lips quivered as she spoke.

"Do you renounce the devil and his kingdom in this world?"

"I renounce."

"Do you embrace the holy Trinity, and Jesus Christ God's Son, and his cross?"

"I embrace it."

"Do you embrace Christ's true people, the church, and the commands of Christ?"

"I embrace it."

"We baptize you, Gretel Schirmer, in the name of the Father, and the Son, and the Holy Spirit!"

And Onkel thoroughly doused her with three full ladles of water, and the water ran down through her brown hair and over her trembling lips and wetted the tips of her fingers, and ran into the ground of Montau. Onkel laughed as he poured, laughed like a victorious warrior on a field of battle. And Paulus knew that Onkel and the others believed that this Gretel Schirmer had just passed from damnation and darkness into a world of light and love. And into a life of persecution. Certainly, Gretel Schirmer had been baptized as an infant in some Catholic church in Austria, with chanting and Latin mutterings and incense. She was throwing that baptism back into the pope's face now. Paulus felt the immense power of this simple woman's repudiation of her Catholic baptism, and he understood better now how the pope and bishops and monks could feel its tremor too, under their feet.

Even though Paulus was there physically in their midst, and so close to Gretel Schirmer that he could have leaned and touched her, he was still in the old world. When he witnessed Gretel's baptism, Paulus felt the first firm tug at his soul. *I want to leave the darkness, I want to live in light and love.*

ONE EVENING, BEFORE supper, a sound of men's angry voices rose near the meeting room. All the people went to the noise. Two young men, Jürgen and Josef, were pounding each other with their fists. Jürgen was getting the better of it; Josef's nose was bleeding and he was retreating. Onkel waded right into the middle of the flailing fists, shouting wrathfully.

"You will both stop, now! You will both stop, now!"

They stopped, their chests heaving, their eyes glaring at each other.

"He was staring at my wife," said Jürgen. Jürgen's wife was, in fact, very pretty.

"So you hit him?" asked Onkel.

"Yes, because he was staring at my wife. I will not let him stare at my wife. He has his own wife."

Onkel sent them to their homes, and the congregation ate supper, and after supper Onkel brought Jürgen and Josef to the front – as he had brought Tilman to the front – and rebuked them. He told them that brothers in Christ do not strike each other. He did not care whose fault it was, or what reasons either of them had. He made them each ask for forgiveness of the other.

"He *was* staring at her," said Paulus to Onkel as they were getting ready for bed.

"What?"

"Josef – he was staring at Jürgen's wife. He deserved his punch in the nose."

"I'm not surprised. She's very pretty, don't you agree?"

"Of course. I was looking at her too."

"So then what is your point, my scholar friend?" Onkel was bending over as he said this, massaging his straw-filled mattress to get more of the filling under his upper body.

"You were severe with them, as if their little fistfight would bring the world to an end."

Onkel stood, turned, and faced him.

"I was *severe* with them? No, I was merciful to them. It

is mercy to rescue sinners from their sins. And yes, such behavior will bring the world – our world here in Montau – to an end. There is only one thing that makes us different here – otherwise we are just like Olmütz – and that is obedience to the commands of Christ. Christ, as you well know, told his disciples to turn the other cheek when struck, and not to resist the evil man, even when he puts them in danger. Jürgen sinned first, he attacked. Then Josef sinned when he struck back. They both deserved rebuke."

Paulus shook his head and made a sarcastic sound like a whistle.

"You are thinking this," Onkel said. "You are thinking that I have an unrealistic standard for my people, that I am acting as if these were perfect people. We have heard the accusation enough to make us sick – *You are perfectionists, You are perfectionists* – but this accusation only shows how little our enemies have listened to us. It is precisely because we are still people capable of any wickedness that the commandments of Christ must not be ignored. Those commandments are the only thing that keeps us from devouring each other in this wilderness. Without them our little family will turn upon itself."

"You are saying, then, that you may *never* retaliate?" Paulus asked this question victoriously; he did not expect Onkel to affirm it, since it seemed so patently absurd to insist that a person cannot defend himself. But Onkel affirmed it.

"Yes. That is what Jesus says. Surely the professors of theology in the Sorbonne must have come across the passages sometime in their lectures."

"Of course, but there were some very careful discussions of the problems."

"Oh yes, how well I know. I am a trained theologian too! But after these – what you call careful discussions – everyone in Christendom is exempted from following Christ's command except the monks. Only the monks have to turn the other cheek. And they are the ones who, because they don't live in a natural world, don't ever have to!"

"And this . . . this is natural?" Paulus' gesture indicated Montau.

"Yes, it is natural. We have children, and husbands, and wives, and we have to work with our hands for our daily bread, and we are in daily danger. The monks are protected from all that."

"Then who will resist evil, Onkel?"

"The men with the swords. Caesar and his minions. But not believers. We belong to a different kingdom, we are only on our way *through* this kingdom of the sword. We will obey the power of the sword as much as we can, and we will suffer under it when necessary. But we are forbidden to wield it."

"It is no wonder that they accuse you people of sedition, then." Paulus was repeating the standard charge.

Then Onkel laughed drily, and spread out his arms in symbolic reference to the whole community of Montau. "These people, seditious? Paulus, nothing shows more clearly that the professors of theology have left right reason behind. How can such people as us be considered seditious? People who ask only to be left in peace, people who work and produce and trouble no one and turn the wilderness into a garden. Are we hurting anybody? Are we ruining the world, Paulus?" At the *p* in Paulus' name a fleck of spittle flew across the room, catching the light of the fire. "No, no, Paulus, here is what they are really afraid of! They are afraid that if too many people in Christendom become Anabaptists and learn to follow Christ there will be no more need for their swords. No more criminals to punish, no more heads to chop off, no more lust to fight wars. It's a foolish, childish fear, because Christ's sheep will always be a small remnant. The way is simply too narrow. But that's what they fear."

Onkel was right, of course. His people were lambs. But what would Paulus' noble family do for a living without war? Gretel Schirmer was a lamb, but her baptism was a thunderous stroke against the interlocking system of kings and nobles and armies and executioners.

"More lambs, fewer wolves," reflected Paulus. "But if there are only a few wolves, they can still devour the lambs, can't they?"

"They can, they can," replied Onkel. "But it's no fun. The men with swords aren't mere butchers. It's not wanton slaughter they enjoy. It's the sport, Paulus! There has to be someone to fight back. An enemy. Christians have enemies, Paulus, oh we *have* bloody minded enemies. But we are forbidden by Christ to *be* enemies. The men with swords hate us because we take the honor and the sport out of their killing. We refuse to play the game."

"If I were one of you," Paulus said slowly, "I would be forbidden to defend myself. My body, my life, completely at the mercy of evil men. Is that your doctrine?"

"Yes. So says Christ, and so did Christ."

"And my family?"

"And your family." Onkel came close to Paulus and lowered his voice. The two men had been speaking loudly. "Paulus, let me tell you the truth. If a follower of Christ could defend his family, I would have a family. Don't you think that this arm could swing a good sword?" It could; it was a thick and powerful arm. "Have you seen any swords, any weapons, in Montau? No, you have not. We neither make them nor keep them. And if someone brings one with him when he comes here, we take it to Willi and he makes it into something useful, like horseshoes or scissors or your wood-axe. *They shall beat their swords into plowshares,* says the scripture, and we do it here. This" – he lifted his weathered Bible from the study table – "is all the sword we need."

ONE DAY IN the middle of November a blustery wind blew in from the west and set the people of Montau talking excitedly about the coming of winter. Strange, how they were always glad to see each new season come, and then glad to see it go. As darkness came they converged on the woodpile to lay in enough fuel for the night, and it made Paulus feel good that his labor would now keep them warm.

He fell asleep listening to the moaning of the wind through the crevices in the shutters. Sometime much later, he came slowly awake because of the chill that had seeped into his bed, despite the mountain of blankets he had piled on. Their fire had burned down to coals. Paulus was about to get up and remake the fire when he heard Onkel growl and stir. The old man threw his bedclothes off and tip-toed across the straw on the frozen earth floor to the hearth. He rubbed his hands against his arms. His naked body was white, his leg muscles lean, and the skin across his back hung limply and gathered above his buttocks. He pulled some logs from the pile, fumbling in the darkness and his own blurred vision, stirred up the live embers with a stick, and arranged the wood on them. Paulus expected him to return to bed, but he lingered near the fire, standing on his toes and apparently waiting for it to ignite. *He does strange things at night.*

Flames appeared, and Onkel stood by the growing fire like some primitive priest before an altar, lost in meditation. *What's he doing? Praying? No, he must be thinking and warming himself.*

Then the old man put his left hand over the flames, held it there briefly and drew it back. He turned to go back to bed. Paulus let his own eyes fall shut. Onkel stopped and went back to the fire and put the hand in it again, and Paulus heard a stifled and prolonged groan and saw the hand open and close several times, writhing of its own accord to get free. Finally the heat won, and Onkel removed the tortured member and cradled it in his other hand against his chest. He let his head drop forward and began to sob silently, and the long gray hairs that were always brushed back over his shiny wise head fell across his face.

He is trying to find out how much pain he can endure. And he is afraid because he can't endure it.

"WHY DID YOU leave Paris? Why didn't you finish your degree?" Onkel kept asking. Eventually Paulus was going to answer. Onkel kept turning the pages of his Bible as he waited for Paulus to respond.

"I lost my faith. It would have been silly to continue."

"Many without faith continue in the Roman church and reach high positions."

"I know. They are leeches and hypocrites."

"What happened?"

"I watched a man burn to death. It happened in the Place Maubert, in the Latin Quarter. It was a drizzly day in March. I was on my way home from a lecture in theology, and there was an execution going on in the Place Maubert. People were thick, and the shutters on the windows all around were open. Women, children, food, wine – like a festival."

"Oh yes, public burnings are fine entertainment," mocked Onkel. "The people are bored! The people have no jobs, no bread! They are restless and surly in the streets, and what can we do? Burn somebody!"

"And I stayed to watch too. Why? I don't know. Maybe boredom, fascination, terror. The stake was ready, piled with brush and faggots, and one of the Provost's men was lighting it. The churchmen watched, huddled in a bunch, muttering in Latin. Everyone, Onkel, everyone was united in this purpose. It seemed like someone should be protesting or screaming or saying something logical like, *We can't do this! It is barbaric and cruel!* How can such a thing be done in the name of Jesus?"

"Of course, it can't," said Onkel.

"But it was. The executioner lit the fire, and the people pressed forward to see how the condemned man would die. He didn't struggle or protest. But when the flames reached him and his paper heretic hat caught on fire, he began to scream like a young girl. Some of the men laughed at him.

"I went home and thought about it. Something in my mind had changed, something large. I had always thought that there was some kind of struggle between good and evil, and that some people were evil and some people good. I think I had assumed that the church, and God himself, were on the side of the good. But this was an evil event, and the church was there, blessing it. The men who speak for God were there, approving it. Onkel, that man died in unspeakable agony *in nomine patris et filii et spiritus sancti."* *In the name of the Father and the Son and the Holy Spirit.* "So where was God, or Jesus, or all the things that the doctors at the university talked about? Where was good, where was love, where was common decency?"

"You were right," said Onkel softly. "You knew more than all of them."

"I let my studies go to waste after that. The rector called me in and I told him the truth. I thought I might be burned myself. But my family is too important. They just expelled me."

"You went home?"

"Briefly. My father cursed me and was ashamed of me. So I left."

"And here you are. Running away from it."

"Just running. There is no escaping it. The people, the peasants, the magistrates, the priests are everywhere. It simply is what is."

"It is not all that is, Paulus. We have left it."

"And it is out there, you say." Paulus waved his hand toward Austria. "Not here?"

"It is true, I admit. We bring pieces of it with us. We bring the weed seeds of the old world into our garden. But we give them no ground to sprout. That's why we have no weapons and no personal property. Without weapons and money it's hard to do much evil to another person. We are capable of sins, but we starve those sins."

Suddenly Onkel seemed exhausted. It was very late and

they would have to sleep. As if signaling the end of the conversation, Onkel shook himself and rose from the bed to rouse the fire. It was a preposterous premise: that one man, myopic, balding, lost in the hills of Moravia, was right and the whole world wrong. Paulus watched him drop his pants to the floor and massage the insides of his thighs before swinging his legs inside the blankets. The straw rustled and Onkel sighed. He did this every night.

"Onkel."

"Hm."

"What about a man with a woman?"

"HM?"

"What about sex, Onkel? Isn't that as much an act of conquest as war, pillage, execution? Isn't it an act of power, one person over another?"

"It can be . . . often it is, you are right. The man is powerfully armed, with his lust and his physical strength. But the woman has her own sword . . . and it is a sharp one, very sharp. No, Paulus, this is a more equal struggle than you think."

"What is this woman's sharp sword?" asked Paulus.

"This is a difficult subject. I'm tired. I'm an old man. Perhaps if I were your age and we lived together at the College des Lombards we could talk until sunrise. Talk theology until sunrise. Young men, talking theology."

Onkel lay down again, and the room was quiet. Onkel usually went immediately to sleep, and took long breaths that rattled in his chest. Paulus knew, by the quietness of the room, that Onkel was still awake, tired but thinking.

CHAPTER 4: BAPTISM
January, 1530. London, and Moravia.

There were audiences for the plays even in the winter. The plays were for the laboring folk and the street riffraff of London, who came out of their hovels bundled against the frost to see another story of cheap chivalry acted out: a virtuous knight, a fair maiden, a villain, swordplay, melodramatic death, and the knight gets the maiden. Flat wagons served as stages in the streets, and at night torches lit the plays.

A young man, Jan Bockelson, loved these plays. He knew that they were formulaic and badly acted, but he loved them. Bockelson was from the town of Leiden in Holland. He had been born illegitimately to a village mayor and a servant girl; not until he was seven did his father marry his mother. Now he was in London as an apprentice in the tailoring business. English wool merchants did a brisk business with Dutch weavers, and there was a Dutch community in London connected with this textile industry.

On an icy night in January, Jan Bockelson crowded the stage in a dirty London street. His blonde, wavy hair glowed in the torchlight, and he smiled gently as he waited for the screeching of the trumpets that would announce the beginning of the play.

"You are here often," remarked a man standing next to Bockelson.

"Every night," replied Bockelson, without looking at the man.

"You are Dutch."

Bockelson ignored the man. A couple of minutes passed, and the trumpets were almost ready to sound, and the friendly Englishman said:

"I think you'll like this one. Some good sword action."

"I've seen this one many times," said Bockelson evenly. "And it's not a very good play. The villain is a bad actor and the second scene goes on too long."

The other man, rebuffed, decided that it was no use trying to talk to this uncivil foreigner, and began to mind his own business. Then Bockelson looked at him and spoke to him.

"You wonder why I am here. I love the crowd. I love it that you are here to watch this bad play. There is a magic about it. I will be an actor one day, in a play much bigger and better than this. People like you, ordinary people, will watch me and I will lift them up out of their dirty streets. I will dignify and glorify their lives. You will hear about me one day. My name is Jan Bockelson, of Leiden."

Bockelson loved the crowds, and the riveted eyes, and he loved the women who forgot their rough and uncouth husbands while they followed the deeds of the hero of the play. He wanted those eyes on himself. He wanted their cheers and their worship. He wanted all the beautiful women for himself.

PAULUS WAS A young man, and because of this he thought often about women. The married couples in Montau seemed happy. But Onkel was not married, and this fact impressed him.

"Marriage is not evil, Paulus. It is blessed by God. But it is for those God calls to it."

"Not you?"

"Not me," said Onkel, and thumped the table.

"Why not?"

"I've explained it to you, but you keep asking. It is too great a burden. It would not be kind for me to marry a wife and then leave her a widow when Ferdinand Hapsburg comes for me." Ferdinand was the king of Austria and Bohemia and Moravia, a zealous Catholic with a well publicized program of persecution.

"Maybe marriage would relieve other burdens."

"Maybe." Onkel seemed sullen.

"You don't know much about this, do you?" This was vicious of Paulus. Onkel swung his big head around.

"And you, wet behind the ears, what do you know?"

"Not much. But I have known a girl."

"You have had intercourse. So what? The dumbest animals can do the same."

"It was more than that, Onkel. It was an exercise in power."

Paulus told Onkel about his sexual conquest of a poor, naive Parisian girl. It lasted a month, and when it was over Paulus took his sin to the confessional and received absolution in Latin. Onkel rubbed his broad forehead – his signal of agitation.

"I have read about the forgiveness of a whore," said Onkel.

"This poor girl was not a whore," protested Paulus.

"No, no, no. Think, Paulus. You were the whore," said Onkel. "The whore is the one who has no love, no faithfulness. The whore is the one who can walk away with no feeling."

Paulus felt at once how evil he was and how much Onkel loved him. But he had nothing to say. He simply lay quiet on his bed.

"There is grace for whores," said Onkel. As he talked he was paging through his Bible. "Our Lord forgave them, and they loved him and served him. One of them washed his feet with her hair and tears. They were at his cross long after the apostles had fled. There was a prophet who married a whore. A young man, like you. Hosea was his name, and here, here is his story." Onkel thumped a page of the Bible with the back of his thumb.

"A strange story," said Paulus.

"Read it sometime. The book is called Hosea. Here, I underline the name." Paulus heard the dry scratching of Onkel's quill pen.

"It was a sin, I know. I confess my sin. But it was also power. Jeannette was my conquest, her body my plunder, and the stories I told my friends were my glory. It frightens me. It seems like power lies at the very source of life. No human has an origin unless there is an act of pillage. The man takes, the woman is taken. No wonder that the rest of human life is about domination."

Onkel let out a laugh that sounded like a grunt.

"Why are you laughing? Don't you think I'm right?"

"Oh, of course," said Onkel. "What you did, it was an act of pillage. But women have their own weapon in this thing. I told you this once but you don't believe me."

"Women don't take men in conquest."

"Oh yes they do! They do it with love. A woman's love, Paulus, is a mighty power."

"Jeanette loved me."

"Ach! Paulus, Paulus, she was sixteen. Old enough to lie with you, old enough to inflame you, but not old enough to love you. You merely fascinated her, and perhaps she lusted for you as you did for her. But one day a real woman may love you, and then you'll know what I'm talking about. The love of a grown and intelligent woman is a fearful and overwhelming power, like an army with banners. You have never known *this*."

How could Onkel know this? Had he not been a celibate Catholic priest, and after that a celibate Anabaptist preacher?

"And you, have you known this?" asked Paulus.

"I know some things," he said. Then he shook his head and snorted. "I know very little."

"So it is worse than I have made it. Men and women conquer each other. Then why marriage, and intercourse, and children? Why are your people married at all?"

"The scriptures do not forbid it," said Onkel.

"So you leave behind the power of the sword, and the power of personal possessions, but you bring into your little protected kingdom the power of sex and reproduction and passion and love? It doesn't make sense."

"You're right. These things create a great attachment to the world. Great joys, great sorrows, great confusions. Very combustible."

Onkel was sounding exhausted. He rubbed his eyes with the knuckles of his forefingers.

"Remember this story of Hosea, Paulus. You'll need it some day." Then he let his Bible fall shut and slid it away from him on the table. "I have chosen celibacy. There is too much danger in having a wife. As for the others, each believer will stand before his own Master. I do not judge them. But still, there is danger."

Paulus wondered whether the danger Onkel spoke of was the long arm of King Ferdinand or the power of a woman's love.

Paulus thought that Onkel was asleep, but then he heard the old man whisper, as he often did to himself when he was reading his Bible. It was soft but audible, and he repeated it several times: *Ich will freundlich mit ihr reden . . . I will speak to her kindly . . . I will speak to her kindly.*

PAULUS WAS HEARING the kind voice, and he knew he was being converted, and he was not able or willing to do anything to stop it. He saw no lights or visions. There was just Onkel Langshammer, talking, talking, talking, and Paulus simply found himself, by tiny irresistible increments, seeing God and the world the way Onkel did. At a certain point, he saw that in order to avoid becoming one of them he would have to leave them. And he had no desire to leave. It was only, therefore, a matter of time. He learned to think, as Onkel and the brotherhood thought, in terms of two invisible kingdoms that lay behind all people, places, things, events, and words, and to see the church in Montau as a tiny but indestructible nugget of God's kingdom projecting into the territory and time of the kingdom of the devil. The God who hovered above the settlement no longer disconcerted him. The way of peace, the way of sharing, the way of strict obedience to the laws of Christ all came to seem natural and right. He knew the songs by heart and hummed them as he chopped wood.

But one did not become a member of the community through assimilation. Paulus was a friend, a helper, and to Onkel a kind of son, but he would not be a brother until he had gone through the watery death of baptism and risen to life on the other side. And Onkel, undoubtedly for Paulus' sake, preached much on baptism. Paulus' mind was full of black, churning swells and spray – of Noah's flood, and the Red Sea piled up in walls, and the deep waters engulfing the psalmist, and the Jordan river. All beckoning him to death and life.

At supper one evening, Paulus said to Onkel:

"I want to be baptized."

Onkel's blue eyes came around to Paulus' face, full of light. He lifted his face up, as if toward God, and smiled broadly, as people do when they are supremely happy, and let out a huge roar and shook his head like a lion. No words, just a roar of joy.

"You make me very happy, Paulus," he said. "I want to be sure – I want you to be sure – of one thing, though. You are not doing this for me. And if I die tomorrow, you still want to be baptized."

Paulus roared back at him: "I want to be baptized!

Baptize me!"

ONKEL PERFORMED THE baptism on the next Sunday, on a morning in late January when flecks of snow swirled about outside. The brotherhood gathered around him in the meeting room and Onkel baptized him with cupfuls of water, not in Latin, but *auf den Namens des Vaters und des Sohnes und des heiligen Geistes*. Then the brothers greeted him with a holy kiss. Nothing changed outwardly except that he could now join in the communion celebration and could give his opinion when the men of the community met in council for major decisions. He was still Paulus the wood gatherer, still found satisfaction in this labor, still wondered about many things and talked with Onkel by the light of hot fires. But the previous summer of wandering and stealing and emptiness receded into a historical past, as a chapter written and closed; his youth at Malbeck and his study at Paris all seemed like part of a previous life. He began to forget his Latin. He was now Paulus the believer, the brother. The Anabaptist.

He still had young male thoughts about women. But his sexual life was part of the past; he would be content with celibacy, like Onkel. He would serve the Lord with a single purpose, an undivided heart; he would not burden himself with wife and children, nor endanger their future should he be called upon to seal his testimony with his blood.

CHAPTER 5: SHEPHERD
1531. January-May, 1532.

Two plantings and harvests had come and gone since Paulus' baptism, and now again it was winter. Others joined Paulus in the important task of gathering firewood, but for the most part it was a time of rest. The community monitored the food supply with great care, and ate sparingly. They sang, and they listened to Onkel preach.

Spring came, and they mobilized. They gave thanks to God that there was enough grain to sow for another year, and the men attacked the soil. Paulus, now familiar with the trails and the undulations of the land, worked at clearing new ground.

And he was devouring Onkel's Bible when he could.

"Onkel!"

Onkel was splashing water from a basin on his face; as usual, it was running down his whole body and onto the floor. He was like a big animal playing in a river.

"Hmm."

"Hosea. I'm reading about Hosea."

"Ah, the prophet."

"The man who married a whore." Paulus was at Onkel's

small reading desk, with Onkel's large Bible open to the prophet Hosea..

"Ah, yes, I recall it," said Onkel, reaching for a shirt to wipe his face.

"This is certainly an allegory, isn't it? God would never tell a real man to marry a real whore." Paulus chuckled. But he was worried what Onkel might say.

"Her name was Gomer, no?" asked Onkel. Paulus nodded yes, her name was Gomer. "Sounds like a real name, doesn't it? And the children, they sound like real children."

"Then you think it really happened."

"I think so. But I confess that it is an unpleasant story, and one that might make a skeptic question the wisdom or the justice of God. But you must remember, it has a point. It is not an allegory, but it has a point. Gomer represents Israel, sinful and straying from the Lord."

"You still have the fact that God told Hosea to marry a whore. What would happen here in Montau if one of the men decided to marry a whore? What would happen if I decided to marry a whore?"

"Then you would be asking for much trouble!" snapped Onkel.

"Why? Because I would be marrying a whore, or because I would be marrying?"

"Both!" said Onkel. He wagged his finger. "Paulus. Paulus." Onkel relaxed and sighed. "You must understand something. Before Adam and Eve fell into sin, marriage was a great blessing. After sin, everything gets turned upside down. Marriage becomes God's great forge of testing. You think that I remain unmarried because I am stronger in spirit than the others here. That is false. It is because I am the weakest of the brothers that I have no wife. They are enduring trials and testings that an unmarried man cannot imagine."

"I was not asking about marriage, Onkel. I am asking about the prophet Hosea."

"I am answering about Hosea. You are making too much of the fact that Gomer is a whore. The hard thing is forgiveness. Hosea has to marry a sinner. Every man has to marry a sinner. To be married you have to forgive. Read on some time, Paulus, finish the story. It's about God and you."

Paulus would have to read it all some evening. Now it was dinner time. He was comfortable in his commitment to celibacy. If it meant that he was weaker than the others, so be it. No shame.

ONKEL LANGSHAMMER CAUGHT a chill one afternoon and put himself to bed. Paulus came home from his work and found the old man shaking and sweating under the blankets he had piled on himself. Paulus went out and fetched Katrina, who came from the kitchen immediately. She felt Onkel's forehead.

"He has a high fever," she said.

Katrina tried to cool Onkel with wet cloths. The old man was in a mild state of delirium. Katrina called in Willi, the smith, who kept the knives, and together they opened one of Onkel's veins and bled him. Still no improvement.

"Paulus, you'll have to preach the sermon tonight," said Willi.

Paulus had somehow known that this time was coming. He was worried for Onkel, but excited to preach.

After some thrashing and moaning, Onkel's fever broke, and he slept. Paulus took Onkel's Bible and began to consider what he would say. Onkel talked about the Bible's *shoutings – God is shouting at me here, I must preach this to the people.* Several times Paulus had heard him cry out in his study, or slap his hands hard on the table with glee. Would Paulus hear such a shout?

Paulus heard no shout, but he did have something he wanted to say. He organized his thoughts, and presented them to the church that evening.

When he returned home, he found Katrina back at the

bedside of Onkel. The old man was sleeping peacefully.

"Is he better?" asked Paulus.

"Yes, praise God," said Katrina.

Claus and two other men poked their heads in. Their eyes were big with worry. "How is Onkel?" asked Claus.

"He is resting," said Katrina. "He will live."

"Praise God!" said Claus, and the others murmured the same with him. "And Paulus. Your word tonight, it was very good."

ONKEL RECOVERED, BUT slowly, and was very weak long after the fever had gone. Paulus led the worship three more times, and then Onkel resumed his duties, but they had to lead him into the meeting room with helpers on both sides. Katrina told Paulus that they should be thankful to God for a special miracle, for she had been certain, that night when they hovered over his bed, that he was dying. She had never felt such a fever when the person had not died. But Paulus told her that she should have had greater faith, since Onkel was their leader, their shepherd, and they needed him, and God would not take him away until his course was finished. Onkel was the great rock in Paulus' life, immovable, steady.

The earth awoke and yawned under the glow of the warming sun. The small brown buds broke open and delicate leaves emerged and the gray winter ground was tinged with green. The men were in the fields from the earliest shades of dawn to the last fading dusk. Paulus and his band of lumberers chipped away at the forest south of Montau. Spring rains, warm and brief, came like embraces.

With the earth, part of Paulus awoke too. He was thinking more and more about sex. During the day his world was one of work and sweat and hard stubborn wood and clean manly labor; at night, while he slept, it was filled with women and scenes that made him feel polluted in the morning. The sprouting of the plants and the blowing of the tepid winds had something to do with this, he knew, and he resented it. He could understand why spring was the time of resurrection and life for the godless and why the world's heathen worship of false gods so often revolved around sexual intercourse. He prayed to the God of Israel, who had purged the fertility gods of the Canaanites, the Baalim and the Asherim, from the land, to clean out his soul.

But it did not happen easily. He ached for a woman. The women of Montau gave him no provocation, but he watched them longer as they walked from place to place, and as they nursed their babies, and as they disappeared into their homes with their husbands in the evening. Paulus and Onkel alone, of all the brethren, were people without a sexual life. This had always been true, but now he felt it sharply. These new thoughts were invading his mind, binding him against his will, and he sensed the freedom and peace he had experienced since his baptism slipping away. He prayed each night for dreamless sleep. He prayed each morning that the Lord would keep his eyes pure.

He talked little of this to Onkel. It was embarrassing, and what would a celibate man know of such things? He cultivated patience. This would pass, and he would grow out of it as he became more like Christ and as time flowed by and gently healed him of this weakness.

ONE OVERCAST DAY in mid-May, as Paulus and his helpers cut trees, a boy from Montau appeared across the clearing, running as fast as he could, darting through the stumps and fallen trees toward the woodcutters. Paulus leaned on his axe handle and wiped his face. The boy stopped before him and said:

"Brother Ketterling, come quickly! They've taken Onkel!"

"Who?"

"Soldiers. Claus Hestermann just told me to tell you as fast as I could."

Before the sentence was done, Paulus had dropped his axe and was running, with the others behind him. When he reached the settlement, the brethren stood in the clearing like a small flock of sheep, huddled together, quiet except for the muffled crying of a woman.

"Claus, what happened?" Paulus was heaving to catch his breath.

"They arrested Onkel." He put his hands into the air.

"Who arrested Onkel?"

"The bishop's police from Olmütz."

"What about von Abersicht? Was he with them?" Claus shook his head no. "Did they hurt him?"

"No, it was all very orderly. They just came in on their horses, four of them, and Onkel met them right here. They said they were here to find Heinrich Langshammer, and Onkel told them that he was the man, and asked them what they wanted. They said that they were from the Bishop of Olmütz, and that the bishop wanted to question him about his beliefs, since the King Ferdinand was zealous to see the purity of the faith established in Moravia. Onkel said that this was Count von Abersicht's land and asked them if they had his authorization to pass, and they said that they did. Then Onkel agreed to go with them and asked if he might get some extra clothes. The police were courteous and let him do this. He went into his room for a few minutes and then came out with a bundle. He prayed with us, right here, while the soldiers watched."

Paulus looked down the path leading out of Montau to the south, knowing that Onkel was long gone but hoping to see something. There was nothing but a mush of hoofmarks.

"Oh God, help us. God, help Onkel."

The group stood silent. The children looked up into their parents' faces to find explanation and assurance.

Paulus went into the room that seemed so strange now with Onkel gone. Onkel's Bible lay on his reading table, open to the psalms. Paulus riffed through its pages with no particular purpose. Onkel's Bible had always seemed to him a mysterious and powerful thing, a source of truth and love and a kind of embodiment of Onkel himself. Now it was all that was left of the man. Paulus closed it and placed it exactly in the center of the table.

When he returned to the group outside, Claus had another announcement. Onkel, he said, had instructed the community to consider and accept Paulus as its new bishop. This they had done. What could he say? The ground had been well prepared for this. Here were the dear people, stripped of their shepherd, and it did not matter much whether Paulus wanted this calling or not, whether he was a shepherd or not. He had been summoned. He was all they had. Not only this, but they were all he had, and he could not contemplate the possibility that the brotherhood would disintegrate and scatter to the winds. A twinge of the old desperation, a glimpse of the loneliness, a memory of the road – of having no people or family – shot through him. So for his own sake he must shoulder the burden that Onkel had handed to him, and hope that it was also for the good of the others.

"Well?" asked Claus.

"I accept."

Suddenly he understood how Onkel must have felt. Their eyes were all fixed upon him, waiting. The passage of authority had taken place in an instant. They were now waiting for him to tell them what to do.

"We have work to do," he said, and he began to move back toward the forest. "The heathen shall not throw us into disorder."

"Yes, Onkel," said Jürgen.

Onkel? Why did Jürgen call him Onkel? Because, he remembered, *Onkel* was not Heinrich Langshammer's name but the official title of the brotherhood for its leader. Jesus forbade his followers to call their leaders *teacher*, or *father*, so the people of Montau had settled on the lesser term *Onkel* – uncle. Now

Paulus was the Onkel of Montau. But to him the name would always belong to one man.

CHAPTER 6: WOMAN
June-August, 1532. Moravia.

Grass was high and thick everywhere. Down within it the bugs bred and came out in their swarms. Through the long days, until the sun finally buried itself in the northwest part of the horizon, the men toiled and sweated and drank water from the skins that the boys brought them. In mid-June there was a stretch of hot steamy weather. Paulus worked long days and slept restlessly at night, sweating in the dark heat. One day a breeze from the west blew and the clouds bulged and as the sun sank the rain came. Paulus listened to it splashing from his roof to the ground. It was a small gift from God.

But he was alone. There was no one with whom to share his childlike delight in a summer rain, the feeling of comfort knowing that the roof was firmly built above him, or to whom he could now say, *Doesn't that smell good!* Onkel was gone. They had heard nothing from him or of him since his arrest. Paulus had gone first to von Abersicht to see if the count knew anything about Onkel's fate. The old noble shook his head; it was obvious he did not know and did not want to involve himself in these things. So Paulus took a tremendous risk and made the journey to Olmütz, where his inquiries were met with consistent ignorance. Nobody knew anything. It seemed that Heinrich Langshammer had never existed.

Paulus grieved, sharply, privately. The duty of leadership seemed an intolerably heavy load. But it had one salutary effect: it purged from his mind the sexual stirrings of the spring, and he was full of joy to be free again. He could even look at Jürgen's wife, with her slender waist and pink cheeks and straw-blonde hair, and think of her only as a dear sister in Christ. He even began to think that he could perceive a larger purpose in God's work, as Onkel had been able to do: if through the pain of Onkel's absence and the new burden of spiritual leadership his sexual pollutions were being cleansed, then that, at least, was a blessing.

"ONKEL."

Claus's voice pulled Paulus up through fathoms of sleep. He awoke chilly; he had fallen asleep uncovered and the night had cooled.

"Claus, what is it?" Claus was leaning over him and gently shaking him.

"There are some people here."

"People?" Visions of soldiers.

"Tyrolians, they say. Refugees."

"Believers?"

"Yes. They say they are from Josef-Albert Roth's congregation."

This was a familiar name, one on the list of persecuted Anabaptist pastors for whom the brotherhood prayed every night. Paulus tried to remember.

"Innsbruck?"

"Yes," said Claus. "Come and meet them."

Paulus threw a shirt over his shoulders without putting his arms through the sleeves and followed Claus out into the clearing. There was enough light from a sliver of moon for him to see four people standing together, near Claus's room, and Claus's wife standing in the doorway looking out. The people had knocked on his door because it was first in the row.

"Grace to you," said Paulus to them.

"And to you," replied the one man among the refugees. Then there was a stretch of awkward silence.

"Claus says you are believers in Christ."

"We are believers in Christ," returned the man. "We follow the way of true baptism, and of peace. May we take refuge with you?"

"You may. What we have is yours. What is it that brings you here, so far from the Tyrol?"

"Our bishop has been arrested and our people harassed. When the shepherd is struck the sheep are scattered."

"Your name?"

"Simon Stubner." He extended his hand to Paulus. "And my wife, Elisabeth . . . Anna, one of the widows . . . and Marga Roth, our bishop's daughter." As Simon Stubner introduced the others, he pointed to them. In the dark, the last one named seemed to Paulus to be no more than a thirteen year old girl. But when she spoke, the voice was that of a woman.

"We are tired. We've been walking for three days without a rest."

Then Paulus understood that it was not right for him to stand there questioning them when what they needed was rest; he remembered suddenly the night he had come as a refugee, and how he had been offered comfort and help without delay. He was ashamed of himself. Onkel would have handled it better.

"Of course," he said. "Forgive me. Claus, you take them to my house, where they can sleep for the present. I will sleep in the kitchen."

The other woodcutters woke Paulus early the next morning and they were out at their work site long before the newcomers were up, so it was not until dusk that Paulus saw them again, this time at supper. Sitting with them over bread and cabbages, he was able to form a better estimate of them. Simon Stubner was a plump and pompous looking middle-aged man whose face showed the strain of their recent experience. He was a gentle man and very protective of the women who had come with him on their trek north. His wife was, like him, rotund, but she was silent. Anna was an older woman who, alone of all of them, seemed to have kept her joy. She smiled often.

Paulus found his attention drawn to the young woman, Marga Roth, although he tried not to show this. He avoided looking directly at her, and he avoided talking to her. Yet, when he thought he could do so undetected, he watched her. She would wonder later why he had not even noticed her that first day. In fact, she looked very nice to Paulus. That was the problem.

He had never seen such hair on a woman. It was dark and thick and rebellious. She had brushed it straight back over her head, but there were tufts of it around the temples that refused to fall into place, and the mass of it swung and shook like something alive. There was something almost Asiatic about her, which had to do with the long dark hair and the almond shaped eyes that were tilted slightly upwards as they came around to the sides of her face. Her cheekbones were prominent and widely spaced. During the conversation Paulus noticed, in his espionage, that her lips were full and that she tended to talk with them half closed over her teeth, and he wondered why. Her skin was white. There was not a spot or blemish anywhere on it that Paulus could see.

Paulus got their story in full. The voluble Simon Stubner began at the very beginning, as if writing a chronicle for posterity, and related to Paulus and others who sat around the men's table the origins of their congregation. Josef-Albert Roth, it seems, had been converted by the famous preacher Balthasar Hubmaier shortly before the latter's execution by burning, and had set out to do his own preaching in and around Innsbruck. The congregation at its zenith had numbered almost eighty members, but in recent years had declined as the persecution became more systematic. In June, the authorities had finally knocked on Bishop Roth's door with an arrest order in their hands and had taken him away. Soon afterwards, two more leaders of the group had followed the bishop to prison. At that point, said Stubner, the remaining believers had decided to follow Christ's injunction – if they persecute you in the cities, flee to the countryside – and had scattered to the four winds, some to Switzerland, some to Bavaria, others north to Bohemia and Moravia. Stubner's band had begun with seven souls; one married couple had relented and decided to return to the Tyrol and face the consequences, and another man had left the group near Vienna to find work. The rest, with Stubner, had pushed on to Moravia, where they had heard that there existed numerous Anabaptist congregations.

Along the Morava they had became convinced that they were being followed, and in desperation they had turned up into the hills, where they had became completely lost. At the first inhabited castle they had stopped to ask for help; it was von Abersicht's. The sour old aristocrat had answered them with his usual sarcastic words but in the end had told them about Montau and how to find it.

Marga Roth interrupted Simon Stubner twice, once as he was describing the arrest of her father, when she wagged her head sharply and said, "No, that's not how it happened!", and again when he was not hiding very well his disappointment with the others who had left them along the way, to which she interjected: "They did what they believed was best, brother Stubner." When she spoke she tended to bob her head in rhythm with her words, and her hair waved and bounced. Paulus wished she would speak more.

Paulus and Claus and the other leaders all agreed that they should be received into the community and that additional housing should be built for them.

PAULUS WOULD NOT have denied later that he deliberately brought about the opportunity to sit down by Marga Roth two evenings after her arrival, but he tried at the time to make it seem fortuitous. It was late in the day, and Marga was beating the dust out of a blanket stretched over the woodpile. Paulus just happened to walk by.

"Oh, good evening," he said, trying to sound casual.

Marga Roth nodded deferentially and smiled without opening her lips.

"The work goes well," Paulus continued, and gestured toward the place where the new lodgings were being built. "Before long you'll have your own place."

"We are thankful."

"You have suffered much."

"Too much," she replied. It was a tough and decisive statement. Her eyes met his firmly when she said it.

"The time is coming when our suffering will be over."

"You sound like my father."

Paulus sensed that he was entering dangerous territory here, and that this Marga would not hesitate to enter it with him.

"Do you like our community?" he asked.

"I am very thankful to be here."

"But do you like it?"

"I like the hills up there. I was up early this morning, looking at them. How blue they were! I like my bed, and I like eating instead of being hungry, and I like not having to walk any more. Walking, walking, I will never walk again when I don't have to. My feet are still blistered."

"But it's not like home. Is that what you're trying to say?"

"What could be? What could be like Innsbruck?"

She swatted the blanket again.

"Will you go back?"

"Someday. And you, will you ever go back?"

"No."

"You are a hard man, I think. Young, but something has made you hard. It seems to happen among us. How do I address you?"

"The people call me Onkel, but only because they are used to it. I let them. But I would rather be called by my name. Paulus."

"Then I will call you Paulus. Oh, Simon Stubner will complain about that, but he can't do anything. He thinks that he is my father now."

Paulus was hurt that she had called him a hard man. He did not think of himself this way, but perhaps she was right.

"You think I am a hard man? Why?"

"That was perhaps too harsh. You seem . . . serious. Melancholy."

"I don't feel melancholy," said Paulus. Then he decided to be honest. "I guess I do. Our pastor was my father in the faith, my best friend. He's gone."

"I know. Like my father."

"And now I lead them. Maybe I'm old before my time. But you, you seem sad too. I've never seen you smile, really smile." Marga averted her eyes. He'd hit a nerve.

"I don't like my smile," she said. "So I don't use it much, and I try not to laugh."

"Why?" asked Paulus.

"I have a big space between my two front teeth," she replied.

"It can't be that bad," protested Paulus.

"I think it is," she insisted.

And Paulus was overpowered by the impulse to say something nice to her. "Marga, you have beautiful hair, and beautiful eyes, and beautiful skin." He decided not to say *beautiful lips,* although that's what he was noticing. "I can't imagine that the distance between your two front teeth could make any difference."

"Thank you, Paulus. A bishop, with all your responsibility for the souls of the flock, should you be noticing a woman's beauty?" Her voice lilted up. *How do women do those things with their voices?*

"Probably not," he said. "Do I get to see your teeth?"

She smiled . She was right; there was an abnormally large gap there. He was right; it made no difference to her beauty.

"I like it," he said. "It's beautiful too."

She turned back to her dusty blanket.

MARGA SMILED AGAIN at him the next day, with her peculiar tight-lipped smile, and they kept glancing at each other across the dinner tables in the evening. When their eyes met, Paulus could feel the muscles in his body contracting.

Their contacts for the next few days were brief and casual, but Paulus' soul was a roiling volcano. *Onkel, what do I do now? My sweet peace is draining away from me. I am squandering my gift of liberation and cannot seem to help it. But I cannot let this happen to me. I have responsibility now – I know just how much because I have seen what has happened to you, and if they came for you they can just as easily come for me. I have held myself in check, I have not lusted yet for this dear sister in Christ, but Onkel, it takes all the spiritual might I possess. I have lost sleep because of the prayers I have made; my knees are raw from kneeling. Certainly this is a test that God has sent my way, to see if I am worthy of him. There must be a way to endure it.*

But the hair, Onkel! If you could see her hair you would understand my problem. You would want to touch it just as I do. The white skin, too. You once said that a woman's skin is one of God's finest creations, and now I believe you. My fingers sometimes tremble to feel it.

Paulus redoubled his efforts to distance his mind from Marga. He avoided her eyes, and skirted the settlement if it appeared that they would meet. Yet while he did these things his heart would pound and a throbbing excitement would suffuse his body. This could not go on: it was as bad as lust.

One of the sheep died, and they were worried that it had been rabid, so some of the men built a pyre one evening outside the square of buildings and began to burn the sheep's corpse on it. Service was over; Paulus sat alone in front of his door watching them arrange the fire in the dusky light. He was exhausted and was looking forward to an early bedtime. Most of the people were inside their rooms already, and the children were asleep. For once his mind was not on Marga, or engaged in trying to keep from being on Marga, for he was thinking about the mill and some problems that had arisen that day. The wheat was coming up; the garden was bearing; the new buildings were almost finished.

Then Marga came out through her door, clad in a long white gown. She did not see Paulus or even look in his direction, but she was curious about the fire and tiptoed to the edge of her house to get a direct view of it. *A childlike thing to do,* thought Paulus, as the mill and the wheat and everything else that had previously been in his mind vanished. She placed herself where she could see what the men were doing. Anna said something to her from inside their room, which Paulus could not hear; Marga answered back but did not move. Like a solar eclipse, she stood squarely between Paulus and the fire, and what he saw now sent his pulse roaring and made him draw up his knees to his chest in an instinctive motion of self protection. The firelight radiated around her form and filigreed her hair with gold and silhouetted her slender form within her gown. She was standing in a firm, boyish sort of way, with her feet spread apart and her hands on her hips.

Paralyzed, he simply drank in the sight of her; seconds seemed like minutes. God and Onkel were somewhere far away, frowning, grieving, maybe shouting at him, but he could not hear.

Anna called again, and Marga turned quickly, away from

the background of the fire and into mere humanity again, and disappeared into the shadow of the building, mercifully, before the sight of her made Paulus explode. But the image remained in his heated mind, like the spot of light implanted on the eye by a sudden flash in a dark place, perfect and vivid.

He would have to get to sleep or this would burn him up. Night was always a dangerous time; things were sharper and more vivid, emotions more intense, fears more primordial, longings more passionate. If he could somehow get to sleep and wake up, with the sun shining in and the sheep bleating for food, and get himself out to the woods to sweat and strain, he was sure he could survive. And Marga would have her baggy blue dress on again and would not seem the demon-angel she had seemed while standing haloed by the bonfire.

But it was not easy. The well defined picture of her degenerated into a kaleidoscope of pieces that he could not excommunicate from his mind; the universal cracked into particulars and he had the desperate sense that he was losing any objective vision of her; she was becoming a phantom. He could not recapture her face. All that appeared were the soft lips and the erotic gap between her teeth.

The night wore on, and it was too warm for blankets. He threw off his shirt and then his trousers, and thrashed about on his bed, searching for a comfortable position, but there was none. He should get down on his knees in his usual spot next to the chair and implore the forgiveness of God. Jesus had said that to lust for a woman was to commit adultery with her, and for this he needed forgiveness. He mouthed the words. *Forgive me, God.* But he was not sure he meant it, not sure at all that his God in heaven was angry at him for wanting Marga like he did now. Had not God brought her here? One tiny woman, and one lonely forest settlement, and God had seen to it that they came together. But what would Onkel say? As Paulus thought of Onkel he was seized with remorse and dread, for Onkel was perhaps at this moment languishing in some dungeon, suffering for Christ, and here was Paulus, in his place, leading the sheep of Christ – burning up with desire for a woman. So his emotions were tossed back and forth and he was unable to direct them or capture them.

Marga is asleep now, breathing quietly. Her mouth is barely open. Her life breath passes silently through her lips and teeth.

He despaired of sleep, and he knew that this despair was a product of the night, but he could not overcome it. The moon arose and threw a square of pale light through the open window onto the opposite wall; Paulus could gauge the passage of the night by the way it moved down the wall toward the floor. Hours had passed. This was no good; he would be useless in the morning if he did not get some sleep. He tried rhythmical breathing, and he forced himself to think about trees, and Bible verses, and Paris, but time and again the vision of Marga rushed back to displace everything else. Disgusted with himself, he got up, put on his trousers and shoes, and slipped outside as quietly as he could. The effort to make himself silent and invisible brought back a startling impression of the time when he had wandered on the road.

Onkel!

Outside, the moon hung over the settlement, about three quarters full. Crickets chirped their moonlight sonatas in the high grass. The remnants of the bonfire glowed red and the faint odor of the sheep's charred body drifted his way. He stepped quietly away from it to the north, where the edge of the trees was closest to the settlement. It was time to fight violently against the lust of the flesh. St. Jerome had advised the recitation of Hebrew verb paradigms to dissipate lust, but Paulus knew none of them. He could try Latin – no, too rusty. Jerome had also, in desperation, flung himself into bramble bushes. Paulus removed his shirt and ran, arms held up, into the thickest part of the forest. The branches flagellated his ribs and belly. Dry stiff twigs snapped apart against him. He tripped and sprawled into a dark and tangled thicket and lay in a painful heap and gasped. He imagined that blood was running from him.

His wounds were not as serious as he had imagined when he examined them in the morning. But, to his satisfaction, Marga noticed the abrasions on his neck.

"What happened to you?" she asked.

"I was chastising my flesh with branches and brambles, trying to overcome the lust of the flesh with St. Jerome's method."

"Of course you were," she chuckled, not believing him.

"ARISTOCRATIC BLOOD?"

"That's right. All the way back to the battle of Legnano, where my progenitor fought manfully and was knighted on the field of battle. Impressive, eh?" Paulus raised his eyebrows in mock awe.

"Paulus Ketterling *von* Malbeck! We burghers chuckle, you know, at people like you. Behind your backs, of course," said Marga.

"Oh? Why?"

"The whole fantasy of chivalry, nobility, excellence of blood, we think it's all a joke nowadays."

"It is."

"Then why did you tell me?"

"Because it's my origin, which I can't change. And it may help to explain some of the things I do or say."

"Such as . . ."

"I don't know. If I knew I would change them. But there are certainly things about me which I cannot see but that other people can. Habits. Mannerisms. I am very self conscious about this. Have you seen any yet?"

"Nothing blatant, Paulus. You hide this very well. But there is a certain assuredness about you that is aristocratic, now that I think of it."

Paulus shook his head in frustration. "That's what I'm

thinking, too. How else could I be the pastor of this congregation after just two years in the faith? Did the people sense in me, from the very beginning, the kind of person they were accustomed to obeying in the old world? Beneath my grime and poverty did I still walk and talk and sound like the son of an ancient knightly family?"

"If you're a leader, you're a leader. It doesn't take people a long time to see that."

"But I'm not sure I'm a leader. Noble manners, noble arrogance don't make a man a leader. It's just a varnish. Now Onkel Langshammer . . . that man is a leader. As common as dirt, but a leader."

"I think you're a leader," said Marga. Then she changed the subject. "What about me? Do I seem like the pampered daughter of a rich Tyrolian burgher?" She struck a pampered pose, her nose in the air and her lips pursed.

"Pampered? I'd say more than pampered. I'd say somebody spoiled you rotten!"

"Oh, they did! And I confess I loved it! I had the best dolls from Italy, and silks from Palestine, not only for my own clothes but for the dolls . . ."

"For the dolls?"

". . . and oranges to eat, from Spain. And I had my own tutor. Can you believe that I can read and write?"

"It's not uncommon these days, Marga, for women to read and write."

"To read and write Latin and Greek?"

"Greek?" he asked, disturbed that she knew something he did not. "Have you read the New Testament of Erasmus?"

"No, actually," she replied. "I only started the Greek. The alphabet, the present and imperfect tenses and the first two declensions were about all I learned." Paulus was relieved. "I had a tutor from Florence. But that all came to an end when my father heard Balthasar Hubmaier preach one day near Innsbruck. That changed everything."

"Balthasar Hubmaier, Onkel spoke of him almost as if he were one of the twelve apostles."

"I never met him." She said this curtly.

"And your father. The one who spoiled you so extravagantly and thoroughly."

"He is a great man, in his own way."

"How did he get his wealth?"

"Silver mines. His charter came directly from the Hapsburgs. We had a house in Innsbruck that probably made your father's castle look like a shed."

Incredible, Paulus thought. He was sitting here with the daughter of one of the silver magnates of Europe, the men who produced the stuff that fueled the wars and conquests and intrigues of kings and emperors.

"But it's gone, all of it," she went on. "The day father heard Hubmaier – it was 1527, I was sixteen – he came home with an ashen face and wet hair. 'What happened?' I asked him. He told me he had heard the true word of God, and that he had been baptized, and that our lives were changed forever. He proceeded immediately to sell the mining interests, the house, my mother's wardrobe, which he had kept carefully since the day of her death. It must have been worth a small dukedom. All that money, I never knew where it went after father got it, but it was quickly gone. I suspect that he used it to buy the release of many of the Anabaptist prisoners in the Tyrol. Once the authorities learned that he was willing to spend anything, they likely put their prices higher and higher. Soon the rich Josef-Albert Roth was a pauper."

"And a bishop."

"Yes, of course. It's what you noted about yourself. Once a noble, always a noble – once rich and influential, always rich and influential. The brethren around Innsbruck naturally looked to my father for spiritual leadership. He didn't seek it."

Paulus thought, *Who in his right mind would?*

"But he paid the price of it, didn't he?" Her voice now

had the strident edge which Paulus had heard several times before.

"There is a price. Hubmaier paid it too." He was referring to Hubmaier's death by burning in 1528.

"But is it a price that God demands? Or is it just sinful *hubris* in another form? This obsession with suffering and martyrdom – isn't it just our own *anabaptist* display of arrogance? *Look at us, look at us, we're suffering and dying for Christ!*"

Now she was stepping into the heart of what was, for Paulus, holy territory. He momentarily lost sight of her as a woman and met the immediate intellectual challenge.

"Marga, we don't kill ourselves, or torture ourselves! It's the work of the world."

"Are you so sure?" Her words picked up speed and spilled over each other. "If you could have seen what happened when father was arrested, you would understand me. One mealy mouthed little constable came to our small house with the arrest order. He had no trouble finding father because father had made no effort to hide himself. As he stepped into the house you could tell by the look in his eyes that he knew he was in the presence of a great man. He was almost apologetic when he read the summons. Now all father had to do was to call upon his most authoritative voice and say, *Out of my house, you scum!*, and the man would have bowed and left. We could have made our escape before someone else was sent, and he would be with us today. He did not have to let himself be taken. Why? What a waste."

Marga's front teeth flashed openly in her passionate words.

"But what does the Lord say? *Resist not him who is evil.*"

"I know the verse," she snapped.

"Then what do you think it means?"

"I am not advocating that my father should have killed the man, or even hurt him. Even if he had refused to leave, we could have tied him to a chair and left."

"But what does the verse say? Does it say, *Do not kill*, or *Do not hurt*? It says, *Do not resist*. What does that mean?"

"Does it say that?" she asked, defiantly, but on the defensive. "You know how such things get said a thousand times, until we all begin to believe them, and when we go to find them in the Bible we find that someone had made them up or changed them. Maybe that verse has been given a martyr's twist."

"Will you believe me if I tell you I have memorized the verse directly from Onkel's Bible, and that it says *widerstreben*? *Resistere*."

"No."

"What?"

"No, I won't believe you. Show it to me."

He fetched his Bible. The reading of the passage proved him right.

"Well, that's what Luther says, that's his translation. Some time when we are near a Greek New Testament we shall settle it for good. Perhaps Jerome and Luther had their axes to grind. I suppose you'll have to trust me for that verdict, since you know no Greek." The almond eyes stared straight at him with no fear or hesitation. Paulus was really angry now but dared not show it.

"Until then," he said slowly, "we will have to go by the German, won't we?"

"And if I don't agree?"

"Then I will excommunicate you from the community."

She began to laugh and put her hand to her mouth. Paulus was more serious than she suspected.

"WHAT A MESS," MARGA said, seeing Paulus' room one day.

It was. Marga and Anna had stayed there on their arrival but were now in their own room; Paulus had returned, and he had put Onkel's things back where they had been when he left. There were woodworking tools everywhere and a heap of shavings between the beds.

"It's not a mess, Marga. It's the way it's always been."

"But aren't you going to pick up all that?" she asked, pointing to the middle of the room.

"The shavings? No, I put them back when you moved out. When Onkel comes back he will find it all just as he left it. He'll want to finish that stool, and he has a hard enough time finding things without my moving them around. His eyes are weak."

"You talk as if it's not your room at all."

"It isn't. It's Onkel's. It always will be."

"What if he never comes back?"

"He will."

Marga whistled between her teeth. "This man has a hold on you. I wonder why."

"Because he loves me. Come, we must get to the meeting room for service." Paulus took the Bible that lay on the table, for which he had come – Onkel's Bible, Onkel's table.

THEY WERE BACK to their running argument about the meaning of Jesus' commandment not to resist evil people.

"You are really saying that God *wanted* father to do what he did, aren't you?"

"Yes."

"That's just so hard for me to believe. I know, I know, you have the texts on your side, so don't quote them to me again."

"Is it just the texts, Marga? Is it just to you a matter of buckling under to something that you think is stupid? Can't you see the wisdom in it? Jesus took the burden out of our hands. Just think about it. If he had said, *Resist gently,* it would be up to our wisdom to decide in each case what is gentle. And do you think for a moment that the definition of *gentle* would not escalate? Next to a blow in the nose, a shove is gentle. Next to the thrust of a sword, a blow in the nose is gentle. Next to death, torture is gentle. Even the Inquisition does its work in the name of Christian mercy. What would you want your father to have done?"

"Nice sermon," she said.

"Now you're baiting me. I don't like that. You want me to defer to you just because you're a woman? Poor little Marga, she's just a woman, so I won't tell her what I really think because she won't understand anyway. Or, she's too gentle to bear it. Is that what you want?"

"No! I want you to listen to what I'm saying. Really listen. I don't mean necessarily to what I'm saying in terms of its logic. You always hear the words, Paulus, you hear them so well, but sometimes you don't hear me. Me."

"Aren't the words an expression of you? I never take them as anything else but . . . you."

"That's what you don't understand. No, the words are not always an accurate expression of me. They get jumbled and confused and they lack logic. They fail all the tests. But in spite of that, I am still trying to say something, and that is what you must look for."

Paulus put his forehead in the palms of his hands. Chopping logic with the Catholic theologians at the University of Paris had been elementary compared to this.

"You want me to feel what you feel. Is that it?"

"Yes."

"Then tell me what you feel. I'm not a brute. I have feelings too. What do you feel?"

"I feel. . ." Her bottom lip shook slightly. "I feel angry with God. It doesn't seem right. Here is this commandment, like a big rock in a river on which the boats break themselves. *Do not resist, do not resist.* It sits there, no matter what happens, no matter how much suffering it brings on those who try in their simplicity to keep it. Why is it the height of piety to keep that commandment, Paulus? Why has it become for us the single greatest commandment? Are there not others? How about the commandment to care for one's family? How about the words of Jesus that the good shepherd does not abandon the flock when he sees the wolf coming? Because that is exactly what my father has done: abandoned his flock, and his family. Is it really better that the church in Innsbruck dissolve, and his own daughter end up in Moravia, than that he shove the constable out his door?"

"Now, what do I respond to – your feeling, or your logic? I can hear what you're saying, and I can see what you're feeling, but they're different things."

Marga dug in her heels. "My logic. What do you say to those scriptures?" she demanded.

"About the flock and the family?"

"Yes."

"I respond by saying that you are setting the commandments of Christ against each other. And you are trying to arrange them in a hierarchy, a system, so that some are more important than others. We cannot do that. Our faith is a rejection of that method of dealing with the commandments of Christ. We are called simply to obey."

"But that's what I'm saying, exactly. How could father obey the commandment not to resist and the commandment to care for his family, for me? Could he have obeyed them both?"

"He had to obey what was right in front of him. As your father stood confronting the constable, there was no question about the method of obedience to the commandment not to resist. It would have been disobedience to resist. He obeyed. But did he know for sure that in order to care for you and his church he had to resist? Did he know what would happen afterward? It seems to me that that is for God to decide."

"You're saying that maybe it's better for me to be here, and God knew that all along."

Paulus nodded. "Is it so incredible?"

"It's hocus pocus. Maybe those years in the Sorbonne warped your reason more than you know, Paulus."

"Maybe they did." This was getting rather rough; Marga was an intellectual mercenary and could fight with any weapon when she had to. She said,

"You're sitting there, with that ridiculous hat on your head, that hair sticking out your nose – can't you trim those hairs, Paulus? – and you're telling me with this scholastic logic that somehow it is better for a man to go to prison and his daughter to be homeless than not."

Her words clipped from her mouth so rapidly that they were almost unintelligible, and she was losing the battle with tears that had been raging within her for the last minute or so. At the same time, her comment about his hat and his nose hairs had set Paulus laughing. So, at the same moment, she began to cry and he to laugh.

"You're a barbarian," she said. She struggled monumentally to stop her crying. "You're an animal."

"What else?"

"A fake aristocrat."

"With a hairy nose," he could not help replying.

But she had started crying and had to finish. Paulus sat quietly by her side until she gathered herself.

"I'm sorry," she said.

"For what? For grieving over a great loss? You'd be less than human if you didn't shed tears for that."

"That's not what I was crying about. For father, I'm all cried out. I was frustrated at you."

"I don't know what else I could have done but keep my mouth shut completely."

"Try it some time."

They did not part that day on the best of terms. But Paulus found that these intellectual and emotional jousts with her stimulated his desire for her in a powerful way.

THEN, THE NEXT day:

"Marga, I was thinking of something else I didn't say yesterday, something I should have said. About your father and our talk."

"Will it make me cry?" she asked. But she was teasing him.

"I don't think so. I was thinking that I should have spoken about Jesus himself. You are right that I often fall back into the old dialectical ways I learned, when I should be talking about Jesus. Isn't Jesus our example? And didn't Jesus do exactly as your father did, when they came to arrest him? That's what I should have said."

"But Paulus, Jesus was on his way to the cross to die for our sins. That was the purpose of his life and everything was directed to that end. Father was not on his way to die for anyone's sins; he was just on his way to prison. Is that the same?"

"He's our example," asserted Paulus. It was what Onkel had taught him: *don't be afraid to bring a simple answer against a complex, tangled problem.*

MARGA WAS ABSENT from the evening worship, and when it was done Paulus sought her out in her room. She was mending something with a needle and thread.

"What's wrong?" he asked.

"Nothing. I had some mending to do and was tired."

"You are a member of our body. You are expected to be in the worship unless you are sick or unable."

"What was the sermon about?"

"The sermon is not the point. The health of the whole community is the point. If you are absent unnecessarily again, I will bring up the possibility of discipline."

Her mouth was hanging open as he turned and left. The next evening she stood of her own initiative and told the others she was sorry. She was not absent again.

ON THE NIGHT Paulus had seen Marga outlined by the fire, he had resolved, in the deepest layer of his will, to marry her. Marriage occupied his thoughts, although he and Marga did not discuss this. Their actual relationship proceeded slowly. As July gave way to August, and the wheat began to stiffen and brown, he had still not touched her. Once, when they were out of sight of the others, Paulus almost took her hand, but his courage, or his certainty, failed him.

He spent much of his study time – which was scant during the summer – in the dining room, where Marga could be with him without scandal or mystery. Usually there was some twilight when they sat down together, and when that ended Marga lit two oil lamps on either side of their table and they continued reading into the early night, she respecting the necessity of his reading the scriptures, he yearning to touch her. When his eyes could no longer focus on the letters in Onkel's Bible, they put out the lights and he walked her home.

Paulus talked to Claus Hestermann one day.

"You can see what's happening with Marga Roth and me, can't you?"

"Of course we can. You are spending time together, maybe even learning to love each other. Am I right?"

"I hope so. What do the brothers think of this?"

"Think? What is there to think? It is what happens."

"Do they talk about it?"

"Yes, of course. But not much."

"Approvingly?"

"Of course. Paulus, we all have wives."

"What would Onkel think?"

"I think he would think as I do."

"I think he would counsel me to remain celibate."

Claus shook his head. "I know some things about Heinrich Langshammer that you don't know. You should trust me in this."

Paulus was not quite convinced. He thought perhaps

that he knew Onkel's mind better than Claus did, even though Claus had been with Onkel much longer. But still it was comforting to hear Claus say this.

What would Onkel think? With this in the back of his mind, and with the desire to learn of Onkel's well-being as the publicly stated purpose, Paulus took another trip to Olmütz in early August. The boat ride down the Morava went quickly. In Olmütz, he questioned the secretary of the Town Council and one of the deacons of the cathedral. He even walked several times around the burg, the bastion in the center of the town that served as a prison, hoping that Onkel might be inside and happen to see him from a window. All to no purpose: he got no answers from any of the officials, and the burg remained dark and silent before him. One day in the town was all he could risk, so he left before dusk and took the road along the river home.

It was a new Marga that met him radiantly upon his return. It had been five days.

"I missed you," she said. "Nobody talks with me like you do." Worship was over for the evening. Paulus had announced to the brotherhood the failure of this second attempt to find Onkel, and they had prayed with fervor for his return and safety. Now Paulus and Marga sat, as they often did, on part of the woodpile.

"I missed you," Paulus replied. "But I couldn't remember what your face looked like. When I saw you this afternoon it was like seeing you for the first time."

She stared unabashedly at him. Sometimes, when she looked straight at him, he felt like his head was being almost physically bored into by her dark brown eyes. It frightened him a little that she was able to do this. He turned away.

"Are you sad about Onkel?" she said.

"More than that. I'm afraid. He's either been transported away, or they are doing something to him in Olmütz that they don't want anyone to know about."

"They're vile heathen. God will judge them."

A wave of emotion came over Paulus, and he felt like crying and putting himself in a woman's arms.

"Let's not talk about the heathen," he said.

He was in such a churning sea of emotions, anger, despondency, unspeakable joy in the presence of Marga, fear for the future, that he reached out and took her hand. She responded with a firm grip. Her hand was small and bony, but strong. The difficult chores of the summer had produced callouses in her palm, but it was a feminine hand nevertheless. They sat without talking for a long time, while the last light of dusk disappeared.

"What will the others think?" Marga asked.

"They'll think that you're relentlessly pursuing me, and that you've finally cornered me here, and that you've grabbed my hand against my will. What else?" She tugged at his hand but he hung on. "They'll think that we . . . like each other. That I need you, maybe that you need me, although that's more difficult to imagine." He lifted their joined hands.

"Paulus!" she whispered in protest.

"Someone rescue me!" he shouted. "She won't leave me alone!" A small child's head poked up at a window to look. Somewhere inside a cabin a woman giggled.

"Paulus!" She was not strong enough to bring their hands down.

"I like her, I need her, I'm glad to see her again!" he shouted.

CLAUS HESTERMANN HAD said, *It is what happens.* Man and woman are drawn together. Holding hands is not the end.

Paulus read the Genesis account of Adam and Eve more often now, and the words of Moses, *And the two shall become one flesh,* made his heart race.

At harvest time the energies of the brotherhood focused completely on bringing in the crop. Paulus and his foresters laid down their axes and took up scythes that Willi had made as sharp as razors. Since the fields were scattered in different places, the men divided into groups to harvest them. On the morning when the harvest began, the brothers stood out in the light of the rising sun and sang one of their hymns and Paulus prayed for God's blessing on the harvest.

It was back-breaking, arm-wearying, throat-drying work. Lines of men advanced through the fields like destroying armies, the long strokes of their scythes carefully measured in relation to each other, and in their wake the golden wheat covered the earth in fan-shaped bouquets. Behind them came the sheavers, who tied the bouquets into bunches and stood them with the grain up. Dust and chaff rose in clouds under their feet and no kerchief, no matter how tight, could keep it out. A boy named Michael followed Paulus' group with a goatskin of water slung over his shoulder, and responded to the calls of the men when they had to rinse their throats. The water was not just for drinking; they poured it over their gritty heads and rinsed their faces with it as often as they wanted, and they doused their chests and shoulders and wetted their felt hats with it. So Michael made many trips to the Plava, and at the end of the day he was as tired as the others.

It went on for four days, under dry blue skies, and there was a building elation because it was the best harvest that any of them could remember. It was not, by any relative standard, a good yield, for the soil they worked was rocky and uneven, far different stuff from the loam that lined the river banks below them. But for them it was life. If they had to work twice as hard as their neighbors in the world, so be it: their bellies would be full anyway, their children would live, and they would have peaceful minds through the winter. So there began to be talk about having a prodigal feast to celebrate the conclusion of the harvest. Two of the fattest sheep would be butchered, and a pig – oh, they talked about the deep grease that would crackle over the fire and the dollops of dough they would drop into it, and how the crisp doughballs would taste with the roasted meat.

There would be crusty tarts filled with blackberries, and hearty sour wheat beer. The anticipation of it produced a ferocity in their work on the last day.

It ended for Paulus when his group had leveled their last field. They plowed through it like men possessed and stood panting at its edge, calling for Michael and his waterskin, while the sheavers finished their work. Paulus dropped onto all fours.

"Michael, here for a moment!" he called. The boy ran to him. "Baptize me, my boy." The cool water hit his sweaty back and took his breath away. This, they all knew, was their last drink in the field. They could return to the settlement, collapse for a while, and arise to the feast in the evening.

Marga appeared and walked, with her delicate straight steps, around the edge of the field toward Paulus and the others. When she reached Paulus the others had started to leave. The sheavers had finished, and the field looked like a village of miniature thatched huts.

"Hello, my friend," said Paulus.

"Hello, my friend."

"What brings you out here?"

"The women sent me to see how the work is coming. Everything is ready, and you are the last to finish."

"Oh, patience!" he exclaimed. "After all this, there is time to sit and enjoy the victory. They can wait a little longer."

He sat on a stump, savoring the relief of sitting and the coolness of the water as it evaporated off his body. There was a strange look in Marga's eyes, though; she was drinking him up with them and he was suddenly aware that he was half naked. He reached for the shirt he had discarded.

"No, no," she protested in a husky voice, putting her hand on the shirt. "Let me look at you."

She knelt between his knees and gazed up at him. Then she put her arms around his waist, and he felt her short fingernails on the skin of his lower back, and he was glad that he was sitting down because his knees would not have held him up.

"Marga, I'm dirty, you'll get yourself dirty." He was. His upper body was covered with clinging dust and chaff and sweat and clean streaks where the water had run.

She smiled up at him and held him tighter. "I don't care," she said. She ran her hands up the two sides of his back, digging her fingers into him like she was trying to pull the muscles away from the bone. The defenses inside him, frail, pathetic, ramshackle defenses, crumbled at the onslaught of her woman's love. He embraced her and the words he had held inside came tumbling out.

"Marga, do you know I love you, I love you?"

"Yes, I know you love me, you stubborn man. Why has it taken you so long to say so? Why must we debate everything first? Why do I have to kneel before you like a serf, to get you to say that?"

"I don't know. It's so easy. I love you, I love you."

"And I love you."

"And I love you."`

"I love you."

What a face she had, with its marble white skin and almond eyes. And what hair. He seized two handfuls of it above her ears and pulled her face right up to his own.

"That crevice between your teeth, I love it. I've always loved it. Now smile for me. Keep your hand down, and smile."

She gave him a big smile.

"I love that crevice."

They began to kiss each other, at first delicately, then violently, like hungry animals, and kept kissing until Paulus began to forget what she looked like and drew back, breathing heavily, to see her face. He was through forever with the diplomatic stolen glances at her, with the effort to take her in with his eyes without seeming to do so, with the attempts to appear civilized and discrete and self-controlled when what he really wanted was to gawk at her like a child at a new toy. Now he gawked. He let his eyes run all over her face, and along her neck, and down her bare white arms, and then back up to her face.

"It's frightening to be studied like this," she said.

"I'm just opening the cover of this book. I'm just beginning my study of you."

"That sounds like an offer of marriage."

"Please marry me."

"When?"

"As soon as we can arrange it. Maybe even next week."

"That's too long. Why not tonight?"

"Tonight?" *What will the brothers think?* He wanted, of course, to marry her that night, but he felt himself squeezed between his private desires and his public position. He offered a feeble excuse: "I don't even know how marriage is done among us. There has never been one here since I have lived here."

She swept it away. "You're the Onkel," she said. "You decide."

She had a good point. "I'll ask Claus," he said. "If anyone knows, he will."

"Paulus, you're not going to *ask* him if we are going to be married tonight. You're going to ask him *how* to do it. We must get married tonight. I can't wait any longer. It would be sinful to wait any longer."

THEY WENT BACK to Montau and found Claus Hestermann gathering in the sheep for the evening, while all around him preparations for the harvest celebration were under way. Paulus asked Claus to perform their marriage ceremony, and Claus laughed.

"We're serious," said Paulus.

Claus subdued his smile and said, "Philip and Anna were married in Austria. Get them."

So they fetched Philip and Anna, Philip from the garden and Anna from the kitchen, and asked them to review how

Onkel Langshammer had done their wedding. It was simple.

"I can do that," said Claus.

Paulus went to his room to wash, while one of the women washed his shirt and held it close by the fire in the kitchen to dry. Marga went to her room with several other women to wash and arrange her hair. Paulus was all alone in his room for a while, feeling in a glorious daze. Then several men came with his clean, dry shirt to escort him to his bride. The women brought Marga to him. They all met outside the kitchen and stood in the tall summer grass.

Marga mouthed the words *I love you* to him.

Claus raised his arms to quiet the excited whisperings of the group.

"Marriage is a covenant, like God's with us," said Claus. "You should make your covenant with each other now, and we will be your witnesses on the judgment day."

Paulus faced Marga and spoke first.

"I want you to be my wife, and I want to be your husband. I promise to stay with you whatever happens and to be faithful to you."

Paulus had finished. He looked at Claus to see if this was the general idea; Claus looked over at Philip, who stood nearby in a kind of advisory role, and Philip nodded. So Claus nodded to Paulus.

"Marga?" Claus primed her.

"I want to be your wife, Paulus Ketterling." It was with full consciousness that she left out the distinguishing, aristocratic *von* from his name. "I promise to stay with you through life and be faithful to you."

Now Claus turned again to Philip and whispered something in his ear, and Philip whispered back. Claus told one of the boys to get his Bible from his room. The ceremony stalled while this went on, but Paulus and Marga stood as they had while exchanging promises, oblivious to the others. Her eyes bored into his. *What am I going to do with this furious woman?* She seemed to him enormous, overwhelming in her power and love. Claus read from the Bible. When he was finished he led the whole congregation in a prayer of thanksgiving. After the amen he hesitated for a moment, then said:

"I suppose you are married now!"

At this he threw his arms around them and the whole assembly cheered and stretched out their hands to congratulate them.

The great feast of harvest victory and marriage joy began. Roasted mutton, fried dough, great chunks of dark bread soaked in the hot grease, various kinds of tarts and pastries, boiled onions and carrots and turnips – in an uncommon burst of prodigality the community of Anabaptists made merry almost the way the world would make merry, with overflowing trenchers and slopping cups and loud laughter. The happy people spilled outside, where they sat on the warm August ground with their food and talked as they ate. As the bellies filled, the conversation slowed, then stalled, and some of the men let themselves fall back in exhaustion and satiation, overcome by the soporific twilight. The children wandered and scattered, untended.

Paulus and Marga ate near the woodpile. Marga didn't talk much and picked at her food as if not hungry, but smiled at Paulus often. The brothers and sisters came by them to congratulate them. Paulus was famished and ate hard as the women refilled his trencher with food, and he had no sense of time. The twilight lasted forever. The sounds of the happy people were sweet to him. Marga rested her head against his shoulder.

Darkness finally came, and the snoozing men roused themselves from the ground as the chill came on, and people went to their rooms.

"Did it seem like a real wedding to you?" Marga asked Paulus as they stepped into his room.

"We're really married," he replied.

"Did it feel like a wedding?"

"Very much. What should a wedding feel like, love? It seems to me it should feel like the people getting married feel. I felt happy, confused, childish, crazy. That's what the wedding was like."

"No bells, priests, formulae, liturgies – you didn't miss that?"

"Not at all."

"That's good. I didn't either."

He blew out the lamp. They became one flesh. The dualities that structured his life – time and eternity, this world and the next, heaven and earth, flesh and spirit – melted, though partially and temporarily, together. He had the sense of heaviness and stasis and silence that accompanies complete happiness. Paulus said, as they lay together in the afterglow:

"For the first time since I became a believer, I am afraid."

"Why?" The sweet gust of her breath passed over his face.

"Because now I have something in this world to lose."

"Now is no time to do theology, Paulus."

JAN BOCKELSON HAD come back to Leiden in 1531. There he married a widow with a nice inheritance and set himself up in the tailoring business. But he was no good at it, or his heart was not in it, for the business failed, and Bockelson took up with one of the town's acting troupes.

At this, he was an instant success. He had stunning beauty, and piercing eyes, and a stage voice that carried like a trumpet. He acted the hero's part in the cheap plays with more than mere professionalism; his tears were real tears, and the swordplay was real combat, sometimes resulting in injury, and the women that he won in the plays were also his women in real life. He took them by their hearts from their husbands and lovers.

And he had ecstasies, or trances. Carried away by some

powerful influence, Jan Bockelson was known to fall stiff to the stage and lie there for hours at a time in a kind of catatonic state, eyes open, lips moving silently. To the crowds that worshiped him, this was awe-inspiring. People came from miles around to see him perform, hoping that they would be able to witness one of these trances.

Then, just as suddenly as he had leapt to fame, Jan Bockelson lost interest in the stage. His acting lost its fire. He needed a bigger stage, larger crowds, and a better script.

CHAPTER 7: EXILE
January, 1533. Moravia.

Just when the memory of Heinrich Langshammer began to be, if not less powerful, at least less distinct in Paulus' mind, when the hurt began to recede and Marga was filling his life as much as the old man once had, Onkel came back.

The winter that spanned 1532 and 1533 was a mild one, which meant that they could work. They fixed their buildings, and they built new homes for people that were not even there yet, and they made the woodpile in the center of the settlement a mountain. The mill on the Plava was choked with the logs that Paulus fed into it, and there appeared near the settlement another hill of unworked logs that the mill could not handle.

Marga had a logical idea for so much timber.

"Why don't we put up a stockade with these logs? Just a wall."

"Why?" asked Paulus, knowing well why.

"To protect us from surprise. To keep the wolves out."

This was not nice of her. She knew already what Paulus would have to say. But she did this because she was an persistent woman. Paulus still did not know whether she fully meant many of the things she said or whether she considered herself an instrument to keep him sharp. It irritated him and he loved it.

"Just like Olmütz? Like a walled city." he said.

"I know your thinking, just like the world."

"That's exactly what I'm thinking. The heathen wall themselves in, and carry swords, and post watches in the night, because they are full of fear. The world is an armed camp, poised like a cat with its back arched, hissing and threatening all the time because of its fear. Are we that frightened?"

"I am. Aren't you?"

"I'm frightened, but not enough to spend my life with my back arched. In any case, what good would it do? Would the brotherhood be willing to fight to defend a wall? If not, it only takes a minute to cut it down."

"Put me on that wall."

"Marga, you shouldn't talk like that, even in jest." He was not at all sure this time that she was jesting.

EARLY ONE MORNING, as the community readied itself for work, one of von Abersicht's household servants rode into Montau on a shaggy plow horse, bundled in furs against the cold. Paulus came out to meet him.

"Good morning, Berthold," said Paulus as Berthold unwrapped himself.

"And to you, Herr Ketterling." The good mornings were perfunctory; it was a dismal morning, with a steel gray sky and a faint fog rising from the frozen, snowless ground.

"May we offer you breakfast? You have been up early and it is cold."

"Thank you, but no. The count expects me back. He is very peevish if he awakes and his own breakfast is not on the table. I have come to give you a message." He lowered his voice and spoke to Paulus. "The count asks you to come to him."

"May I ask why?"

"The authorities have returned Heinrich Langshammer to us."

Paulus was about to shout for joy.

"Wait!" said Berthold quickly. "He is not himself."

"What do you mean?"

Berthold shook his head. "You must come. I suggest you come alone."

"I will come immediately."

"Certainly, you may come with me."

Paulus had one of their own plow horses fetched and saddled for himself, and it plodded off down the muddy frosty path behind Berthold. So Onkel was back, somehow, resurrected from the dead, regurgitated from some stinking prison, but he was not himself. *Not himself.* The phrase tormented Paulus, and his mind raced in jagged circles as they made their way through the forest.

They arrived at von Abersicht's small castle, which sat on a knoll, gray against a gray sky. It was crumbling at some of its corners, and roof slates were missing. Berthold led through the high front door in the main hall, but not before momentarily barring the way to Paulus with his arm and saying:

"Be ready for sadness."

Paulus nodded.

So they went in, through a hall and into a large, cold bedroom. An iron brazier sat in the middle of the room, smoking, but the room was cold. Von Abersicht sat in a high-backed upholstered chair, at a table, next to the brazier, wrapped in quilts. There were some papers before him on the table. The old man reminded Paulus of a hound dog, with his puffy jowls and sad eyes, and his blubbering way of talking. He was an average man and knew it. He never attempted to exceed his capabilities through war or dabbling in high diplomacy, as most of his kind did these days. He was thankful for his tottering castle, and knew it would fall down one day, but he believed that it would last long enough for him to die in it. He just wanted to be left alone to die in his castle. To be left alone – that in itself took some skill in these times of uproar. In a roughhewn sort of way he was an ethical man; he had never lied to the brotherhood or taken advantage of them, as he could have done with impunity.

"My lord," said Paulus with deference, and bowed, as commoners had often bowed to him.

"Herr Ketterling, good day to you." Von Abersicht scanned the papers before him, making Paulus wait for a moment. Then the count said:

"What is this world coming to?" He looked up, his gray eyes peering through folds of flesh.

"My lord, is it true that Heinrich Langshammer has come back?"

"You might say, rather, that they have sent him back. But he is a broken man."

"What happened? Tell me what happened to him."

"Come see for yourself."

The count hoisted himself up on swollen, gouty legs and hobbled, with Berthold's assistance, away from the table. Paulus went behind them. They entered a side room which had a brazier of its own and was much warmer than the count's bedroom. Von Abersicht then extended a hand and said:

"*Ecce homo*. You know any Latin?"

Paulus knew the Latin. It meant, *behold the man*. There Onkel lay. His grizzled face stared up from the cot. The blue eyes were the same color; the deep wrinkles extended from them outward in every direction, and the big bumpy nose stuck up like a bulb.

"Onkel," said Paulus.

There was no answer. Onkel had to squint to see, and Paulus knew by the wide-open eyes that Onkel was not seeing anything. Paulus then touched Onkel's arm and spoke his name again, to which there was still no answer.

"He doesn't talk," said Berthold. "He has been here since

yesterday afternoon, and has not said a word."

"What's happened?" asked Paulus.

"Well," said von Abersicht, "to begin with, he's been in prison for several months. There is no describing what effect that has on a man's mind. Some men harden, others soften, others just break. The hard ones are usually the ones that break. If you don't bend, you have to be awfully tough not to break, and few men are that tough. Now I always took Heine Langshammer for a soft man at heart. A soft man with hard convictions. So they had him in a vice. They pressed him between his body and his heart. He wasn't made to be a martyr. God, what is this world coming to?"

"Judgment day," said Paulus, almost automatically. Never mind that Onkel did not hear this and that von Abersicht and Berthold did not understand or believe it. It was the right answer to the question.

"Here's what happened," continued the count. "I can just about reconstruct it for you. I've seen it before. Here is a good man, with convictions that run deep into his soul. They torture him, maybe even just a little. Maybe all they do is get out the instruments and dangle them before his eyes or rattle them around a bit. He sees right away that he will not be able to bear up under it. He sees that he will inevitably betray his deepest beliefs. He is helpless and they can make him do or say whatever they want. God, what an agony! What a struggle! He can't endure the torture, and he can't betray his faith. So something snaps inside. I've seen it before. Something breaks. Like a thong pulled too hard."

Paulus listened to this analysis with dread, and the listless body on the cot seemed to confirm it.

"Are you saying he's mad?"

"Mad? Maybe. What is mad? The world is mad. I'm mad. God, I've lived too long, that I should lay my eyes on . . . this."

"Is he mad?" Paulus demanded.

"Of course he's mad!" barked the count. "He's somewhere else now, somewhere safe, where the fire and the machines can't reach him. He saved his soul and lost his mind. What is it with you people? You are like the rest, mad already. Is anything worth believing this much?"

Although Paulus appreciated the righteous indignation of the count, he now looked him in the eyes and said:

"My lord, if I may respectfully reply, God will make up all our suffering in the day of his kingdom. It is for that glory that we wait."

"I know, I know," the count grumbled. "You must take him now. I don't know what to do with him. Why did they bring him here?"

"Of course we will take him. Only let me return to Montau and get some help. Unless you can spare some of your own servants."

"No, you use your own people."

"Can he walk?"

Von Abersicht pulled back the edge of the blanket that covered Onkel's body.

"No, they've burned his feet."

Paulus saw, and averted his eyes, and saw again. Onkel's feet were red and misshapen and covered with shiny gnarled scar tissue. Some of his toes had been almost welded together. Paulus thought of Onkel holding his hand over the flame. And of the man at the stake with his flaming paper hat. He thought of the flames of judgment, cascading torrents of pain, and he wished these flames on those who had tormented his friend. But it was Count von Abersicht who spoke for them both.

"May they burn in hell."

The rest of the morning was filled with the ride back to Montau, the return trip, with several of the men, to von Abersicht's to get Onkel, and the final journey home.

Von Abersicht said, as they were about to leave:

"Herr Ketterling, take care. They know your name."

THEY PUT ONKEL Langshammer on a sled with thick wooden runners and the horse pulled him home. About noon they arrived at the settlement and the brethren crowded around the sled, anxious for a glimpse of the long lost bishop, frightened of what they would see. Paulus had already told them of his condition.

There was no talking. The brothers and sisters knew instinctively that it would be destructive to talk about such suffering. They could teach about it, from the Bible. But they could not gawk at Onkel's shattered person and say things about him. They would undoubtedly think such things, but they would never say them, because spoken words made the thought forever irretrievable, both to the one who spoke and to the one who heard.

To the children, they gave simple, straightforward answers, with no details. A little girl asked:

"Papa, is that Onkel, the other Onkel?" Heinrich Langshammer had already become dim in her memory. "What's wrong with him? He doesn't look right."

"He has suffered for the sake of Christ."

Of course she didn't understand all that this meant. But her father did not say, *They put him in prison and burned his feet and asked him questions*. He simply said, *He has suffered for the sake of Christ*.

So the brotherhood gathered around the old pastor, their father in the faith, the man who had led them out of the Egypt of Roman Catholicism, through the Red Sea of Zwingli's Protestantism, out into the desert of the world. Now he had fallen in the midst of the journey. They discussed how he should be cared for and where he should be kept. Then they took him indoors.

MARGA WAS PREGNANT. They had known this since

November, when Paulus had not reached for her in bed because it was the predictable time of her menstrual period, and she had said:

"Have I done something to anger you?"

"What?"

"Don't you want me tonight?"

"Of course I want you. I want you all the time. But it's the time of month."

"Not tonight, young man."

"I thought . . ."

"I know. Maybe I'm pregnant."

It jolted him. "How will you know for sure?"

"I asked Anna about it. She said I should miss two monthly cycles before I can be sure. But I don't believe that. I've never missed one in my life. Handsome barbarian, you got me pregnant."

That was the first sign. Then her internal temperature changed. Always she had been the cold one. Now she was always too warm. Her cheeks flushed magnificently pink and behind her smile was a new spark of joy. She became sexually voracious and Paulus gladly met her need. The women told her she would be sick in the mornings – they always seemed to know just exactly how it would be and were delighted to hand out advice to her – but she never was. They told her she would be tired, and they tried to take over some of her work, but she felt extraordinary and abounded in energy. They suggested that she should be cautious and prudent in the matter of lovemaking; she told Paulus this and together they laughed uproariously and then made love. Old wives' tales.

It was into the midst of this beautiful time that Onkel Langshammer came back. Paulus insisted that the old man stay with them since it was, after all, his house and because Paulus thought that if anyone could pierce the opaqueness of Onkel's mind it would be he. Onkel required little care. A bed was set up for him on the vacant side of the room, and Paulus finally cleaned up the mess that Onkel had left there on the floor. Onkel lay on his back most of the time, but he was able to get up to relieve himself with the aid of a pair of crutches. It was pathetic to see him put his ruined feet to the ground. They were stiff and lifeless, like boards of wood rather than living things. He ate well, and slept well, and seemed to be physically comfortable. But he never talked. The people talked to him as if all things were normal, and Paulus made a special effort to assault him with words. Perhaps Onkel really could understand, but Paulus never knew.

After a couple of weeks Paulus built a wooden partition wall with a door to separate Onkel from himself and Marga. He felt guilty and uncomfortable about this, as if he were shutting Onkel out of his life. He could not shake off the sensation that this was Onkel's room – how could he bring himself to wall Onkel into an almost closet sized space and take the largest share of the room for himself?

Because Marga insisted on it. Onkel was not a friend to her, only a strange, demented old man. He never looked at her, or at anything, in his labored, squinting way. His perception was a haze. Marga could have run around naked in the room and Onkel would not have noticed. But he was there, while she dressed, and slept, and while she and Paulus made love, and it was not the same with a man in a bed across the room, no matter how distant his mind was. They loved under the blankets, silently, but without their customary freedom. Paulus thought she might eventually learn to disregard Onkel, and he tried patience, but it only got worse. He wanted her back. He hung a curtain across the room but that was not enough; she asked him to build a wall.

Paulus built it one day, shut the door with Onkel behind it, went to bed with Marga and found his passionate wife again.

"A wooden wall makes a big difference," he said to her as they went to sleep.

"Yes."

"Even though he can't see and probably can't hear us. You realize the only difference is that our room is now smaller, don't you?"

"Why don't you go knock your head against your new wall and get smarter? You're so objective you're stupid sometimes."

He raised his head to be able to look at her.

"Enlighten me," he said.

"You really don't understand? No, you really don't. Here's how it is, Count *von* Malbeck. The wall is not just a wall. It's a symbol."

"Of what?"

"Of the fact that this is my room – mine and yours. Onkel Langshammer is welcome, but it's our house now. Until you built that wall I wasn't sure you felt that way."

Then he understood for the first time that Marga saw Onkel as a rival for his affection, even though the old man saw nothing and said nothing. He wanted on the one hand to laugh at how ridiculous this seemed to him, and on the other hand to tremble a little at the ferocity of her love for him. And Onkel had said that the love of a woman was like this. Marga went quickly to sleep, and Paulus disengaged himself from her warm embrace, feeling the need to be by himself even in the small space of the bed. He felt guilty about the wall. Later, when he was almost asleep, he shifted and brushed against her and felt the dry warm satin of her skin and took her into his arms.

Thus crumbled the most reasonable predictions of the past. Heinrich Langshammer, the man who had kept himself celibate and free so that he would not be a burden to anyone, was now a burden. Paulus, the man who would never marry, was married and about to become a father. Together they had tied themselves to the world. Never before had Paulus dreaded so much the midnight sound of horses or the clattering of armor in the clearing outside his door.

A NEW BISHOP came to rule in Olmütz over the diocese which included the lands of Count Otto von Abersicht. He was anxious to please his superiors. Bohemia and Moravia were notorious dens of heresy, and he intended to clean them out.

When the soldiers came from Olmütz and milled around in the clearing, Paulus heard the noise and his first thought was that Ernst had not shut the gate and the plow horses were loose. It was a frosty, clear, moonless night in January. He must go and wake Ernst and they would put the horses back into the pen. As he shoved his feet into his boots he instantly knew the truth; their horses were not loose, for he had seen Ernst put the horses away earlier that evening. *It's the time, it's them.* Nothing happened: no panic, no hysteria, no aching in the chest. Just a dry, frozen calm in his heart, the resignation to inevitability. Montau suddenly seemed infinitely fragile, brittle, and chimeric to him, and he could almost feel it evaporating around him. Then came the sound of a man's rough voice calling out something he could not understand. He opened the door and saw the figures on horseback. One of them carried a torch. The clearing was full of steam from their breath.

"Paulus," said Marga.

"Soldiers, love. Get dressed."

"Oh, no!" she hissed and sat up.

One of the soldiers had heard the door open and walked his horse toward Paulus, the leather of his harness groaning and squeaking.

"Where is Paulus Ketterling?"

"Right here."

"You must leave this place."

"I will come with you."

"All of you, the whole bunch of you, out."

"By whose orders?" As if it mattered.

"The bishop of Olmütz."

It was so simple and prosaic. They just rode into your home, the place you had hacked out of the forest, the place where you had spilled your sweat and buried your children, and they told you to leave. They had all the power. There was nothing to say in reply.

"We will leave in the morning."

"You will leave right now."

"There are children. Would the bishop punish them too?"

"If the bishop had wanted you to leave at your convenience he would have sent a letter. No, there will be no heretics here when the sun rises again. Be thankful, heretic. We have orders not to hurt you unless there is resistance."

"Do you know that little about us? There will be no resistance."

"Perhaps you know little about yourselves, heretic. Yes, you will fight. Someday you will give up this nonsense and you will fight. Like the heretic brother of yours down the hill, who came after us with a scythe."

"There will be no resistance here."

"I trust not."

Others besides Paulus now poked their heads out of their doors. A small child cried in one of the houses, and the sound of it made Paulus glad that he had no children.

"Will you withdraw your men so we can gather our things?"

"I will give you room, but I cannot leave. My orders are strict."

Paulus dressed, and Marga sat up in the bed with the blankets pulled up around her shoulders, saying nothing, watching him, and he was glad that he could not see her eyes, for those eyes, now dark and hard, would be saying: *Do something, Paulus. Resist. Yell.*

"Where are we going?" she finally asked in a lifeless voice.

"Into the woods, maybe down to the Morava."

"How about the count? Would he let us stay there?"

"No. Believe me, the count has his head almost on the

block because we are on his land. The soldiers will watch him tonight, maybe longer. Get dressed."

"Like sheep to the butcher," she spat. But it was a silly thing to say. Of course the believers were sheep.

"Exactly, love." As she dressed he said, "Put on everything you can wear, then gather up all of our blankets and belongings. But especially the blankets, anything to cover a body and keep it warm. We'll need them all."

Then Paulus went through the settlement. Many were already awake and stood at their doors wondering what to do. Others had to be roused. Sheep. Paulus repeated his instructions again and again: gather blankets, clothes, rags, rugs, straw, anything to keep the cold away from the children.

Paulus also sent several of the brothers to gather up food and to dump it into the community's large two-wheeled cart. They hitched the cart to the horse and piled one end high with sacks of foodstuffs from the shed – grain, and onions and turnips dug out of their protective earth bins. They drew the cart over to the kitchen and loaded into it everything they could find there, from unbaked dough to last night's soup in buckets. The brethren, who ordinarily took such quiet pride in their orderliness, were now forced in the rush to spill, throw, crush, and strew their precious food pell-mell into the wagon. The ground around it was littered with scraps. One of the soldiers meandered over, dismounted, and foraged on the ground for something to eat. Then he looked into the wagon itself and took out a piece of bread. He tore one bite from it and dropped the rest on the ground. They ignored him.

Thirty minutes later Paulus' people converged in the center of the clearing, near the woodpile, carrying their piles of blankets in their arms and looking like huge beasts under their many layers of clothes, enormous dark shapeless forms in the night, waiting there to be told what to do. The soldiers sat on horseback some distance off, growing impatient because they themselves were growing colder and wanted to ride again. The captain shouted, at shorter and shorter intervals:

"Let's go! Off with you!"

They were going as fast as they could.

Finally the men with the cart joined the group and they were complete. They spread straw across the cart and laid Onkel on it and covered him with blankets. Fathers strapped small children to their backs. Paulus said a prayer for protection and guidance, and the sounds of his voice intermingled with the shouts of the captain calling again for them to leave. But where would they go? The points of the compass lay open before them. To the south lay Austria and the bloody maw of the Hapsburgs – almost certain death for Anabaptists. To the north lay the kingdom of Poland, but the Carpathians stood in the way. To the east were trackless forests and the Turks. It seemed to Paulus that their best decision would be to turn west, to populous, confused Germany itself, where they might be able to hide themselves in a corner, or perhaps find other believers like themselves, and where at least they would be in familiar territory and be able to speak the language. Paulus suggested this to the group, and when there was no objection they set their faces toward the path that led down the slopes of the foothills toward the Morava.

The cart creaked as the horse lowered its head and pulled. The wheels had frosted fast to the ground and snapped as they came loose. Onkel's body lurched and rolled toward the side of the cart and several helping hands reached up to set it straight again. They were off.

Paulus glanced back as the path entered the forest. Montau lay black and dead under the starlight, the buildings mere mounds of darkness against more darkness. He heard, faintly and thinly in the cold, the voices of the soldiers, following. Then Paulus, for the first time, felt the backlash of hate in his heart. He had done well: no slaughter, no bloodshed. But now these better, artificial instincts were exhausted, and in the face of a dark cold night and a gray earthly future, he was angry. Montau was the sum of their earthly life, their work, their pain and joy. Now it would rot, or burn, or thieves would pillage it, or the spiders and mice would slowly cover it with webs and hair and dirt. He could see no sense to this. Nobody gained. It was wanton, nasty cruelty.

"Bastards." Marga whispered the word to him as they walked.

"Yes," said Paulus. "They are. Keep quiet."

"Paulus, do something."

"What? Resist? Resist these, kill these? Then more will come!" He snapped at her, and the anger in his voice subdued her.

"It would just feel so good to do something."

They tramped, crunching, feeling their way, for about an hour. Paulus knew they were near the river. There was level ground now, and the soldiers had disappeared, and Paulus' people stopped to sleep. Paulus built a fire and the people huddled on the cold ground in their families. Then the soldiers appeared again. They had dutifully followed the refugees through the night, under orders to be certain that the Anabaptists really vacated their settlement, and they had tethered their horses somewhere in the dark behind them. They were terribly cold and were seeking the warmth of the fire. Paulus swallowed hard and came to meet them. How much like children they seemed now, down from their horses, their faces lit, teeth chattering. Paulus was taller than any of them.

"We've come to warm ourselves," said the man who had spoken with Paulus earlier. He hardly got it out, so violently was he shivering, and though there was some obvious effort to make it sound martial and authoritative, it came out more nearly like a plea. Paulus extended his hand toward the bonfire, and turned from them. He found Marga, nestled into the cocoon of warmth created by her pregnant body, and pulled her close. In her deep sleep she moaned in protest and tried to change position, but Paulus held her fast and said softly in her ear, through the dark female-smelling hair:

"I love you, Marga."

She cleared her throat and shifted, which meant: *Don't bother me, I'm trying to sleep.*

"I love you, Marga," he said again. He did not care whether she responded or not; he loved her and felt like telling her so. He was light-headed and irrational, exhausted, numb from adversity, and she was all he had on this earth. To this second expression of his love she replied, more consciously:

"M-m-m." This meant: *I'm still very sleepy but I acknowledge your intent.*

"Marga, do you love me?"

Paulus said this and then buried his face in her hair at the back of her neck, where her aroma was exquisitely strong, and waited like a child for her reply. He would wait as long as necessary. He would ask again and again, because now he needed to hear her say that she loved him, even if it were dragged from her. He thought, after some seconds, that she had gone to sleep. But then she turned her head toward his face and moved her body slightly to be able to keep it there. Her eyes were shiny with tears.

"I do," she said.

"In spite of everything?"

"Yes."

"Even though I didn't fight?"

"You fought," she said.

So she did understand, after all. Yes, he had fought. Fought as Jesus, and Stephen, and the martyrs, and the Anabaptists Sattler and Hubmaier had fought.

The soldiers remained quietly at the fire and in the morning were gone.

The next day, an Anabaptist from the village of Landshut, also in Moravia, arrived in Montau with a report of events in more distant places. Part of what the messenger would have told them, had they been there, was that Marga's father,

Josef-Albert Roth, had been executed in Innsbruck.

CHAPTER 8: BLOOD
November, 1533. Leiden, Holland.

Two men entered the tavern and stood just inside the door, looking around while their eyes adjusted. It was a cellar room, close by the Leiden docks, and it was lit by a few oil lamps on the walls and a glowing charcoal fire in the center of the room that vented up through a wide iron hood. It smelled of charcoal smoke and yeasty beer and salted fish and the spices in the wine punch which simmered over the fire. And it smelled of the working men who sat at benches and stood in small knots. The two men were Jan Bockelson, whose wheat-colored hair had grown long and whose beard had grown out, and a sullen, silent, nervous man named Piet Bruinsma. It was the day before All Saints' Day, on October 31, 1533.

They saw the man they were looking for, sitting at a table by himself in the far corner, and made their way to him through the tables and benches and customers.

"Are you Jan Matthys?" asked Bockelson. The man at the table nodded yes and the two others sat.

"I am Jan Bockelson, of Leiden, and this is Piet Bruinsma. He doesn't talk. It's kind of you to meet with me. I've had a dream, and it is from God. I want to tell you about it."

"In time," replied Jan Matthys. "There are questions about you to be answered first." Jan Matthys was long, lank, fiftyish, with a big black twisted beard. He wore a floppy black broad-brimmed hat and a black coat. His long back slumped over the table but he held his head straight up, like a buzzard.

"I have no secrets," said Bockelson and smiled. "Especially from you, brother Matthys. You are God's prophet in the Low Countries. You are filled with the Spirit."

"It is reported that you have left your wife."

"I have left her," said Bockelson. "It is true, and public. She hates God's kingdom." After spending his wife's inheritance, Bockelson had abandoned her as blithely as he had abandoned tailoring and acting. "You should understand this, brother Matthys. It is well known that you too left your first wife for the sake of the kingdom." Bockelson was saying this dipomatically. The report – and the truth – was that Jan Matthys had left a sick wife of his own age to the care of her family and had married a much younger, much more beautiful and bosomy brewer's daughter named Divora. It was part of the danger and mystery that surrounded Matthys as the leader of Holland's illegal believers, small bands of brave souls who rejected infant baptism and looked for the imminent return of Christ.

"We cannot allow the work of the kingdom to be polluted by unbelieving wives," said Matthys.

"Never!" said Bockelson, with a flourish of the hand practiced on the stage. "They say you were a baker."

"They say you were a tailor."

"A tailor, yes . . . and an actor. Now . . . I've had a dream, and I want to tell you about it."

"Tell on," said Matthys. "I will determine if it is from God."

Matthys and Bockelson stared straight at each other's eyes in a skirmish for control. Matthys' gaze was grim. Bockelson's was playful.

"Yes, you are God's prophet," said Bockelson, and he laid his hand on Matthys' arm in a gesture that was at once friendly and condescending. Then, quickly, he went into himself, stiffened, and delivered the contents of his dream.

"In my dream I see the globe of the earth. The wicked encircle the righteous in the holy city, to destroy them. The righteous have swords in their hands. They throw open the city gates and march upon the godless hordes. There is divine power in their arms, and though they are vastly outnumbered they march through the ranks of the unbelievers and slaughter them. Slaughter them. Slaughter them. And as this happens the globe turns red and drips blood."

Matthys' eyelids drooped and quivered. His hands flattened onto the table. "What does this mean?"

"What do you think?" asked Bockelson. He knew already.

"Saints with swords," mused Matthys. "Which city is the holy city?"

"What do you think?" prodded Bockelson. He knew which city, but he wanted to create the illusion that the ideas were coming from Matthys.

"Hoffmann proclaims Strassburg as the city of God."

"Can that be, brother Matthys? Hoffmann is in prison. Nothing has happened in Strassburg."

"Hoffmann led us to faith. We must be faithful to his message." Melchior Hoffmann had been the first preacher to bring the message of true baptism and of the second coming of Christ to Holland. He had preached, however, peaceful non-resistance to persecution.

"These are different times!" Now Bockelson warmed. His voice rose in volume and pitch and urgency. "When Hoffmann preached, the enemy was still in his lair, but now he has risen up against the saints! Brother Matthys, they burn us! They stretch us! They break our bones on the wheel! They tear our tongues out!"

On cue, Piet Bruinsma leaned forward into Jan Matthys' face and opened his mouth. Matthys glared into the tongueless hole and Bruinsma waggled a clump of scar tissue at him. The Catholic authorities, uncomprehending, thought that they could silence men by removing their tongues, but men like Bruinsma, with their mutilated mouths, were louder than sermons.

"How long, really, brother?" pleaded Bockelson. "How long can the innocent sheep of God endure this? Is it possible that Hoffmann's message of patient endurance was a message for his time, but that there is a new message for us?"

Matthys was getting it. "The bloody earth. It means that God exercises his judgment through the hands of the saints."

"Yes, that's what I think it means!" said Bockelson. "But I need you to confirm it."

"The people of God are dying. We need champions."

"Like Joshua."

Matthys took Bockelson's cue. "And Samson, and Gideon, and Samuel. All champions of God with bloody swords."

"And Phinehas, remember him?"

Matthys grinned. "He found an Israelite man and a pagan woman fornicating and speared them both through!"

Now Bockelson climbed, in one smooth motion, onto the table and stood upon it. The room was low and he had to bend his neck. He mimed Phinehas impaling the two bodies and lifting them both on his spear into the air with superhuman strength. The drinkers began to watch.

"There is the world, brother Matthys," said the actor, and swept his hands in an arc around the room. "Ripe for the harvest, ready for God's judgment. And how do you think it will come? As Hoffmann has taught, while the saints wait and suffer and die? Or as in my dream? At the hands of the saints?"

"I will pray," said Matthys.

"How many more burnings?" shouted Bockelson, now to the whole crowd. A few paid attention. Most thought he was drunk. "How many more rackings? How many more?"

A large-faced, gray-headed man lifted his beer cup and huffed, "As many as it takes!" and the other men at his table laughed. The gray-headed man flung his cup at Bockelson across the room, and it missed and clattered in the corner.

"You will see the kingdom of God come and the rivers run with blood, old man!" shouted Bockelson. He laughed and jumped lightly down from his stage.

"I have been in the city of Münster for the last few months," he said. "It is like gunpowder waiting for a spark! The preachers, Rothmann, and Rol, and Staprade are already preaching the true baptism. The guilds are coming over to our faith. The guilds hate the nobles, the Lutherans hate the Catholics, and they all hate the new prince-bishop, Franz von Waldeck, who is determined to make his city Catholic again. He will not use gentle methods. It will all get hotter and hotter until it explodes. The parties will destroy each other, and into the confusion you will step with your message from God."

"It is a bold idea. I have pondered it." Matthys was now thinking that this was his idea.

"There is also a mighty man named Bernhard Knipperdolling, a leader of the drapiers' guild, who has been baptized. I have spoken with him. The guilds will be with us. They are a field white for the harvest."

"The scripture speaks of cities of refuge. Münster might be our city of refuge."

"It might. The walls of Münster are thick and high, built in the most modern style, with bastions and a moat."

"It could be a place for the poor Dutch sheep of God to find rest from the suffering they endure now." Visions of torture and execution, most recently of the extraction of Bruinsma's tongue, marched continually through Matthys' mind, keeping it on the boil and driving him to new ideas and expedients.

"There will be violence," said Bockelson. It was a simple analytical statement, coldly made. "We do well to acknowledge that the struggle of the kingdoms of God and the devil is a mortal one, and the weapons we use must be appropriate to such a struggle."

"The red earth."

"Yes, as in my dream, if it is from God."

"It is."

This was the endorsement that Bockelson wanted to hear. "Then you accept the truth that the saints have been given the sword of justice to wield in the name of God?"

"I do. But!" Matthys seized Bockelson's arm across the table. "It is not yet time to announce this truth to the sheep. The weight of events, and of suffering, must pile up. Sadly, more of the saints must be slaughtered before they will be ready to take up this righteous sword."

"Very wise counsel," flattered Bockelson. "But we must stop – right now – telling them to suffer peacefully. We must let Hoffmann's teaching die. Then they will eventually demand the sword."

Matthys shook his shaggy head around in a circular motion. His eyes rolled up into his skull, and there was a slow release of breath between his lips. It was several minutes before he spoke. Then he said:

"Let us see whether Münster can become the city of God. Let us watch God's work. And if it is his work, let us call the saints there. Then we shall see if this prince-bishop, von Waldeck, means business. If he does, we put the swords in the saints' hands and tell them to fight. Then they will understand."

Bockelson smiled deferentially. "It is a glorious thing that the Lord has chosen to speak through you, brother Matthys."

At the next preaching of the prophet, Jan Bockelson allowed himself to be baptized at Matthys' hand and was immediately let into the inner circle of those who went everywhere with the prophet, did his bidding, knew his mind. And had his ear.

CHAPTER 9: DUST
February, 1533. Thuringia.

Onkel's dead body, withered almost to skeletal thinness, lay as if in state near the grave. His cheeks were no longer round. The pink tinge on his eyelids was gone, as was the oily sheen on his nose. Even before his death he had been far on the journey that takes men's bodies back to dust.

They stood around the grave, those who still remained of the flock that had left Montau some six weeks before: Paulus, Marga, Claus Hestermann, the Anna who had come from the Tyrol with Marga, and Krem and Hansi. A pile of gray, rocky earth lay to one side of the hole, Onkel on the other. Claus Hestermann had prayed and now they stood silent with their thoughts. A fine mist covered their hats with tiny jewel-beads of water. Paulus and Claus picked Onkel up, Paulus by the shoulders, Claus by the feet, and they lowered him with great respect into his grave; his head was tilting awkwardly to one side, and Paulus straightened it, pausing to pull the long white hairs back over the forehead where they belonged. Then Paulus placed Onkel's hat over his face, for he could not bear the thought of the earth falling directly upon it.

They had no shovel. They filled the grave laboriously with their hands, and the last they saw of the man who had remade their lives was the crown of his hat and the toes of his felt shoes. To protect the body from wolves they covered the grave with large stones and dragged a fallen limb across it.

The others went down the slope of the hill to the place where they had made a fire and slept the previous night, but Paulus stood by the grave and savored the memory that was his alone, of the words that Onkel had spoken during the night and which only Paulus had heard. For at least three weeks they had known that he was dying: he would not eat, and his complexion grew pasty, and he slept almost all the time. Still they carried him along in a hammock slung between the shoulders of the men. On the night before his death they made their camp close to the bank of the Main, about a day's journey upriver from the city of Bamberg. There was no longer any real purpose in their traveling except to escape from the constant hostile pressure that came upon them whenever they encountered people, so they had zigzagged westward into Germany like a ball being kicked from one player to another.

That night, by the Main, Paulus had awakened to the sound of Onkel's voice speaking incoherent words.

"Onkel, it's Paulus. Say something to me."

More babbling. A word or two, but no sentences. Paulus put his mouth right up against Onkel's warm ear, so that his lips were pressed against it.

"Onkel. I'm Paulus, your son in the faith. Onkel, your church is vanishing. The sheep are wandering away. I can't hold them together. I'm sorry."

Onkel said nothing to this. Paulus rose and jabbed at the embers of the fire with a stick; they broke and glowed, and Paulus swept them together in a pile. Then he heard Onkel again.

"Speak to her kindly," said the old man. It was very soft.

"What, Onkel?" And Paulus now put his own ear to

Onkel's mouth.

"Speak to her kindly." To whom? What was he talking about?

Paulus waited for him to continue, but Onkel was silent. Looking closely at him, Paulus saw that his eyes were closed. But it was not sleep. There was something different about Onkel's face. Paulus put his hand under Onkel's blankets, next to his chest; the cavity was warm, but there was no beating of the heart. It was what he had partly hoped, partly dreaded: Onkel Langshammer was dead.

The only tool they had carried away from Montau with them was an axe, and Paulus now got it and climbed the hill overlooking the river, finding his way reasonably well by the moonlight that filtered through a ceiling of clouds. Onkel should be buried high, he thought, near God, above the villages and cities and roads of the world. He began chopping at the brittle frozen surface of the ground with the axe, and when he had loosened enough earth he got down on his knees and shoveled it to one side with his hands. Part of the way through this work he found himself shouting angry words while he struck long arching blows – unnecessarily violent, vengeful blows – at the ground.

When the others woke in the morning, the grave was ready and Onkel's body was lying beside it.

"WE'VE BEEN TALKING," said Krem to Paulus, with quiet Hansi standing next to him. Paulus knew immediately what it was about. When anyone had approached him like this during the last three weeks it meant that they had decided to leave. He had lost the heart to argue. He felt like saying it himself.

"We've been talking about staying in Bamberg. Hansi has an uncle here, a kind man, not a believer as far as we know, but a kind man."

"You know that Bamberg is ruled by a bishop."

"Yes, but what does it matter? Everywhere we go it is the

same – we are unwelcome. We will hope to find shelter under the roof of Hansi's uncle, and live quietly in God's will."

"Not too quietly, Krem. You cannot lose yourselves completely in the world and remain the people of God."

"We know. We will seek God's guidance. Perhaps there are believers in Bamberg."

Krem and Hansi left before noon. Now there were only Paulus, Marga, Anna and Claus, no Onkel in the sling to slow them down, no small children like Krem and Hansi's to worry about. They could travel quickly, and they did, perhaps to get as far away from Onkel's grave that day as they could, finding the footpath along the Main toward the west.

CHAPTER 10: CHILD
June, 1533. Nassau.

Paulus kept Onkel's Bible in the leather bag with his other things. It was heavy, and it knocked incessantly against his side as they walked, but it never crossed his mind to get rid of it.

After burying Onkel they followed the bank of the Main river through the ecclesiastical territories of Bamberg, Würzburg, and Mainz, all of them ruled by powerful worldly bishops, heavily populated and laced with towns and villages. To eat they foraged in the woods, scavenged on what was dumped outside the towns at night, and begged for charity at small monasteries along the way.

The weather warmed with spring, and instead of snow and sleet the rains came down on them. Claus had lost his wife along the way, and he and Anna talked quite openly about their affection for each other and their desire to marry. They were not young but it could be that they had many good years ahead.

The Main eventually poured its waters into the Rhine near the city of Mainz, seat of Germany's oldest and most prestigious archbishopric. They were traveling the north bank, but the cathedral, solid and confident, was clearly visible across the river. Paulus got a weak feeling looking at it, a feeling which had something vaguely to do with the permanence and immovability of Catholicism.

They entered the territory of the counts of Nassau. To their right were the Taunus mountains, blanketed with trees, and between the river and the mountains the rising piedmont was checkered with vineyards and small hamlets built around winepresses. Paulus was ready to stop here; Marga was almost too pregnant to travel any further. Near the tower of the castle of Eltville they turned north and followed one of the countless little brooks that tumbled out of the Taunus into the Rhine. It led them through vineyards and dense glades, past cottages and ruins of cottages, and into a valley whose sides grew steeper and darker, where the light of the sun rarely pierced the trees and the ground was always damp and rank. Here the brook was rushing past them over sharp rocks.

When Paulus was beginning to think that they had passed the line of human settlement, they came upon a sawmill that straddled the stream. Beyond it the stream had been dammed, and beneath it the flow of water had been channeled through a narrow passage that forced it through the cups of the wheel that drove the saw. The wheel was engaged and the saw was grinding. All around the mill in disorganized bunches lay four-sided beams of various lengths.

Paulus climbed the ladder that led up to the mill and stood at the open door. Inside, a single man with short-cropped blonde hair and a huge red beard worked at the saw. He was shorter than Paulus, stout, bare to the waist, and shiny with sweat. He was feeding a log the length of two men into the teeth of the saw and the chips were flying into his face. When he saw Paulus he finished the cut, kicked loose the clutch that connected the saw to the wheel, and smiled.

"You are not from the duke, are you?" he asked.

"No, I don't think so. We are not here on business."

"Then what?"

"We are traveling. I, my wife, and two others. They are outside. We mean no harm."

The sawyer raised his eyebrows. "So? What do you want?"

"Work."

"Strange place to ask for work. Very little to do here but chop down trees."

"That's what I do best."

The sawyer laughed. "A young man came to me last week, sent up here by his father, I presume, because he was a no good brat. Put him to work, said the father. Well, it was not a half a day and the whelp was asking for mercy. You don't look much bigger than he." He kicked the clutch in and the saw started with a groan.

"I don't expect you to believe me until I've proved myself. Let me work a day for you." Paulus was shouting over the saw. "I ask nothing but a place to sleep for the four of us, no money – for now. What can you lose?"

"No wages? No food? Do you have food?"

"No, but we've been hungry before. We won't die."

The sawyer looked at him quizzically. He put his knotty arms around the lumber, now squared on all four sides, lifted it off its carriage and carried it to the back end of the building, where he dropped one end to the ground and pushed the other end over. It landed with a thunk on others like it. "Fine! You can all sleep here in the mill tonight. There's the axe. I'm working on a stand of pine just over that knoll, you'll see it when you get there. And take the others with you, they'll be in my way."

Paulus took the axe from its resting place on two wall pegs, and before he was out the door the man said:

"Don't think of stealing my axe from me. It's not a good idea to steal from Max Holzmann."

When Max hiked up to the knoll late in the day to check,

Paulus had done a good day's work, and Max knew it. They slept in the mill that night. Paulus worked the next day and at the end of the day Max took all four of them on a circuitous path to a cluster of ramshackle buildings at the foot of a steep slope. This was, he explained, where he lived – he pointed to the largest of the huts – and they were welcome to stay in one of the smaller ones. It was a wreck, but they accepted.

MAX HOLZMANN WAS a talkative man, and Paulus soon heard his story and learned exactly what the four of them had stepped into. Max manufactured structural beams for a man who was somehow distantly related to the counts of Nassau but who had been driven from the court of Nassau in disfavor. This man, who styled himself "The Duke", was building a castle nearby, on one of the rocky eminences, from which to defy and probably harass his family.

"And you are a friend of this man's?" asked Paulus.

"Heavens, no! I hate the man. He needs my beams, I need his money, that's all. Desperate men band together. Very few men up in these mountains who are not rogues or outlaws or moonstruck."

"Which are you?" asked Paulus.

"I'm a rogue, I guess," said Max. "And you?"

"Moonstruck."

The Duke sent his own men about once a week, with big wagons and many horses, to take away the beams and pay Max Holzmann. They were dirty and rough men who cursed at Max, but Max cursed back and held his own with them, and he always got his money. They often brought with them women who were obviously prostitutes, and once Max disappeared with one of them for several minutes while the Duke's soldiers loaded the wagons.

While Paulus worked, Marga, Claus and Anna tried to improve their hut. Its walls were made of closely stacked stones, which were abundant on the mountainside, and it was chinked with mud, and its roof was made of thickly packed branches. But one wall was down, and half of the roof had collapsed into the cottage and was composting on the dirt floor. Bit by tedious bit they fixed it, having as their goal a dry warm place for Marga to have her baby. They fashioned beds from pine needles and covered them with the blankets they still had with them from Montau; they cleared the floor; they rebuilt the roof and reinforced it with off-cuts from the mill; they designed a simple chimney to take the smoke out of the room.

Other people lived in the cluster, but it was a strange silent kind of society which seemed to sleep during the day and go about its business at night. Peddlers came up from the Rhine valley with food and drink, but they too came at night, finding their way on the path by lantern light and waking the people when they arrived. The first time this happened Paulus woke up alarmed, remembering the night they had been driven from Montau.

Marga grew bigger and more uncomfortable; her back hurt and her right leg swelled and ached. But this was to be expected, said Anna. In the midst of her discomfort Marga was radiant and hopeful, and she and Paulus dreamed together of their child and their future. They spent long hours with his hand on her distended belly and her little hand on his, feeling the baby turn and stretch inside. As her time to deliver came nearer, her world contracted to a point: the baby, the baby.

IN THE DEAD of night he heard her voice: "Paulus."

The word hit his ears and he was awake with a start.

"What?"

"I think I just had a pain." Her voice was unnaturally smooth and even; she was trying to sound calm.

"A pain? A birth pain?"

"I think so. Twice now. Very mild, strange feeling. I went back to sleep after the first one."

Paulus propped himself up on his elbow, his heart

pumping.

"Now, remember, what did Anna say?"

"About what?"

"About the pains . . . that they sometimes come but it is not yet time?"

"Yes. So let's just wait and see."

"Should I wake her?"

"No."

Paulus climbed up out of his bed and looked around, at what, he did not know. Claus and Anna were asleep, and the fire they had built was smoldering in the corner. He stuck his head outside. No sign of daylight yet, only the bright stars visible here and there through the treetops. The sound of the water tumbling down the ravine. The old man in the cottage opposite sitting in front of his door next to a small fire, as he always did at night. Paulus stirred up the embers of the fire and put on some wood. He crawled back into the bed with Marga and put his arms around her from behind as she lay on her side.

"Marga, Marga, beautiful body, maybe this is the time."

"M-m-m-m, don't touch me, not now. . ."

"Again?"

"Yes," she whispered. Her eyes were shut and her forehead crinkled. She held her breath. Paulus watched in amazement. Then she let out her breath in a long sigh and smiled at him.

"There, it's over!"

Paulus kissed her on the forehead. "What can I do?"

A silly question. Nothing. There was nothing either of them could do about any of it. The womb received some secret signal when nine months had elapsed and went about its work.

They lay together quietly. Marga took his hand and let her eyes close. Paulus watched her parted lips, and listened to the breath pass softly, back and forth, through them. Another pain came and went.

"Paulus, Anna says that I am small."

"Small?"

"Small in the hips."

"And . . ."

"I don't know. She didn't say any more. But I think she meant that when a woman's hips are small, it's harder for the baby to come out."

"Anna likes to talk and show off her vast knowledge, I think. I wouldn't worry about it." Then, after some silence: "I like your hips, Marga."

Marga said, "Pff!"

"I do. These women with their broad hips look like milk cows from behind. I like you better."

"Well, Paulus, your preference in hips is of no account now."

He put his head down and dozed, while she endured her mild pains silently beside him. Occasionally he awoke and asked, "How are you?" and she replied, "Well," and he dozed again. They would not awake Anna until they had to.

Paulus heard a yelp beside him and opened his eyes. Marga's legs were drawn up and her back arched and she was in the middle of a pain. Little beads of sweat shone on her forehead. When the spasm passed and Marga could move again, she pushed the blankets off and felt beneath her with her hand.

"Paulus, it's wet!"

Paulus did not comprehend.

"It's the water. Anna said to watch for it, that when it happens the time is close. Something inside me broke and my insides changed. And it hurt, really hurt."

"What does it mean?"

"That the baby is really being born."

She lunged for Paulus and hugged him, a vibrant animal, her hot face grazing and dampening his own; her body was moist and flushed. She kissed him full on the mouth and tongue and he tasted the salt.

"Shall we wake Anna?"

"Not yet. Not as long as I can do it myself."

The next pain came much more rapidly and took Marga by surprise and wrenched a gasp from her. She groaned involuntarily. Paulus was already getting out of bed, and when he accidently jarred her with his knee she yelped again and cried through clenched teeth,

"Don't touch me!"

"Anna!" said Paulus loudly.

When Anna took over the dawn was coming. Claus got up too and took Paulus outside. "Come, Paulus, this is woman's work, not for us. We'll walk. When we come back you'll have a baby to hold." They walked along the path toward the sawmill, between banks of trees filled with singing June birds, and Claus told Paulus how his wife had been pregnant three times but had never borne a live child.

Max was beginning his work for the day.

"Ho, Herr Ketterling! Herr Hestermann! Do you both need work today? The Duke is coming."

"Perhaps later, Herr Holzmann," said Claus. "This man is becoming a father today."

"For what?" said Max Holzmann, never concerned about the niceties. "What a stinking world it is. If you need help, a woman in the village is very good. Her name is Varani. Some kind of gypsy, I think, but very good with childbirth. In the cottage next to the fallen tree – you know where it is?"

Paulus nodded. A gray pall was falling on him. Claus had had three dead babies; Max thought it was a stinking world to be born into. A small point of fear formed in his mind on which other fears began to congeal, and suddenly he wanted to go back.

They had been gone perhaps a half hour, and they found Anna on her knees, bent over Marga. When she heard them she turned, and her face showed perplexity and terror.

"I'm worried," she said. "The pains are severe, and there seems to be no progress." She shook her head, almost angrily.

"She's so small, so small." She shot a hard, accusing look at Paulus. While Paulus and Claus stood dumbly looking on, another labor pain came upon Marga and Paulus knew, from the cry that she let out and the sound of her dry frantic breathing, that all the beauty and romance had gone out of this event. Marga coiled up like a ball during the pain and unwound limply when it was over.

"Anna, can't you do something!" he exclaimed and went to the side of Marga.

"I'm not God!" barked Anna. "I can't open her up!"

Marga's head was back, her eyes closed, her mouth open. She was sweating heavily and breathing hard. Hearing Paulus, she lifted her head and opened her eyes, and then let it drop back on the bed again. Paulus saw exhaustion, pain, and fear. He also saw that he was an outsider, that she was wholly within herself, and that the things that were happening inside her were monumental and consuming, beyond his understanding. Like a garrison under attack, she had gathered all her resources together and bolted the doors. No one else could struggle with her.

"It might be better if you went out for a while," Anna suggested. Paulus nodded and obeyed, on his way out taking his wife in with his eyes, not really believing that she would die in childbirth, but knowing that many women did, especially with the first child. The black hair lay spreading on the gray blanket beneath her, one shock of it across her forehead, held there by the perspiration. Her arms lay straight along her sides. Her legs were together and bent and tilted to one side. The bulge of her stomach stuck up from her little body. That must now come out between her legs, somehow. No wonder women died. But Marga would not die.

Claus had already gone outside, and Paulus suspected that Claus's memories of his own lost children were tearing at him.

"Would you like to take my place for Max today?" Paulus

asked him. "We need the food, you know, but I should stay close."

Claus's eyes said *thank you*. "Yes, I suppose I could do that," he said, and set off down the path to the sawmill to get the axe, leaving the screaming and crying and aching flesh behind him.

While the light of day filled the valley, Paulus alternately sat and paced by the cottage where Marga lay. It was a hellish time for him. The cries came at regular intervals from inside, chilling his blood and paralyzing him until they ended, and sometimes the half shouting of Anna's voice mingled with Marga's in an eerie double soprano. Women's work, women's anguish. In spite of the tumult of his soul he was rational enough to be glad he was not a woman. The anguish of women was so lonely. Men faced death in comradely fashion on a battlefield, enduring pain, but surrounded with glory, bravery, duty, and other myths designed to prod them more willingly to their deaths. Men died of quick killing diseases and fevers. But women died in bed, trying to have babies, trying to empty themselves of new life, fighting themselves. The more Marga screamed, the more he thought about death.

He set off running, along a seldom used path that led up the mountainside. If he could not endure being near, he would get away, and when he returned, the baby would be born. He listened to the clomp, clomp of his heavy shoes, watched the swerves and bends of the path slipping by him, felt his thigh muscles stiffen as he propelled himself up the slope. *Forget Marga. Forget Marga. Think about anything else. You can't help. Just let Anna and Marga and God work it out. Run until you are tired enough to sleep. Run through the friendly forest.* Soon he was gulping for air and the sweat was trickling down the center of his chest to his belly.

He stopped when he reached the crest. It was still forest here, but through the trunks of the trees he had a view of the Rhine valley below him, and to his left he saw for the first time the rising castle of the Duke. The sun shone directly upon him as it broke above the ridges to the east.

When he got back to the hut it was still shrouded in gray shadows and there was no Anna standing to greet him with a baby in her arms. Instead, there was the sound of Marga's crying inside, and the sight of Anna sitting dumfounded outside, her back against the wall.

"Anna! Anna! What's happening?"

Anna shook her head. "I'm sorry, I've done all I can. I had to get away. I was shouting at her in my frustration. I've done all I can do."

Paulus went to find Varani, in the cottage near the fallen tree.

He had never seen her, had never had any idea until this day who lived in the low, almost cave-like shed on the opposite side of the cluster from him, but he had noticed that a small amount of smoke came constantly from the chimney. The people here were eccentric, and Paulus asked no questions. Two yellowish dogs lay in front of the faded scarlet tapestry that was her door; they looked up languidly and put their heads down again, dazed by the warmth of the morning.

"Varani?" Paulus half asked, half called.

When there was no response he pulled the tapestry aside and looked into the single room of the place.

"Varani?"

"A woman in travail," said a woman's voice from out of the darkness.

"I need you. My wife needs you."

"I know. We'll go now."

Paulus waited just outside the door for her. One of the dogs sniffed him around the knees and went back to his warm spot on the ground. Then the woman Varani burst out through the tapestry, looked this way, then that, and finally at Paulus. It was difficult to tell how old she was; her skin was dark and smooth and most of her head was covered. She was clothed with a fantastic assemblage of brightly colored rags, sewn, pieced, tied together. It seemed, beneath all this, that she was a fat woman, but when she set off for Paulus' house, having analyzed him in a hard quick stare, she moved with astonishing speed. From behind she looked like a whirlwind of autumn leaves coursing along the ground. Paulus did his best to catch her.

Anna still sat despondent on the ground when the two of them returned.

"Paulus, no!" Anna said. "She's a gypsy." Anna rose and stood between Varani and the door. Marga shrieked inside.

Buffeted by these powerful feminine storms – Marga's agony, Anna's superstition, Varani's confidence – Paulus made his decision.

"Anna, move out of the way. Let her in."

"She will use magic."

"Anna! Let her by! Marga belongs to God!"

Varani stood calmly, as if being talked about this way was nothing new to her, and waited for Paulus and Anna to settle their feud. Paulus had never shouted so loudly to any of the people since he had come to Montau. There was a ferocity in his tone that made Anna silent, and she meekly stepped out of the way. As Varani ducked her head to go inside, and as Paulus started to follow her, Varani turned, catlike, and put her hand on his chest:

"Alone," she said. "I do my work alone. This is where a man cannot come." And Paulus obeyed her, as Anna had obeyed him.

Paulus staggered to a small pile of straw by Max Holzmann's house and fell upon it. It was cool and prickly against the hot wet skin of his face and neck. He had turned the burden over to Varani. The gypsy woman was God's provision. When his head rested on the straw an almost palpable wave of relief engulfed him, and in spite of the sounds that came from his cottage his mind disengaged itself partly from the present anguish.

Paulus was drifting off to sleep when Marga's voice cut into his peace like a dagger. It was an unnaturally high, almost artificial, tremulous tone, something from an animal's throat, or out of the abyss, scarcely human. He shook his head, saw the sun shining above him, felt his limbs moving unbidden, and was running clumsily toward the place where Marga was. When he reached the doorway he was afraid to go in or even to look. But he heard:

"One more, little sister, just one more."

"Oh, it's not coming out!"

Paulus had never heard such sounds from Marga before.

"Just one more." Varani's voice was deep and calm.

Marga screamed again, hoarsely. Varani sang a song underneath the screams. Paulus went in. Varani's huge bulk was between him and Marga's prone body, her back turned to him, but she sensed his presence and turned.

"Out! Out!"

Paulus saw one slender white calf and foot, in the air, quivering like a leaf in the wind.

He backed out and fell to his knees. He saw Marga in her baggy blue dress, with her dark mane of hair, with her self-conscious smile, outlined by the fire, kneeling in front of him in the field, making her marriage promise to him, plump with child – the whole story unrolled in his mind. His soul was holding a funeral for her already, remembering her.

The song and the scream continued together and suddenly stopped. Marga began to sob loudly, and then Paulus heard the tinny wailing of a baby, using its voice for the first time, shocked by its own sound and the sounds around it and the feel of dry air upon its naked body. Paulus wanted to go in but would wait until Varani invited him.

Claus was back. He and Anna were sitting together on the wreck of an old wagon that lay at the edge of the forest. They were far away, but it seemed to Paulus that Anna was still crying, and that Claus was speaking gently to her, and that both of them were also keeping their eyes on the house where Marga lay.

Varani came out the door of the house, and she was holding in her hands a naked baby still coated with the white creamy stuff of the womb and speckled with blood. Paulus scrambled to his feet, astonished, and looked and saw a little penis on the baby. Varani had the severed end of the naval cord pinched firmly between a thumb and forefinger.

"Your son," she said simply.

Paulus first took the baby in with his eyes, then cautiously touched him on his face with his fingers. The sun was shining brightly down and the baby was squinting and shaking his head from side to side, and the little limbs were moving aimlessly. He was fully alive.

"Should he be covered?" Paulus asked.

"The sun is warm, the sun is life. He likes it."

After a minute Varani took the baby inside again, saying that she had to tie the cord and attend to Marga. Paulus did not ask her about Marga's condition. A healthy baby did not necessarily mean a healthy mother. Suddenly he became frantic to know how she was, and he realized that though the baby was his son and was new and fascinating, Marga was his wife, his love. He went into the house, prepared to overrule any objections that Varani might have.

The baby lay on a cloth on the ground, squirming, his naval tied. Varani had her hands in a pail of water and was wringing out a towel. And Marga lay still, her eyes closed and her head tilted to one side, her face still wet. There were covers over her body, but they were not carefully arranged, and Paulus could see that under her hips the bedclothes were the dark maroon of blood. Varani saw him come in and had no objections.

"You see?" she said, and threw a blanket over Marga's legs.

"Is she alive?"

"Yes, but she's bleeding badly."

"Will she live, do you think?"

Varani said firmly, "How should I know?"

Paulus took a seat on a stool in the corner of the hut, his back pressed against the cool stone wall, while Varani patiently swabbed Marga and washed the bloody cloths. He was able to pray a little, and when the comfort of this took hold, he thanked God for his baby son. Would it be a fair trade, a son for a wife? Many men had made it, some gladly, since sons were more important than wives as the world saw it. Paulus would rather have the baby die and Marga live. He would make that trade in a second. But perhaps a gracious God would give him both.

Varani kept Marga clean and warm and sometimes just watched. There was nothing she could do to stem the bleeding that came from deep inside. But Paulus learned to watch carefully for the bloody tint each time the clean rinsed cloth came away from her body. There came a time in the afternoon, when the warm sunlight disappeared as the sun sank beyond the mountain ridge, when Varani brought the rinsing cloth away clean three times in succession. Paulus' hopes leaped.

"It's stopped," announced Varani. "I think she will live. She has lost much blood, but she is still breathing strongly and she is young."

Paulus let himself down to the ground, overcome with tiredness and relief. The last thing he felt was the blanket dropping on him from Varani's hands. When he awoke it was night, and he was still curled where he had fallen, and a small fire burned on the hearth. Varani was sleeping on the ground next to the bed where Marga lay, with the baby wrapped warmly and securely under her outstretched arm. Paulus went to Marga and knelt by the bedside. She was beautiful again; some of the color was back in her cheeks, or maybe it was only the dusky shadows. Varani had brushed out her tangled hair and washed her face and straightened her body on the bed. Under the bedclothes her belly still bulged abnormally, which surprised Paulus. Bloody bedclothes and towels were piled together in a corner next to the water pail. Paulus was reassured. Reality was seeping back. This was Marga, and the ordeal was over. He came close to her and felt the warmth of her neck and forehead and put his own face next to hers with his ear against her cheek and held it there while he listened to the whisper of her breathing, and it was the sweetest sound he had ever heard, the sound of life. He moved his face over hers, lightly touching her eyes, nose, and mouth with his lips. He marveled that her breath was sweet. And the Marga-smell emanated from her skin and hair.

Then Claus and Anna came in. It was, after all, their house too, and they had been waiting all day and far into the night outside. Paulus put a finger to his lips to signal quiet. Anna had a nervous, unsettled look on her face and kept glancing at Varani's sleeping form. She circled the room, inspecting everything, touching everything, looking, as Paulus knew, for some signs of magic or sorcery.

"She's done this by sorcery!" Anna said, in what was supposed to be a whisper but came out as a loud hiss.

"Anna," said Claus quietly, as if he had been discussing this with her already.

"She's a gypsy, Paulus!" The same loud whisper. Paulus noticed that she did not call him *Onkel*. The sound of her voice woke Varani, who sat up and handed the baby to Paulus.

"I will leave," said Varani quietly.

"Tell us what you have done!" demanded Anna, leaning down aggressively.

The woman Varani was not afraid. She arranged her tattered clothing about her and stood, and then faced Anna and spoke slowly and clearly, in her grammatical but strongly accented German:

"When I came, this woman was having a great problem. She is small, and the baby was coming feet first. I pulled. I thought I might have to kill the baby to save the mother's life, but the baby came out whole. If anything happened, it happened because this young man was praying."

Then she simply turned and left.

"Thank you, Varani," said Paulus.

"You let a gypsy in to tend to my Marga," said Anna. She was furious.

"Anna!" said Claus, and put his hand on her shoulder. She knocked it away.

But Paulus had had enough. It was her saying *my Marga* that made him snap.

"She is not your Marga! She is *my* Marga! Haven't you learned anything of Christ? You bitter and suspicious woman! This woman Varani saved Marga's life, don't you understand that? You bitter woman! You would rather have *my* Marga die than let this woman help her, wouldn't you!"

Hot tears came into Anna's eyes and she began to wail, and Claus took her to their corner of the house.

In the morning they were all calm but grim. Claus and Anna talked to Paulus, politely but distantly, and explained that they had decided to return to Claus's home in Switzerland. Before last night, they had wanted Paulus to help them marry, but now they would wait until they could find another community of believers to make their vows. Paulus had made an enemy of Anna, it was clear, but he was also certain that Claus still loved him very much, in spite of his need to go with his woman. Paulus wished them well, read from a psalm even though he knew that Anna would resent it, and blessed them.

Onkel, the flock is gone, gone to the four winds, scattered by the enemy. Could you have kept us together?

The rest of that day Paulus spent his time watching Marga sleep, and caring for the baby when it awoke. Varani came again in the afternoon.

"The baby needs to eat," she said. "Put it to the mother's breasts."

"Even while she is asleep?"

"Of course."

When Marga finally awoke, the baby was nursing at her breast. "Boy or girl?" she asked softly, seeing Paulus next to her.

"Boy," said Paulus. "His name is Heinrich."

"What else?" said Marga.

WITH THE ENTIRE congregation now dispersed, Paulus felt strangely free, glad, youthful. His eyes popped open in the mornings and he was full of joy at the coming of each new day. One warm evening he did something he had not done for a long time: he went off into the woods and prayed, not officially, not with a heavy heart, not for the long list of names that he had continually prayed for after most of them were gone, but simply pouring out the gladness of his soul to God. He was glad for the health of his wife and baby, glad for the tumultuous summer life of the forest around him, glad for the strength of his body and the work that Max Holzmann had given him to do. When he was done praying he felt warm and strong.

CHAPTER 11: PROPHETS
January-February, 1534. Münster.

Three men picked their way through the debris of the Market Street just before noon on the fifteenth of January. Nobody had cleaned up the rubble of bricks, broken furniture, and charred wood, results of sporadic bursts of violence. Across from St. Lambert's church, they stopped at the door of a brightly colored house and knocked. A large man with a jovial, intelligent face opened the door. He was well dressed; his tight, knee high stockings, white linen shirt and tailored green coat put him well into the city's merchant class.

"I am Jan Bockelson, of Leiden," spoke Bockelson, one of the visitors, in clear but deliberate German. "This is Gerrit Boekbinder, also an apostle of Jan Matthys. And this is my friend, Piet Bruinsma. The Catholics took his tongue." Bruinsma opened his mouth.

"And I am Bernhard Knipperdolling," said the man in the green coat, extending a right hand to Bockelson while his gaze remained on Piet Bruinsma's mutilated mouth. "The saints have been expecting you. Come in out of the cold. In the name of Christ."

They went to the kitchen and warmed their hands by a hot tile stove, and Knipperdolling's wife served them bread and beer and salted fish.

"How does it stand with our cause?" asked Bockelson.

"Rothmann and Rol received true baptism a few days ago," reported Knipperdolling.

"The preachers?"

"Yes. And more and more nuns, from Overwater and St. Aegidius and Niesing, are leaving the convents and being baptized."

"Nuns," mused Bockelson. "Captive virgins, escaping their prison."

"And new people, more every day, mostly from Holland," continued Knipperdolling. "The last two apostles that Jan Matthys sent really stirred up the crowds in the streets. Riots, fires, lots of sermons and songs."

"There will be more of that," said Bockelson factually. "There will be blood in the streets soon."

Having eaten, they went immediately to the marketplace between Knipperdolling's large house and St. Lambert's Church, where the people came to purchase their daily groceries. A pale winter sun forced its way through a layer of clouds, and the single Gothic tower of St. Lambert's Church shone white and unnaturally large; the leering gargoyles on the church's sides seemed to look with sinister delight on the scene below them. Along the street were the opulent homes of the city's patrician class, their facades painted orange, or pink, or blue, their doors heavily bolted. Inside them, fat nervous people made plans to get out of the city. Smells came from the hot vendors, smells of boiled soups, fresh cakes, and warm cider. Charcoal smoke hung in a barely visible layer just below the gargoyles.

A butcher hawked his wares from a large wheeled cart. Its top was a broad, greasy, wood table on which he had spread his sausages.

"Friend, we want to rent your cart," said the next

customer. It was Bockelson, He held out a hand with several coins.

"What is it?" asked the butcher, not understanding.

"We want to rent your meat cart."

"My meat?"

"No, no, stupid one, the cart itself!" Bockelson slapped his hand on the table, where the butcher's meats lay. "Put the meat underneath. We want the stand." The butcher looked at the coins. "There are ten pfennig here, ten pfennig for an hour."

It was not a bad offer, but the butcher was suspicious. He scratched his neck nervously and watched Bockelson and Bruinsma.

"The price is going down as you delay. Eight pfennig."

Still the butcher eyed them.

"The Lord has need of this stand," said Bockelson in a thin, high voice, and placed an index finger on it. "I think we should just take it, brother Bruinsma, in the name of the Lord, the way Israel took the land of Canaan."

With his dark, bruised looking eyes, Bruinsma said *yes*. The butcher had lost his chance. Now Bockelson swept the meats off the stand with his arm, and glared around him with white teeth showing.

"Stop!" roared the butcher. Heads began to turn. "You, pick up my meat!" As he said this he took a heavy cleaver from the shelf beneath the stand and shook it at his two assailants. Piet Bruinsma bent down, took a sausage, and threw it with all his might at St. Lambert's Church, against whose wall the sausage slammed and burst into bits. There was some applause in the marketplace.

"Seize him," said Bockelson quietly, and from behind the butcher three men came out of the crowd and knocked him to the ground. The cleaver flew from his hand. A boot on the back of his neck held him helpless against the cobblestone pavement.

This carefully orchestrated incident got the attention of the people in the marketplace like trumpets before a play; all around, they stopped and watched. Then Jan Bockelson climbed onto the butcher's stand. Around him a cordon of men formed, young, stern looking, half bearded men, most in tattered clothing. The butcher's stand had become Jan Matthys' first piece of conquered territory in Münster. And Bockelson's first stage.

"Good people of Münster," cried Bockelson in his trained voice, which cut through the air and reverberated against the walls, "it is now your turn to hear the word of the Lord." A hush fell over the marketplace.

Bockelson preached, and as he preached he pulled his audience with him into the drama of an unfolding redemption. He reviewed the troubles and sufferings of the common people, and they nodded their understanding. He identified the pope, and Luther, and the prince-bishop Franz von Waldeck as agents of the devil. They gaped in amazement. He listed the sins of Christendom and brought a heavy, wrath-loaded heaven down over their heads. They trembled. Then he gave them hope. Jan Matthys of Haarlem was, he announced, the Elijah of the last days, with a prophetic message straight from God. Jan Matthys would tell them how to be saved from the imminent collapse of the world. So the people must listen to Matthys as they would listen to Christ himself. The people buzzed.

At this moment, nothing better could have happened for Jan Bockelson than the sudden appearance of one of von Waldeck's magistrates, Berthold von Wessel, a minor knight who served the prince-bishop as a vassal. He now came down the market street from the north with a company of about ten horsemen. The banner of the prince-bishop flew above them on a pole, with its chivalric symbol, a black falcon perched on a battle axe – no gentle, otherworldly bishop, this Franz von Waldeck. The heads of the people turned in one motion toward the staccato sound of hooves on pavement.

"My lord!" cried Bockelson, smiling, across the sea of heads. "Have you come to hear the word of God?"

"No," shouted von Wessel, "but rather to see who it is that disturbs the peace of the prince-bishop's city."

"Jan Bockelson and Piet Bruinsma, apostles of the prophet Jan Matthys, of Haarlem. This city is not at peace. We bring it peace!"

"Does this prophet have no respect for the laws of our city? Does he not know that preaching in the streets is forbidden?" It was a lame and crippled statute, broken every day now, and it was pathetic for von Wessel to cite it.

"God has commanded us to preach, and his command supersedes the law. The streets belong to him after all."

Von Wessel stared from under the brow of his helmet. "The streets may belong to God. But they are patrolled by my horsemen. Keep it in mind."

The horses pulled against their bits and puffed. One lurched forward unbidden and its rider drew back the reins with all his strength to stop it, and the crowd stumbled back upon itself in fear. Bruinsma hopped onto the cart beside Bockelson to see.

"I want you out of my city, Dutchman, or, by the saints in heaven, I'll have your head!" cried von Wessel.

The rider next to von Wessel was a dark-haired, swarthy man with hairy bare arms. He spoke to his commander: "But give the word, and I'll have his head in three minutes, and save us all another saddling of the horses."

Von Wessel hesitated. The man's suggestion was a good one – ten armored knights could sweep across the square unimpeded and catch the Dutchmen before they got away. But he hesitated to shed blood without the direct command of von Waldeck. He lost his nerve.

"No," he finally said. "There must be order, and law." He turned his horse away and the rest followed him, back up the market street toward the cathedral.

"You see! You see!" shouted Bockelson with his hands in the air. "The soldiers of the Beast ride away! The power of the word is too great for them! God has frozen their hearts and sealed their swords in the scabbards! The time is coming to an end when the fat and strong trample the weak!"

The people cheered.

"Now you must choose which kingdom you will belong to! There are only two kingdoms, the kingdom of God and the kingdom of this godless world! No middle ground! The prophet Jan Matthys declares that soon, very soon, the last vengeance of God will sweep away the chaff! He is God's prophet and I am his spokesman! Believe him and save yourselves! Believe him and receive the salvation of God! Believe him and you will wash your feet in the blood of the wicked!"

This peroration was lost in the din of a huge shout. The crowd milled now like a mass of ants, condensed, and pressed forward toward the two apostles. Bockelson raised his arms to quiet them.

"Now, it is time for you to be sealed with the sign of God's covenant. Forget, renounce, and abominate your popish baptisms and wash them away with the true baptism of God! Place yourselves inside the safety of his true kingdom and church! Come! Come to the true baptism!"

They came, while two of the young wild men held Bockelson's arms aloft, as Aaron and Hur had held Moses' arms while the Israelites had slaughtered the Amalekites, and Piet Bruinsma baptized them as they passed before the butcher cart. He poured water on their heads, and another, one with a tongue, pronounced the Trinitarian baptismal formula over each one. Most of those who came for baptism were young and ragged, and most were women. The ancient convents of Münster were still emptying themselves out into the new revolution, and four nuns in a group approached the butcher's cart with their heads still covered by their habits.

"Uncover your heads before God," said Bockelson, sensing a dramatic moment. The women obeyed him.

"Now throw them down and step on them," ordered Bockelson, and the nuns trampled on the symbols of their loyalty to pope, church, and holy orders, looking like boys with their close-cropped hair exposed.

"Now see what the Beast has done to womanhood, cutting their hair, turning them into men!" cried Bockelson. "God reclaims you from the prison of the convent, dear sisters. God will make you women again." They were baptized, and hugged each other, and wept, and laughed, and one tried to reach Bockelson's face to kiss him but could not. Still, his eyes sparkled as she tried. "Glory to God for such great deliverance! Here are four who have been rescued from the certain damnation that will come to the kingdom of the Pope! They have cast off the marks of the Pope! It is not too late, dear people! Come!"

The sight of bare-headed, wet-headed nuns unhinged the crowd; its motions now transcended any individual thought, decision, or reservation. They came in a crush of warm bodies to receive Bockelson's baptism. They came in anxiety that the world would come to its end before they could reach the butcher's cart.

Through the week the baptisms continued; the Anabaptist cells which had met secretly came out into the open; preachings were held in public squares. A growing flock of ex-nuns followed Bockelson wherever he went, as his admirers had once done in Leiden; the abbotesses of St. Aegidius and Overwater complained bitterly and sent frantic letters to the bishop. Six hundred years of history in the city whose name stemmed from the word *monasterium* were being erased at a stroke.

BOCKELSON'S ARRIVAL IN Münster, and his butcher-stand performance, escalated the spiritual tension to a new height. The damp February cold, and the sleet from the silver-gray sky, and the dearth of food and fuel could not squeeze the pulsing life from the streets, where the newly baptized rabble loafed and sang and debated. The Lutherans and the Catholics stayed indoors. More of Matthys' agents filled the countryside around the city, preaching impending judgment and imploring the simple folk to flee to Münster as the only safe place on earth, and the city gates remained open wide to receive peasants and artisans with superheated minds. Various kinds of German, and Dutch, and Walloon, and even some garbled French mingled Babel-like in the streets. By the bonfires at night they talked about the end of the world.

Münster's ruler, the prince-bishop Franz von Waldeck, gave them something else to talk about when, on the twenty-third of February, he had his agents in the city post notices that all rebaptized persons were to be arrested and imprisoned. Of course, it could not be enforced. It gave the people by the bonfires something to laugh at, but it also made them angry.

Underneath the appearance of chaos, Jan Matthys was at work through his apostles, giving direction to the chaos like a cook tending a boiling pot. The sermons in the streets, and the tubs of soup which appeared, and the knots of bellicose young men marching and shouting, and the bursts of violence and vandalism were all by design. Matthys, lucid and pragmatic, also saw to it that the cellars, bins, and closets of the poorer neighborhoods of Münster were filled with weapons more worldly than the word of prophecy, weapons of wood and steel. There was now no contradiction in this for him. The kingdom would come as the saints turned these weapons against the godless. From a cleansed, sanctified Münster, sweeping outward in concentric circles, the judgment would gobble up the whole world, leaving a globe smeared with blood, purged of sin, ready for Christ.

On the eighth of February those who still worked for a living went through the mist to their shops and workhouses. Those who waited more eagerly for the end gathered in their groups. The ex-nuns sang martial psalms and prepared to distribute food as noon approached.

Then a commotion arose. Jan Bockelson and Bernhard Knipperdolling issued from the door of Knipperdolling's house, shouting judgment. The merchant and the apostle. They ran at a jog towards the cathedral square and shouted, at intervals:

"The wrath of God is at hand! Repent!"

"Turn now to the mercy of the Lord!"

"The kingdom is coming and is here!"

"Repent and be baptized!"

"This city is the footstool of Christ's feet!"

By the time they reached the cathedral square they were being followed by a small crowd. They ran under the shadows of the monstrous, squarish cathedral, symbol of an earlier, quieter time, circling it almost like vultures as if it were prey. As they did so, their following swelled. Along the streets that fed into the cathedral square came the frightened and the fascinated, the repentant and the curious, the bored and the vengeful. People cried out things, and some sang, and many wept. Then Bockelson and Knipperdolling led them on a winding path through the city's neighborhoods, and as they passed under the windows of the houses they cried repentance. Windows flew open, and slammed shut. Middle class citizens nervously fingered their swords and axes.

Bockelson's rabble circled the city and turned back toward the cathedral square, from the east. As it came into the open space it lost its momentum and cohesion and broke into little clusters. Many of the women were prophesying in ecstasy.

"O God in heaven!" screamed a young woman with two weeks' growth of hair. "I see him, I see him!" She fell to her knees and her breasts heaved up and down. "I see him in his glory! Lord Jesus, Lord Jesus, I see you now!" Her vision set off other experiences among the women. Some cried loudly, others fell silent and foamed at the mouth like epileptics. A tailor, Georg thon Berge, looked into heaven and screamed, in a broken voice, things about sin and heaven and more sin, and jumped up and down, trying once to fly by leaping from a bench and clapping his hands in the air, and then he spread his body on the frozen cobblestone pavement in the form of a cross.

Standing on a wagon in a curiously casual pose for such an intense event – shoulder against a wall, weight on one leg and the other crossed in front of it, fingers doodling with his beard – Jan Bockelson watched with satisfaction the collective emotional climax which he had induced. When its energy began to wane, he walked calmly back to Knipperdolling's house.

CHAPTER 12: CONQUEST
February, 1534. Münster.

"I'm worried, no matter what you say," said Gertrude Fettbauch while she dusted the surface of a Venetian dining table. She was a tall, angular young woman with large, almost masculine facial features. Her drab brown hair was pulled tightly back and tied in a knob at the back of her head; her clothing was clean, ironed, and dull.

"Sister, sister," smiled Julius Fettbauch from his green upholstered chair, which had come from Lyons in France. He was a round, buttery man. "You frighten too easily, as do our beloved parents."

"But if they have gone, why should we stay? If it's dangerous here for them, then why not for us?" She began to wring her hands.

"Father is the proprietor," Julius said with deliberate slowness, exasperated, "He is the logical target of any action against Fettbauch Goldsmiths."

Gertrude went to the front window of the house, which looked out onto the Market Square street as it curved from St. Lambert's church northwest toward the cathedral square.

"Just look at them," she said. Outside, in a lightly falling snow, the Anabaptist rabble huddled around their fires. "The logic of it doesn't matter much, Julius. Those people frighten me. Are you so sure that the bishop will be able to control these violent people?"

"Absolutely. . .When heresy's a threat to the order dear,
Our bishop with his troops will soon be here."

"You and your stupid poems!"

"My poems are brilliant. I am the mouth of the Muses. Gertie, stop dusting, for heaven's sake! There's been no dust on that table for years. You're wearing off the finish. Now, that's right, sit down." Gertrude sat down on a couch opposite Julius. "Do you want to hear the rest of the letter?"

"I suppose."

Julius read her the rest of a letter from their parents, who had fled to Dortmund.

"They are cowards," said Gertrude.

"Shame! You shouldn't talk about them like that."

"It's true."

Julius folded the letter and picked absently at the wax seal on its back. "I'm surprised that he still tells me to deliver the goblet to Mayor Tilbeck. I told him in our last letter that I had already done so." He did not know, of course, that much of the mail that left and entered Münster was opened and read by Anabaptist censors.

Gertrude went to the window again, fascinated and frightened by the desperate characters that now populated the street. She had watched Jan Bockelson and Bernhard Knipperdolling run by here; she had watched Gerrit Boekbinder preach and baptize. And the glass of the window through which she looked distorted the images and added to the sensation she already had, that she was peering into another bizarre world. She and her older brother had lived in this well-kept house all their lives, and they had always assumed that there would be food on the table and wood in the fire and that there would be the necessary order around them to pursue the family business and sustain their lives in the customary manner.

The city had changed. Soft, orderly people like her parents were gone, people interested only in their own small kingdoms, and were being replaced by coarse, hungry people with bigger kingdoms to build. Gertrude was not hopeful about the future. Julius was funny, but she had doubts that he could run the business in the absence of his father.

While she was gazing out the window, a man in the street saw her and shouted at her.

"Ho, rich pig!"

Gertrude stiffened and caught her breath. Through the swirling translucence of the glass she saw him lift his arm toward her with a stiff middle finger on its end. She didn't tell Julius. He would make a joke. Or a poem.

Julius arose from his chair and filled his cup with beer from a metal pitcher. His belly spilled over his belt like a huge soft mound of bread dough.

THE FETTBAUCHS COULD see from their front window most of the important things that happened in the next couple of weeks.

On the ninth of February, a large gang of Lutherans and Catholics assembled by the Overwater church and an even larger gang of Anabaptists, with Bockelson at its head, marched past the Fettbauchs to confront them. Nothing happened.

On the tenth of February, a party of the bishop's police, led by von Waldeck's bailiff Wolbeck, tried to arrest two city councillors, Tilbeck and Judenfeld, who had joined the Anabaptists. Angry Anabaptists filled the street and forced Wolbeck and his men to gallop away. After this, the prince-bishop had to face the truth: decrees and police and normal coercive measures did not work. He would have to gather himself a real army and win the city with the sword. He summoned his vassals to a war council in the town of Telgte, east of Münster, and wrote to Duke Johann of Cleves and his fellow ecclesiastic, the prince-bishop of Cologne, as he had to Philip of Hesse.

Gertrude and Julius could watch, at almost any time of day, citizens of Münster leaving town with their possessions piled in wagons and on their backs in bags. Julius scoffed at them for their fear. But Gertrude had a good observation.

"You can scoff, Julius, all you want, and maybe you're right. But there go father's customers. Who will be left in the city to buy goldware and silverware?"

On the twenty-second of February the Town Council ordered that the ground immediately outside the city walls be cleared of trees and brush and debris. This meant that the city was preparing for a siege. Julius was conscripted for this work. He found himself out in the muddy ground under the walls with underfed, unshaven men, who saw his big belly and sneered quietly at him.

JULIUS FETTBAUCH BURST through the door of his house around noon on the twenty-third of February.

"Gertie, Gertie!" he called into the house. He was dressed in work clothes and covered in mud.

Gertrude came down the stairs. "You're filthy, take off your coat right there." Julius dropped it near the door and pulled off his shoes. He had come from just outside the city walls, and his shoes were caked with mud from the defense works ordered by the Town Council.

"Gertie, the prince-bishop is moving with a cavalry force near Telgte. I told you, I told you, he's coming to save his city."

"Well, he'd better come fast. As of today, the town council is completely in the hands of the Anabaptists. Just look. The streets are full of riffraff again. I don't like it at all."

Julius cleaned himself, ate a bit, and for the rest of the afternoon they sat – she nervously, he curiously – watching the Market Street. Crowds of young men congealed and dispersed, and regimented bands of women passed by singing. The street was now in sunlight, now in shadow, as batches of clouds blew over. The city was in the hands of common men, butchers and tavern-keepers and tailors and chair-makers and smiths. And they were in the hands of the preachers. And the preachers were led by the prophet, Jan Matthys, for whom they all waited.

Late in the afternoon, there was a new commotion outside.

"What's going on now?" asked Julius.

"Another procession," said Gertrude.

"It sounds louder than usual."

Gertrude stood in her usual spot before the window, with her hands clasped before her. "It is," she said. "There is something coming. Everyone here is looking back, toward the Town Hall."

Julius came next to her and put his hand on her shoulder.

"Come away from here," he said. "There's nothing to be gained by watching. You'll only upset yourself. Let them go from worse to bad, They'll only get our bishop mad." He smiled, pleased at his talent for rhymes.

"Look!" she said. "That must be what this is all about."

"What is it?"

It was Jan Matthys, coming into view through their window with black hat, black gnarled beard, and recessed eyes, and his hot breath shot frosty into the winter air as he shouted, and he shook a long wooden staff above his head. He stood in a plain country cart with wooden wheels, drawn by four large and restless horses. Walking alongside the cart were twenty-four truculent looking men, twelve on each side, dressed in black like Matthys and carrying spears. The Market Square street was a narrow street here, and the spearmen were marching with their shoulders against the houses on each side. Several dark heads passed by the Fettbauch house before Gertrude was overcome with anger and frustration and pulled one side of the window open.

"Away from our house! Don't you filthy creatures touch our house!"

"Gertie," gasped Julius, leaping forward too late to prevent her outburst.

A black-clad spearman halted before the window. He had a half-grown dark beard but was very young, perhaps seventeen or eighteen, and his nose and ears were red from the cold.

"Close the window, fat cow," he said in scarcely intelligible German. When she did, he jabbed his spear through it. Broken glass exploded into the house and Julius and Gertrude stepped back, unhurt. The procession moved on. It was one small incident lost in the din. Up and down the Market Square, vandals in Matthys' procession shattered windows and sank their spear points into doors and woodwork.

Now Julius was nervous too. As darkness fell, crashing, breaking sounds came from all directions, with jubilant male voices, and luminous glowing nodes appeared in different directions.

"What are they doing now?" Gertrude kept asking.

The next day they found out. Matthys' gangs had attacked the churches and monasteries and had vandalized, stripped, and burned much of the city's religious art: paintings, statues, relics, sacred furniture, and stained glass. This was pagan idolatry to Matthys, and it all had to be consigned to destruction like the graven images of Canaan. In the greatest symbol of the despised old order, the cathedral, Jan Matthys personally supervised the demolition of the statues, the altar, the baptismal, the windows, and even the old mechanical clock that rang out the time.

ON THE TWENTY-FOURTH, Knipperdolling hosted a dinner for the preachers, prophets, and leaders. Jan Bockelson and Matthys' beautiful wife Divora happened to sit where they could see each other well, separated by only two other people. While

Matthys preached, with the eyes of the guests riveted on him, Bockelson feasted his own eyes on Divora's bare white shoulders and neck, crimson stained lips, large eyes outlined with black pencil, and fine straight nose. She was a little, but not too much, on the plump side, and made no effort to hide her conspicuous breasts. She caught Bockelson's glance several times and returned it hard.

"I have heard about your run through the city," Divora said to Jan Bockelson later that evening, when the party was breaking up and the guests were saying their farewells with bloodshot eyes. "Is it true you took all your clothes off?"

"No, of course not," he laughed. "The common people embellish these things. But I could have. The Spirit was heavy upon me."

"H-mmm. I have never yet received an impulse from the Spirit to remove all my clothes, but it could happen, I suppose."

"I should think it would happen often to you, being the wife of such a prophet."

"No, not often."

FOR A FEW DAYS, Münster was a city without an official religion. The Town Council declared all faiths to be legal. But on the twenty-seventh Matthys commanded the cleansing.

It was a Friday. The temperature hovered around the freezing point all day and cold stuff fell from a slate-gray sky, sometimes wet, sometimes frozen. Matthys first preached himself into a holy state in a private house by the fish market, then he called the faithful together in solemn assembly in the cathedral square and announced that it was God's will for all citizens of Münster to receive the true baptism or leave the city. Those who refused to do either would be driven out by force. Matthys sent his enforcers into the various districts of the city with lists, and they went systematically from house to house making the ultimatum. And the streets were suddenly full of people again, people with colorful clothing and fat stomachs, making their way through the cold slush toward the gates with a few of their goods slung over their backs, huffing and puffing people who were not used to carrying things themselves. Gangs of Anabaptists followed them with whips and clubs and cried at the top of their lungs: "Get out! Get out, you godless ones!" Not all left, though. The repentant ones were brought in small bands to the cathedral square for baptism.

Julius and Gertrude knew what was happening and were expecting the knock when it came. Julius opened the door and two men pushed their way in. One of them was the spearman who had put his weapon through their window four days before.

"Yes, it's she," he said to the other, who was consulting a list.

"Fettbauch, Julius and Gertrude," he read, and then laughed. "Fettbauch – " he began to translate for his comrade " – means fat belly."

The spearman sniggered and reached out to take a handful of Julius' belly and pulled it up and down a few times. Julius smiled with the two men as if he were really amused at his own paunch. "Too much beer," he said.

"The prophet has decreed the true baptism for all citizens of Münster," said the one with the list. "The blessing of God cannot abide on the community while there is impurity and unbelief in it. You will either receive baptism or leave the city immediately."

"I will not," stated Gertrude, looking at Julius.

"You will not what?" he asked.

"I will not deny my Catholic baptism. It would be blasphemy, a reproach to God and to our parents."

"And the reproach of leaving this house and our father's business behind?" asked Julius, fidgeting.

"Those are worldly things!" she snapped.

"Stop bickering," said the man with the list, "and decide."

Gertrude did not hesitate. "I'll leave."

The dark Hollander was looking around at the house and its comfortable furnishings while the others talked. He poked a thumb into the cushion of Julius' favorite green chair, and ran his hand along the smooth wood paneling on the wall.

"And you?" The other Anabaptist pressed Julius, who had one eye on the Hollander. Julius searched for help in Gertrude's face but his sister looked mulishly at the floor.

"I'll stay," he finally said, without much conviction.

"And receive Christian baptism?"

Now Gertrude looked up sharply at him.

"Yes, of course," Julius said. "I've always suspected that infant baptism was . . . incorrect." He laughed nervously.

They allowed Gertrude five minutes to gather some clothes. Julius tried to give her a kiss on the cheek as she stormed toward the door, but she lifted her arm to prevent it, and he gave up, shrugging his shoulders at the Anabaptist with the list as if to say, *Ach women*! The door slammed and she was out on the street, headed toward the Ludger Gate on the south side of the city, thinking to get herself to her parents in Dortmund.

So Julius Fettbauch was about to be baptized. The idea struck him strangely, but he could get through it, he thought, if that was what it took to keep the peace with these people. So he put on his heavy fur coat to go with the two Anabaptists. On their way out, the dark Hollander noticed an exquisite silver candy dish on a shelf next to the door, stopped, touched it as though it were poison, then put it in the pocket of his coat. Julius was shocked; the piece was especially precious to the family.

"No, please –" he started to say, when the man with the list drove a hard clenched fist into his nose. Julius Fettbauch had never been struck like this; there was the dull stunning of the impact, then the swelling surge of pain, earth shattering, incapacitating. He sank to his knees and held his face, while tears came from his eyes and blood and mucous from his nostrils.

Somehow he staggered with his tormenters to the cathedral square and felt through his pain and dizziness the water poured onto his head. He thus became an Anabaptist. One of the men in black informed him that he would have a new place of residence, for the Fettbauch house was to be used for other purposes. He thought for an instant of protesting but remembered the blow to his nose and kept quiet. They led him to a dilapidated narrow house on the New Bridge street, built directly against the fortification wall in the northeast corner of the city, within a stone's throw of the Aa river as it oozed out of town under the tower. By the time the river left the city it was loaded with rubbish and garbage and stank; Julius had a delicate sense of smell and was glad that because his nose was so swollen he could not smell it now.

"A Homer with his pen and ink, Could not describe such horrible stink," he muttered involuntarily.

"What?" asked his surly escort, balling up his fist.

"Nothing . . . Just the Muses again." Not everyone appreciated his poetry.

So Julius had a new home. For the time Julius was the only one in this particular house, but the Anabaptist explained that he would probably have companions soon. Julius shrugged and sat down to dab his bloody nose. The bishop would certainly be here soon, he thought.

GERTRUDE NEVER GOT to Dortmund. The prince-bishop had seven fortified camps around the city now; his knights were building blockhouses against the cold, and supply wagons were coming and going. When the gates opened and the refugees began to make their way across the frozen plain, he ordered his horsemen to prevent their passage. He was determined to shut the city up as completely as possible. Chased back toward the walls by the bishop's cavalry, Gertrude, with others, pleaded to be let back into the city. They were met only with stones and jeers from the walls and sent back out into the winter night. Gertrude was not well dressed for such an ordeal; she contracted a severe cough and died four days later, after the bishop finally relented and received some of the refugees into his camp.

CHAPTER 13: PILGRIMAGE
March, 1534. Nassau, the Taunus mountains.

It was too wet to work, so Paulus stayed with Marga and the baby and built a roaring fire on the hearth. Fitful rain, driven by a stiff wind, pelted the house, but Paulus had made it weatherproof, and they stayed dry. The brook that flowed through their valley was swollen with melting snow and was running too fast for Max Holzmann to work his sawmill, so he too, for once, sat in his house. They could hear the sound of his singing occasionally; he always sang.

Paulus had improved their little house. It now had a good roof and a strong door, but it still had a ramshackle look, like something made by ten-year-old boys as a playhouse. In the small room there was now a proper bed, with a wooden frame up off the floor, a table for them to eat on, a couple of benches, and a cradle for the baby. Paulus had done his best to construct a vent for the hearth, but it worked well only when the fire was very hot, and by morning the room usually smelled of smoke. He worked on this problem but could not seem to solve it. The only solution, he said often, would be to raze the whole house to the ground and begin again. Like what Christ would have to do with the world.

Sometimes Max Holzmann paid Paulus for his labor in real coin, but more often he told Paulus to simply take what he needed when the food peddlers came into the squalid little settlement every few days with their bread and salted meats from the cities by the river below. In his own rough way Holzmann took care of Paulus. Even when Paulus had to stay home to care for Marga after the childbirth, Holzmann paid him. When Marga had recovered, they invited Holzmann to eat with them, but he refused. He was a very private man.

Marga was happy in the core of herself. She did not care that they were existing on the fringe of the world. She was a mother. Paulus, for his part, though he was filled with love for the child, was conscious of his natural distance from it. The child knew its mother from conception, but its father it would have to learn about through touch, and voice. Paulus was good with the baby, and because his connection with it was less intense than Marga's he was sometimes able to calm it when she could not.

Paulus was also happy. But it was a happiness that consisted in large part of the absence of things – society, responsibility, the church – and it made him uneasy, when he thought about it, that he could be happy without these things. Still, the fact was that he was happy. They had found an island of tranquility.

PAULUS WAS MARKING trees on a slope above the sawmill when he heard bellowing male voices below. A wave of fear passed through his body and almost buckled his knees, and when he had caught himself and had taken a deep breath, he was leaping and sliding and clawing his way down the slope as fast as he could. The river came into view through the trees, then the mill, then the figure of Max Holzmann standing by the mill with a big wooden staff as thick as a man's wrist in both hands. Over against him were four armed horsemen who seemed at the moment undecided how to attack. One had drawn out a mace and was untangling its chain, while another was reaching for his sword while his nervous horse turned in tight circles.

"You go back to your idiot duke!" roared Holzmann. "Tell him to come himself if he wants his beams for nothing! I'll kill you all!"

And the riders were shouting back at him curses and insults.

Paulus halted with difficulty before he was close enough to be noticed. The mill and the fight were between him and the cluster of houses where they lived. He would have to find a way around it and get to Marga before the duke's men killed Max Holzmann, as they certainly would, and went up the trail to sack his house. He scrambled along the steep side of the mountain using bushes as handles, moving downstream, keeping an eye on the mill.

The rider had pulled his sword clear, had gotten control of his horse, and now with bravado charged at Holzmann. "Kill, Dieter, kill!" cried one of his companions, laughing. With a powerful, catlike motion, Holzmann lunged forward and swept the horse's legs out from under it, and horse and rider went down in a broken heap. With another lunge Holzmann brought his stave down on the man's head, breaking it like a clay pot. The horse tried to right itself on its injured front legs but could not.

"Who's next?" growled the sawyer. Paulus had reached the river and was waiting until the next flurry of action to break into the open and cross it. Two of the knights attacked at once. Paulus charged through the river with two steps, wetting his feet. Over his shoulder he saw one horse fall and its rider tossed like a sack against one of the piles that supported the mill, while the second assailant closed with Holzmann and raised his sword. There was a flash and a whine and a yell; Holzmann's leather cap flew off in pieces and he clutched his head. The fourth attacker was not far behind. He came straight at the wounded Holzmann, whose damaged body went down under the horse's chest like a sapling. The fight was over.

Paulus had gained the path to his house and was running with all his might, still afraid to shout. Maybe the knights would spend some time at the mill, ransacking it or setting it on fire. Perversely, he hoped so. He had only one thought: to gather up Marga and the baby and run, to get up the mountain where the horses could not follow.

Marga was sitting in front of their door, enjoying the sun that poured through the trees around noon. She stood as she saw him running up the path, and she sensed danger and dashed into the house and came out with the baby in her arms.

"What's wrong?"

He had trouble talking since he was so winded. "The duke's men. They've killed Max. Let's go."

"Go? Why?" Paulus saw something strange in her face.

"Because they will certainly come up here to plunder everything. They had some kind of falling out. Marga, we're Max's people in their eyes."

"How many are there?" she asked evenly.

"Two, maybe three."

"If two, we can stand our ground." She wanted to stay and fight.

"Marga, no!"

He took her hard by her shoulders and felt them tense and taut.

"The baby," he said. She let her head fall to her chest.

"It was too good to be true, wasn't it, Paulus. We're Anabaptists, we can't be too happy too long, can we." She turned away from him and started toward the thick forest behind the house, and he took her arm and went with her.

They did not leave too soon, for there was immediately the sound of hooves coming up the path. Two of the knights were on one horse, leading the way, and the third had Max

Holzmann's body tethered to his saddle and was dragging it behind him. Other people were leaving the hovels and shacks around Max Holzmann's house like bugs from a flooding weedpatch and slipping into the forest; Paulus caught a glimpse of Varani's red and purple back, the last he would ever see of her. The Duke's men stopped by Holzmann's house and dismounted. Paulus and Marga crouched behind a thicket of fallen branches and brush, and Paulus saw now that Holzmann was not dead – battered and dazed, but alive, he moved and twitched as he lay on the ground with his face in the leaves. Two of the duke's men knocked in the door of the house and entered it while the third stood outside and scanned the village on all sides.

"Anything yet?" he called in to them. He was nervous alone.

They did not hear him inside, but the sounds of their rampaging could be distinctly heard outside, even where Paulus and Marga hid.

"Come on, go in, go in and see," whispered Paulus, wanting the lookout to vanish for just a moment so they could lose themselves in the woods beyond his field of vision. But the knight stood his ground. Then the others came out, one of them with a canvas bag in his hand, which he swung around and shook with delight.

"The duke's money!" he said. "Looks like every last coin of it. This fool should have spent it while he was able."

"This place is totally deserted," said the man who had been the lookout. "They must have run into the woods when they heard us coming."

"Anything of value here?"

"Doesn't look like it. Pitiful place, not fit for the pigs."

"Well, we don't need him any more, since we found the money." The helmeted knight who seemed to be the leader among them walked to Holzmann and in a detached manner placed the tip of his sword between two ribs and drove it in with all his weight. Holzmann twitched once and was still. The knight extracted his sword from Max's body and wiped the bloody tip, pulling it slowly through his leather-gloved hand and whistling as he did. Marga watched with narrowed eyes, her teeth set, her lips thin, the corners of her mouth quivering with tension. Her white hand closed around a fist-sized stone.

"Get fire," said the leader. They found fire in Paulus' and Marga's house, and with it they ignited the roofs of all the buildings in the village. Paulus watched his painstaking labor burn, and felt a twinge of shame as their jerry-built house fell all at once, collapsing as if it had been held together only by its own confusedness. Still, there was too much risk in their leaving their cover and running, so they stayed.

When they had set fire to every flammable thing in the village, the knights gathered again. They mounted their horses and found the narrow path that led out of the settlement up the mountain. It was the path that Paulus and Marga had taken, and their hiding place was only thirty yards away.

"We must run for it," whispered Paulus.

"They'll run us down," retorted Marga.

"Now! While there's time!"

"No! I refuse! Here, take the baby."

He didn't know why, but he did what she asked. The knights were approaching, the features of their faces visible. Marga stood up noiselessly. She held the stone that filled her hand, cocked her arm, coiled her body, and launched the stone at the closest knight with all her strength. She was not a powerful woman, but the stone was heavy and her aim was perfect, and when it hit the leader of the group on the side of his face with a smacking sound, he went limp and slid from his horse to the ground. He lay there with both hands to his bleeding head.

"Where did that come from?" said the leader.

"Up the hill," said the other. "There could be others." Now the forest held new terrors for them. They dismounted, tossed their comrade across a horse, mounted quickly and went back down the hill.

Paulus and Marga waited for more than an hour before they crept down through the smoldering ruins of the village and searched the wreckage of their house for anything that may have remained. Paulus found the axe that Max Holzmann had let him use. Its handle was slightly charred but intact. He also found Onkel's Bible, its top cover darkened by heat but its insides intact. Their blankets, furniture, and Heine's cradle were gone.

They followed the little path along the river down to the Rhine.

CHAPTER 14: COUP
April, May 1534. Münster.

In the cathedral square, flanked by his henchmen, the dark prophet Jan Matthys confronted the Münster blacksmith, Hubert Ruscher.

"Are you an imbecile, or are you full of the devil?" shouted Matthys at Ruscher. Matthys' black-shirted guards had Ruscher bound, but the blacksmith's restless muscles rolled under his shirt. A large crowd had formed around this confrontation.

"It is you who are full of the devil!" roared Ruscher. "Who but the devil would want to burn all of our books? And who but the devil would burn our property records?"

Matthys had ordered the burning of all books but the Bible, and had decreed the communal ownership of all property and the destruction of the city's ancient property records. The smoke from these burnings had scarcely drifted away. Ruscher had a huge voice, and went on:

"You are not interested in helping the poor, false prophet! You are interested in taking our goods and giving them to your dirty Hollanders!"

Matthys roared in indignation and frustration. "You must be cut off from the holy people! God will not bless us if there is grumbling!" He took a sword from one of the guards and brandished it above his head. He approached Ruscher, aimed the sword at Ruscher's throat, retracted it, growled deep in his throat, and paced, cutting the empty air with the sword.

Jan Bockelson whispered to Piet Bruinsma: "Our prophet fears to strike the blow. Do you think the prince-bishop would fear him in single combat?" It was a safe sarcasm, since Bruinsma could neither speak nor write.

Matthys came near Ruscher again. He pressed the captive's body into a bowed position. He raised the sword, and he retracted it.

Bockelson to Bruinsma: "Our prophet stinks, my silent friend. Can you smell him? He wears the same shirt, the same trousers, the same coat every day. He never washes." Then, abruptly, Bockelson sprang into action like an animal. He pulled a halberd from the hands of a young guard, strode past the hesitating Matthys, and drove the tip of the halberd into Ruscher's back. A gasp went up from the crowd. Everyone watched the wounded man roll and groan on the pavement.

"It's not enough?" cried Bockelson. "It's not enough? This will do, then!" He took a hand-arm from a man in the prophet's bodyguard, and he checked its powder and priming, and he held it against Ruscher's back and fired. The smith's large body jerked and a small billow of smoke – powder smoke, cloth smoke, flesh smoke – went up toward heaven.

As Bockelson walked past Matthys, he said: "Brother Matthys, we cannot hesitate to shed blood." And as he and his lackey Piet Bruinsma walked past Divora, who had watched the whole thing, Bockelson said to the silent one:

"What use does our prophet have for this gorgeous young thing, Piet? She is a bundle of grapes needing to be pressed for her juice, and our prophet would not know how to proceed."

It took poor Hubert Ruscher eight more days, days of bleeding, swelling, and gangrene, to die.

JAN MATTHYS LED his flock of some ten thousand people ever closer to the millennium, aware of but not really concerned with the very secular siege that Franz von Waldeck was mounting against Münster. There were sentries on the walls who reported regularly the troop movements outside the city – their reports told a story of growing numbers of both soldiers and stockades on all sides – but this was to Matthys a laughing matter. What could iron guns do against the Spirit of the Lord? Bernhard Knipperdolling suggested that they make military preparations, organize the manpower, and watch the prince-bishop around the clock, but Matthys scoffed; instead, he said, they should pray.

ON THE THIRD of April, with the sound of the prince-bishop's newly acquired cannon thudding in the distance, Jan Matthys and the other spiritual leaders attended a wedding banquet hosted by the converted patrician Lambert von Luettich, whose U-shaped table was buried in food and drink, some of which was served on finely crafted silver plate confiscated from the Fettbauch house. All those of spiritual and political importance were present: the prophet, the Dutch apostles, the mayors and the council members, the preachers, and their wives. Matthys was proud of Divora and displayed her prominently at his side. There was much drinking at the table. Public drunkenness on the streets was now punished by flogging, but here, among his friends, Matthys ignored the sin.

"So, how shall we celebrate Easter in the city of God?" said Gerhard Kippenbroick, already well lubricated, to no one in particular.

Jan Bockelson had been thinking about this moment for a long time. "I think we should attack the prince-bishop's camp," he said.

Jan Matthys, sitting next to him, did not hear, or pretended not to hear. But Knipperdolling replied: "Indeed! We have two thousand young warriors, armed and full of faith. Certainly that is a sufficient force."

"It's too many," said Bockelson.

"Too many?" ranted Knipperdolling. "Von Waldeck has at least three thousand!"

Bockelson held up his hand for quiet.

"Let him speak!" barked Divora.

"It's too many," said Bockelson again. "The Lord does not give the victory to those who are mighty in the flesh, but to those who are mighty in faith. Remember Gideon" – and Matthys' eyes smoldered a bit, since Gideon was a favorite biblical hero for him, Gideon who had, with an army pared down to three hundred by the Lord, put to flight the Midianite hordes – "and David, who faced Goliath with only a sling and stone."

Matthys straightened up. Bernhard Rothmann watched the prophet nervously: Matthys, incited by Bockelson, was forging in his own mind a plan to attack the besiegers with only a handful of men.

"We must be wise," Rothmann urged. "The Lord has given us our people here for a reason."

"Silence!" snapped Matthys. "If we attack with our whole army, it will be too many." Matthys' eyes seemed to sink back further into his skull, as they always did when he communed with his own mind and spirit. Bockelson drank daintily from a steaming cup of sugared wine, trying not to burn his lips. Divora's eyes widened and danced and lit on Bockelson.

Rothmann's face fell. He had lost. Now the idea of reducing the attacking force was, in Matthys' thinking, his own idea. This is what Bockelson did so well.

"Too many men?" Bockelson asked, prompting Matthys. Divora was smiling.

"Too many for the Lord to get the victory. Too many for the Lord to get the glory. So it was with Gideon's three hundred."

Something was happening to Jan Matthys. His eyes were rolling around inside the sockets. The festivities stopped, and the groom took his lips off the bride's neck and watched in apprehension with the others. Knipperdolling seemed unaccountably sober. After some minutes, Matthys hit his clenched fists together and began lifting his shaggy head up and down, and groaning deep within himself. Then out of him, though as if not out of him but someone inside him, came the words of Christ on the night before his death:

"Oh dear Father, not as I will, but as you will!"

The whole company watched silently, suddenly sober, while the prophet groaned and swayed and leaned, full of the Spirit. He sank to his knees for some minutes. Then up he stood, taking Divora's fleshy pink arm, and made the rounds of the other guests with handshakes and kisses.

Rothmann said, "You will not endanger your own life, we trust."

"I will lead the elect warriors of God to the tent of the Beast of Waldeck with my own staff. There is no danger. The only danger is relying on the power of our own flesh." And he went out with Divora, who shot back a hot glance at Jan Bockelson. Bockelson winked.

NOBODY SAW JAN Matthys the whole day before Easter, since he was secluded in his room in prayer. The prince-bishop's gunners practiced their marksmanship against the west wall with little effect but to keep the city in a state of suspense, for the word had circulated throughout the population that a great deliverance was awaiting them on Easter, and the booming of von Waldeck's cannon seemed like a portent of judgment day.

Before daylight appeared on the morning of April fifth, twelve picked men assembled in the torchlit street by the east gate. There was foggy haze; the men talked in subdued tones, their voices bass from much sleep, and tried to shake the drowsiness out of their heads. Younger boys held the horses by their reins, and the horses stomped and urinated in the street, sending up steam and a heavy animal smell. The men were checking their harness, saddle straps, and stirrups, buttoning up their gray peasant coats against the chill, and handling their weapons. Some women went among them with a pot of hot drink and a ladle, saying, "God be with you."

Peasants, artisans, beggars, criminals, going to battle for their prophet. Finally it had come: the time for the saints to take up the sword. The dripping red earth.

Bernhard Knipperdolling cantered up to the group on a black horse; he was dressed in a bright red coat with green trim.

"Hurray for the mayor!" said several.

"The prophet is coming," announced Knipperdolling.

Out of the fog the figure of Jan Matthys appeared, coming on foot down the street with several others behind him, striding long, the clunking of his shoes a conspicuous sound. The collar of his black coat was pulled up around his neck. Rothmann was with him in his scholar's robe and beret, and Bockelson came also, bundled up in fur. These men stopped in front of the preparing riders.

Matthys was delirious with zeal. He dropped to his knees on the street and prayed to God with arms outstretched and head thrown back. His prayer went on at length while more people quietly assembled around him and the warriors, and the rising sun began to turn the sky to a faint gray.

The prayer was over. Matthys stood and attendants strapped armor around his chest and hips, and placed a glossy black helmet on his head. A sword on a belt was buckled at his side. Matthys took the bridle of a horse that was being held for him and mounted it. His legs were longer than the average man's and the stirrups had been set too short, and his long coat spread out behind him on the horse's rump like a cape. He carried his staff in his right hand.

The rest of the attacking party mounted with a racket of wood and metal and followed Matthys toward the opening west gate. Matthys took his horse out onto the causeway that spanned the moat, and the others bunched behind him. The light fog of the night was thinning, and the first morning's glow was rising in the sky to the east.

"Where to?" Jonas the bodyguard asked the prophet.

"Straight ahead. God will guide us to him." Then he said, "Follow me," and kicked his horse in the ribs.

Once across the causeway, Matthys' horse broke into a canter, and the prophet's crotch thwapped against the saddle; he veered and rolled, an old baker on a careening warhorse. The twelve men followed him in no particular formation but tightly packed, some with swords, others with lances, none with any armor on their bodies.

The people of Münster flowed up to the battlements on the walls to watch.

The little band headed towards a swell in the landscape called Miller's Hill, into the deep morning gray. Waiting for them there was the prince-bishop's heavy cavalry, armored in black, predatory and grim. Matthys and his twelve met these five hundred just over the hill. For the black riders it was not even an exercise. A few seconds of combat. Anabaptist riders splayed dead or dying on the cool ground. Their horses rounded up.

The black knights gathered around the still living body of Jan Matthys.

"Ha! Ha! You cannot touch me!" he cried, and laughed until the tears rolled down his cheeks.

"What is he saying?"

"That we can't harm him."

"Why?"

"That silly staff, I guess."

"This must be their prophet," said the captain of the

company. His men stared at the insanity before them on the ground.

"Kill him, and take his body to the bishop," said the captain, shaking his hand as if to be done with the thing, and walked away. The knights dismounted for this work.

LATER THAT DAY a heavily armored horseman came across the empty zone from the siegeworks and dumped a large canvas bag to the ground near the city wall. Matthys' bodyguards fetched the bag. Inside it were the dismembered remains of Jan Matthys. But there was no head, and the sentinels looked again out at the bishop's camp, fearing to see what they did see: the hoary dark head of Jan Matthys being mounted on a pike.

The city fell into a shocked silence. Even the women were saying nothing, singing nothing. The pieces of Matthys were placed into a plain wooden coffin which was set on the south side of the cathedral where the sun shone. The leaders congregated around it, and the shepherdless flock of the population collected in the cathedral square. Nobody knew what to expect, or do. There was no plan or precedent. Matthys had led them by his personal power; the old institutions were gone, and there was nothing to put in their place. Then Jan Bockelson turned and faced the people, and spoke, seizing the moment as he had done already so many times.

"God's prophet has met his glorious end!" he exclaimed. "He died as prophets die, did he not? Does not the scripture record how the true prophets of old sealed their testimonies with their blood? And our brother Jan Matthys now stands in the company of the glorious martyrs, with beheaded John the Baptist, with stoned Stephen, with crucified Peter and beheaded Paul and flayed Bartholomew. What company! What glory! His message was complete. His task was done. It was his time, and God took him with great honor!"

The reinterpretation was in process; heads were nodding yes; hope was flowing in where there had been only despair.

"Do you think this was a surprise?" Bockelson continued. "Does God act without revealing his work to his prophets? Eight days ago, as I was studying the scriptures in the house of brother Bernhard" – he nodded to Knipperdolling – "I was given a vision, in which I beheld a pikeman stabbing a man through the middle, and his intestines falling out, and I was horrified until the pikeman called to me, *Fear not, man of God, but be faithful to your calling! For the vision deals not with your life, but with the life of Matthys, whose wife you must marry after his death."*

It was outrageous, so outrageous that it had to be the word of God, and Knipperdolling promptly stood to confirm it.

"This is true," said the mayor. "The apostle told me of his vision a week ago."

And the people grasped at it because they had already given too much of themselves to their leaders to turn back.

"We have our commission!" cried Bockelson. "The purpose of Christ will not be set aside! The death of one man, even this last Elijah, is not the end of the work of God in this city!"

By now he had their hearts.

"Think of it, people of God! See it all with the eyes of faith! Right now the prince-bishop and his drunken lackeys are laughing at God, and holding God's dead prophet in contempt! How easy it was to kill him, they scoff. They drink, and sleep. But who is laughing? The Lord sits on his throne in heaven and laughs, and on his left hand our brother Matthys stands and laughs, and together they make their plans to send this prince-bishop . . . to hell!"

A volcanic roar of cheers and applause.

"Now let us go about our task!"

And now not even Matthys' death, not even the obvious failure of his word, could halt the madness he had nurtured.

JULIUS FETTBAUCH SHARED his humble house against the wall with a small, feral man whose name he did not yet know.

The man had come in the middle of the night and had set his bundle of personal things on the floor of the main room, and Julius had not seen him for several days after that. One evening Julius walked in and the man was sitting by himself on the floor with a thin blanket over his shoulders. He looked up at Julius.

"Well, there you are," said the man in good German.

"You're German," said Julius. "What a relief. I had assumed you were Dutch. Not that I have anything against the Dutch, of course." The house was cold, and Julius began to arrange a fire in the tile stove. "My name is Julius Fettbauch."

"My name is Arndt Manns. Fettbauch?" The man smiled.

Julius was used to it. "Some name for a man with a *fett Bauch,* eh?" He grabbed his belly above the belt and slopped it up and down.

"It will get thinner in this city. You know we're going to starve, don't you?"

"Softly, my friend," said Julius Fettbauch. "There are many ears."

But Arndt Manns seemed not to care. "Mark my words, this place is doomed. That blonde fool Bockelson will see to it. It doesn't matter that Matthys is dead. Mark my words, we have seen only the beginning. That blonde fool has plans. The prince-bishop would have been wiser to send the old man back here alive."

"Why are you here?"

"The food is free. What's the slogan . . . one egg, one bread . . . ?"

"One pot, one egg, one kitchen," said Julius. "The preachers say it in every sermon."

"One pot, one egg, one kitchen. And there are lots of women." Arndt Manns' grin made him look like a gopher.

MATTHYS' FATAL EXPEDITION became quickly a great victory in the minds of the Münsterites: they sang songs of it, and told and retold the story, and the witnesses on the wall remembered seeing angels by the prophet's side as he rode out of the city, and it was reported on good authority that the prophet had slain a hundred mercenaries with his staff before laying it down and allowing himself to be martyred. So things had never been better.

Still the siege was not tight. The prince-bishop's position was porous enough for new refugees to slip into the city at night. He was having problems getting military aid from his fellow princes in the region, and besides, it was not campaigning season yet.

On a balmy May night, Jan Bockelson ran naked through the city. People lined the streets and watched in silence. He sang psalms and summoned the people to repentance and spoke in incomprehensible languages. Finally he fell to his knees as if to pray, straightened out as if hit by lightning, and lay motionless in the street. It was the ecstatic trance, lost on the stages of Leiden and now recaptured. As before, in Leiden, the watchers came to see if he was dead and found his eyes wide open and very much alive, the fire shining through the ice, and they drew back in awe. They watched him through the night and covered him with blankets to keep his body warm, and by day they shielded him from the sun. The suspense was almost unbearable. On the third day he rose, dressed, shaved, combed his hair, ate meat and bread, and called the people of Münster together in the cathedral square to tell them what he had heard from God.

CHAPTER 15: MEMORY
April, 1534. The Rhine.

The boat was on the Rhine at night, and Paulus was dreaming. In his dream, Onkel was preaching. Again. The old man's words were effortless and fluent and eloquent, like music.

He woke and what he saw first were the stars, promiscuously scattered in the night sky. Then he felt the undulating rhythm of the boat and heard the tender lapping of small waves against its sides. He remembered: he and Marga and the baby had boarded the boat in the afternoon. The oarsman had argued with them, saying that his craft was already too heavy with its cargo of books from Basel, but he had in the end been unable to deny passage to a mother with a baby. The oarsman was still at the stern of the boat, guiding it in starlight, the side to side movement of his oar giving it its rhythm. Paulus put his hand out to touch Marga, and she was there, next to him, asleep in her usual position with legs drawn up and back against Paulus' side. Heine was in the cradle made by her curled body.

"Marga," he whispered. Even though he said her name, he hoped that she would not wake up. He only wanted to hear the sound of his own voice. Marga slept on.

Onkel kept storming into Paulus' inner life. He tried to review the previous day: had he thought about Onkel, spoken his name, longed for him? No. But it was more complicated than that, for Paulus knew well that he was always conscious of Onkel, the way he was conscious of his mouth even though he never saw it. There were the small reminders, like the Bible. Sometimes when the light was good Paulus found dirty finger smudges on certain pages and could imagine Onkel stopping and puzzling over a passage while he held the page between his greasy fingers. And the church. It had been Onkel's church, then Paulus', and then it had blown to the winds. And it felt to Paulus, when he reflected on it, that the dispersion of the church was when Onkel had really died. For the church had been Onkel's heart and soul, his labor, his love, and something which he had needed as much as the people of the flock had needed him. Paulus could live without it, as he was doing now, but he could never imagine Onkel living without it. These were the things Paulus felt, and to do so was sometimes a poignant comfort, sometimes a sorrow.

The dream left him with a sense of burden. He had done his best, but it was not enough. In Onkel's gnarled face he saw strength, faithfulness, wisdom, singleness of purpose; when he thought of himself he saw weakness and division and the lust for tranquility. But even if the memory of Onkel made him feel inadequate, it also continually told him who he was.

He tried to sleep again but could not. His memory raced, and he told it to stop, and it kept going, from Paris to Moravia to Marga to the Taunus and back in crazy detours to his childhood, and it all seemed so exquisitely sharp and emotional. Where was he going? Was he really on a pilgrimage, or lost in a circle? He wanted to be a child again, to be held, to be cooed at. He knew that in the darkness all his sensitivities were heightened, and that with the coming of the daylight everything would seem less giant to him, but he could not force himself to see it all that way now. Besides, he wondered which was truer, the routine beaten world of the daytime or the exquisitely painful world of the night, which opened up when the clamor of the day stopped. Did the night, the loneliness, and the fresh impact of the dream muddle up the truth, or expose it?

Eventually his eyes stung, and his head felt heavy.

"Marga," he said again, and took her shoulder in his hand. "Wake up, please."

"O-h-h," she moaned.

"I need you."

She rolled onto her back and extended her legs.

"What's wrong?"

"I dreamed about Onkel."

"Why don't you tell him to leave you alone."

"I don't want him to leave me alone."

"Dream about me."

"I do sometimes."

"You dream about him instead of me."

"Not always."

She turned back to the baby and put her back to him.

"Marga, I can't stop thinking, thinking. Wishing that I were an old man with my life behind me and death coming soon."

"You talk like an old man."

It was her last word for the night. She was angry with him because he had done nothing to help Max Holzmann against the duke's knights. They had debated it, logically, theologically, practically, and she was still angry. So she went back to sleep and he lay on his back with his eyes on the starry sky, waiting, like a night watchman for the morning, for the first hues of gray, for the stars to fade away.

CHAPTER 16: VORTEX
June, 1534. Wesel, Cleves.

Like draining flood waters, the forces which had uprooted them subsided; like debris, Paulus and his little family settled onto the firm earth. This time it was near the city of Wesel, in the Duchy of Cleves. The boatman had learned that they were Anabaptists.

"There are many like you in Wesel. Besides," the kind man added, "further down river you'll have trouble understanding the language."

The country along the lower Rhine, where it poured out of northern Germany, turned west into the Low Countries and fragmented into several rivers like fingers coming out from a hand, was honeycombed with Anabaptists. They had heard Hoffman, and they had heard about Matthys, and they knew all about Münster. It was a land of many languages, where German and Dutch and Flemish and French converged like the rivers, a land of movement and commerce, and of towns.

The boatman let them off a short ways upstream from where the river Lippe ran into the Rhine. It was a flat land they were in now, where the horizon all around was straight like a ruler. And it was a wet land, with no place for the rain that fell to go except to drift lazily toward the Rhine, and even the Rhine flowed slowly here, as if it had grown old. The confluence of the Rhine and the Lippe was swampy and ill-defined, and they got their shoes soaking wet as they walked from the river bank toward the church steeple that the boatman had pointed them to as the center of Wesel.

Marga insisted that they seek out the believers as the first thing they did. They had talked about this again and again on the boat, for Marga was feeling a deep need to be in the midst of others like themselves. She felt lonely and unprotected. Heine, she said, needed other children; she needed other women. Paulus was less sure that seeking out the believers here was a good idea, for he had come to love the solitude of their life in the mountains even though he felt guilty about it, and he thought that they were probably safer alone than they would be as part of a visible Anabaptist community.

But Marga insisted, and when they had entered the little town of Wesel she asked the first person she saw on the street:

"Are there Anabaptists in this city?"

It was a middle-aged woman with a basket of clothes in her arms. She winced a little when she heard Marga's hard, Austrian German.

"Everywhere," she said and gestured with her chin because her hands and arms were loaded. "Like spring flies in a pig pen. But you'll find most of them in Münster." She lifted her chin again, this time to the northeast.

"Thank you," said Marga without smiling, and they went on. "Münster, where's Münster?" she asked Paulus.

"Two, three days east, I think," said Paulus.

Marga kept asking questions until they learned about a leather worker named Matthias Forder who was reputed to be an Anabaptist. They found him in his place of business. While they talked to him he avoided eye contact and kept his hands busy with his work, and he seemed reticent to give out information. He asked them many questions before he finally told them where the believers met.

"There is a bad road leading out of the town, by the old ruin of the tower to the north. It will go north about a quarter of a mile and then turn sharply west, like a hook. When it does, if you look straight west, you will see a barn. That's where we meet. Dusk on Sunday."

"And until Sunday?" said Paulus. "We have a baby."

Matthias Forder sighed, as if such a request was an imposition. "And you're on your way to Münster. Why don't you just go on to Münster without further delay and be done with it? They have streets of gold there, and the cabbages grow on the sides of the houses. Or so they say." He sliced a piece of leather with more force than was necessary and kept his eyes on his work.

"We are not on our way to Münster," said Paulus slowly. "Why should we be on our way to Münster? We are in Wesel, and we are believers in Christ and we want to find our brothers here. That's all."

"Then you don't know about Münster?" For the first time the man looked them in the eye with some warmth.

"We know that there is a city called Münster."

Matthias shook his head. "You'll soon learn, I'm afraid. And I'm sorry. It's the fear, I guess. I've seen so many wild-eyed people claiming to be my brothers, on their way to Münster. I was assuming you were more of the same."

He put down his work, took their hands, and offered them lodging in his own home until they could find their own. It was a plain place, absolutely unadorned, small and tight, but dry. Paulus and Marga and the baby slept up in the attic where the rafters met.

They told Matthias Forder their story, and he told them his. He was a widower, and childless, and a believer since the time four years before when Melchior Hoffmann had passed through Wesel and preached. The church which sprang up in the wake of Hoffmann's preaching grew, thrived, and shrank. Persecution thinned it first, but most recently many of its members were caught up in the enthusiasm of the Münster experiment. And Matthias Forder told Paulus and Marga about Münster. Paulus was dumfounded. Anabaptists fighting the prince-bishop, executing people, stoning people – it was unthinkable, unimaginable. Paulus was sure that Matthias must have received some twisted information. Marga listened, mesmerized, to this strange report.

THEY WENT WITH Matthias to the church meeting on Sunday night, in a dilapidated animal barn that still smelled of hogs. To prevent suspicion, the people arrived by twos and threes over about an hour.

When all had arrived, they covered the windows and brought out a lamp and lit it from a smoldering firebox, stark light and shadow fell across the room. Now Paulus could see faces, and sex, and size, and found himself hungrily taking in face after face and saying to himself with each one that this was a brother, or a sister. His experience had been so small, really. The brotherhood of Montau had been his whole spiritual family until now.

A man with a dense black beard, which reached up over the points of his cheeks and down almost to his collar, took charge of the meeting; he prayed, and gave a short exhortation, and served the communion with bread and wine taken from a cloth bag. The liquid, vowel-filled sound of his language lulled Paulus, and the sharp light and shadow made his eyes hurt. Paulus was tired. Things would not be right, not until he and Marga had a bed of their own with room to sit up without bumping their heads, not until he had some productive work with which to busy his hands and his mind, or until the world stopped pursuing him, or until Christ came to give rest to the saints.

He was beginning to sway toward Marga. She took his

arm at the elbow and shook him.

"Paulus! Wake up."

The place came back into focus. The man with the black beard was looking at him, his mouth was moving, yes, he was speaking to Paulus.

". . . have some word of exhortation to give to the brothers and sisters of Wesel."

Matthias Forder, who had introduced Paulus and Marga to the others, was looking at him too.

Paulus managed to say: "I have . . . no word of exhortation. Only greetings, from the brothers and sisters of our community, now scattered to the south."

"We have heard that the oppression is hard in the south."

"It seems hard, yes," said Paulus. "It seems like a storm that never ends." He could hear the things he was saying and knew that they were not completely coherent. "We walk and walk and walk, so far have we walked, brothers, and we never arrive. We're always in the middle of the journey."

The people were staring at him. Marga was staring at him. The leader finally cleared his throat and rubbed the side of his nose.

"The Vogels have left us," he announced.

"To Münster?" asked one from the group.

"Yes. We remove them from our membership."

"And God from the book of life," said Matthias Forder.

"You have no right to say that!" said a woman. "They have done what they thought was best!"

"What they thought was best?" said the leader. "God does not promise his blessing to those who do what they think is best. The magistrates and the pope do what they think is best. The Vogels have rejected the covenant, it's that simple."

The leader spoke with authority, and was not afraid of the storm that this issue unleashed among them.

"It is not right that this should make us bitter to one another."

People were speaking swiftly and in no order.

"We should withhold judgment on the brothers of Münster until we see what God does."

"What! They have already trampled all the commands of Christ!"

"But who is perfect?"

"That's not the point."

"Jan Bockelson is a demon-possessed man."

"No, no, no."

"No, I have heard him preach, and he is a man of faith and the word."

"So much confusion!" cried Matthias. "Can we hear ourselves talk? Can you hear yourselves? We used to have a belief about this matter, one that we were willing to die for, and one that some of us died for. Brother Hoffmann taught it to us, from God's word. And it was not so long ago. Our Lord forbids that we take up the sword. And the men of Münster have taken up the sword. Why this confusion?"

"Perhaps brother Hoffmann was confused."

"Perhaps he was wrong."

"But is the Lord wrong? Never mind brother Hoffmann!"

"I am tired of this, this, hair-splitting!" shouted a young thin man with a sharp voice, who stood in his place in a corner and shook his finger across the room at Matthias and the pastor. "Now I am no doctor of theology, as you all know. And I stammer and don't have the right words. But I wonder to myself, I do, if the Lord wants me to stand by and let my family be taken, put in prison, tortured. I'll tell you, I think about it at night, I do!"

"Brother, we all do," said the pastor, but his last words were lost.

"Yes, that's right!"

"The man speaks truth."

"Brother Katzenbach, do you want to take up the sword in your own defense?" Matthias was putting this question to the thin man. "Because there's no sense talking about this for the sake of argument. Is it what you really want, to carve human flesh?"

"Is it what you want, brother Forder, to have your flesh carved? Is it any different?"

"It is! It is! If the other man does the carving then it's he who goes to hell! I'll say it is!"

"Hell? You talk about hell? The strappado is hell, my friend, the rack is hell, the hot iron boot is hell, the wheel is hell."

"No," said Paulus suddenly. "The rack and the wheel are not hell. Hell goes on forever and ever. The brothers and sisters who have suffered their pain are now in heaven."

"And why do you think you may speak here?" shot back Katzenbach. "What do you know of what we've suffered?"

Blood pumped into Paulus' head and he felt suddenly clear and lucid. "I know. Believe me, I know."

"Let's not play this game, who's-suffered-more-than-who, brothers," pleaded the pastor. "Only the word of Christ, that's all that we can live by."

"Jan Bockelson has some scripture on his side too."

"Yes, Old Testament scripture."

"Scripture is scripture. Who are we to take one part over another?"

"Our Lord abolished the old covenant."

"Were not David and Moses and Elijah godly men?"

"And they held swords, didn't they?"

"Of course!"

"Of course!"

"This is all ridiculous!"

"We are ridiculous! We are ridiculous, to let the heathen chase us and carve us! What could be more laughable?"

"Fighting, that's what. Saying we follow Christ and still fighting."

"Brothers, don't fight each other!"

"Listen, please listen to the pastor!"

"Listen to the pastor! Let him speak!"

The pastor held his two hands aloft to ask for silence and the right to speak.

"The Vogels have gone," he finally said. "It makes us sad to see them go. We understand the great fear and confusion that is in their hearts, which is also in our own. But we cannot for that reason leave our gospel behind or change it. We have believed in peace since we first gathered together, and I for one will continue to believe in peace. May God give me the grace to do so. And brother Katzenbach, do you think you should ask forgiveness from our new brother, Ketterling? You have no idea what he has suffered."

Katzenbach shifted back and forth on his feet.

"I don't know what he's suffered, it's true. But I believe... I believe that when a man has suffered enough... he will fight."

"Our Lord didn't," said Paulus.

"He was the Son of God. You're a mere man, and so am I."

The people kept talking about Münster, and peace, and violence, and most of all about their constant fear of arrest, through most of the night. Paulus was tired, and slipped in and out of periods of attentiveness, and ventured only a few more remarks of his own. He thought at first that these must be a peculiarly contentious people, these northerners on their flat plains; maybe there was not enough sunshine. He thought that if Onkel were the pastor there would be order and love – the brothers in Montau had never yelled at each other like these did – but as a picture of what was happening in Münster gradually congealed, from snippets and pieces of the debate, and from what Matthias had already told him, he was not so sure that even Onkel could keep the peace.

In Montau, one could think about revenge, retaliation, and retribution – but there was little to do about it. Here, there was Münster, not far away, where persecuted Anabaptists at the end of their patience were doing something. Onkel had talked about starving sins to death. In Münster, the lust to fight back was nourished and fed.

On the walk home, Matthias Forder denounced Münster, and wished that all those who sympathized with it would simply go there and be done with it, so the church in Wesel could have peace.

"May God give the prince-bishop success!" Matthias said.

"That is unworthy," replied Marga. "You're asking God to slaughter our brothers."

Paulus was tired of controversy. He wanted to rest. He wanted to pull a quilt up around his pounding head and sleep. Already he had had enough of Wesel, and he wanted to go back to the Taunus mountains, or even to what was left of Montau. This flat crowded country made him sad. There was something evil about it.

One thing worried him more than the rest of it. It was what Katzenbach had said, full of intelligence and logic and the wisdom of observation, and it stated what all the saints, however committed to the doctrine of peace, felt and feared in their hearts: *when a man has suffered enough he will fight*. Or a woman. What worried him was what Marga had done in response to Katzenbach's statement. She had shaken her head yes. It frightened him, because there was nothing he could do. He had given her all his arguments and all his love. He wished he had never brought her near Münster.

THE NEXT DAY was a good day to sleep, and they did, while a boisterous wind from the northwest shoved piles of clouds across the Zuider Zee and Gelderland and on across the small duchy of Cleves. Matthias awoke to open his shop, and took Heine downstairs with him when the child cried, so Paulus and Marga could sleep.

Just before noon there was a terrific racket in the street below, so loud and constant that it penetrated even to the attic where Paulus and Marga lay. Marga awoke and scrambled down the staircase with a blanket thrown over her shoulders. Heine ran to greet her and she picked him up. Matthias was at his open door, watching the street. Outside, soldiers marched by, and drums beat in chaotic individualism, and people shouted to each other.

"What's happening?" she asked.

"Looks like the prince-bishop von Waldeck is getting some help from the Duke of Cleves. Mercenaries, lots of them."

"They're going to Münster?"

"Seems so."

Rough men, these German mercenary foot-soldiers who now filed by, ruffians paid to fight the wars of kings and princes. Young men, barely grown, and many mature men too, since once a man sold his spear and his body this way it was hard to do anything else. Scarred, maimed, souls cauterized to violence and pain, these men had no cause except their own pay. They dressed as individuals, with brightly colored fluted trousers, one leg red and the other yellow, and gaudy plumes and painted leather jerkins, and they armed themselves as they preferred, with swords, axes, halberds, and pikes. When they marched together in a body they made a fearsome sight. There was no discipline among them. The only thing that made them behave was money.

They were behaving today, for the prince-bishop Franz von Waldeck had sent a chest of money to the Duke of Cleves; the Duke had taken his cut and sent it on to the organizer of this particular company, who in turn took his cut and gave half of the rest to his men, withholding the balance so the mercenaries would stay on the job. The mercenaries were happy because they had money in their pockets, money to buy pleasure from prostitutes while they camped in the muck around Münster, money with which to gamble away the endless dreary hours of waiting or to buy their freedom if they were captured. Many of them limped from sore old wounds, and many had fingers missing, but they were all smiling. And they were talking, as much as Marga could understand them, about the share of the spoil that the prince-bishop had promised them when Münster fell and about the Anabaptists they would butcher in the process. It was as if they were going to a picnic, a fair, a hunt.

"May they do their work well," said Matthias Forder grimly.

"May God smite them," said Marga.

"Long live the prince-bishop! May his coffers always be full!" shouted a mercenary, and others around him laughed.

CHAPTER 17: KINGDOM
August, 1534. Münster.

Jan Bockelson rose from his three day trance – and the women of the city noted the similarity to Christ's own resurrection, while they also noticed Bockelson's physical beauty – and took control of the city. He had seen it all, he said, in a vision. Through the late spring and summer he refashioned the city.

He abolished the ancient Town Council and appointed, instead, twelve elders, whose names he had received from God in the vision. They were all men of the inner circle, veterans in the struggle, saints with scars, and men who would listen to the new high prophet of the city obediently. He promulgated a new code of justice and punishment, in which death was the automatic penalty for a host of crimes from adultery to complaining. He organized and rationalized the administration of the city's physical and economic life. Bernhard Knipperdolling became the Swordbearer, with the job of executing condemned criminals. Foodmasters would set up public kitchens. There were two Fishmasters, two Meatmasters, three official Shoemakers, masters of ironwork, nails, clothing, liquor, leather, oil, beer, and bread, a master of the city's firearms and a master of its wagons.

The big explosion happened in late July, when Bockelson announced, as a revelation from God, the institution of polygamy. There were eight thousand woman and two thousand men in the city, and when God granted them their great victory and the unbelievers had been eradicated from the face of the earth, a new holy seed would flourish. So begin, he said. Take wives and multiply.

He made this revelation in the cathedral, where the elders, the Swordbearer, and the preachers were assembled. These leaders were dumfounded. Political and social innovations were one thing, but polygamy was another. In a rare outburst of independent thinking, they voiced their objections, and the argument began. It continued for several days, Jan Bockelson against them all, revelation against tradition. He reasoned with them at first, but they proved unreasonable, so he threatened them with the fury of God.

"This city is the city of God and I am his apostle, as you have seen and heard! You remember that – God does not need you! He can raise up saints from the cobblestones if need be! If you disobey his revelation he will damn you and your bodies will rot outside the wall just like the bodies of our enemies! If only I am left, this will still be the new Jerusalem of God, and I and my wives will inherit it. Through me and the holy sisters a new seed will arise to take your place!"

Their fear was greater in the end than their inhibition. They did fear him, because his blue eyes shot out lightning bolts, and because they did believe that he was the mouth of God. So, on the fifth day after they had sequestered themselves in the cathedral, they emerged, baggy-eyed, pale, and announced through the voice of Bernhard Rothmann that God willed all godly men to take several wives, as many as their dwellings could accommodate. The people murmured.

There was a brief insurrection, a few hours of danger

during which Bockelson's ascendancy could have toppled, but in the end the city was with its prophet. There were some executions, more sermons, and then polygamy became law in Münster. There followed an avalanche of new marriages, in which most of the former nuns from the convents and some very young girls, twelve and thirteen years old, were snatched up by the men of Münster. Elaborate ceremonies were not necessary to finalize these new marriages, only a simple transaction before a couple of witnesses and the prompt recording of the marriage to a clerk who sat at a desk by the St. Lambert's Church. Such marriages now became daily, even hourly occurrences.

Jan Bockelson himself led the way by marrying Divora. After their marriage he requisitioned a spacious and stylish house on the cathedral square, which had once belonged to a wealthy canon of the cathedral, Melchior von Büren – he intended to keep a large household with many wives. Within days of his marriage to Divora he had taken fourteen more wives, all of them nubile and very young. There were plenty of rooms and beds in his house for all of them.

WHILE JAN BOCKELSON consolidated his city, outside, in the old world, the prince-bishop built his camps and kept writing letters. He built supply depots around the city, and conscripted thousands of peasants in the vicinity of Münster and put them to work, as befitted their station in life, in the ground, digging trenches, throwing up earth walls, and carving out canals to drain the moat which surrounded the city. To feed his army, he set up camp markets, where local merchants and farmers could sell the goods that would ordinarily have been taken to Münster.

Von Waldeck assaulted the city half-heartedly on the morning of Pentecost Monday, the twenty-fifth of May, but this assault was thrown back. It was humiliating. The prince-bishop let loose a fearful rage when an investigation revealed that the plan had been given away the night before by some drunken mercenaries. In the wake of this defeat, some of his own mercenaries ran off to Münster. His army was melting away. Only the promises of the Archbishop of Cologne and the Duke of Cleves to supply laborers for the trenches and ten thousand gulden for the purchase of powder kept his hopes alive.

Then, in early August, the prince-bishop and everyone else heard about Bockelson's decree of polygamy. Now he had something to write about to his fellow princes.

HERALDS FROM THE prince-bishop's tent roused his motley army, part feudal, part mercenary, at dawn of August thirty-first. For four days previous, through a soaking rain, the cannon of the bishop had pounded the city gates on all sides. Now, after one final bombardment, his army would move.

Franz von Waldeck had been a furious letter writer; his messengers had been in the courts of Saxony, Mainz, Trier, Brandenburg, Braunschweig, Lueneburg, and Luettich; he had even appealed to Ferdinand, Duke of Austria and King of Bohemia, the emperor's younger brother. But in the end it was the prince-bishop of Cologne, and the landgrave of Hesse, and the duke of Cleves who finally came through for him with substantial contributions of troops and war material. The prince-bishop's camps were suddenly awash with men and equipment, and he decided to attack.

The prince-bishop had two monstrous guns, courtesy of Philip of Hesse. The largest was nicknamed The Devil and its slightly smaller companion The Devil's Mother. With these two weapons, the prince-bishop had bombarded the city and its main gate, the St. Mauritz Gate. It appeared from a distance that the gate was now in shreds. But thousands of hours of work to drain the city's moat near the St. Mauritz Gate had been undone by the rains, which filled every crevice, every depression, every ditch. So the prince-bishop equipped his mercenaries with straw bundles as flotation devices to cross the moat. He was determined to attack.

His army stood in their companies, dressed for battle in bright colors, rested, fed, ready to earn their florins and guldens by throwing their bodies against the gray wall of Münster. They carried shields to protect themselves from the hail of projectiles that would inevitably meet them at the wall; they carried crossbows, and spears, and daggers, and many carried the arquebus, the clumsy musket that fired a heavy ball. Ladders were evenly distributed among them, and each man bore on his back several bundles of straw moat-fillers.

The musketeers would sweep the wall clean; the lightly armed men with the ladders would scale the wall where it had been blasted low to a V-shaped notch and engage the enemy; and the heavily armed pikemen would enter the city through the gate. That, at least, was how the prince-bishop had it planned.

The Devil and The Devil's Mother sent a few more missiles at the wall, and the buildings within a mile of them trembled. This last salvo was more symbolic than strategic; it was the signal for the attack. The heads of Anabaptists were visible along the top of the wall, still, like the teeth of a saw, faceless from the distance where the mercenaries now stood. Von Waldeck's field captain nodded to his drummer, who pounded the advance on his drum.

Fifteen hundred men set out across the four hundred yards of denuded field that lay between them and the gate. The kettledrums pounded away. On the wall near the St. Mauritz Gate, Anabaptists commanded by the elder Gerlach von Wullen waited. These defenders knew that the mercenaries were headed for the blasted notch, and they had stones, arrows, logs, buckets of boiling pitch and lye, and loaded muskets ready. Among von Wullen's warriors, armed with a short sword, was Julius Fettbauch.

The drums stopped beating when the attackers reached the moat. Thousands of straw bundles went into the rising water, and soldiers followed them in, while from the wall, and answering from below, came the ragged crackling of musket fire.

Brown smoke, bitter and hot, filled the air. Bodies choked the moat, but the wave of the attackers came up on the other side, and ladders and weapons came along, and a swell of hopeful shouting erupted from the prince-bishop's troops as they reached the wall. Up to the wall, and into the softened notch in the wall, went the ladders. All the while the muskets ripped in both directions.

All along the threatened section of the wall, Bockelson's people fought. As attackers climbed their ladders, they were met with heavy logs from above, which stripped the ladders of their men and broke bones and heads on the way down. Furious Anabaptist women flung buckets of hot pitch and lye, which found the naked faces and hands and crevices of the attackers. And at the all important notch, von Wullen's fighters stood at the ready.

Poor Julius Fettbauch was sweating profusely, and his heart was jumping in his chest. His head was just below the firing line of the prince-bishop's musketeers, and he could hear the balls singing above him. Beneath his feet was the slippery earth ramp which the city's workers had quickly thrown up behind the wall. If the mercenaries should reach the top, he and his unit would counterattack. Ahead of him the women were fighting with screams and songs, and the steam from the hot pitch went up.

But the assaulting army had concentrated its might on this point, and gradually the ladders found a firm grip, and the sheer weight of the attack drove the women from the wall. The superior firepower of von Waldeck's musketeers kept the Anabaptists hidden in the rubble until the last moment, when the first climbers came to the tops of their ladders and set foot on the wall. Then, amid flying balls, the Anabaptists counterattacked with a shout. Bareheaded, ragged, armed with everything from spears to clubs, they came at the panting mercenaries from three sides, from along the walls and up the mountain of rubble that backed the gate. There were five or six attackers who had gained their feet already, and they braced and met the charge. They knew their job: to stand fast, to survive, until behind them their companions could mount the wall too.

Men on the ladders waited for movement, watching the struggle above. The captain bellowed, "Stand fast! Push it, push it! Help them up there!"

In the notch, swords flailed, metal and wood crashed, men grunted and puffed and sweated under the noon sun. There would have to be some forward movement on the part of the mercenaries or the attack would be at an end.

Certainly by no planning of his own, Julius found himself in the very middle of this struggle. He had been among the first to rush into the broken sides of the notch to meet the attackers. Beside him, half-crazed men charged the mercenaries and met unyielding shields and steel points. More than once he heard bullets sing past him, and once he even felt a whiff of air against his cheek. He slipped his sword finally into the gut of an enemy fighter and saw in surprise that the man sagged forward and then fell. Julius took the fallen man's shield and had just gotten it in front of him when he felt himself being pushed forward by the eager Anabaptists behind him. The crazy elder who had ordered him here in the first place was behind the whole group with a stave, driving them forward, and most of them were more afraid of the elder than of the mercenaries in front of them.

"Get back!" cried Julius.

No one heard. Julius knew he would have to go forward. He thought he would probably die. He thought about how the men he would meet were professionals. But, strange to say, none of this made him panic. In front of him was a squat ugly mercenary with a short sword, purple trousers, and a protective leather hat with an outrageous orange plume. The man was fighting for his life, protecting himself on all sides. A decorative crucifix made of some cheap metal hung from his neck by a string.

Their shields came together, and they were face to face, pinned, crushed. They could only move as the forces behind them moved. Inches away, they cursed each other. Julius caught the smell of alcohol on the other man's breath. Then the mercenary laughed. Julius thought he was not so ugly when he smiled.

"Did my best," said the man through his teeth, as he felt himself being moved to the precipice of the wall.

"Did your best, Take a rest," said Julius. He still had the poems. It was as if the conflict had sharpened his senses and his mind.

The Anabaptists were winning the shoving match in the narrow defile. Hemmed in and engulfed in confusion, Julius did not know that his fellows were dumping buckets of boiling water on the attackers from high up on the sides of the notch, though at a terrible cost to themselves as they exposed themselves to the fire from below; this new device was breaking up the assault. The men behind the mercenary that faced Julius panicked, the line moved, and Julius was hard pressed to move his feet forward amid the tangle of legs and bodies beneath him. He saw fear, then resignation, on the face in front of him. There would be no way to get back down the ladder, no way to retreat. Mercenaries were being pushed off the wall, one by one, then in twos and threes. Their resolve melted.

"Holy mother of God!"

"Help! Help!"

Men in dying anguish. Lives unrolling before minds' eyes. Scenes from remote childhood, hearts suddenly penitent for sins, flashes of visions of purgatory waiting, souls trying to get right with the Creator. And still the relentless captain at the base of the wall exhorting them to *hold, hold, hold,* cursing them for their cowardice, stamping his feet and knowing in his heart that they had lost, already counting in his mind how many men he would have to replace after this campaign. Julius' foe was a better man than most and struggled until the end, shoving against Julius with all his strength, glaring at him steadily right up to the crumbly edge of the notch where it yawned out over the moat and the ground twenty-five feet below, and when there was no place left to stand he said, "Go to hell," and let himself fall. Julius feared for an instant that the pressure would drive him off too, but hands took him from behind and pulled him back.

"Good fight!" said the man who held him. Julius Fettbauch was seized with a rush of elation and pride. He had fought well.

The Anabaptists threw down the ladders and the battle was won. Many of the companies were already in retreat. The pikemen had never really joined the battle because the gate had never been thrown open to them. A final salvo from the muskets along the wall blew away those who remained like leaves before a wind.

The Anabaptists had won!

All along the wall the attack of the prince-bishop had been repulsed. Cheering wafted across the city. The defenders streamed down from their posts and were joined by the women, who had boiled water and tended the wounded, and went toward the cathedral square. There Jan Bockelson waited for them all with arms aloft.

"See, the Lord fights for us!" He said it again and again, as the saints cheered.

Celebrations went on through the night. A deeply distressed Franz von Waldeck could see from his station on the plain the glare of bonfires against the summer night sky.

The prince-bishop's men were demoralized and broken. They had all expected a rabble of religious fanatics, and had found instead an organized community, armed and resourceful. The approach to this siege would have to be rethought.

THE REVELATION CAME through Johann Dusentschuer, the fiery prophet from Warendorf. He said that God had identified for him in the dream the last David, the eschatological king foretold by the Hebrew prophets. It was, of course, Jan Bockelson.

The coronation of Jan Bockelson, illegitimate son, actor, and tailor, was held on a rainy day, with the main events in the cathedral and the rest of the populace gathered outside in the square. People filled the damp gray interior of the building from wall to wall, climbed to the sills and sculptured tops of the pillars, stood in the places where candles, relics, and saints' statues had once stood, even up on the nave where the altar had once stood in holy loneliness. The twelve elders, some of them still bandaged from the battle, sat on their chairs in a semicircle and around them stood the bodyguards in black and the preachers. As usual, the women were at the front of the crowd.

It was a short, programmed ceremony, with Dusentschuer presiding, but there was a moment of tension. For the kind of king which Dusentschuer described – undoubtedly at Bockelson's instigation – was the king of Old Testament prophecy, the messiah, the one who, according to traditional Christian interpretation, would be fulfilled by Jesus Christ. Some in this frantic city were still thinking, and when they realized that Jan Bockelson was claiming to be, not merely a prophet but the messiah, there was murmuring in the cathedral.

Bockelson heard it, shouted it down in wrath, and proceeded to reign over his tiny kingdom of God.

CHAPTER 18: HELL
September, 1534. Duchy of Cleves.

Life with Matthias Forder was not pleasant. There was too much tension between Matthias and Marga, who wrangled about Münster. The victory of the Münsterites was well known, as was the crowning of Jan Bockelson as king, and it was becoming more difficult for the congregations that held the old peace ethic of Hoffmann to resist being sucked into the current. Paulus hated all this. He lay awake nights worrying about it, and he knew that Marga was more attracted to Münster than she would tell him. The meetings of the church were always filled with stress and fear.

The August victory of the rebels in Münster also put fear into the hearts of dukes, bishops, abbots, lords, and town councils throughout the whole region. They thought of heresy, as the church had taught for centuries, as an infection, a contagion, a contamination. And it seemed obvious now where it led: to sedition, revolution, and fanaticism. No city wanted to become another Münster. The infection must be cut out. Arrests, searches, interrogations multiplied.

The town fathers of the city of Wesel, together with their

bishop, recognizing with some wisdom that arrests and burnings only produced more Anabaptists, decided instead to remove unbaptized children from heretical families. Imperial law allowed them to do this. The parents would probably end up in Münster anyway, but at least the new generation could be salvaged for the Catholic church. They had an uneasiness about the whole idea of taking children away from their parents; it offended common decency, but the specter of revolution, communism, and polygamy was worse.

PAULUS FOUND ODD jobs, but nothing steady. He had become one of the urban poor, and if it had not been for Matthias and the help offered by the brotherhood of Wesel, he and Marga would have been very wet and hungry. He swept and dug and gathered and carried things. He spent long hours walking the country paths from manor to small manor, asking for a day's labor in the field or mill or forest. And every penny he earned he gave directly to Matthias. He realized that he had very little pride left. And he could understand why other prideless people had decided to go to Münster.

He suggested to Marga that they go back to his home in Malbeck and throw themselves on the mercy of his father. At least there they would be safe. She refused. He knew that it was because she was fascinated by the new kingdom in Münster. The times were difficult for Paulus and Marga. It was hard for them to be kind to each other.

But there were also times when the old warmth and joy came back, for they were too young and strong for the heaviness of life to completely paralyze them.

Paulus came home one afternoon with a young pig on a length of rope. The pig wanted to stop along the street and nibble on the flowers and grass.

"Marga! Look!"

Marga was upstairs. She put her head out the open window and looked down. "What in the world?"

"A pig," smiled Paulus. He was extremely proud of himself. He felt like a prosperous townsman, coming home with something nice for his wife. "It's ours."

Marga ran downstairs and met him at the door. "What are you doing with a pig?"

"I worked today, Marga. My employer paid me with – a pig!"

"So it's really ours!" Marga's eyes were bright. Paulus was happy for her. She could cook something besides porridge and cabbage..

"You can eat like an Innsbruck spoiled girl again, for a while."

"Meat!" She went into the small kitchen of the house and came back with Matthias' largest knife. "What shall we do?"

"Where's Matthias?"

"Gone to speak with the pastor again, I think." She shrugged.

"We need to share it with him, of course."

"Of course."

"But there is so much of it –" he spanked the pig's round back affectionately "– and I feel selfish tonight."

"Oh, I do too!"

"Let's eat it."

Marga's dark eyes flashed with joy. "Yes, let's eat it, let's eat as much as we can."

Paulus took her face in his hands. "Let's carve a big roast, and eat ourselves sick tonight, and do the rest early in the morning. The sausage can wait."

She raised herself on her toes and kissed him with a smack. "A big roast!"

They took the young pig behind the house and hung it by its hind legs from an apple tree. The pig squealed at the indignity and arched its back as if trying to right itself. Marga gave Paulus the kitchen knife. She held an iron pot to catch the pig's blood.

"I hate this part," he said.

"Who doesn't?"

Nobody that Paulus had ever known enjoyed butchering animals, even some people who did not mind butchering humans.

Paulus clamped the pig's head between his side and his left arm. It shrieked and jerked and almost lifted him off his feet once by the sheer strength of its arching back. Marga held the forelegs together with one hand and the pot with another. After a minute or so of wrestling Paulus had it in the right position – head firmly held, throat toward the ground. He had the knife in his right hand. He placed its point carefully at the pig's throat, in the soft hollow just below the jawbone, sucked in a breath, and drove it in. The pig went silent and its body quaked. Blood shot from the wound and pumped into the pot and spattered on their arms and clothes. As the pig died, its legs went limp in Marga's hand and the spurts of blood became a dribble. Its mouth froze in an almost human grimace. They let it go, and it swung slightly as it hung head-down, and the last of its life blood sank into the soil beneath.

Paulus took the pot of blood inside and hung it on its black hook over the fire. He put more wood on the fire. He stirred salt into it, a spoonful at a time. They would mix it into the meat and it would yield, when boiled, a delectable rich dark-brown sausage.

Paulus skinned the pig and gutted it. He brought the carcass into the house and dumped it onto the table. He scratched his itching eyebrow with the middle of his forearm; his hands were covered with gore.

"Now, my love," said Paulus. "Now, my love, I am about to extract, to carve, to gently separate from this bloody mess the roast of the evening."

"Make it big."

"Enormous. Fit for a king." And, because he was in a festive mood, he added: "Even the king of Münster." Because she was so happy, she laughed too.

He cut through the vertebrae and along the rib, taking the best and meatiest part of the animal's body in a slab that was five ribs wide.

"Paulus, that much!" she said. He was pleased that he had astonished her.

"We are wealthy burghers tonight." He pretended to be a fat merchant by sticking his bottom lip out.

"Rich! How rich?" she laughed.

"Filthy rich!"

"Rich from what?"

"Rich from . . . from gold from the Indies."

"Oh that's sinful!"

"And our ship, my dear soft-breasted woman, has just come in, so full of gold that it could hardly dock in Rotterdam. They thought it was sinking, but it was just so full of gold it looked that way."

"How much did we profit?"

"It would be sinful to say. Let's just say that I never want to see you in the same dress twice."

She giggled. "Let's eat. I'm hungry, aren't you?"

"Like a bear."

Paulus spitted the roast sideways with two metal rods and set it over the fire with the ends of the rods resting on the sides of the hearth. This way he could turn it over from time to time. Almost immediately the fatty edges turned clear and began to sizzle and drip into the coals.

Together, silently, they watched the meat cook. Paulus had been so preoccupied he did not realize how empty his stomach was. He had worked hard that day and eaten nothing since mid-morning, and now the aroma of pork fat burning in the coals made the saliva come to his mouth and his stomach ache. Something like euphoria came over him. He wished he could preserve the moment forever. Marga's profile, as he saw it in that moment, was extraordinarily beautiful to him, especially the place where her lips met. Heine was holding her dress with one hand and trying to see what she saw; he could sense the excitement in her. The room was warm, the light soft, and there was the expectation of a full stomach, which was somehow more satisfying than the full stomach itself. So Paulus savored the waiting.

Marga cut pieces off the roast with a knife as it cooked and they ate them with their hands. Heine was not fully weaned yet, but he got a small tender piece and fingered it and put it in and out of his mouth while they laughed at him. And they ate and ate, past the point of comfort, past the point of satiation to what Paulus knew was gluttony, burgherish gluttony. But their ship had come in.

Matthias Forder came home while they were finishing. They invited him into the kitchen and he ate some of the roast, but he seemed preoccupied. Marga never looked at him.

“The magistrates in Wesel are making housecalls,” said Matthias. “Trying to find Anabaptists.”

Paulus looked up, trying to be polite but refusing to allow this uncomfortable news to spoil their happiness. Then Matthias went to his room upstairs. And they kept eating.

"O-h-h-h," said Paulus, "my poor belly."

"It's wonderful. Are you finished?" Marga licked her fingers.

"I was finished long ago. I'm a glutton. A little taste of the kingdom."

"Do you think we'll eat like this in the kingdom?"

"I don't know," he laughed. "The grain and the vines will grow on the mountaintops. Maybe the cattle and the pigs will be there for the taking."

"I don't think so. There won't be any death."

Of course not, realized Paulus, too bloated to think straight, and the image of the young pig in its death struggle appeared. The present world was one of futility. For every step forward there had to be a step backward, for every life, a death.

They fed on the stems, the leaves, the seeds, and the flesh of their fellow creatures. Paulus' euphoria was the pig's destruction.

"No, love. You're right. No death."

Glutted, exhausted, thankful, still euphoric, they climbed to their attic and went to bed. Paulus lay and thought for a long time about things he could do to make Marga happy. There would not be pork every day, but there were many little things he could do, now that he really thought about it. Making Marga happy made him happy.

SHORTLY AFTER MIDNIGHT, two constables in the service of the Wesel town council and a priest knocked on Matthias Forder's door.

"Is this the one? Are you sure?" asked the priest.

"Yes, father. It's a leatherworker's shop. The man's a leatherworker." The constable had a list in his hand that he held almost against his face to see. "Hans, give me some light." The other official had a lamp which he held close to the list.

"And the child?"

"Belongs to a man named Paulus Ketterling, from the south."

"Will they resist?"

"Ha, these are the kind of people that are going to Münster," said the constable with the lamp. The priest was calm, but the two constables shifted around nervously. "And they send only two of us! There could be a whole nest of them in there. And all armed. And crazy."

"Sh-h! Someone's coming." The constable who had knocked on the door spat into his palms and gripped his halberd tightly.

Paulus opened the door. He was still awake and had heard the knocking and the talking in the street. He wore nothing but his pants.

"Are you Matthias Forder?" asked the constable.

"No."

"Are you Paulus Ketterling, then?"

"Yes."

"We would like to come in."

"It's not my house, I'm a guest."

"Then we will come in," said the constable, and the three of them walked in.

"I am a priest of the church," said the priest, although this was obvious from his robe and the crucifix around his neck. "Is it true that you have a child?"

"Yes, I have a son. Heinrich."

"Has Heinrich been baptized into the true and Catholic faith?"

Marga's clear voice came with a desperate lie: "Yes."

Paulus whirled around, and the man with the lamp lifted it higher. Marga stood at the base of the stairs with Heine in her arms. When the baby tried to look around, she pressed his face into her shoulder.

"Marga," said Paulus softly.

"Tell them nothing," she said.

"Herr Ketterling, I ask you, as the father of the child" – the priest looked straight at Paulus – "has this child been baptized into the holy Catholic church?"

This must be how Onkel had felt, pressed between his faith and his safety, lost if he lied and lost if he told the truth. Paulus heard himself say:

"No, but we pray that he will be baptized into the true faith when he is able to confess it for himself."

"It is a sin in the eyes of the church, and a crime in the eyes of the emperor, to withhold baptism from a child," said the priest. "Lying will not help. There are records, you know. They can be traced."

"Forgive my wife. She is very frightened of you, as you can see. You must know that we are not Catholics, or you would not be here."

"You play games with the child's soul, man. He is born with original sin. How do you help him with that?"

"We are not so sure of original sin as you are. In any case, we don't believe that baptism helps it."

The theological debate was useless, as they both knew, and the priest dropped it.

"We are not cruel men," he said. "I have not asked you about yourselves, whether you are rebaptizers or not, and I don't plan to ask you. But we must demand that the child be baptized."

Paulus' eyes tingled and moistened. He could feel the cross being strapped to the back of his soul, and he could see his Golgotha hill destination, and he felt angry and stubborn.

"Why must you come to us in the middle of the night?"

The priest swallowed. "Those are the bishop's instructions. There is much unrest."

"Come back in the morning. We'll be here. Let us sleep."

"We have our orders," said the constable with the halberd. The priest chewed on the inside of his cheek. He produced a small roll of paper and a vial of baptismal water and proceeded hopefully, as if Paulus had agreed to the baptism. "We can be done with this in no time. I will baptize the child and you will sign this paper, promising to be faithful to the holy Roman church. Then we will leave. Please."

"Paulus, sign it," said Marga. "It's no trouble." Her eyes were larger than he had ever seen them, her mouth thin, her nostrils spread wide. She had the look of a she-dog with its pups, coiling to strike, ready to take on any attacker. The baby was small and quiet in her arms. Paulus knew exactly what she was thinking. *Just get them out of here. Appease them. The baptism is nothing, just a few drops of popish water. The paper is just a piece of paper.*

"Paulus, sign it," she said again.

"I will not submit my son to the pope's baptism," Paulus said to her. Their eyes met, and through their eyes their wills, colliding and burning, and Paulus could feel across the space between them the incineration of their marriage.

"I'll sign it," said Marga to the priest. "Give it to me, I'll sign it."

The priest shook his head. "I'm sorry, the father must sign."

Marga was standing by Paulus now. He felt her burning eyes on the side of his head, and from above, the gentler but more compelling gaze of Christ.

"Please leave us alone," he said. "You've awakened my baby, my wife, in the middle of the night."

"Fool, sign the paper and be done with it!" said the priest. Now the priest and Marga were together against him. *Just sign. You don't have to believe it. Don't lose your child over a scrap of paper and a few drops of water.*

"I cannot! Don't you understand? Why can't anyone understand when a man must do what is right?"

"What if he won't sign?" asked Marga.

"We take the child."

Marga's eyes darted from the priest to the constables and back to the priest again.

"What? Is that true?" She appealed to the priest; he seemed to be softening.

"Yes, those are the instructions. The child will be baptized and raised a Catholic."

"God in heaven! Paulus, sign the paper! Please, Paulus, or they take my baby!" She went back to the stairs and sat down with the baby on her lap. She tightened the blanket around him and encased him with her arms.

The two constables edged closer to Paulus and the priest.

"Please sign the paper and let me baptize your son," said the priest, and by the tone of his voice it was clear he was making his last plea.

"I can't!" bellowed Paulus, leaning forward into the priest's face.

The priest glanced at the constable behind him, then down at his feet, thinking. Then he nodded. At this moment Matthias Forder, awakened by the noise of their conversation, appeared on the stairs. One constable took two long steps and blocked the stairway with his weapon, holding Matthias away. The other constable gave the lantern to the priest and gripped his halberd with two hands and moved toward Marga and the child. Marga eyed him like a cornered animal and wrapped her arms more tightly around Heine.

Paulus stepped between the constable and his wife and child.

"Don't take my son," he said.

The constable stepped to the side to go around Paulus, and Paulus shifted to meet him.

"Don't take my son," he said. "I tell you, in the name of Christ, not to take my son." He could fight with words. Christ had not forbidden that.

The constable had had enough. He struck Paulus in the gut with the butt end of his halberd, with a slap of wood on flesh, and the blow doubled Paulus over and dropped him to the floor. With Paulus out of his way, he approached Marga and the baby. Marga got smaller and tighter. Paulus, coughing to gain his breath, crawled to Marga and put his body again in front of her.

The constable said, "Give me the child." There was anger and frustration in his voice.

"Don't take my child," said Paulus.

"Give me the child, man!"

"In the name of Christ, don't take my child."

"Paulus, kill him! Kill him!" Marga raged. Her enormous voice came unnaturally from the small ball of woman and baby.

At this provocation, the constable flew into a rage. He drove the blunt end of his halberd into Paulus' unresisting body again and again and again, grunting with each stroke. "You . .

." To the ribs. "Will . . ." To the arm, raised in defense. "Give . . ." To the ribs again. "Me . . ." To the head, a glancing blow. "The . . ." To the soft part of the back, beneath the ribs. "Child . . ." To the hip. Until Paulus' body rolled away from Marga.

The priest could not watch. He held the lantern but looked at the floor. He had lost control of the event.

The assailant reached out with his right hand, into the dark ball of Marga and Heine, and took the blanket that Heine was wrapped in. Snake-quick, Marga had his hand in her teeth and was biting with all her might, snarling deep in her throat. The man howled and recoiled. He tried to pull his hand from her mouth. He dragged her from the stair to the floor, still fastened to him with her teeth and holding the baby with both arms. The baby cried. The priest crossed himself. Matthias Forder shouted, "Let her alone!", and the constable in front of him shouted, "Shut up!"

The constable began beating on Marga's head with his left fist. Still she snarled and held on, and Heine wailed.

Paulus heard this, vividly. His body would not respond to his will any more. His cross was crushing him into hell: the night, the smoky lantern light, the bestial sounds, and evil here, incarnate, and overpowering like a juggernaut, evil that could only be overcome by receiving receiving receiving from it until its fury was spent. Maybe Marga was right: he was a deluded fanatic, and he held an unreasonable view of the commands of Christ, and he was blind and deaf to the natural instincts of preservation and self-dignity. If she were right, he would find out on judgment day, when all things would become clear and the dark convoluted glass through which all was now seen would be gone. Then, to stand and have one's eyes and face bathed in the light of truth! But for now, the darkness ruled, and Paulus carried his cross into it.

He managed to say again, "Don't take my child." But the blows kept falling on Marga's head, the constable's filthy hand on that lovely black-brown hair. She finally let go of his hand

and screamed:

"Paulus, help me!"

Her hair was tangled, her teeth were red with the man's blood, and she was sobbing. She lay on her side on the floor with her legs drawn up, as if to protect the baby on as many sides as possible. The constable stepped back and examined his hand – it was limp and bloody. Paulus now gathered his strength, raised himself up on his hands and knees, and tried to place himself again by Marga. The constable by Matthias Forder brought his halberd staff down on Paulus' back and the heavy wood crushed Paulus flat to the floor on his face. When the constable with the bloody hand recovered his wits and breath, he drew a sword awkwardly with his left hand.

"You she dog witch. Now give me the child or, by the saints, I'll put you out of your misery."

He put the swordpoint on the white skin of Marga's throat. She closed her eyes and waited. He would have to kill her to get the baby, it was clear. But there was a better way, and when he thought of it he put the swordpoint against the baby. Marga's eyes opened.

"Karl!" said the priest.

"We have our orders, priest."

The threat was clear: he would run the baby through if Marga did not give it up. It was illegal, and he would probably hang for it, but he was angry and ready to do it. Slowly, she unwrapped her arms from the child.

"Come get the child," the constable said to the priest, who did as he was told. His legs were wobbly. When he picked Heine up, the child looked at him with curiosity and reached out to touch his clean-shaven face.

The constable tore a strip of cloth from a curtain and wrapped it around his hand. Then they left.

In the darkness of the house, nobody spoke. Marga still sobbed quietly and lay where she had fallen; Paulus was stretched out in the middle of the room like a broken table, his arms splayed to each side. Matthias wandered from place to place, sat, rose, sat again. Eventually he went back to bed. Darkness and stillness enshrouded the room like a tomb.

There was a little dawn when Marga finally stood and walked into the kitchen. Paulus was still on the floor, now lying on his back. She pulled the strands of her hair from off her face. She wiped her mouth, and dried flecks of the constable's blood came off on the back of her hand. She whispered something and ran to a bucket and Paulus, who was awake, heard her gag and retch. The sounds of it produced a wave of nausea in him, and he reeled out through the front door, fell to his hands and knees on the street and vomited out a bellyful of half digested pork.

CHAPTER 19: PASSION
October, 1534. Duchy of Cleves.

The first thing Paulus saw when he opened his eyes was the familiar sight of roof beams. It was already morning; light was coming into the garret through a small shutter in a gable that faced east. He closed his eyes. The tingle of waking up flowed from his head through his torso to his arms and legs. His head hurt, and the bruises from his beating still ached, a month later. He flexed his feet to stretch his calf muscles. He yawned, and felt his mouth dry and fuzzy and his breath sour. Why was this? Why did his head hurt?

Then he remembered: Marga was gone. He looked to his left. The place in the bed was indeed empty. He remembered: the wine.

The previous night a messenger from the city of Münster had visited them at their meeting in the shed. When he first knocked, they thought it was the Wesel constable. He came in and announced himself as Johannes Essen, apostle of Jesus Christ from the city of Münster. He was an uncouth man with bowed legs, and a limp, and no front teeth, and he could not pronounce a decent S. But he spoke with extraordinary boldness. He was one of twenty-five apostles who had been sent out in every direction through a prophecy received by Johann Dusentschuer. God's wrath on a wicked world was at hand, he explained. Only in Münster was there safety.

How did he find them? the pastor asked. *Alfred Lasthaus,* Essen replied. Lasthaus had fled recently to Münster with his wife, after his two children, like Paulus' son, had been taken away by the authorities. Lasthaus had gone to Münster with vengeance in his eyes.

Essen had a document called *A Restitution of Christian Teaching, Faith, and Life through the Church of Christ at Münster.* It had fourteen points of doctrine, among them the outrageous assertions of polygamy and the righteous use of the sword by the saints. The pastor read them to the people, and a loud, vitriolic debate ensued, with the man from Münster shouting for those who said they had their bellies full of punishment and fear. Katzenbach and his wife had had two children taken away; they screamed abusively at the pastor when he spoke, and supported everything the apostle from Münster said, and breathed out their desire for revenge. They were not alone.

Essen urged them to come quickly to Münster. There was food, and drink, and plenty of warm housing for them all. Matthias Forder said that the king, Jan Bockelson, only wanted their money and their bodies for the defense of the city. Essen shouted him down. Then Matthias Forder left.

Marga suddenly entered the fight on the side of the apostle from Münster. She was eloquent and passionate and instinctive as she argued, and it was hard to contradict her since, as everyone knew, she had seen her baby ripped from her arms. Paulus tried to quiet her, but she screamed at him, and he gave up. He knew already that he had lost her to Münster. He was not feeling panic and grief like he thought he should. He was feeling that there was a sense of justice in it. He deserved to lose Marga; he had never deserved her in the first place, for she was too beautiful and passionate and he was too plain and dull. She deserved a man on a large horse, with houses and lands, with power to protect her and the wealth to dress her body in satins.

He had done his best since their child had been taken away, going from magistrate to magistrate, and even to the bishop himself, to find out where they had put the boy. The bishop was honest, and told Paulus what he had told the council earlier: that if he thought it would do any good he would burn Paulus and Marga at the stake – he had no compunctions – but that this was a more effective way to silence the heresy. The child would be, had probably already been, baptized by a Catholic priest and placed in a good Catholic home with pious and loyal parents. Paulus asked where. The bishop shook his head at the stupidity of the question.

Paulus wrote letters of supplication and protest to the town council. He even wrote a letter to the Duke of Cleves. None of these letters was ever answered. He was a simple, powerless man trying to break down an immense fortification with his bare hands. He knew this, of course, but he had to try. He reported his efforts to Marga, and she received his reports coldly. He hoped that she counted his efforts as courage, love, and dedication.

"They understand only the sword, Paulus," she said once. He could feel this, too. There were times, thinking about his son, and reliving the abduction in his memory, when bloody and brutal imaginations filled his mind, as they certainly filled the minds of the people who were now flocking to Münster. But if he beat to death the priest who had taken his son, would he get his son back? If he went to Münster and took up the sword, would he get his son back? Paulus just wanted his son back. That was all. These others, including Marga, wanted some kind of divine, comprehensive justice.

As the argument continued in the shed, the pastor slipped away, and one by one those who still agreed with him followed. Only Paulus, of the advocates of peace, was left when Johannes Essen gathered his converts around him and explained to them carefully how to proceed to Münster and how to sneak into the city through the prince-bishop's siege line. All Paulus could see of Marga was the back of her head, her full, extraordinarily heavy dark hair hanging down almost to her waist. He was taking the sight of her in as he had those first days in Montau, when she did not belong to him and the thought of her ever belonging to him was too much to imagine. She was simply a distant, astonishing, beautiful woman. He wanted to touch her but did not dare, for he had no right. He was outside the core of her life now. Essen led the group outside to say a prayer with them.

"I'm going to Münster, Paulus," she said calmly to him as she passed.

"I know."

"You won't fight for me, will you? You won't even try to stop me from going, will you?"

"I fought," he snapped, suddenly angry. "You're blind now, you can't see that." *One more look at her face.*

"I'm going to become part of the kingdom of God, Paulus. The real kingdom of God. With *justice.* Not a silly dream of peace. The peace will come after the wicked are gone, then there will be peace."

Paulus, after this, had gone back to Wesel and had spent the small amount of money he had on wine and had drunk too much. He knew it was a sin but he did it anyway. That was why his head hurt and his mouth tasted so sour.

PAULUS SPENT SIX days pretending that he could live without Marga. He told himself that a great burden had been lifted from him, that now he could be free again to serve Christ as he had originally intended, in celibacy. He told himself that he had no obligation to bring Marga back, since the apostle Paul had instructed believers to let their unbelieving spouses leave if they desired – and Marga he now had to consider as an unbeliever. He told himself that he was now following the pattern left to him by Onkel. He wondered if the whole interlude of his marriage had been some terrible, selfish mistake, and if all that had happened to the brotherhood of Montau had been the visitation of God's anger upon them for Paulus' lack of restraint. He did nothing but read Onkel's Bible, and pray, and walk in the country. Matthias Forder left him to himself.

He missed his baby, with a missing that was like a huge, heavy weight. But his missing of Marga burned like fire. On the seventh day after Marga's departure, he tried to remember the shape and color of her face but could only remember the fragments – the eyes, the nose, the lips, the slight bit of downy fuzz above the lips, the wisp of hair that always hung down by her ear, the space between her teeth – but not the whole. This frustrated him so much that he began to cry, and once he began to cry his whole soul came apart within him for love of Marga and missing Marga and wanting to touch Marga and wanting to have Marga naked and moving underneath him again. He was alone in Matthias Forder's house at the time. There was no one to hear him. He cried as he had not cried since he was a boy, with long howls of anguish and the stuff coming out of his nose and mingling with his tears. When it was all over, he knew that he would have to get himself to Münster and find her, and have her back as his wife or die in the attempt. If this was a sin, God would have to forgive him.

Within an hour of making this decision, and without saying farewell to Matthias Forder, Paulus was on the way to Münster. He had the bag of his possessions slung over his shoulder on a stick. Following the road to Münster was easy; it was crowded with the footprints of the soldiers and zealots who had gone there before him.

CHAPTER 20: WALLS
November, 1534. Münster.

Getting into Münster was easy. Paulus followed the instructions that he had heard from Johannes Essen and came in with a group of women. He was surprised at the porosity of the prince-bishop's lines, as they walked through the dark between two bonfires around which the mercenaries seemed to be clustered, laughing, coughing, not caring at all what happened. The ground they walked on was well trampled, slick, filth-littered mud. Once a shot from a musket rang out, and they fell to their faces, but there was no sequel. It was just soldierly horseplay.

Paulus' imagination of what he would find here was corrected. He had envisioned a tense, Armageddon-like conflict, desperate and bloody battles, zeal on both sides. What he found was the slogging, dreary reality of siege warfare.

After a cold, quick swim through the waters of the moat, the group stood beneath the Budenturm, the stone tower that anchored the defenses of the north wall, and were greeted from the top of the wall by a lookout. To his greeting, one of the women in his group answered, "Melchizedek". The man on the wall disappeared and moments later let them in through a small door near the tower.

They stood, still dripping and shaking, in the former chapel of the Monastery of St. Johannes, stripped of its religious decorations and filled now instead with ropes, barrels, muskets, crates, buckets, and people sleeping on the floor. Paulus could almost hear the mournful chants of the monks that had once filled the place; he somehow longed for them. An unshaven, hard eyed man interrogated them.

"I am Heinrich, from Osnabrück, one of the king's bodyguards," he said. "It is my duty to welcome you to the city of God. I must ask you each some questions."

The questions were the same for all of them, routine questions about name and place and baptism. Then, the hard question, at least for Paulus:

"Why are you here?"

Paulus had considered his answer to this question all the way from Wesel. "To find a wife and to fight for the kingdom of God," he said. It was the truth, if he could interpret it in his own way, and he hoped that it would satisfy his interrogator.

The bodyguard laughed. "In that order?"

"Absolutely," said Paulus and managed a smile.

Heinrich from Osnabrück riffed through several pages of his book. Paulus could see that it was full of names and strikeouts.

"You will live . . . on the New Bridge street, with the brothers Arndt Manns and Julius Fettbauch, and their wives. You will go tomorrow to the Holy Cross Gate to receive your labor assignment. You will take your meals at the common house by the Holy Cross Gate, beginning with breakfast tomorrow. You will find your wives by going to the St. Lambert's church. You will obey the laws of the city of God and be happy, but disobedience will be punished quickly. Blasphemy against God or the king will be punished with death, and avoidance of duty will be punished with flogging. Glory to

God." He handed Paulus' a scrap of paper with *Holy Cross Gate* and the initial *H* written hastily on it, and went on to the next person.

Armed guards stood at every street corner, and by asking them along the way he was able to find New Bridge street. The street paralleled the river, which he crossed on a narrow wooden bridge. He found the house easily, since they were all identified now with large numerals in white paint. Behind him, the river gurgled and stank; behind the house loomed the east wall, against which the house had been built, and on it a sentinel stood; to his left he could see where New Bridge street ended at the northeast corner of the city, where the wall turned sharply west.

Paulus felt lonely and lost; waves of fear rushed up from his stomach but he quenched them one after another. This place was beginning to seem more like he had imagined it, blacker, more sinister, like the inside of a huge coffin. Then he knocked on the door, and for some time there was no answer.

Julius Fettbauch opened it. He was bare-skinned from the waist up and his hair was disheveled. He smiled.

"I'm sorry if I've disturbed you," said Paulus meekly.

"No problem. I was just having sex with one of my wives. Actually, you've rescued me. They all want to have children. I'm exhausted." He chuckled.

Paulus did not know what to say, since he had never disturbed a man in the middle of sex, at least that he knew of.

"I'll come back."

"No, no, no! What is it?"

"I was told to come here . . . I am to live here."

"Ah-h-h," said Julius Fettbauch, not delighted but trying to be polite. "Helga, cover up. Come in . . . brother."

"Paulus Ketterling."

"Julius Fettbauch. These are Helga, you see her there trying to cover herself – ha! – and Hille, Katie, and Susanna. They're asleep, they can greet you in the morning."

Fettbauch's wives were strewn around on the floor of the sitting room of the house. To Paulus' relief, none of them had long black hair.

"We'll have to work something out," said Julius. "Arndt and his wives stay upstairs. Can it be possible that the city is so crowded that they are putting three families to a house now? I suppose it can, if the king and his court keep taking the best and biggest houses for themselves." He caught himself and shot a wary glance at Paulus. "But then, that's only proper. The king should live in fitting splendor, don't you think?"

"Of course," said Paulus.

PAULUS HAD A mat and a blanket and a spot on the floor, and he fell immediately into an unsettled semisleep. His head felt larger than normal. He woke once, and he heard the sound of breathing all around him and someone snoring softly. Then he was able to recall where he was, and he went to sleep again. Later, still in the dark, he heard male voices. One was Julius Fettbauch's, the other was new. Probably the other man in the house, Arndt Manns.

"Back from the watch?" asked Julius.

"We all take our turn, except you."

"If you were a war hero you'd be exempt from night watch too." Julius chuckled.

"War hero, right. You were stuck in the wrong place at the right time."

"That's how war heroes are made."

"When do you go on?" asked Arndt.

"Eight o'clock. What's out there?"

"Nothing at all. The prince-bishop's camp is dead."

"They say his vassals are going home." Julius sat up, keeping the covers over his shoulders. Arndt Manns was unbuckling a cuirass and a sword belt.

"I believe it. One of the blockhouses to the south is deserted now."

"Maybe this whole thing will end."

"Don't believe it, war hero. Von Waldeck is making the rounds of the courts of Germany. Now is not a good time to hire mercenaries – too cold, too close to Christmas. But come spring, you'll see. How about some dice?"

"At this hour?"

"Why not?"demanded Manns.

"Because I'm sleeping. My wives are sleeping."

"The best time to play dice. The mind is clear. You can hear the dice thunking."

"No, I owe you too much already."

"No worry, you can pay me back when Bockelson conquers the world and we're all as rich as the Fuggers." This sounded sarcastic to Paulus.

"Ha, ha. Let me sleep."

Arndt Manns dropped the swordbelt to the floor. "What's that in the corner? Did you go and get yourself another wife?"

"His name is Ketterling. He lives here."

"There's no room as it is. What's he like?"

"Quiet, I think . . . from the south, by his accent. Alone."

"Bockelson and his lackeys are snatching up all the housing in this city. His whores, they have the old house of the cathedral provost now, the nicest house in Münster."

"They're queens, after all," said Julius.

"They're sluts, Dutch sluts, most of them."

"You should watch your mouth. Our friend in the corner may be a spy from the king, who knows?"

"Bockelson is a raving stud horse, he goes through a passage in the house each night, giving them each a turn with him."

Julius began to laugh, wheezing, trying not to be too loud. "Can you see it, can you see all the stupid little blonde Dutch pups around here if the prince-bishop doesn't find a way in?"

"That's nothing to laugh about. They'll all be crazy like him."

Listening to the two men talk made Paulus feel much better. They were obviously not in sympathy with the program of the Münster kingdom. Maybe there were more rational people around.

In the morning Julius went with Paulus back to the armory.

"I heard you talking last night, you and the other man . . . " said Paulus, as they passed the saints of Münster on their way to their daily tasks.

"Arndt Manns," said Julius, worried now at their loose tongues.

"You are not great believers in the king."

There was no point in dissimulation now, thought Julius. "No, we are not."

"But you are here. Why?"

Julius shrugged. "I can answer for Arndt. He's a soldier, and there's a warm place to sleep, and women to make love to, and plenty of food. He says out in the prince-bishop's camp there's dysentery and typhus this time of year. I can't really answer as well for myself. I'm a Münster man, evicted from my house, separated from my family, but in some strange way I'm having fun."

"I'm here to look for my wife. She came here about a week ago."

"Ah," said Julius. "She will already have been married off to one of the saints. Women have to be married, you know, it's the law. The men, they have more choices."

"She's married to me," Paulus insisted.

"Now that's a new one! One woman with two husbands, in Münster. I promise you, my friend, you're sharing her with someone else. Especially if she's pretty." They were at the bridge over the river. "Watch your tongue, my friend," said Julius as he turned to go to his watch on the wall. "Or the

Swordbearer will be doing his work on you. He loves his work!"

The Holy Cross Gate was the north gate of the city. When Paulus found it, there were about forty people, both men and women, working with shovels and wheelbarrows, both inside and outside the gate, building huge earth mounds for defense. A very thin man named Gert was in charge of these earth mounds. Gert took Paulus' papers from the bodyguard and pointed Paulus to the outside mound.

They were building a ramp of earth and debris from the ground to the top of the mound. Paulus got a pickaxe and went to work loosening the ground for those with shovels. It was a good day for him. The work was invigorating, and the pace was rather slow, and there was time to exchange remarks with the others who worked side by side with him. They seemed kind and human. Before noon he had some good blisters along the tops of his palms, where the fingers were attached, and he had a satisfying muscular tiredness in his lower back.

There were three general signals: one for assembly in the cathedral square, one for the clearing of the streets, and another for attack by the enemy. This last was the most important, and if he heard it Paulus was to immediately report to the St. Johannes monastery, take a spear and a shield, and run to his place on the wall. Anyone found not responding to these signals would be arrested, and few people survived arrest in Münster.

In the evening the trumpeters blew the signal for assembly, and Julius and Arndt and Paulus, with the seven women of the house, went to the cathedral square. It was only the reading of another decree that had something to do with the apportioning of the food supply. The king was not there, so the decree was read by the chancellor, Heinrich Krechting. Paulus scanned the crowd for Marga but could not find her. Then they went home. Arndt told Paulus that this happened almost every night.

The next day there was some daylight left when

moundmaster let the workers quit, and Paulus walked around the city looking for Marga. Work helped, but it could not completely eliminate the awful yearning that surged up in his body and mind when he thought of Marga. Listening to Julius Fettbauch coupling with his women did not help either. He could live without Onkel, and he could even live without his son, but how could he live without his wife?

He went through the heart of the city, from the Holy Cross Gate through the cathedral square to the Ludger Gate on the south, and then he went counterclockwise around the perimeter, hugging the wall the whole way. Men in black military uniforms were more numerous near the center of the city, women on the outskirts. It was overwhelmingly a city of women and children, and most of the women were pregnant. The old open markets were gone, replaced under the rational regime of Bockelson by a centralized food distribution system. In a typical city, people stood around, being lazy in the marketplaces, haggling over groceries or firewood, but here the people were always in motion, with a purpose. And they seldom laughed. The clothes they wore seemed to Paulus uniformly dull and shabby; all display of color or wealth had been forbidden to the people and reserved for the court.

Wagons plied the streets. Every open space held a vegetable garden, and in every garden, it seemed, was a woman with a hoe. Pigs and horses grazed on the autumn grass. And the streets were clean, even the Kellerstrasse. Laborers patched and strengthened the walls, and even the large breach made on the west side had been repaired and was now bristling with guns.

There were many women with dark hair, whom Paulus could imagine from a distance as Marga. Closer, they were not. The hips were too wide, or the steps too long and masculine, or the skin too dark.

"Did you find your wife?" asked Julius when Paulus came home.

"No."

"Are you sure she's here?"

"Sure enough."

"You must love her."

"Oh, I do."

The wives prepared supper and they ate.

"You will see the king tomorrow night, when he holds court in the cathedral square," said Arndt Manns.

"He is magnificent," said Hille.

"The city is like any city," said Paulus. "I went through it all today."

"You're wrong, Herr Ketterling," said Helga. "By day, the city is like any city, the people grumble through their chores and their pains. At night they come alive. Wait until you see Jan Bockelson at night."

CHAPTER 21: QUEEN
November, 1534. Münster.

Around the cathedral square a ring of light, a circle of torches, contained the congregation like the walls of a building. They were all here, including the children, bundled in woolens against the November night air, staring expectantly toward the empty, multilevel platform in front of the cathedral. They waited for the entrance of the king and his court. Earlier, the trumpets had blown the assembly signal, and runners had gone through the streets crying, "Come see the king!" And the people all came because the assembly at night was what made everything else meaningful. They had given up their freedom, their property, their finest clothing, even their homes, and had received instead a daily routine of work. There had to be something more, and Bockelson knew what it was: spectacle, entertainment. This was his stage, and he gave them himself as spectacle.

The throne on the highest level of the platform was draped in cloth-of-gold which mirrored the hues of the torchlight. When the king sat, nothing but gold would touch his person. Behind the throne a banner hung on a pole. Against its dark background, in gold, was emblazoned the symbol of the city since it had become a kingdom: the orb of the world pierced by two swords. Above the world stood a cross, and running the length and height of the cross were the words ONE KING OF RIGHTEOUSNESS OVER ALL. For a thousand years the people of Catholic Europe had been taught that there existed two swords, two dispensations of power, the secular and the spiritual, and that these swords had been given to the emperor and the pope, respectively. Now, said the banner, in Münster the two swords had come together in the hands of one king. Beside the throne, a smaller banner stated GOTTES MACHT IST MEIN KRACHT, *God's power is my strength*. It was the personal motto of the king.

Below the king's throne were seats for the members of the court. Around the platform, shrouded and anonymous in their dark uniforms, stood the members of the bodyguard; every third man held a torch, the others held drawn swords.

The spectacle was carefully orchestrated. At some invisible signal the trumpeters that stood directly before the congregation at the base of the platform put their instruments to their lips and blew a fanfare that shattered the silence of the cathedral square and rebounded back and forth between the buildings that lined it. The trumpet was the sound of God and of power. Whenever Bockelson appeared, the trumpets blew. It was the sound of armies on the march. It was the sound of the second coming.

Paulus went to the assembly to look for Marga. When he saw the hot mass of people in the torchlight he felt a strange thrill. At the sound of the trumpets he sensed the quickening of his pulse.

The first members of the court appeared from the direction of the cathedral, coming out of the dark and entering the circle of light by the platform. This was the new aristocracy of Münster, created by the fiat of Jan Bockelson during the first few days after his coronation as king. The government of the elders was gone, and the city, like old Israel, had moved from patriarchy to monarchy. There came Knipperdolling, still the Swordbearer, and Bernhard Rothmann, now called Chief Preacher; the king's chief councillors, Gert tom Kloster, Bernt Krechting, Heinrich Redeker, and Gerhard Reyninck; behind them, the Horsemaster, the Palacemaster, the field captains of the army, the chancellor, the Schoolmaster, the Cabinetmaster, the Kitchenmaster, Gatekeeper, Winemaster, the Armormasters, Meatmasters, Chief Tailor, Buttermaster, Royal Baker and the Royal Barber. And still they came – horsemen on their nervous white-eyed mounts, musketeers with their unwieldy weapons, foremen of the walls, of the defense mounds, of the buildings, masters of grain and of shoes and of saddles and even of the city's firewood. With the sure instinct of leadership, Bockelson gave them titles which transformed menial tasks into noble callings, and simple men of action, who might otherwise have pondered rebellion, now basked in his reflected glory and had a stake in the kingdom. Now they stood with him in torchlight, dressed in confiscated finery.

But they were, after all, only the garnish around the king. After another pause and another fanfare, Bockelson himself emerged into the light, sitting on a dark horse with a glistening oiled coat. He wore a heavy gold crown on his head, and the large golden orb of the earth pierced by two swords hung by a chain from his neck, and he carried a scepter with a gold knob. His coat was bright yellow, tightly tailored around his torso but full in the sleeves and the skirt, and lined with ermine fur at the neck. His trousers and shoes were white. The king was a glowing node of light against the blues and purples and greens of the court. A shining sun in a twilight sky.

Paulus felt the king's entry so viscerally that he held his breath. He strained like the rest to see.

The king dismounted and ascended the throne, while two pages in blue held the back of his robe off the ground. When he sat, the congregation fell to its knees. Then Bockelson raised his scepter and the congregation stood again.

It was time for the entry of the king's favorite queen, Divora, covered like the king with white and gold, and behind her came Bockelson's other sixteen wives. Divora led them to the topmost level of the platform and they sat around the king like rays of light from his sun.

Rothmann stood and prayed. Heinrich Krechting the chancellor rose and began singing a psalm, and the people joined him as they heard and recognized it, until the unison sound of almost ten thousand voices carried up and over the walls to the few mercenary troops that still kept the siege alive outside the city. It went on to some twenty verses and became faster and stronger near the end. When the last note had lingered and then died, some of the women moaned.

Bockelson surveyed the people as a shepherd would a flock, his eyes moving calmly from one side of the cathedral square to the other and from the faces that pressed close to the platform to those lost in the darkness, with mingled severity and benevolence, until every person could feel that he had been seen. His eyes were large and their delicate blue was completely lost in the torchlight.

"Do you remember the mockers?" he said, and paused. "They scorned us to shame from the very beginning. Simple holy people will never prevail against the vast evil machinery of the pope and the devil and world, they said. That was less than a year ago, when we still met in dark rooms. They mocked when we stood against the well fed burghers, but we prevailed. They mocked when the laws of this city were purified and said that no people could ever live by such laws. But we have lived, and prospered. Then the great beast of Waldeck began his siege – ha! a siege he called it – and the mockers began again like stupid mooing cows to repeat their mockery: they will die now, the authorities have taken up the sword and the game is over, they said. Then what happened?" Pause, hands raised. Scattered responses. "We again prevailed and drove the enemy hosts away! And where are they now? Gone! Gone! And this city grows in strength and holiness from day to day. Who fears the prince-bishop? Where are the mockers? What is left to mock? Where is the fool who says now, after all the great deliverances of God, that this is not the city of God?"

Paulus felt the power of the king and the power of the numbers concentrated shoulder to shoulder, condensed and organized, pointed to the king and held quivering by his power like iron filings by a magnet. It felt good to be part of this. Something in him rejoiced at the prospect of a mighty blow against the pope and the potentates of the world. His thinking mind, calling to him from a remote distance, reminded him that this king was nothing more than another of the world's bloody tyrants, but his eyes and his intestines told him to rejoice. This was not ordinary any more. Maybe when the sun rose it would be. Maybe such things could only happen at night. But now it was night.

"We go from strength to strength. The fury of the enemy will increase, and as it does the righteous power of the Lord will increase to meet it and overcome it. And I say to you, by Easter of next year, you, the saints of God, and I your king, will be marching far and wide as the victorious army of God. Our time in the wilderness is over. The time of conquest has begun. Let the King of France beware, let the archbishops of Mainz, and Trier, and Cologne fear, let Kaiser Karl and all of Germany and Spain and Burgundy prepare to meet their doom! Let the Turks and the Muscovites and the savages of the Indies tremble! Let the pope say his rosary one more time! We are coming! Your eyes will see it! This generation will see all these things take place – not your sons, but you, you, you!"

The congregation erupted in a roar, and Paulus felt a hot tingle run its way up his body from the base of his spine to his head. The sound was swirling around the cathedral square like water in a pitcher, rolling over him again and again, and he became aware that he too was shouting.

"In Rome by June! In Rome by June!" cried the king. "This is the word of God for you!"

The cheering rolled on. The white king stood with his arms raised, holding the scepter between them. The trumpets launched a solemn fanfare.

Then Paulus saw Marga.

First it was her hair. There was a woman among the king's wives whose long dark hair was flying in all directions as she rejoiced. Paulus couldn't see her face. He shoved his way through the crowd to get a better view. The face could be Marga's. The king lowered his arms and the queens stopped their jumping and dancing, and the woman with the dark hair shook her head slightly, tilted it back and brushed the hair away from her forehead with her two hands – twice. It was what Marga did; no one else would do it just that way. Paulus knew.

Marga was one of the king's wives.

The ceremony was coming to an end. The whole court below Bockelson rose to its feet, and the queens organized themselves once again around their lord, and Paulus had finally an unobstructed view of her face, from the side. Somehow Paulus had expected her to look different, but there were the same features, the same half smile that Marga so often had when she was pleased with life. But behind the face, Paulus told himself, was a strange and foreign mind.

PAULUS WAS THE first one to the house; the others continued in the spontaneous celebrations – prayers, songs, sermons – that kept going in the cathedral square.

He's like a raving stud horse, Arndt had said. He sleeps with a different wife each night, maybe more often with those whom he prefers in bed. And Marga? Was she one of his favorites? How could she not be? Paulus' mind ran out of all control. Perhaps even at this moment, in the flush of the ceremony in the cathedral square, in the great patrician home where the queens lived, she was loosening the buttons on her dress, and he was admiring the handfuls of her hair and the soft whiteness of her body, as Paulus once had. And what was she thinking? That now she had a real husband, a man of strength and purpose, and some dignity as a woman, even if she had to share him with others. Even a share of Jan Bockelson was more than the whole of Paulus. Did she even remember Paulus? How could the pale memories of life with Paulus hold their own against the glory of Münster? Paulus himself had come close to feeling that he could follow the king of Münster – how could he expect Marga not to?

Paulus bellowed a wordless bellow into the emptiness of the house.

The others came in laughing, with their arms draped over each others' shoulders. Neither Arndt nor Julius believed in Münster but they were enjoying it.

"Paulus . . . is that you? What are you doing sitting in the dark?"

Dying, he wanted to say. "Thinking," he actually said.

Arndt's wives went immediately upstairs, and those that belonged to Julius made their beds for the night. Julius told one to stoke up the fire.

"You see what we meant," Julius said. "About Bockelson."

"Yes, the man has demonic power," said Paulus. "I felt it."

"Rome by June, what drivel," said Arndt. "He is insane and ignorant both. Do you know that there are now less than – *less than* – two thousand men in this city? The rest are women and children."

"But the people believe him," replied Julius. "That's all he cares about anyway. Did you see him up there, when they were cheering? That's what he wants out of this. Not victory, or the coming of Christ. He wants to be king, that's all."

"Perhaps. I've often tried to guess how much of his own talk he believes, and it's hard. If he's a hypocrite, he's such a brazen hypocrite that it's believable."

Julius pulled his shirt off and looked at his belly. "I'm still fat," he said. "Arndt, you lied to me, you promised me that staying in this city would get rid of my fat."

"Julius, I'd like to stick my knife right in through your bellybutton and see what squirts out."

"The nectar of the gods," said Julius.

"Dirty, half rendered lard, more likely. I stick to my promise, you'll be skin and bone before you die." Arndt went upstairs to his wives.

"I saw my wife tonight," said Paulus. Julius looked up. "She's one of the king's wives."

"Oh no, don't tell me. The new one, long black hair, small?"

Paulus nodded.

"They had the ceremony about a week ago. Every time he takes a new wife, there is another one of these torchlight meetings. Silly, I think. After wife number ten, or twelve, what's the point?" Paulus raised his hand in a gesture that said, *Don't tell me any more.* But Julius was talking. "She's pretty. He was bound to find her. What is it now, seventeen?"

"I didn't count them," said Paulus.

"Yes, I think it's seventeen now. Your wife is the seventeenth queen."

IT HAD BEEN some time since Paulus had really prayed. The tumult and unrest of his life, the complete concentration of his energies on Marga, the noise and traffic of Wesel, had all squeezed prayer from his life. In Moravia there had been time for prayer, but here whole days would go by, and Paulus would put his tired body and frustrated mind to sleep at night, and it would occur to him that he had not spoken to God. And shame about not having prayed would smother the impulse to pray that then arose. *Salvage the day, Paulus, pray. No, it's too late; God knows that such eleventh hour prayer is really the dregs, the crippled lamb of the flock offered as a sacrifice when God desires the best. Tomorrow I'll start afresh.*

There had been also a decaying of his desire to ask God for anything. God seemed to be in a removal, rather than in a bestowal, mood, at least in the case of Paulus Ketterling. He had learned the very difficult lesson of thanking God for tribulation, but he had forgotten how to ask for blessings. There would be plenty of blessings later. It would all be fine in the new heavens and earth. Paulus would gut it out.

But now God had deprived him of one thing too many. He wanted Marga. Now. In the world to come it would be too late; there would be no marriage or sexual love. That new day of finished perfection would not be unwelcome. But now he was not finished. And God had not called him to celibacy or he never would have brought Marga into his life. So he determined that he would pray that night, after the others were asleep and snoring.

Paulus got on his knees and leaned forward with his forehead on the floor. And he prayed, in a whisper, that God would relent and give him back his wife. He pleaded, he reasoned, he repeated himself. He knew that he should accompany this prayer with the words *if it is your will,* but he did not honestly feel that submissive. If it were God's will to take Marga away from him, Paulus would not acquiesce. *O God, give me Marga, give me Marga, give me Marga.*

If he were sinning by refusing to accept God's will, then God would have to teach him that. He only knew what was in his heart, and could only pour it out before the God who saw into it.

CHAPTER 22: PRINCE-BISHOP
December, 1534. Cologne, Münster.

The *Kreistag* was the regional council of the princes and rulers of the Upper and Lower Rhine. When it met in Koblenz, on the thirteenth of December, a delegation from Franz von Waldeck, prince-bishop of Münster, was there to ask these most excellent princes for money with which to continue the siege of his wayward city. The members of the *Kreistag* – princes, dukes, bishops – grumbled and groused about this but in the end coughed up the funds. The *Kreistag* also insisted that the seasoned commander Wirich von Dhaun take over as the director of the siege. They knew von Waldeck would not appreciate this, but it was their way of refusing to seem docile, having given the prince-bishop his money.

In early January of 1535 the first locked, guarded chest of silver ducats arrived on the outskirts of Münster – the agreed upon first month's pay for the besieging army. Wirich von Dhaun arrived two days after the money chest. He entered the country house which von Waldeck used as a headquarters and approached the prince-bishop with his hat in his hand, a middle-aged man of slight build and hawk-like features, more scholarly than bellicose.

"Prince-bishop," he said to von Waldeck.

"Ah, von Dhaun, you're here. You come highly recommended by the *Kreistag*." The prince-bishop had been miffed by the *Kreistag*'s insistence on von Dhaun, which he took as something of an insult to his own military skills.

"I have had some successes in Italy, by God's grace," said von Dhaun. "Modern warfare is largely a matter of calculation, not of valor."

"Well, we will need both. When can we begin?"

"When I see the money," said von Dhaun. "It's a habit I've developed. I always see the money first."

"Surely you know that I could not pay my mercenaries in September and that that is why my army melted away."

"I had not heard," said von Dhaun, lying.

Von Waldeck took him to another room of the house, opened a door that was guarded by four fully armored halberdiers, and showed him the chest. Von Dhaun opened the lid and plunged a hand into the coins.

"This much every month until June," said the prince-bishop. "The *Kreistag* has guaranteed it."

"The sound of success," said von Dhaun, and let the ducats fall from his hand. "And plunder when we take the city?"

"Half for me, half for the army."

"You take an unusually large portion. One quarter is customary."

Von Waldeck's face darkened. "I have expended every last coin of my own fortune on this cursed siege. In August I sold my family plate. No, Wirich" – a mild insult, calling him by his first name – "I take half."

Von Dhaun bowed politely. "Half it shall be, then."

"You have seen the money. When do we begin?"

"Today, of course. We get these reprobates shoveling. The shovel is mightier than the sword. I will be clear, my lord. No more frontal assaults. Too bloody."

"And too expensive. Report to me once a day."

Wirich von Dhaun took three steps backwards, then turned and left

Von Dhaun had a plan. He proposed to cut the city completely off from the outside world through the construction of blockhouses and connecting ditches. He believed that starvation would do its work without ruinous and expensive direct assaults. He believed that no more zealous refugees should enter the city. Within days, Anabaptist sentries on the city wall spotted the mercenaries and the poor crews of peasants as they began to dig and saw and bore. They were not many yet, since von Dhaun and the money had arrived ahead of the troops, maybe three hundred and fifty in all, who were attacking the vastness of the plain. The sentries laughed and called into the city, and soon there was a small crowd of Anabaptists on the wall hooting in derision.

"What are they doing?" asked von Dhaun, his feet sunk in mud.

"It sounds like laughing, my lord," said a mercenary soldier.

"Why?"

"They're crazy. They laugh all the time, sometimes you can hear it coming from the city at night."

CHAPTER 23: SIEGE
January and February, 1535. Münster.

Inside Münster's walls, the king canceled Christmas and then held a feast of his own on the twenty-sixth of December in the cathedral square. The weather dampened the ardor of this celebration.

Outside the walls, mercenaries, ammunition, blankets, lumber, shoes, food and drink arrived. The siege line took on the cluttered, crowded appearance that von Waldeck had desired for months, the messy, noisy, dirty blight of an army on the land. And more and more of the dormant sod was chewed to semi-frozen mud under the hooves of the mules and oxen and the tramping of the men. They dug and dug, and they cursed von Dhaun for making them dig, but he paid them, so they dug, and ugly black mounds of earth arose on every side of the city.

Bockelson went to the top of the wall once each day and looked out. He knew what this meant.

As each day passed, the pattern became more perceptible, the links in the chain more numerous and closer together, and the black mounds became long dark ridges which reached out to each other, straining to touch. Shovelfuls of earth flew up.

Along the siege line at regular intervals arose blockhouses of rough-hewn timbers from the surrounding forests; in these blockhouses supplies and a few moments of warmth were available to the prince-bishop's men. By the beginning of February the line had closed. The martial clutter was now a complete circle.

THERE WERE TRUMPET signals for everything now: waking, eating, resting from work, military drill for the men in the cathedral square, and church services. Before dawn Paulus would rise to the sound of the trumpet, drag his shivering, somnolent body somehow to the warehouse by the Holy Cross Gate, where those who labored on the defense mounds were fed, chew on his dry bread and cheese among the other quiet workers under the shadow of the earthwork, and would be handed his tool for the day. The king did not allow the tools to be taken home. Everything was controlled. Shortly before noon, trumpets would sound again and women would come by the earthwork with a food wagon, drawing it themselves because of the shortage of animals, and the workers would eat. After this noon meal they would have time to rest, and one of the preachers would come to them and read the Bible, and lead them in the singing of a German psalm. At dusk, at the signal, the Moundmaster would wave his arm and the people would disperse to their homes where they might find a modicum of warmth, to wait for the next trumpet which would signal supper. Paulus was finding a certain comfort in this predictable routine; the king, he thought, was an intelligent man who understood how hard it would be for people accustomed to an orderly life to contemplate rebellion against the leader who gave it to them.

Paulus came home one evening with a Münster wife. Paulus' supervisor, Gert the Moundmaster, had simply ordered him to take a wife. He went to St. Lambert's church, where there had once been a lively matrimonial traffic, and found only the clerk and one lonely, homely woman. Her name was Ari, and she was from Deventer in Gelderland, in the Netherlands. The clerk wrote down both their names – surprised that Paulus Ketterling had not yet recorded his name in the marriage register – and pronounced them married to the glory of God.

Ari was plainer and older than most of the women in Münster. She was short, with a shapeless figure and rounded, sloping shoulders. Her dull blonde hair was chopped off at the level of her neck. Yet she had a happy smile, Paulus thought.

"You should have taken wives when the selection was good," said Julius, when Paulus had brought her home and given her a place on the floor. "The man will certainly grow tense, Who has a wife with a face like a fence. Does she understand me, do you think?"

"I don't think so. She's Dutch."

"They're all Dutch," said Arndt. And they were, all the wives in this house, Dutch. Three German men and eight Dutch women. "But it's good to watch what we say, in any case."

"Paulus, come sit with us. Play dice with us."

"I'll sit for a while."

They sat in front of the stove, with the door open to give them some light, and the small fuel ration for the day beside it waiting to be used up.

"Helga's pregnant," said Julius.

"Is that why she's up every morning before the trumpeter, throwing up in the Aa?" asked Paulus.

"It's about time she got pregnant," said Arndt. "I've suspected you of slacking, Julius. Thinking about reporting you to the king for shirking your saintly duty."

"No danger of that now, I guess," said Julius absently.

Paulus said, "So we have in this one house seven pregnant women?"

"And in this city four thousand pregnant women. Can you imagine what it will be like if the prince-bishop doesn't get in here soon? Julius, your turn to throw."

"Do you think he'll spare the women if they're pregnant?" said Paulus.

"Heretics? Of course not."

They played for a while without talking, and Paulus watched. Arndt picked at his nose, and coughed.

"Where are you working now, Paulus?" asked Julius.

"On the earthworks at the Holy Cross Gate, as before."

"Stuck with a shovel."

"It's not bad. I don't mind it."

"I would," said Arndt. "I like the armory. Better than masonry on the walls."

"And I like guarding the Swordbearer's wives," said Julius and smiled. "Which is what one does when one is a hero."

"How did that happen?" asked Paulus.

"Come, Julius, tell the story one more time."

"In August – "

"Roll, Julius!"

"I did nothing. I was lucky. I was in the forefront of the fight for the wall in August. I became famous and important in a day! And privileged duties – sentry duty only during the day, and guard duty over the wives of the Swordbearer. While the rest of you get blisters and sore backs. All because I was stupid enough to be in front."

"You make it sound like nothing," said Arndt.

"You have told me a hundred times it was nothing."

"I am teasing you, war hero. You did what every soldier does. You tried to save your own life. And you did it well. Any man in the same position would have had the same fear and confusion, though he had fought a thousand times before."

"Did you kill?" asked Paulus.

"Yes, I killed, one man at least, with my sword. Others were pushed to their deaths."

"How did it feel to kill?"

Arndt was shaking the dice in his hand, but stopped. "What's your problem, Paulus?"

"Paulus believes in peace," said Julius, casually..

"That kind of an Anabaptist," said Arndt. He shook his head. "You are in the wrong place, Paulus, the wrong place. They will force you to fight when the time comes."

"No, they won't," said Paulus.

"You'll die, then."

"And you, and you, and these pregnant women. You'll all die. What difference does it make if I fight?"

"It makes a difference. I don't intend to die. I don't think about death. I intend to live to a ripe old age."

"You are the one in the wrong place, Arndt Manns," said Paulus and laughed dryly, trying to calm himself. "This is a place of death. You have all decided on death. Those who live by the sword will die by the sword. Jesus said that."

Arndt laughed, looked at Julius, and pointed to Paulus. "So I get a sermon, as if we don't have enough of those already. If Jesus said that, he was wrong. Those who die by the sword are those who don't have swords. So it is and so it always has been. You look around you and you'll see that that's the truth."

Paulus could not think of a reply to this. He often thought of good replies to things like this later, but hardly ever on the spot.

Julius spoke. "When they put that sword in my hand on the wall, it felt good. It felt good, Paulus. Not that the other man died, but that I was still alive. It felt like life. And I think that may be why I am still here. I never felt life before like I did in that battle. Never saw my own life so clearly, and how much I really love my own life. I probably should have left the city earlier, but being here has given me a new kind of life."

Paulus said, "How many of these poor people are just like you two, do you think? You don't believe the prophecies. You're just here because it's interesting."

"Lots of us are here for that," said Arndt. "And the blond fool knows it too. That's why he keeps us entertained, and busy."

Julius said, "Maybe Jan Bockelson is bored too. Maybe this whole thing is *his* entertainment."

They kept playing dice, and Paulus eventually left them and went to his bedroll on the floor. His feet and hands were cold and there was little prospect of their getting warm tonight, with the wood ration so small. He had not seen Marga since the first time at the great assembly in November, and he had that desperate feeling that his memory of her was almost too weak now to sustain him. The sound of the trumpet in the morning would be welcome, he thought. He lay down next to Ari, and for a while the muffled sounds of Julius and Arndt registered in his mind – their endless wagers with each other, and the clicking of the dice on the floor, and their dry coughing – but then it was all background to the cloudy semi-thoughts that preceded sleep. Ari reached over and put a hand on Paulus' back. She did it so gently it was as if she did not want Paulus to notice, but he noticed.

The next thing Paulus heard was the breakfast trumpet.

CHAPTER 24: LETTER
February, March 1535. Münster.

A dog stood outside the front door, politely, as if it had knocked and was waiting to be invited in. It was a small dog, no longer than Paulus' forearm, black with a white streak from the chin to the chest. When it saw Paulus, its ears went up and it cocked its head to one side. Münster was full of dogs, large half-wild yellowish creatures that ran in packs, hunted for scraps of food, and were themselves now hunted by the people for their flesh. This one, despite its pitiful appearance, had some manners.

"Good day," said Paulus. It was a good day in some respects: the sun was out, the grip of winter was loosening, and the king had given his subjects the afternoon to rest. When Paulus spoke, the dog tilted its head to the other side. Paulus knelt down to the dog's level.

"Little dog, little dog," he said, and the tail wagged. He put out a hand, and the dog rolled onto its back, exposing its belly and looking back at him from an upside-down angle. He lifted a leg and looked – it was a female. Then he scratched its belly. The dog's eyes went dreamily shut and its mouth opened.

"You pitiful thing, your belly is as bare as mine. How did that happen?" He kept scratching. "What's your name? Why is it you're not eaten already, eh?"

"Too thin," said someone behind Paulus. It was Ari, speaking her German, which was clear but very slow.

"Maybe too fast," said Paulus.

"Or smart."

"Where are the others?"

"Sleeping," she said.

"Come, Ari, sit." She responded quickly to this invitation, closed the door behind her, and sat cross-legged with her back against the wall of the house. Paulus leaned back against the door. The dog righted itself and went toward Ari with its tail swinging and its body low to the ground, seeking approval. She picked it up and let it lick her neck.

So they sat, with the sun shining warm on their faces. People in Münster did much of this, sitting languidly and talking slowly, often about the same things again and again. Their bodies were weak from much labor and little nourishment.

"I have a question," said Ari.

"Ask."

"Why do you not touch me? I have been your wife for almost a week, and you have not touched me. It is my right to bear a child by you."

"You really want to be pregnant?"

"I am the last woman in the house to be without child."

"There are others."

"Because they cannot. I can."

"And you want to bring a child into . . . this . . . this starving kingdom?"

"I want to have a baby. I came to Münster to have a baby for the kingdom of God."

Her face was still utterly sincere, like the dog's.

"For the kingdom of God, or for Ari?"

"For the kingdom. I never thought of it until the

kingdom came. I never thought of it before I heard Jan Bockelson preach in Deventer."

"You were not married in Deventer?"

"No. I was in a convent, the convent of the Holy Family. Since I was ten years old."

"I am your first husband, then."

"Yes."

"You are a virgin."

"Yes."

"You could have done better than Paulus Ketterling, Ari."

"I would like to carry the baby of the king," she said. "He is so strong and holy. His seed will be mighty in the kingdom as it spreads over the earth. But I am too ugly, I know that. It is better for the seed of such a man to be planted in beautiful women. The king has only beautiful women."

"Only beautiful women," said Paulus. *Like the woman who used to be my wife.*

"I was never beautiful. Not always so ugly, but never beautiful."

"I was never beautiful, either," said Paulus.

"You are a beautiful man. I never expected a handsome man to come marry me, as you did. I stood there day after day and even the ugly men did not want me. Your child, and my child, would not be ugly. Maybe not beautiful, because of me, but not ugly either – because of you."

"You should not speak like that."

"How?"

"So plainly. About yourself, about a child that does not exist. You should not call yourself ugly."

Ari gazed at him patiently and politely. She scratched the little dog around its ears.

"Can you find the dog something to eat?" he asked.

"I will try. It will not eat much."

THE MONTH OF March began with a string of rainy days.

A pewter sky hung over Westphalia and the rain fell straight down, and the chewed ground on which the prince-bishop's army camped became a morass of human and animal filth. Brave men began to worry now about the great spring enemies of any army – typhus, cholera, plague. Men who could face guns and pikes often deserted at the appearance of disease, with its long hellish death by fever and vomiting and bloody diarrhea. They had some vague sense that these diseases were connected with filth, so von Waldeck kept moving them around to drier ground and filling in the privies.

To an army living in this slogging misery, the smell of roasting meat, coming from the besieged city in late March, was a grievous blow. Franz von Waldeck summoned von Dhaun.

"Herr von Dhaun, the soldiers are restless. They smell the heretics roasting meat in the city. If they have that much food left, they are certainly not starving to death."

"Your grace," replied von Dhaun with a deferential nod. "If I may explain. This happens in sieges. They have run out of fodder for their animals, and they have slaughtered them all before the animals starve to death. It's their last feast."

He was right. Food was running low in Münster. But Bockelson assured his subjects that the Lord would deliver them at Easter, which was coming in mid-April. After the March feast, the Münster saints were reduced to a meatless diet. The worst enemy of Jan Bockelson's little kingdom in March was not the prince-bishop, or even hunger, but boredom. There were more assemblies, frequently at night, and the preachers churned out their sermons by the hundreds, and they all sounded more and more like the last.

THE HOUSE OF Julius and Arndt and Paulus now reeked of urine. Piles of ashes sat heaped or scattered around the stove. Blankets covered the floor in disarray; pregnant women slept and woke and dragged themselves around at all hours of the day and night and talked among themselves in Dutch or shouted at the men in truncated German phrases. There was no fun or novelty left in polygamy. The women were not only pregnant but they were weak and sick, and eyes that had once been pretty were now drooping and bagged. Their bellies swelled while their legs and arms and faces lost shape and the skin began to scale and wrinkle. Ari was thinner, and her cheekbones showed.

And the air stank, because the prince-bishop's army threw its garbage into the Aa river, and in the city the people had nowhere to take their offal but to the river, and the detritus of both sides collected on the banks and in the corners.

Now spring was coming to the fields, and the mercenaries could watch flowers trying to grow, and listen to the birds, if they wanted to. The breezes from the west were warm, and the days were longer. The prostitutes came back when von Waldeck paid the men, and there was much lounging around the fires into the evening, and drinking. It was not an easy life, but it was getting better. For the citizens of Münster, there was only more stench, and less food, and now some deaths. And everything that came up green was picked immediately and made into soup.

Paulus' stomach and intestines were not right. Sometimes he could not hold down even the small food rations he ate, and sometimes when they came up, it was speckled with blood. But there was nothing he could do, and others were far sicker than he.

One of Julius's pregnant wives, Susanna, began shouting deliriously in the middle of the night, and everyone in the room woke up. Julius barked at her to shut up. She did not. He went to her, leaned over her in the darkness, put his hand on her face and said, "The fever."

In the morning they saw that her face and hands and ankles were swollen, and that her whole body was turning faintly yellow. She shook and sweated. The other women tried to act routinely but were very nervous. Susanna repeatedly pushed her tongue out of her mouth and it was dry and large and white. They gave her water, but she did not seem to want it.

Julius Fettbauch sat by her side through the whole thing and was nervous and upset. Then, when she died late in the morning, he cried and shook his head again and again as if he could not believe it.

"Come, we'll take her to the graves," said Paulus. "It's good not to keep her with the others, they might be infected too."

"Yes, you're right."

They rolled Susanna in her blanket and each of them took one twisted end of it and they carried her out the door.

"Wait, is her head up?" asked Julius.

"What does it matter?"

"It matters. It's indecent to carry her face down."

So they carried her as if she were lying on her back, face up, through the city to the burial ground behind the Overwater church where the animal pens had once been. Ramshackle wooden walls had been put up around this graveyard. As they came to the entry way they were confronted by one of the king's men in a black uniform, who insisted on unrolling their burden and looking at Susanna's face. He asked her name, and Julius told him. He scribbled something in a book, not words but the rough strokes of symbols, and then two women came to take the body through the door to the graveyard.

Paulus looked briefly through the gate as the women carried the corpse away. A large, deep ditch. Bodies, some wrapped, some exposed. Tiny bodies. Babies.

"They're digging mass graves now," Paulus said softly to Julius at home, so the women would not hear.

"I had assumed it. It's happening, isn't it."

"What?"

"We're starving."

"The pregnant women are suffering the most."

"I never thought I'd starve. I never imagined I'd ever go

hungry."

"Nor I. Do you know, I am a noble?" Paulus lifted his chin in aristocratic arrogance.

"Ha! Look at you now, a noble. It doesn't seem to matter much. This city changes everything, doesn't it. The blonde fool promised us a new world, and here it is."

"Not really. There are new nobles, and new poor. Everyone's changed places but the end result is the same."

"I never think about such things. I wish the prince-bishop would attack. O prince-bishop please attack, For Julius wants to smack and hack. I want one more good fight before I die. Some soldier is going to pay with his life for Susanna. I'm going to designate him – you there, come here, let me kill you, it's your fault Susanna is dead."

There were always surprises in Münster: it seemed that Julius had really loved Susanna. And it seemed that he was becoming more bellicose, absorbing the violent spirit of the place.

"I WANT TO contact my wife," whispered Paulus to Julius. "Can you help me think of a way to contact my wife?" Julius moved regularly among the royalty and high officials. "You know where she is and who come and goes."

Julius was almost asleep. He stirred at Paulus' questions. It had been a long time since Paulus had spoken with Julius about Marga.

"Your wife," said Julius, at first confused.

"The wife of the king."

"Oh yes. Can't this wait?"

"Another day, and another day, and soon we all die."

"Which one is she?"

"Short, slender – "

"Isn't everyone."

" – long very dark hair."

"Oh yes, I know her. Abishag."

"Abishag?"

"That's her name. They all have these ridiculous names now, like Abigail, and Tirzah, and Deborah."

"Old Testament names. Like the streets." A surge of acute jealousy went through Paulus. Jan Bockelson had given his wife a new name, Abishag, the name of the young girl they put next to King David when he was old, to keep him warm.

"Can I get a letter, a note, to her?"

"Not easy. The king keeps his wives shut up pretty tight, I'm afraid. He's in one wing of the house and they're in the other. There's a hallway for him to use when he . . . visits them. They never go out except for the ceremonial things."

"Will you try? Will you just think about it?" Paulus pressed a small square of folded paper into Julius' hand.

"I'll see," said Julius. "But listen!" He pointed a finger at Paulus. "I'm no hero, despite what Arndt says."

Now one of the wives said, "Sssst!" and rattled off something in Dutch. Julius climbed over two sleeping bodies and cuffed her on the side of the head a couple times, and mumbled to himself as he got back beneath his blankets, "We may have nothing here, but we'll have respect."

It was familiar, Paulus had heard it somewhere else . . . the Swordbearer had flogged a woman on the pillory in front of the Rosental Convent for some petty act of theft, and the woman had shrieked in pain and terror and protested that she had nothing to give her child, that there was nothing in the whole cursed city, and the Swordbearer had said, "We may not have much, but we will have respect." They were starting to talk alike and act alike in this city, like rocks tumbled endlessly in a barrel, all becoming round like the others. Paulus wondered if this was happening to him. He wondered if he would recognize himself. He wondered if Onkel would recognize him.

IT HAD BEEN a wretched night, with little sleep, because two of the women had been violently sick with coughing, and another woman, half crazy with hunger and anxiety about the baby she carried, shouted at them for keeping her awake. Arndt was upstairs and shouted down at all of them in a bellowing voice that one would not imagine could come from his slight, emaciated body, and his wives shouted back at him like screeching cats. Julius, for once, was on duty for the king at night, and Paulus was in the sitting room with Ari and the three others, and he had no heart to say anything to them.

Paulus tried to imagine what the house had been like before. It was not a bad house, though it was small. It had, perhaps, belonged to a struggling merchant, who fetched wood from the forests and sold it in the city, or to a cobbler, or to some civic official, a notary or scribe or even a hangman. Maybe the man was young like Paulus. Maybe he had small children who ran through the house and played on the stairs. The floors were plain but solid wood, noticeably worn along the path from the front door back to the kitchen; the ceiling beams were well built and straight; on one wall of the sitting room, by the tile stove, there was wood paneling that reached halfway up to the ceiling, as if the owners had started in on this project and never finished.

Maybe there had been furniture, comfortable furniture, in this room – a soft chair here, a bench, a table for flowers and ornaments. Maybe people had sat and talked here, clean, calm, fundamentally happy people, people not especially excited about anything. What had become of them?

Now the room was a stark expanse of floor, except for the stove, and the stove, once a nice one, had been hit and chipped and the dust and ash had settled upon it and turned it from cream to gray. The oak paneling had been ripped out piece by piece, taken away by the Woodmaster Heinrich Havickhorst, because it was useful for defense, and a part of the wall itself had been used for firewood. And the kitchen was no kitchen now but a closet piled high with debris. People collected debris in Münster; when they saw something for the taking, they took it, whether it had any use or not, for the old instinct to possess something to call their own had not been entirely rooted out of their hearts. In the kitchen were pieces of clothing, and broken dishes, and flowers, and children's toys, and rope, and scraps of iron and chain, and plants in pots, and papers and books and ruined shoes. Paulus found a tin tube one day, lying in the street, put it in his pocket, and took it home. No one knew what it was, but it was at least something the elder did not want.

So Paulus had blocked out the pandemonium around him by fantasizing. Then Julius came in.

"Paulus," he said, beneath the bawling of the women.

"What?"

"I think I got your note to your wife." Paulus sat up. The fantasy was gone. "There is a crippled man who delivers firewood to the king's wives every day. I persuaded him to put your letter with the wood he takes to the queen Abishag."

THE WINDOWS OF the queen Abishag, laced with expensive lead patterns, faced to the east. To keep out the early morning sun they were covered with green velvet draperies. There was no reason for her, or any of her sister queens, to rise early; their chief work was at night. She lay asleep under fine quilts with roses embroidered in them, in a high bed with posts and canopy and curtains all around that could be drawn shut. The king had cleaned the city of its best furniture for his wives. On the floor lay a heap of gowns; Abishag and her maid had been up late the night before, trying to decide which one to wear tonight, when the king would present himself again to the people.

But the maid had drawn the drapes poorly, and a vertical sheet of sunlight fell through a crack onto Abishag's face, a milky white face, well nourished, not sallow and gray and pimply like the complexions of most of the women in the city. She squinted her eyes against the sun in unconscious defense. But the glare was too strong, and she awoke and turned her face into the pillow and rolled onto her back with eyes open and enjoyed the sensations that flowed through her well rested body in a warm bed.

She sat up in bed and shook her head and dug her fingers into her hair, separating the tangles. She ran her fingers many times from front to back: it was the ritual Paulus had loved to watch while she thought he was still asleep. She stepped out of the bed, naked, stretched her back with her hands on her waist, covered herself with a gown, walked to the window and threw open the drapes. Light filled the room.

She went toward the door and saw the usual bundle of wood tied with a piece of twine, and she saw the folded note resting between two pieces. She took it and opened it.

"Marga, I am here . . ." she began, and put her hand to her mouth, reading on silently. "The stupid fool," she whispered. "He's here."

There was a soft knock on the door, and the voice of the chambermaid saying, "My lady, my lady."

Abishag was jostled out of her repose by the knock and put the letter behind her back.

"I don't wish to rise yet."

"Yes, my lady."

She returned to the letter and read it again. Two small lines just above the bridge of her nose deepened into scowling furrows. When she was done, she folded it again and placed it under the leg of her table. Then she put her fingers in her hair, and let out a long, tension-relieving breath. She arose and went to the open window.

"Fool," she said softly.

She knocked on the wall, and her chambermaid, a homely young girl with dark eyes and a wide nose, instantly entered.

"My lady," the girl said and bowed.

"Well, Greta, what shall we wear today to please the king?"

"My lady, I've been thinking of the scarlet one all night." Greta giggled.

"That . . . or the blue gown with the white trim. It makes my breasts look bigger."

"The king likes that," said Greta.

"That's what we'll wear tonight, the blue one."

This was not the response that Paulus had prayed for.

CHAPTER 25: JUSTICE
March, 1535. Münster.

The king's heralds blew the trumpets that night to call the people together to the cathedral square. The sound of the trumpets excited Paulus. The natural markers of time had largely lost their meaning, and the people lived by the trumpets. Among the others, quiet slow-moving specters in ragged clothes that hung from skeletal bodies, Paulus made his way obediently to the cathedral square.

The eyes and faces of the people around him were distant and preoccupied. They talked softly to each other from time to time – trivial gossip, petty complaints, but few were talking about the kingdom of God. It reminded Paulus of Catholic parishioners at mass. Bockelson was losing their hearts, though he still had their bodies. He now owed his kingdom to the surrounding wall of the prince-bishop's army.

The king stood and spoke.

"We come to thank God for his good blessings to us. We thank him for his law, and for this city, and for the promise of deliverance that is only weeks away. And we thank him for the sign of future blessing and prosperity – our children!"

This was a cue, for as the king continued to speak, a line of women holding babies emerged from the shadows and went up onto the platform, and eventually there was a large crowd of them.

Now the wives of the king appeared, brilliantly clad. Among them were three carrying babies in their arms and several others whose advanced pregnancies could not be hidden even by sumptuous robes. The king was ecstatically proud that he was a father, and he was now displaying his reproductive accomplishments to the people. The mothers of his babies gave the children to him and he held all three at once like trophies, their faces to the crowd. Again the people clapped and there were *ohhhs* and *ahhhs* at the sweet domesticity of the scene. Only nine months and they had practically forgotten their initial horror of polygamy; it seemed so natural and beautiful now, this vignette of a strong male flanked by his adoring wives and holding his own children in his arms.

The king began a ceremony of blessing the children. One by one their mothers brought them before him, beginning with his own, and he spoke words of dedication and blessing on them, laying a sword carefully across their faces.

Paulus had a direct view of Marga. She was one of the few wives with a flat, unpregnant belly. He thought her dress was beautiful, that it accentuated her wasp-like waist and made her breasts look high and large, and that the pale blue color complemented her skin and hair. And he liked the bonnet she wore, even though her hair was all gathered and stuffed into it, because it revealed the shape of her neck. She was one of the most beautiful of the king's wives. Paulus loved what Greta had done to Marga's face with cosmetics – the bold arching lines over the eyes and the blue powder on the eyelids and the red powder on the cheeks and the throbbing red paint on the lips – and he should have been ashamed to admit to himself that he loved it, but he did. He knew too that such powders and blushes were scented with perfumes, and he wished he could smell her face, that he could bury his nose in her cheek or neck and breathe in. This was how Marga deserved to look.

But something troubled him. Paulus had expected her to be the same beautiful face and body, because that beauty was something objective and physical. But the person inside, the person who leaked out through the body and the face, seemed the same too. He saw her look at the babies the way she had once looked at Heine. The woman next to her whispered something in her ear, and Marga responded with a quiet laugh – Paulus could not hear it but he could see it – and then she closed her lips the way Paulus had seen her close her lips a thousand times. She ran her fingers lightly from her throat to the back of her head, a motion designed to sweep away her hair from her face; he had seen it a thousand times. She had a way of lowering her face and staring at things upward, with her eyebrows raised. This she did while the king blessed the babies.

All normal Marga things. Marga mannerisms, Marga emotions.

Paulus returned home depressed, for reasons he did not really understand. Something about the way he had been thinking about Marga was wrong.

"Your wife was very beautiful tonight," remarked Julius.

"She is beautiful. Maybe if she weren't so beautiful, it would be easier for me to forget about her."

"Forget about her? I thought you were madly in love with her."

"Tonight – tonight I feel like forgetting about her."

"Then forget about her!" Julius laughed. "You have a wife that wants you badly, right here." Julius gestured toward the sleeping Ari.

"She seems so happy."

"Abishag?"

"Marga is her name, Julius. I guess I expected her to look angry or upset. Or insane. It seems insane, to me, for anyone to want to come to this place. I thought she was crazy. I expected her to be wild-eyed. I expected her to be someone else. And if she has already read my letter, then I expected her to be either crazy or weepy eyed. She was . . . normal."

"You thought your letter would break her heart, huh?"

"Yes."

"Wake her from her spell?"

"Yes."

"Paulus, you need to understand something about these people. They're not insane. They just believe what they believe. Lots of people think that you and your kind are insane, the way you refuse to defend yourselves. But you're not insane either, you just believe what you believe. Listen. These people are here because they like it! I'm here because I like it. Not for the same reasons, but I like it. If none of them liked it, they would turn on the blonde fool and throw his body to the prince-bishop in ten minutes."

"Why do you like it?"

"I want to fight again. That's honest. Those five minutes on the wall were the best five minutes of my life. I was a fat, worthless burgher, and those five minutes made me into a man. I want to experience that again."

Paulus felt the immense power of the world weighing down on him. He could understand what Julius was saying. The intense taste of combat, danger, comradery, and victory sounded good to him too.

"Marga likes it here." When Paulus finally said this, everything inside him that had to do with Marga shifted around into a different position.

"I'm afraid so, my friend. How could she not like it here? She lives a wonderful, pampered life, she has plenty to eat, and she is part of something she really believes in. What could be better than that?"

"My letter probably made her laugh," admitted Paulus, feeling ashamed.

"I wasn't there," said Julius, trying to spare him. "Good night."

The Marga whom Paulus had pursued to Münster was, in his mind, a crazed woman, out of her mind. But Paulus had been the crazy one. Now he was embarrassed at the way he had written to her. *Remember,* he had said – as if by simply reminding her of the past he could cure the present. As if she were a child with a ten minute attention span. As if – and this hurt – she really had any pleasure in remembering their life together. *Marga likes it here.*

PAULUS WAS EMBARRASSED, but he was also relieved. He had been trying to live by a falsehood, and everything that the falsehood touched had been bent and contorted. In his false construction of things, Marga was not really responsible for her sin, and Paulus was. He had pronounced himself guilty for being an inadequate husband, and for failing to give her a real home, and for losing their son to the godless authorities. It was all his fault, all his fault . . .

She's not insane. She just believes what she believes. She likes it here. Before these simple, true words, Paulus' painfully constructed falsehoods dissipated like smoke-wisps before a strong wind.

He was not guilty for Marga's coming to Münster, or for her heretical beliefs, or for her adulteries. He had followed his faith. Marga had known all about that faith, and its consequences, when she married him. She was a grown woman, and she was not insane. He had never deceived her. His only wrongdoing had been his silly effort to exempt her from her own cross-carrying, as if the fact that she was pretty and soft and loved by him should exempt her from her own personal discipleship. She was as responsible to Christ as he was. She had denied Christ. Now Paulus was able and willing to leave her all alone before Christ, with her own real apostasy and guilt.

And he was angry. Angry for the first time, really angry

at her, for her apostasy and her adultery and her disregard for him and his love. She was a violent Münsterite.

A clear, steel horror settled into his mind. It was so clear now. It was good that he had gone to the assembly and seen her face close. It was good of God to speak to him through Julius.

And a new question: *Do I want her back?*

Paulus lay for what must have been two hours like this, the whole chain of thoughts clanking through his mind again and again, making the path smoother each time. Daylight came and still he was the only one awake. He felt wonderful, purged and simple. He put the blankets over his shoulders and sat outside the door of the house. The little black dog, which Ari had named Anika, rose from its sleeping place in the dirt nearby and came to sniff him.

"Anika, you must be my congregation," he said to her. The dog tilted its head. "We need a witness for this."

Paulus raised his hand in a formal, pastoral gesture. He was trying to remember how Onkel would have done it. He tried to imagine himself in Montau, in the meeting room, with the believers gathered around him.

"Marga Roth, you are here before this holy assembly of saints because of scandalous and unrepented sin. You have denied the doctrines of Christ by taking up the sword, and participating by your approval in numerous acts of bloodshed and murder. You have entered into covenant with godless and violent men. And you have broken your marriage covenant by adultery. In the presence of Christ and the angels, we excommunicate you from Christ's church."

Paulus clenched his fist in righteousness.

"WE'RE GOING TO leave this place," said Arndt.

Julius nodded. They had brought Paulus outside, away from the women, to tell him this.

Arndt was pitifully thin, his eyes sunken, the stubble of his beard graying. His head shook slightly from side to side as he spoke; hunger was doing something to his nerves.

"How?" said Paulus.

"Beneath the wall," answered Arndt.

"Right through the floor of the kitchen, down, under the wall and out," said Julius. "Like sappers, right Arndt?"

"Right. Paulus, will you help us?"

Paulus did not hesitate. "Yes, of course."

"Things not working out with Abishag, eh?"

"No."

"Women, you stay clear of women and you'll survive," said Arndt with a smile, knowing it was stupid advice from a man with four wives.

At night, when the women were sleeping, Julius and Arndt and Paulus picked their way through the debris in the kitchen to its back wall, which was actually a layer of plaster laid on the city wall.

"I've thought this through," whispered Arndt. "Our biggest problem is where to put the earth we take out. There's some room right here in the kitchen, if we keep the door well cluttered with this stuff. Nobody ever comes here anymore. But then, we'll have to put it out the window, between the two houses, and spread it out so it's not obvious. And listen! We can't get impatient. We have to be slow and careful, and take what we can get each day. If we're discovered . . ."

"No thanks," said Julius. "I don't want the quarters of my body nailed to the four city gates." He was remembering the February executions of six people, three men and three women, who had been caught in a plot to escape from the city.

"When should we begin?" asked Paulus.

"Now," said Arndt.

The floor in the kitchen was made of wood; its rusty nails came easily and quietly apart, and the bare ground was exposed below. "Straight down, maybe six, maybe eight feet," said Arndt. "Paulus, you go back to bed. If someone wakes up, talk in a loud voice. Lie to her. Tell her we were called by the king, or something."

They dug, night after night, taking turns. It was hard, painful work, and it was slow work because their strength had been starved from them, but it made all three of them happy in a juvenile sort of way. For Paulus it felt like being naughty; it made his heart race when he had to dump each bucket of dirt out the kitchen window, climb out, and spread the dirt on the ground. The watchmen made rounds at night, and once he saw the dark form of the sentinel walk past on the street and froze where he was. There was also the danger of being seen from the sentries on the wall above. For a few nights the danger petrified him, but after that not so much. The whole city seemed perpetually sleepy, and its senses dull. People so hungry were withdrawing into themselves, not caring what happened around them.

After about a week, they came to the base of the wall. Paulus and Julius were working at the time, Arndt sleeping. Julius was clawing at the earth in the hole and Paulus was evacuating the dirt. Waiting for another full bucket, he heard Julius say something.

"What?" he whispered down.

"The bottom! The bottom!" Julius said.

"Shhh!"

"I think it's the bottom, Paulus."

"Keep digging, we've got to get under it, and there has to be room for a body to bend."

"I know, I know. How stupid do you think I am?"

"Stupid enough to be down there while I'm up here."

"Then come down here and do this for a while."

They exchanged places. Paulus fit much more easily in the narrow shaft than Julius. There was barely room for him to squat and insert his hand beneath the bottom course of masonry in the wall. Yes, that was it, the bottom.

THERE WAS ALMOST nothing left in the communal

granaries. The people now went only once a day, and when they went they received a watery gruel that was made of nothing but boiled and crushed grain and water. Sometimes there were roots in it. Even clean water for the soup was hard to find. When rain came they collected it.

And as the ability of the king to feed his people dwindled to almost nothing, the people began to return to their own wits and resources. It was, after all, spring, and things were growing, and they ate anything that grew. Grass, and weeds, and dandelions, and flower bulbs all went into soup. The rats and mice were multiplying too, and the people learned to catch them, and new recipes for rodents circulated among the women. In April the communal kitchens simply stopped functioning, without any announcement, and there were suddenly two separate economies in the city, one of the king and his court, who still had something in the storerooms to eat, the other of the populace, who lived by forage like a horde of locusts.

Give us this day our daily bread. Had Jesus imagined a place like Münster when he taught the disciples to pray this way? Was it not a prayer for normal times and places when a man had access to the soil and could put feet and hands to his prayer by working? As Paulus trudged to the house one day, having gone out to look for something green and having failed to find it – whatever was growing was picked first thing in the morning and he was too late – he laughed inwardly at himself. What had he expected to find? Someone selling sausage in the marketplace? Two of the women in the house were desperately sick; one had already miscarried her baby, and the baby had been taken to the burial ground. But he had nothing to give to them. He would just have to say it straight out. They would understand. Then he saw Anika near the door, nose in the dirt. Poor thing, its hipbones and ribs protruded and the hair along the top of its back was thinning and falling out. Still, when it looked up it had a pleasant and exuberant look in its eyes. He petted the dog, as he always did, and had a shocking thought.

This is the daily bread. He led the dog between the houses, where he was scattering the dirt at night, and held it in his arms for several minutes. It would be just as well for the dog to die now as to starve. He cupped his hand over its dry little muzzle and smothered it to death. It struggled a bit but gave up quickly, glad, perhaps, to die in the arms of someone it loved, knowing with animal wisdom that the struggle for life in Münster was a waste of time.

Ari was attached to the dog and Paulus did not tell her that it was Anika's flesh they chewed on that night. Dogs were being hunted down all over the city now. In the forest, packs of wolves hunted men. In the city of man, packs of men hunted dogs.

CHAPTER 26: SPRING
March, 1535. Münster.

The prince-bishop wanted action. Von Dhaun was adamant against it: there would be no assault on the walls, or he would resign his commission and report to the *Kreistag*. He suggested a bombardment – lots of noise and smoke and at least the feeling that they were fighting. It would give the mercenaries something to do. Von Waldeck cursed and assented.

Von Dhaun rolled out the guns and the wagons and arranged them around the city. The gunners had instructions from the prince-bishop to stay clear of the cathedral. He intended to celebrate mass in his cathedral some day.

They began with some fun, shooting canisters filled with pamphlets into the city, which rolled in the streets and sometimes burst and spewed the leaflets out. The gunners imagined the people in Münster scooping them up and reading them, but that was not what happened. For as soon as the first one fell, and its contents were examined – SURRENDER NOW, THERE IS NO HOPE, THE EMPIRE IS PAYING FOR THE SIEGE – the decree went out that anyone reading them would be executed. As fast as they fell, the young women cleaned them up and carted them away to an oven to burn.

The next day real iron balls came hurtling into the city, making whirring noises, rattling and clattering through the streets with little effect except to damage some roofs. The Master of the Armory and his men collected them and hauled them to the magazine of the city. This was exactly what the king needed at the time to stir the fighting morale of his people. The cannonballs were reminding them that there was a world outside the city, a world which was their enemy; the bombardment was a welcome diversion, and it made the blood flow. To show his invulnerability, the king rode through the streets on his horse and shouted imprecations at the prince-bishop, and the women followed him cheering.

The bombardment went on into the night, but Paulus heard little of it because he was down in their shaft, digging. They were making progress laterally now, along the underside of the massive city wall, where the earth was hard packed clay. Paulus was on his knees, his back bent, in complete darkness. He chipped away enough of the clay to fill the bucket, dragged the bucket to the vertical part of the tunnel, and called for Arndt to pull it up by the rope that hung there. Again, and again, endlessly, without any idea of how far he was actually getting. To keep the tunnel straight they stretched the rope along it periodically.

"Will this really work?" Paulus asked Arndt.

Arndt shrugged. "With enough time . . . if we don't become too weak to work . . . if we don't go too far and come up in the river and fill the tunnel with water. . ."

"Lots of ifs. Wake Julius, it's his turn." Paulus hauled his beaten body to the sitting room and went to sleep. He heard the hammer of a gun and the song of the ball over the wall.

EXHAUSTED, DIZZY, AND numb, Paulus tried each day to read his Bible, Onkel's Bible. But his eyes danced around on the pages and the words seemed to be decorations rather than symbols with meaning. He spent a part of each evening remembering Onkel, which, unlike the reading of the Bible, seemed to get easier as his physical condition declined. Some kind of inversion was taking place: as the real world around him became more deathlike and fantastic, his inner world of memory and sentiment became sharper and more powerful. It became easier for him to retreat into it, even during manual labor in the tunnel. It was almost as if his soul were beginning to detach from his body, getting ready for death.

IT IS MORNING. Two birds, unaware of the siege, sit on the sharp peak of a roof and sing riotously to each other. They can see, as the sleeping people cannot, the horizontal slash of cloud that lies just above the eastern edge of the earth and turns the sun's light pink. The sentry on the wall does not see it. He is dozing.

Bodies litter the floor in no apparent order. There are the three starving, pregnant wives of Julius Fettbauch: one is curled up with the blanket over her head; another has thrashed in her sleep and lies partially uncovered with an arm thrown back, an arm that is skin and bone, with every ligament in the elbow revealed; the third is up against the wall, and has been sitting against it and fallen to her left, her fine blonde hair hanging over her face, her hands on her belly. Ari is next to Paulus, as always. Paulus is on his back, his head on the hard wood floor. His mouth is open. The blanket is bunched around his middle. His feet stick out; he has his broken, brittle shoes on; his exposed shins are white and thin. His hands are dirty, the fingernails broken and black and the fingers curled like claws. There is dirt in his beard, on his cheek, in his hair. Close to his head Onkel's Bible lies open.

Arndt is upstairs with his wives. Julius is in the hole, digging.

While Paulus is asleep, Ari nuzzles next to him and

begins to tenderly kiss his cheeks. Paulus glides softly across the river between sleep and wakefulness. He understands.

"Ari, no."

She speaks in his ear. "Paulus, give me a baby."

"Ari, no."

"You will give me a baby. You are my husband."

"We are dying."

"We will live. My child will live. Give him to me."

"Ari, stop, you don't know everything."

"Give me a child."

"Ari."

"Paulus, give me a child."

"I can't."

He interposes his hand between their two faces.

"Why?" she demands.

And what will Paulus say? *I am already married.* But he isn't anymore. *We are all doomed to death.* She doesn't believe that; she still believes in Bockelson's prophecy of a great Easter deliverance. *Ari, you are too homely.* But he is not willing to say that. Some things are true but should not be said.

"I can't," he simply repeats.

"You will want a child for the kingdom soon, when you see what the Lord is going to do!"

What faith she had! Faith that made her patient, and humble, and full of hope.

The sun is shining on the steeples and battlements and the gables of the high houses in the center of the city. It will be a brilliant intoxicating spring day.

CHAPTER 27: HOSEA
March, 1535. Münster.

Dinner was finished. It had been a humble fare of plain bread and some bones boiled into soup, but compared to what the populace was eating it was sumptuous.

"Brother Rothmann, we thank you," said Jan Bockelson and put down his cloth napkin. The food on the royal table on this evening had come from Rothmann's portion; he nodded to the king. It was a great privilege to be thanked by the king. "And who entertains the court tomorrow?"

In the fashion of feudal kings of an earlier day, Bockelson imposed himself on the resources of the nobility he had created, requiring them in a certain order to provide for the evening meal around his table. Johann Kursener, the Horsemaster, raised his hand.

"It is my turn," he said. "Tomorrow we will have cheese."

"We will look forward to that! And now, to bed with us," said the king. His wives, sitting around him in their places, became attentive. Knipperdolling chuckled salaciously – *ho, ho, ho* – and rolled his eyes. Bernhard Rothmann, embarrassed at what was about to take place, found some crumbs on his plate to pick at. The king stood, pushed back his chair, and began to walk around the clustered tables, behind the guests.

At each wife's place at the table, a small hole had been bored in the wood, next to that wife's name. Jan Bockelson kept a peg of wood by his place throughout the meal each night; sometimes he handled it thoughtlessly, sometimes it sat untouched until the end. But always, when the meal and conversation were over, he would announce the end of the evening, take the peg, and place it in the hole of one of the wives. This was the revelation of his will to spend the night sleeping with that particular woman. The suggestiveness of this method was hard to miss; the king had a flair for the symbolic. On this night, he let the peg drop softly into the hole of Katherina Averweges, a brown haired smiling Dutch girl whose nickname was Rahab. The others applauded, even the other queens. It was forbidden to show displeasure with the king's choice, since it was inspired by God. So Rahab and Jan Bockelson arose, he helping her chivalrously and stylishly by the hand and then brushing it with his lips, and two of the guards led the way out to the passageway that led across to the queens' house. Everyone knew that bedtime would be preceded by a hot bath for the queen and her careful perfuming by the maids.

But Abishag had transgressed the rule of politeness and sisterhood. She had not clapped in approval at the king's choice, and the king had seen it, as he saw everything around him with an infallible judgment.

Abishag and Greta were in Abishag's room, undressing the queen for the night, when the door flew open and a large man walked in. It was Jürgen Fromme, of the king's bodyguard.

"Queen Abishag, you will come with me to the king."

Greta smiled; she thought it meant that the king had changed his mind and wanted her mistress; it sounded like good news. But Abishag knew better. She had perversely hoped that Bockelson would notice her displeasure even though she knew the risks. She had been in a nasty, belligerent mood for some days. Unaccountably, some of the king's eccentric performances, which had charmed her, now irritated her.

"Abishag, you were angry tonight, weren't you?" The king spoke.

Jürgen Fromme had brought Abishag to Rahab's bedroom, where Bockelson was pulling off his pants, and Rahab was already in the bed. No one thought anything of things like this, since the old privacy was considered prudish and effete. Strong sweet smells hung in the atmosphere.

"I was not angry, my lord, but I was . . . disappointed."

"No, you were angry. Don't ever lie to me again." Bockelson's gaze was utterly without emotion.

"Forgive me."

"Abishag, there is a problem. You are obviously a barren woman, and the scripture clearly denotes barrenness as the curse of God – "

"My lord!"

"Silence! I am a merciful king. I will not attempt to find out what sin it is that has brought this judgment of God upon you, but for you to remain my wife is impossible. The king, and the family of the king, must remain scrupulously holy or our cause may be lost. You will understand this, I'm sure." He was completely naked.

Abishag sank to her knees and circled his knees with her arms.

"Touch me not," said Bockelson firmly and removed her from him by her hair. "The scripture enjoins the writ of divorce, and I give it to you now." Jürgen Fromme brought a sheet of paper from inside his jerkin and held it out to Marga.

"Divorce?" she said in disbelief.

"It is the law of God."

"This is right, and holy?"

"The law of Moses provides for it."

"Doesn't our Lord Jesus Christ set this law aside?" In

Abishag's mind the teaching of the sermon on the mount was filtering back.

"A temporary measure, not intended for us," said the king simply. "Take it, Abishag." She did, and stood. "And leave your holy name behind when you leave my presence. You will be called . . . whatever you were before you came here. You will be the wife of another, but you will not be Abishag."

Jürgen Fromme led her out.

"What is your name?" he asked.

"Marga," she said.

"Marga, come with me, you are my wife now. I have wanted you for many months."

"But I don't want you," spat Marga.

The palm of Jürgen Fromme's large hand splatted against the side of Marga's head. Her knees crumpled and she went straight down, and sat. He leaned over her and yelled in her ringing ear:

"Don't you ever defy me again! You are my wife now! Don't you know I can have your little head cut off?"

He lifted her by her arm and pulled her, his new trophy, to his own house on the cathedral square.

THE VOLCANO OF Paulus' soul erupts one night in a tangled, barbaric dream, spewing, roiling out of his heart. He has wandered to a far corner of the city, has ignored the trumpets and has missed the evening assembly because he does not want to see Marga again, for fear he will want her, has seated himself in a stinking little alley where no one can see him, has tried to think but has been unable to make his thoughts cohere. This crippling of his mind frightens him more than his physical deterioration. He has fallen asleep and is slouched with his head hanging over his lap. In this condition, he dreams.

He is in the middle of an epic, gigantic festival. All around him are tables made of planks on barrels, tables for hundreds, maybe thousands of people, bending and groaning under the weight of food. On one table is a large pig, roasted whole, melted fat running down its body onto the table and congealing there in pearl-colored pools, two men swabbing it up with pieces of white bread; on another, roasted ribs lying in stacks, steaming; on others, deep meat pies, thick with dough and running with gravy, black bread, brown bread, bread with cracked grain sprinkled on the surface, bread with artistic knife gashes baked in, barley pudding, mounds of salted cucumbers, thick slices of yellow onion, berry tarts. There is a table of hungry men enjoying fresh cooked beef liver dipped in hot vinegar and butter and salt, and a table creaking under extraordinary wheels of cheese, white, yellow, and laced with blue, and plump healthy red-cheeked children skimming foamy cream from the surface of milk pails with pieces of bread. All around there is the lilting sound of laughter and talk and happiness. Paulus goes everywhere, even into the side streets, and everywhere there is food and steam and satiation.

Julius Fettbauch is there in the dream, sitting at a table among others, eating and laughing. His mouth is greasy, his stomach enormous. He has a pork butt on the end of his sword and brandishes it in the air with superhuman strength.

"Paulus! Paulus! Rest your feet, Sit and eat. Plenty for all, Great and small. Shame on you so thin and lean, Eat until you can be seen." His face is flushed with wine; red spidery veins show on his nose and cheeks. Paulus feels happy for him.

"One king of righteousness," says Paulus, not knowing where the salute comes from.

Julius raises a wine glass. "Amen! Amen!"

"One pot, one egg, one kitchen," says Paulus again, not knowing what it means or why he has said it.

"Wine! Meat! Eggs! Fish!" cries Julius in jubilation.

Paulus sits. Across from him is Ari, plump and talkative, and next to her is Arndt, working on a plate full of ribs. His arm is around Ari's waist, and they are laughing at something that Arndt has said, and Arndt's gopher teeth show. Paulus eats with one arm thrown over Julius' shoulders and the other wrist-deep in a meat pudding jammed with pieces of heart and kidney. Warmth and comradery are overwhelming him. All is well.

Along the street comes a simple cart drawn by a horse, and on the cart stands the most beautiful woman Paulus has ever seen, so beautiful that a glow of light seems to play around her head like a halo. She is small and plainly dressed, and her hands are tied with ropes in front of her, and her face is stark white like sunlight off a mirror, her lips dark and wide, her eyes large. The people eating and making merry hardly notice.

"Who is that?" Paulus asks Julius.

"The queen Abishag," says Julius.

"The nicest body in Münster," says Arndt, butting into the conversation.

"She's so beautiful," says Paulus.

"That's her problem," says Ari. "These beautiful women have nothing but problems." She looks at Arndt and smiles.

"Give me an ugly woman any day," Ardnt says and kisses her on the cheek. "One who can cook and clean and conceive." Ari kisses him back with a loud smack.

"Never mind how plain they look, Just so they conceive and cook," sings Julius.

"Where is she going?" asks Paulus.

"To trial for adultery," says Julius.

The cart turns a corner and Paulus rises to follow it. The queen Abishag's hair falls like black lava from her head over the rail of the cart and drags behind her like a royal train. Paulus trails, holds some of her hair in his hands and smells it, and the fragrance is sweet, not artificially sweet like perfume, but like wild weeds and mown hay after a rain, sweet with female oils. He is weeping with pure pleasure. His sobs rack him and he can hardly walk.

After winding through the streets, the cart comes to a halt before a kingly personage on a golden throne. His appearance is majestic; his robes are of red-dyed mink fur, and his neck is weighed down with gold chains and medallions. He has a spectacular crown on his head. To his right and left are lines and lines of uniformed attendants with flags and spears and halberds and trumpets, all standing stiff and doll-like.

"Come forward," the king commands in a powerful voice.

The queen Abishag comes down from the cart and approaches him. Her hair slides along the pavement of the street with a quiet rustle. Paulus stands behind her.

The king's eyes are calm and cruel. "You are a whore," he announces. "What does the law of the Lord command in such a case?"

A man in scholar's robes comes before the king with a large, bound Bible in his hands, unfastens its iron clasps and says: "The law commands stoning, your majesty."

Abishag crumples and falls to her knees. She says nothing in her own defense; it is as if all protestation is in vain.

"Whore," states the king. "It shall be done to you as the law commands. Take her to the place of execution and stone her."

Paulus now speaks. "Let us show mercy! Surely there is mercy for sinners!" But no one hears him.

"Whore!" says the king. Abishag shakes as if the word is a blow.

"No!" cries Paulus. "There is mercy for whores! It is written that the Lord Jesus said to an adulteress, 'Go and sin no more'!"

"Whore!"

"No! No! No! Don't speak to her this way! Speak to her kindly!" Paulus is shrieking the words, pouring them forth with every muscle in his chest, but he is like a man underwater. The words are going nowhere; they do not exist; all that comes from his open throat is a roar of silence.

"Whore!" Battered Abishag is on her face at the king's feet.

"Speak to her kindly! Speak to her kindly!" screams

Paulus.

They can't hear.

He wakes. The words *speak to her kindly* are stumbling childishly from his lips. His body is shaking from the cold, but his head is hot and wet. He feels his face with trembling fingers, and then his head, greasy and flea infested. His back and legs are cramped, his left foot numb. He untangles his bony limbs, straightens out his legs, and lets himself down on his back. He stretches out his arms. He can hear the blood shoosh, shoosh, shooshing through his head. Above him, a strip of star-washed night sky, slung between the houses that rise on either side of the alley, hangs like a banner.

Speak to her kindly. Where do the words come from? Onkel spoke them as he died. They must be from the Bible, but where, where, where?

Is my dream from God?

Paulus went home and slept the rest of the night. In the morning he opened Onkel's Bible and began to turn the pages. His mind was full of energy, but it was a centrifugal kind of energy that pulled him from page to page, from book to book, without allowing him to dig in somewhere and read. He read Onkel's glosses in the margins.

In the afternoon he went to military drill in the cathedral square. After dark he took his turn in the tunnel. Julius went down after him. It was quiet in the house. Paulus lay on the floor with a blanket roll under his head and a fragment of candle lit behind him. He opened the Bible again. He turned it once, twice, and on the page before him was the name Hosea, underlined messily by Onkel, and beside it the words *Paulus muss das lesen. Paulus needs to read this.*

Paulus remembered. This was Hosea, the young prophet who married the whore. The words came from this story.

First, he rushed ahead, looking for the words. There they were: *Behold, I will allure her, bring her into the wilderness, and speak to her kindly*. Then, he read the whole story.

The Lord tells the prophet Hosea to marry Gomer, the whore, because Israel has made herself a whore. Not content with the love and blessings of her husband, the Lord, Israel has given herself to the detestable gods of Canaan, the Baals and the Ashterah. On the hills, she has sacrificed to them and offered prayers. And the Lord is enraged, as a good husband is enraged who finds his wife in bed with different strangers, night after night.

The Lord sends her away. He removes his blessings from her. *There, go and see what your new lovers can do for you now. You committed adultery in my bed; go and make your own.* The Lord will make her miserable in her whoredom, and her lovers, the gods of Canaan, will be of no comfort, for they do not exist. The sweet taste of adultery will turn rancid in her mouth.

But it is not the end. The purpose of God's wrath on his adulterous wife is not to destroy her but to bring her back to himself. This is what Paulus sees for the first time. *Therefore, behold, I will allure her, bring her into the wilderness, and speak to her kindly.* The kind words of the Lord are the words of an offended husband to an unfaithful and punished wife. *Come back to me.*

Out in the wilderness, alone, naked, bereft of her trinkets and baubles, thirsty, dying, she will see the Lord again. She will remember him, and the love he had for her. She will remember that as his wife she was never hungry, or cold, or abused, that he always spoke gently to her and treated her with dignity. The whore will remember the warm bed and the loving words and the husband who was still there in the morning. She will wonder why she ever left.

The Lord, his wrath spent, his love hot, will speak kindly to her. The phrase was full of an ineffable tenderness. *Ich will freundlich mit ihr reden.* Paulus read it again and again. The Lord speaks kindly to the whore. He wants her back. She is his wife.

I must speak kindly to my adulterous wife. I must woo her home from the wilderness. I cannot do otherwise, for I too am a forgiven whore. The Lord spoke kindly to me. I remember the words.

Come, friend, eat with us.

MARGA WAS ASLEEP in a bedroom with seven other women, the wives of Jürgen the bodyguard. Jürgen had used her roughly that evening, in the presence of the others; she had resisted him, acting like a queen though she was not, and Jürgen had cuffed her on the face and bruised her lip and nose. When he was through with her, she had asked for something to eat. There would be nothing until the morning, he said, and laughed.

"You're not the wife of the king," he said.

"He treats all the new women this way," said one of the other wives to her after Jürgen Fromme left. "Don't feel bad."

But Marga felt very bad. She wept softly, from pain, and humiliation, and fear. She thought about Paulus. He was rising up out of the grave in her mind where she had buried him. Her inability to conceive was the result of the birth of Paulus' son. Her sudden citation of the sermon on the mount to counter an argument from the law of Moses was pure Paulus. Bockelson had sent her away without an ounce of compassion, and Fromme had beaten her. Paulus had never touched her except in love. And Paulus had come to find her. Marga dug in a small bag of personal things she had been allowed to bring with her, and brought up the tiny folded note.

Marga, I am here. In Münster. Do you remember me? I am your husband, Paulus, who loves you. I want you back as my wife.

Marga wept more, trying not to disturb the other wives of Jürgen Fromme. It seemed like they were used to weeping, for they ignored her.

Then the adulteress, lonely in the wilderness, hearing the kindly voice, will say: *I will go back to my first husband, for it was better for me then than now.*

CHAPTER 28: EASTER
March, 1535. Münster.

A woman approached the king of the New Jerusalem with a dead child in her arms. It was difficult to know how old she was; her eyes were sunken and edged with dark circles and her walk was slow and tired, but she could have been very young. The child was a boy, about five years old, with starvation-hollowed cheeks and open glassy eyes.

She was coming to Jan Bockelson as he sat near the old Town Hall on one of his thrice-weekly days of judgment, not on a throne but on a plain wooden chair, as he imagined the ancient judges of Israel to have sat in their gates hearing cases. This was a time to get close to the king, to ask him for a favor, to voice a grievance, or to just touch him and kiss his hand. As a demagogue he knew he had to give his people the illusion of intimacy.

The mother stood in a line, and when her turn came she held the frail corpse of her boy out to the king.

"My boy is dead." The tone of her voice was flat.

"My sister," said Bockelson. His eyes flashed bright, then tender, and he reached out for the child's body, which tumbled lightly into his arms like hollow reeds, except for the wobbling heavy head. He enfolded it in his arms and stared into the face. The small crowd of people, petitioners, guards, preachers, saw him begin to weep. The delicate features of his white face reddened and distorted and sobs shook him in his chair while the little emaciated body quivered. This display of grief and love unhinged the mother; she cupped a hand to each breast and uttered long, dry-eyed cries while the king wept.

And the hungry, childlike people joined in the grief, as if they had not seen emaciation and malnutrition until now. They were in symbiosis with Jan Bockelson; when he laughed, they laughed, when he cried, they cried; he was flesh of their flesh and mind of their mind, their king, their slave, their deliverer.

When this had gone on long enough, he stood and gave the boy back to his mother's arms, and spoke.

"Lord, God! See from heaven how the heathen rage! Show yourself mighty to avenge the blood of the innocent! Why should the heathen say, *Where is their God?*" The starvation of this child, in other words, was not the fault of Jan Bockelson but of the prince-bishop's besieging army. "Salvation will come by Easter!" He had been saying this for weeks. "The Lord will then reveal his strength in the sight of the nations. This suffering, which seems so deep at the present, will then be flooded over with joy and glory, and you will look back to this short time of testing and wonder whether it ever happened."

The people listened obediently. There was very little shouting and gesticulating any more, as there had been in the first flush of the kingdom's power. Jan Bockelson needed the shouting and devised ways of drawing it out. He could not live without their faith, and they could not live without his promises.

"I say to you that the salvation of the Lord will come by Easter! If it does not, I will die! In the cathedral square! The Swordbearer will behead me!"

It was a brilliant promise. It would cause the people to

forget their hunger for a few more days, and it would draw on whatever residue of passion they felt for him. They would now pray for the salvation of the Lord, not only for their own sake, but for the sake of their king's life. He had taken the whole burden upon himself.

The news of this announcement spread throughout the city almost as fast as a single man could walk from one gate to the other, and the people talked more than usual. Later that day a crew of carpenters was at work building an execution platform, directly in front of the royal platform by the cathedral.

Predictably, the level of zeal rose, and the cathedral square again became the place of expectation of the divine apocalyptic presence that it had been for so many months earlier. All through the week crowds milled nervously around the platform, sermons were preached, and prayers were offered for the city and the life of the king. More children died but their deaths were not noticed as much.

Paulus and Julius and Arndt debated the possible outcome of the king's death, should Jesus not return and should Bockelson really take himself to the chopping block. Arndt and Julius wanted to see the king's beheading. Julius thought that Bockelson's death would propitiate the prince-bishop, but Paulus disagreed.

"It's too late for his death to help us, I think. The people will keep following his dream even if he dies, but they will do it poorly, and there will be terrible confusion and civil war within these walls, with no one strong enough to stop it. And I don't believe the people will find mercy from the prince-bishop. He has too much to avenge, and the other princes who have paid for this siege want something to show for it. Blood, lots of blood."

"We'll be gone anyway," said Julius. "Sssst! Out through our hole."

"I don't want to see more blood," said Paulus.

"I do," said Arndt. "Bockelson's."

"Maybe Christ will really come," joked Julius.

"Maybe he will," said Paulus.

THEY PREPARED FEVERISHLY for Easter, and once again it seemed a good thing to be in Münster. The field captains drilled the fighting men in the cathedral square, anticipating the hour when the saints would be turned loose on the world. Paulus would have drilled, had he not volunteered for the great work that was going on next to it, the construction of several large armored gun-carrying wagons. He would rather swing a hammer than heft a pike. It seemed a contradiction to him that the city would need these imposing and terrifying wagons if deliverance were really coming from the Lord. Some whispered that it was not the Lord for whom Jan Bockelson waited, but an Anabaptist army coming from Holland.

EASTER OF 1535 came on the twenty-eighth of March. Even before the sun rose over the east wall the city was awake. People paced and lit small fires to warm their hands and their soup and drifted toward the cathedral square. Groups of women clustered together, for the promise of the king had given them new hope, and the sound of their voices was happy; children with bony legs and bare feet threw dirt clods and drew pictures in the ground with sticks. Men stood with their backs resting against the buildings. While they talked, or napped, or stood in silence, they could never forget for long that this was the day of salvation, nor could they keep from casting glances at the stake on the platform.

A few lucky horses still survived, and the bodyguards rode them through the streets as a symbol of confidence. But the king was not to be seen. He was in his house. Around him were the preachers and the highest courtiers, attentive and silent in their waiting. What, actually, were they waiting for? Did anyone know? Bockelson had never revealed it in detail. Indeed, the usefulness of Bockelson's theology was its imprecision. You could believe many things. And now the important thing was not so much what you believed, as that you believed; not how the deliverance would come, but that it would come.

Jan Bockelson had let himself drift into a semi-hypnotic state, and he sat in a relaxed posture in a chair that faced out a third storey window, and he did not move a muscle all day. The others kept quiet, as he had commanded, and tried to wait.

Von Waldeck inadvertently added to the suspense by firing a salvo of leaflets into the city shortly before noon. The reverberation of the guns got people up off their haunches, looking frightened and delighted at each other and up into the blue sky. In the room with the king, the advisors jumped and ran to the windows.

"Cannon, just cannon," said Knipperdolling. He was overwrought, contemplating his possible role as the executioner of the king. As usual, the leaflets lay on the ground unread.

Noon passed. It was a logical time for deliverance to come, and many had pinned their hopes on it.

A thunderstorm passed over the city and wetted the crowd. There was great excitement. Perhaps this was the cloud from which the Messiah would descend; the rumbling of thunder suggested the voice of the archangel. It went by and the people dried off.

Late afternoon was warm and humid, an afternoon for planting barley or rye, or for drinking cool beer. But they lived no longer by the rhythm of the earth. They discussed with overwrought interpretations and open Bibles the significance of a late afternoon deliverance. Appropriate, that the end of history would come at the end of the day.

Then dusk, and night. The fires flared again, the children went to sleep, the adults nodded off from hunger. God was surely testing the patient faith of his people. Some people were looking every now and then over the walls for a Dutch army. Christ would come at the eleventh hour. The fire of it would illuminate the night.

There was no precise stroke of midnight, since the mechanical clock in the Town Hall was out of order, but they all knew more or less when it had passed and when it was no longer Easter but the next day. Most of them, exhausted from the vigil, slept where they were. Some went home.

In the morning the carpenters were out again. This time they were dismantling the execution platform. The people awoke to the sounds of hammering.

"What are they doing?"

"Taking it down."

"What day is it?"

"Is the enemy still there?"

"Yes."

"They're taking it down. Where's the king? He must not know. He must be told!"

Some went to the tops of the wall, to see if the prince-bishop's army was still there, and it was. Many more, without any plan, formed in the streets and moved toward the king's residence. There he still sat. The others had finally slept, giving up their pious efforts to watch and pray with him, but Jan Bockelson had watched out the window all night. While the darkness was still thick, he had given the order to take down the platform where he had promised to have himself beheaded. As the awakened populace gathered outside and the sound of their inquiring voices grew louder, the preachers and nobles awoke too.

"It's morning," said Bernhard Rothmann dumbly.

Hermann Tilbeck looked out a window with bloodshot eyes and said, "The enemy is gone! Praise God!"

Rol, Knipperdolling, Heinrich Krechting, and several others looked from one to another and then at the king.

"No," said Knipperdolling. "The enemy is still there."

"Fools," said Bockelson. "You are fools like them. What did you expect?"

What did he expect them to expect? Had he not said that

the city would be delivered, yesterday? But none dared to speak so plainly.

"You are all – the whole city is – infatuated with the flesh and with what the eyes can see. You are fleshly, fleshly, fleshly! You are bellies and eyes and mouths and wombs." Bockelson ejected the words like bullets, through glistening lips. "It is of spiritual salvation I have spoken. I have seen this people lusting for a fleshly deliverance. But before the flesh can be saved, the spirit must be purged. After all that the Lord has done . . . to fail to perceive this . . . unbelievable."

The reconstruction. It had happened before. But this was once too much. There was no reserve of faith to draw upon as there had been in the past. There was no food, no glory, nothing to make the city seem like a grand place even though the predictions of its leader were failing. The momentum had vanished. As Bockelson addressed the whole people later in the morning there were audible shouts and murmurs. The king railed and raged at them and glared at them, and for the first time they glared back.

It was a turning point, just as the victory of August had been a turning point. Then he had fully won the hearts of the people, and now he lost them. Faith was not completely gone, but the monolithic obedience that had been the rock of Bockelson's kingdom was now full of cracks. They criticized him in public and were not arrested. Some of the most loyal subjects made requests for the evacuation of women and children, as starvation deaths mounted sharply and it became impossible to hide the fact that a generation of holy seed was dying. The king listened, morose and righteous, and gave permission for the west gate to be opened and for all the women and children who desired to do so to leave. At the appointed time about forty women with a larger number of children gathered at the gate. They had nothing to take with them but the clothes on their bodies. Knipperdolling was there with some guards to preserve order. The king arrived after keeping them waiting almost an hour past the time, and then the gate was opened. As the group left the king called after them:

"You are eternally lost, you fools! You walk from the kingdom of God into the arms of the devil! Tremble and weep and gnash your teeth, you are condemned!" And so on, until they were beyond the reach of his voice. Several, weeping pathetically, did return. Then the gate was closed.

This could have been the small trickle that begins a flood. The moral bond between Bockelson and his subjects was about to snap. But the prince-bishop blundered, as he had at the beginning, when he should have been firm and was not. After so many months he had learned to be firm, and now he could not be merciful. He had accepted the funds of the Imperial Council on condition that he receive nothing but unconditional surrender. There were to be no terms, since the people of Münster had put themselves beyond the pale of law and fair treatment. In this attitude, embittered by the bitterness of the Anabaptists and driven crazy by the sight of his still inaccessible cathedral, he decided to make an object lesson of the new refugees. Not more than an hour after the women and children had reached the siege lines – and Bockelson watched them from a turret on the wall, hoping for the worst – some knights on horseback came from the earthworks, riding so close to the wall that the observers could see the features of their faces. But attention was elsewhere. The riders carried, on four long poles, the severed heads of four women, open-eyed, loose-jawed, blood-matted, shoved the ends of the poles into the soft ground beyond the city's moat, where once vegetables had grown, and rode back to their camp.

"Majesty," said Knipperdolling, "shall I have them taken down?"

"No, it is the judgment of God. Let the people see and fear."

The heads still stood the next day, covered by birds.

CHAPTER 29: CAPTIVITY
May, 1535. Münster.

Paulus had become so accustomed to the feel of the solid stone underside of the city wall that he was surprised when he encountered, above him, a kind of damp, foul smelling rubble which came apart when he picked at it. He tore at the stuff in the dark and felt it come falling down at his feet, and the sensation of this, after the plodding handful by handful labor through the clay, was like flying after walking. He shouted hurrahs, whoops, and disjointed pieces of psalms, because it meant that he was past the wall and that above him was ground outside the city. He was not sure now whether he would leave the city; that depended on what happened with Marga. But it felt good to succeed at something, to finish something.

He crawled back through the tunnel with a bucket of the rock and gravel and showed it to Arndt, whose gopher face hung out over the opening.

"It's a good sign," Arndt said. "We're out."

But Arndt was sick. He coughed incessantly and had great difficulty catching his breath, and could not sleep. Paulus had noticed that when he walked his knees wobbled, as if there was not enough strength left in the legs to keep the bones straight. Arndt joked about himself, but he knew he was dying. He switched places with Paulus – Paulus offered to continue, but Arndt insisted – and disappeared into the hole. Paulus rubbed the grit off his hands and wiped his blackened face with a cloth that they kept in the kitchen.

It was early morning and everything was quiet. Paulus tiptoed into the room with the women and let himself down to his bruised knees, then he rolled onto his side and fell asleep. Ari was there, beside him.

There were three new women sleeping on the floor, since Julius had divorced two of his first wives and taken three new ones in marriage. People as far from the center of the city's power as Paulus and Julius did not know what had sparked the city's newest diversion: divorce. But the king's sudden divorcing of two of his wives had set off a wave of imitation, and within a few days men were divorcing and remarrying, and the clerk at St. Lambert's church was busy again with his book. As life became cheap, so did the moral bonds which had previously held Münster's polygamous marriages together. Unions became short, and men bartered wives almost like currency. There were marriages that lasted only for a night. The penalty for adultery and fornication was still death, as it had been since the rule of Jan Matthys, but there was no adultery in Münster, because there did not need to be. If you wanted someone, you simply married. Legally, it was the most moral city in Europe. In fact, it was a barnyard.

When the people were not changing partners at St. Lambert's church, they were hunting rats and cats. They had systems now for driving the pests into nets and corners, and they had recipes for cooking them; there was even a market where the slaughtered rodents hung by their tails and could be traded for other kinds of food. The women did most of this hunting. The men drilled in the cathedral square and then came home and sat or slept.

The king tried new ways to keep the people entertained. It was, after all, his specialty. There were elaborate dances in the cathedral square, with the courtiers strutting stiffly in their finery and the people watching, or pretending to watch.

"Look at them," whispered Arndt to Paulus, and he coughed. "They think they're dancing."

"The king is quite good, actually," replied Paulus, noting that Bockelson alone carried himself like an aristocrat in the midst of his makeshift aristocracy.

"But look, look at the Saltmaster! He stepped on that girl's foot!" Arndt's sputtering laughter quickly turned to racking coughs.

"Shh!" Paulus was afraid that someone would see Arndt laughing.

Dancing, and athletic events – footraces, fencing, wrestling. The king often won these events, and the people applauded him politely. Always, Paulus scanned the crowds for Marga's dark head, but she was never there, not even when the queens appeared. Was she sick, in trouble? Could it be that she was pregnant by the king? He began to fear.

The propaganda went on, too, without remission, and became more vapid and grotesque as Bockelson's kingdom decayed. One of the most memorable displays of theater was a fantastic parody of the Catholic mass, at which a well known half-wit named Karl, whom Herman Tilbeck kept around his household like a pet, was put in front of an entirely authentic simulation of the eucharistic table and commanded by the king to read mass. As he butchered the words, the people howled with laughter.

From the mass they went outside and fenced with swords, spears, and halberds. The Royal Tailor had been hard at work: there were new, colorful banners hung out the windows of the great houses around the cathedral square.

ARNDT IS LATE, thought Paulus, waiting in the middle of

the night for him to emerge from the tunnel with his last bucket of scourings. Paulus dozed, then woke, and thought again, *Arndt is late. Why is he taking so long*? Then he knew. All through the day, Arndt had coughed almost to the point of suffocation, and when each long bout ended his face was blue and there were flecks of blood on his lips. *He must be dead*.

Paulus did not want to enter the tunnel and find a dead man at its end. He waited in the kitchen and fought with his own mind. Eventually he let himself down and proceeded, feeling fearfully in the blackness. Arndt was dead, at the very end of the path; he lay face down on the rocky stuff they were pulling aside. Paulus spoke aloud to hear his own voice: "He's dead, dead." He returned to the mouth of the tunnel, got the rope they used to lift the bucket out, carried it back to Arndt's body, and tied it to his feet. He pulled Arndt through the tunnel, climbed to the kitchen with the rope, and tugged. He did not think he could do it, and he was prepared to wake Julius, but the body was extraordinarily light and he managed to hoist it up. All this was in the dark. He could not see Arndt's face and was glad for it.

Then, surprising himself, he went down to work. And as he channeled up toward the surface of the earth, he thought of Arndt and felt pity and sadness and a nostalgic sweetness. Arndt had not been a great man, or even a good man. He was ugly. He was selfish, lustful, and lewd. But he was funny, and he was humble enough to find himself funny. *Poor man, he was my friend*. It all felt so, so sad.

When morning came, Julius carried the dead body outside and they waited for what everyone called the Bone Wagon, a flat cart that four men pulled through the streets each day to collect the dead. They put him on it, and his two wives sat with their legs dangling off the back and went with him. By the law of the kingdom, they were required to marry again before the sun set, or face punishment.

"I liked that man," said Julius, as the Bone Wagon

vanished around the corner of the New Bridge street. "He helped me."

"It's good he died," said Paulus.

"Yes, he was suffering, it's good he died."

"If we get out through that stupid tunnel, it will be his doing. We owe it to him, don't we."

"I'm going to kill two of the prince-bishop's soldiers for Arndt," said Julius coldly.

Standing there, eulogizing a dead man. In the daylight, it appeared more clearly to Paulus that Arndt had been a very ordinary wicked man, and that there was little good to be said about him. But God would pass judgment. At the moment, Paulus felt a lot like Arndt; the legs that joggled on the Bone Wagon were pieces of Adam's humanity which death had conquered and claimed and which hell would probably now devour, and it seemed fitting to say some good things about the man, even if they did Arndt no good.

PAULUS HAD TO make contact with Marga. He had the feeling that everything was collapsing and that he would lose her in the confusion. On the nineteenth of May, he looked all morning for a scrap of paper, finally finding one in a puddle. By nightfall it was dry. He rubbed a piece of charcoal sharp on a stone and wrote.

> *New Bridge street, fourth house from the wall. There is a way out. Come with me. I am your loving husband. You are my Gomer, I am your Hosea.*

Now he had to get the letter to Marga. He spent several days loitering around the cathedral square, ostensibly observing the pathetic athletic events that the king presided over, but actually Paulus was watching the movements of the man who carried wood into the great merchant houses where the members of the court lived. He did not feel like asking Julius to do this errand for him again; Julius was quickly becoming more lonely and bellicose and speaking violently to everyone, talking about what he would do to the prince-bishop's soldiers when the time came.

One evening, having followed the man's movements all afternoon, Paulus trailed him into a dirty nameless alley in the southern part of the city and saw him duck into a space between two wooden buildings. Coming closer, he saw that the man was living under a leather awning nailed to the adjacent walls, with a piece of blanket for a door. Paulus poked his head in; smoke and stink hit his face.

The man was startled and looked up. He was old, perhaps in his forties. His face was mere skin draped over bone. Paulus felt pity for him, since the man undoubtedly thought he was being visited by a bodyguard, or a deacon, or someone who had found something wrong with his conduct.

"I come as a friend," said Paulus. The man cleared his throat and coughed a little. Now Paulus noticed that the man's right eye was blind.

"For what?" he said. They both knew that such an unsupervised meeting was illegal, but Paulus crouched and came through the opening, letting the blanket fall closed behind him. The man had stirred a pile of ashes toward the back of his shelter, from which a ribbon of smoke curled up. He was alone.

"For this," said Paulus and held out his letter, folding into a tiny square. "Some time ago you took a paper to the queen Abishag. Could you do it again, once more?"

He shook his head. "The queen Abishag, she is no more."

"What?"

"There is no queen Abishag. The king divorced her."

"And where is she? How is she?"

"A sad story," the old man replied, twisting his head unnaturally to bring his good eye to bear on Paulus. "And why should I tell you?"

"I'm her husband, her real husband."

"Ah. *That's* a sad story."

"Please tell me."

"The king divorced her, and Jürgen the bodyguard married her. She's with him."

"Where?"

"Oh, next to the cathedral square."

"Is she well?"

"I don't know. Jürgen is hard on his wives, he keeps them pretty well locked away, uses them often. I place wood by her door but I have never gone in."

Paulus had his forehead in his hands, and his head was aching. It was hard to think again, to start new, to absorb the reality of a situation that was not as he had imagined it for so long. His life was a tenuous fragile stick house, and the only thing that held it up was every tiny piece being in its predictable place. He was frightened that things were not as he had planned. He felt like giving up, running home and into the hole he had dug. But for Marga, he had to try.

"Will you?" He held the letter out.

"Why not?" said the one-eyed man. "They can only torture me, kill me, and string the pieces of me from the cathedral." He chuckled and took it from Paulus.

"Not much to worry about, with hell coming. Thank you."

As Paulus went out, the man returned to his fire.

THE KING WAS running out of things to do. In May, the play was over but the audience was still stuck in the theater.

Bockelson restructured the government of his kingdom by appointing twelve dukes and assigning them to twelve districts of the city. He renamed the gates. Then, he called upon whatever faith was left in the hearts of the people, and in his own, and reenacted the ecstatic run through the city which he had performed the year before. Naked, with only the gold orb and chain around his neck, he went about the city preaching, saying that the time was at hand for their deliverance, that the testing of God was almost over, and that God would turn the very cobblestones to bread to feed them. The drama of such a display was somehow diminished; the people were jaded and had seen too much nakedness and heard too much preaching, and the effect was not what Bockelson would have desired. Still, incredibly, the old magic worked on certain of the inner circle of women, including some of the queens, who followed him weeping with joy. The small procession ended in the cathedral square, where Bockelson sent himself into a trance – it had been a long time since he had done this – and the women gathered around him singing and praising God. A hysteria built among them as they waited for the cobblestones to become bread; desperate mothers congregated with their children around the prone king and explained to the children what was about to happen.

Late in the afternoon the king regained his consciousness and went, with Divora and Bernhard Rothmann, back to his palace. From his bedroom window he watched the people milling in the square, still waiting. Some cried in frustration and scratched the pavement with their fingernails.

"There will be no bread, will there?" said Bockelson.

No one answered. Divora sat on the edge of the bed and Rothmann in a chair against the far wall.

"Why does God play games with me?"

"Majesty!" said Rothmann.

"Speak honestly, brother Rothmann. I tire of the fawning and adulation. I know how you all hide from me your inner thoughts."

"Honestly, majesty? How honestly?"

"Tell me I am a fool, a fraud, a false prophet, if that's what you think. That honestly."

Rothmann approached him.

"Our cause is righteous. But it is possible that we have misinterpreted the scriptures in some points."

"But what about the Spirit that filled me this morning? Like a fire in my bones! And the only release was to speak the word he put on my lips. Now, having spoken it through me, he refuses to honor it. What have we done wrong? What have we neglected to do?"

Rothmann tried again. "Is it possible that we have not fully understood the scriptures?"

"God in heaven, the scriptures, the scriptures! You keep harping on this book, brother Rothmann! Haven't we gone beyond a mere book? What is there in the scriptures that we have not heard directly from my mouth, or felt in our souls?"

"Perhaps many things."

"Such as . . ."

"I tremble before the king."

"I commanded you to speak as you think."

"It is not easy after so many months of speaking as *you* think."

Their eyes met, and Bockelson's gaze was angry, but Rothmann had gained courage with speech and did not wince under it.

"You told the people that deliverance would come by Easter, and it did not."

"You didn't understand the spiritual meaning of it."

"And what about this one? Will you tell them now that you meant spiritual bread?"

Bockelson left the window and walked about the room. He stopped by Divora and kissed her on the forehead and said, "My sweet and glorious queen." Then he paused by the large copy of the Bible that lay open on a reading stand. He flipped through some of its pages, reading none.

"No, brother Rothmann, no talk about spiritual bread. God has deceived me this time."

"If God deceives us, then let us surrender not only this city but our faith as well."

"Fool, your views are still from the books, are they not?

You pass yourself off as a prophet and a preacher of the living God, but you have never grown up beyond the books. You have never felt the heat of the word of God within. Would you withhold from almighty God the right to deceive? Do you not understand that he is bound by no laws, not ours, not even his own?"

Rothmann gulped.

"There is no speaking to you, my king. You seal my mouth with your power. I defer to your wisdom."

"Leech," sneered the king. "I know what you all think. You think that I am mad. You remain here because you cannot leave. And I remain king because none of you has the courage to voice his doubts. So be it, it is the hand of God upon you. God promised bread, but he looked upon the heart of this people and he saw only lust and greed and doubt. So he withdrew his promise. If he cannot conquer this people with mercy he will chastise them with the stick. And if you had shown some faith, perhaps the cobblestones would now be bread. Now go."

Rothmann backed out of the room and closed the door.

"Come, my love," said the king to Divora, "take off your clothes for me." He went to the curtains and pulled them shut.

AFTER THIS FRESH disappointment, many clamored to leave the city. With fierce imprecations, the king gave permission for the Holy Cross Gate to be open for a few minutes each day so those who wished to throw themselves upon the mercy of the prince-bishop could leave.

But there was no mercy with the prince-bishop. The Münsterite men who reached the siege lines were immediately executed and their heads put on poles all around the city. The women and children were refused access to the camp, pushed back into the zone between the city and the siege lines. Coming back to Münster, they were pelted with stones and cries of "Go away, apostates!" and worse. They wandered in the green meadow, and slept in the open at night, and foraged in last year's vegetable gardens for roots. Eventually they were eating grass. No one else left after this.

CHAPTER 30: GOMER
June, 1535. Münster.

Franz von Waldeck and one of his field captains, Wilkin Steding, reined in their horses near the entrance of a wooden blockhouse and dismounted. As they approached the door, two guards lifted the iron latch and stepped aside. The bishop and the captain bent their heads and entered.

Inside, illuminated only by natural light that came through slats in the log ceiling, was a man on his knees, leaning over a model city made of earth. He had a trowel in his hand. When the prince-bishop entered, he stood.

"Your grace," he said and bowed. He was dirty and ragged and exhaustion showed in his eyes.

Von Waldeck did not reply, but glared at the earth city on the ground and then walked slowly around it. "This is north, I take it," he remarked and stuck his swordpoint in the ground.

"Yes, your grace, the Holy Cross Gate."

"It appears very accurate, my lord," said Steding, as the prince-bishop continued to circle the model city.

"I was stationed at the Holy Cross Gate," said the man with the trowel. "I worked on the earthworks here, and here, and the armory is here – " the man was frantically climbing among his dirt buildings and walls, trying to impress the prince-bishop.

"Silence," growled von Waldeck. "I believe you. I believe that you know the city well, and that your model is true. You say that this key unlocks a door near the Holy Cross Gate." He held up a large key made of wood.

"Yes, your grace. I fashioned it myself, from oak. As I told you, I am a cabinetmaker by trade. The key is a duplicate of the one I carried at my side while I guarded that door."

"Tell us more about this door," said Steding.

"A small hatchdoor near the base of the gate. From there a tunnel leads into the gatehouse."

"With access from there to the city."

"Yes, your grace."

"And guards?"

"Several, of course, on the gatehouse wall. But they can't see the door below. One guard in the tunnel."

Franz von Waldeck scratched his black beard. "Tell me again about the gun wagons."

"Sixteen of them, your grace. Four-horse wagons. We constructed new wheels for them from oak rafters, and then sheathed them in iron. The entire body of the wagon is also sheathed in iron. Racks of muskets are arranged all around, pointing out through slots. They have their fuses united, so they can be fired together. The horses are likewise armored."

"Good heavens," said the prince-bishop.

"If they were to break out of the city, your grace, it would be difficult to stop them from going wherever they chose," said Steding. "I wouldn't want to send my soldiers up against them."

"Where are they now?"

The cabinetmaker answered, "In the cathedral square, circled like a fortress."

"We must take the city before they decide to bring the gun wagons out into the country. Cabinetmaker Gresbeck, you have bought a reprieve from execution. For now. We are going to test your word, however. Tonight you will take the captain to your little door and show him. You will place your key into the lock and show him that it works. Then you will be freed. If any part of what you have told me is false, you will be executed."

"Yes, your grace. Everything is true."

Von Waldeck stepped into Gresbeck's mud and sand city, with his feet in the cathedral square.

"Bockelson is in the house of Melchior von Büren, is that not true?"

"Yes, your grace," answered Gresbeck.

"With his whores?"

"Yes, your grace."

"I will execute him here," muttered the prince-bishop, sliding his sword into the earth in the Market Square by St. Lambert's church. "This is where he first defied my authority."

AS JUNE BEGAN, the people of Münster were learning to make soups of leather, old paint, and tree leaves. The kettles boiled at all hours and the people filled their pots as they wished and put the nourishless stuff into their bellies. There was some relief when, by command of the king, the storerooms of the nobles were opened for public distribution, but all this, when spread among the eight thousand inhabitants, was not much. It only prolonged their starvation. The remaining horses, used for ceremonial occasions, were slaughtered. A strict ration was put in place even for the king's friends.

It happened almost daily that the king and the Swordbearer marched to the platform in the cathedral square with some poor wretch who had broken a law. There was only one form of punishment: death. The dukes did their job: men who met together were arrested, women who disobeyed their husbands were arrested, children who stole were arrested. Then the drums beat and the women assembled and the entourage climbed the platform to the black-stained chopping block. Jan Bockelson performed many of these executions himself, once upon one of his own wives, Elisabeth Wantscherer. For especially heinous crimes, the victim's body was quartered and the sections fixed to the gates. But it did no good. The people were not in love any more with life. They had seen too much.

The prince-bishop too had his problems. He and von Dhaun debated their strategy endlessly: Von Dhaun still believed that starvation would bring an effortless surrender, but the prince-bishop was worried. They considered Gresbeck's plan many times. The money from the *Kreistag* would soon dry up; several of his cannon had already been sent back to their suppliers; the mercenaries were bored and itching for blood and booty. Von Waldeck wanted to attack.

Paulus, by the middle of June, was seriously preparing for death. He was no longer simply gaunt; he was listless, and for long periods of time lay staring into space. The people that lived in the house no longer talked much with each other; they had retreated into themselves. Julius Fettbauch was hardly ever around, but spent his time near the armory and on the walls, glaring out at the enemy. Paulus had stopped digging because he was afraid he would break into the open air and the scheme would be detected; he did not care much, anyway. But he had grown to enjoy the quiet and the cool of the tunnel, and went into it often at night when the others were sleeping, and listened for hours to the sound of his own breathing.

He thought about the woodcarrier, and whether his last letter had reached Marga.

He thought about Onkel, and he tried to remember the old man's words and teachings. He thought about death, and weighed various outcomes of his situation against death to see which he would prefer.

He thought about Marga's face and its features, and the shape of her figure, and the smell of her cheek, and the sound of her voice in his ear.

ON THE TWENTY-FOURTH of June, Paulus stood in line at the soup kettle. There was no strength at all in his body; the remaining strings of muscle that held him together felt like paper. He was wondering, like a scholastic theologian with an axiom, what was in the kettle, with its grayish color and solid matter that swirled in the bubbling surface. Sawdust . . . twigs . . . cloth . . . bones.

Someone touched him on the elbow. It was the woodcarrier.

"Something from your wife," he said and pressed an object into Paulus' hand. Then he was off.

Paulus left the soup line and went home. Two women sat and talked – whose wives they were he could not remember. Everyone looked alike now. He went upstairs. The thing in his hand was heavy and solid and wrapped in a piece of cloth. He untied the cloth and found three things: a hard dry piece of cheese about as large as an egg, a bone with a little meat still clinging to it – probably horse, he thought – and some papers rolled and tied in a tube, like the ones he had sent Marga. The food made the saliva flow stinging under his tongue; the papers made his heart pound. He put it all down, and let his forehead rest against the floor.

"Oh God, thank you," he said.

Oh God, finally a great miracle has happened in Münster. The pagan prophet has been screaming at heaven for miracles, and his gods of blood and iron have been mute. But you, God, the one true God, have answered your suffering servant with fire.

He broke the cheese into two pieces, placed one in his mouth, and slid the string off the roll. It was, as he had known, his fire from heaven, a letter from Marga. It was written on real, smooth paper in Marga's careful handwriting. Luminous summer light fell through the single window of the room and enabled him to read.

Paulus, my first, beautiful husband. I love you, I long for you,

I give myself back to you with repentance and subjection and loyalty. I will come to you, at your house, on June 25. We will leave this dark place, if God wills. Take me away, Paulus. Your Gomer. June 22.

Paulus felt the happiness of heaven.

He ate the cheese slowly, taking small pieces and allowing them to melt inside his mouth. It was stale and spoiled and delicious beyond comprehension. With each bite he thanked God silently. He could feel his body leaping upon the nourishment and soaking it up. Then, the meatbone. But this he wrapped again in the napkin and put inside his shirt. Asserting that he had a future. For so long he had lived like everyone else in Münster, rabidly, as if each day were the last and there would be no others, but now he had a hope and a tomorrow and he would begin again to live like a real human being, with history in front of him. Marga's letter was dated June 22. Today was the twenty-fourth. Tomorrow he and Marga would leave.

CHAPTER 31: ARMAGEDDON
June, 1535. Münster.

The day of judgment that the city had brought upon itself began on the twenty-fifth of June, while Paulus was asleep. On the previous day, the heavens had pelted the city and its plain with tumultuous wind, driving rain, and egg-sized hail. The guards on the walls were wet and lax.

It began before midnight. Up to the Holy Cross Gate, in padded shoes and muffled armor, and led by Wilkin Steding and the refugee Anabaptist Heinrich Gresbeck with his key, marched about four hundred picked mercenaries. They swam the outer moat silently, entered Gresbeck's tunnel and overcame the tunnel's single guard, and then methodically butchered the sentinels on the inner wall and crossed it. Still padded, and still undetected, Steding's force crept southward through the city toward the cathedral square. There – so the plan went – they would seize the main armory and the gun wagons and then return to open the Holy Cross Gate for Wirich von Dhaun's main army, three thousand strong, waiting on the plain to the north.

For a while it went well. Steding's men overwhelmed the

guards at the cathedral and commandeered several large guns, which they trained across the cathedral square in case of counterattack. But now, before they could return to the Holy Cross Gate, the plan went to pieces. Trumpets began to sound in different parts of the city – along the Market Square street, and from Bockelson's own palace, and from the armory of St. Johann. Voices reverberated metallically through the damp air. To the mercenary soldiers huddled in the dark cathedral, the new sound of women's voices singing songs, drifting through the night, was eerie and outlandish.

"WAKE UP, WITCH!" shouted Jürgen Fromme to Marga, and he took her by the hair and pulled her head roughly. She gasped and tried not to scream.

"Why? What's wrong?" she asked.

"An attack."

"Oh dear God, no," she said softly. "Paulus." *God, what are you doing?*

"You will come with me and hold my matchstick," said Fromme to her. "To the cathedral square we go." He hoisted his musket onto his shoulder. He unrolled a length of fuse rope and tied one end of it to his own belt and the other end around Marga's waist.

He woke his other wives in the same manner, and in a minute he and his little bevy of women were running through the streets to the cathedral square.

THE TRUMPET THAT called them to battle woke Paulus, but it sounded different from the drills. It was hurried and fractured. Ari lifted her head and groaned. Julius came running through the room.

"Up, up," he said to them. He kicked his wives to wake them. "Paulus, up. It's time to fight."

It was the day he was supposed to meet Marga, and the

prince-bishop had chosen it to attack. *God, what are you doing?*

"Out to the wagons," Julius was saying to his wives. Paulus reached for his shoes, such as they were, but Julius kicked them away, across the room to some dark corner. "No time for that, Paulus. Time to fight. Let's get going." Julius' whole life had spiraled down to this one moment.

Julius kicked Ari from behind and took Paulus by the sleeve of his shirt, and out they went into the New Bridge street. Others were doing the same. Paulus looked down the street, up the street, back at the house, with a feeling that he might not see the place again. Even this squalid place in the city of death had become home for him.

This was not a drill. Everyone sensed it. Their steps were quick, their words whispered, their eyes nervous. In a ghostly procession they went to their posts.

What will I do with a pike in my hands?

The diffused pinging of musket fire now reached Paulus' ears, as did the sound of many human voices, like the loud rustling of leaves or rushing of a brook. In the midst of it he heard a crow cawing. The bird was angry for being awakened in the middle of the night; it was living a normal life, and even if the city burned to the ground it could fly away.

Julius delivered Paulus to the arsenal, where he would be watched by the guards to make sure he found his way to the battle line.

"He doesn't want to fight," said Julius. "See that he does."

The guard had a deep, dry voice, and was already sweating. "We won't have to, brother Fettbauch. The bishop will do that." He issued Paulus an iron-tipped pike. That was all he got. There were a few helmets and other pieces of defensive armor in the city, but they had all been given away already. He was wearing only a threadbare shirt that hung down halfway between his hips and his knees, and his trousers. Paulus allowed himself to be carried with the hot flow of humanity toward the battle, half running with them all, feeling dizzy in the dark, trying to keep his weapon out of the way. The upheld points of the pikes clacked together above them, dry, dead, and bony sounding.

"HERE THEY COME!" spat Wilkin Steding with irritation. He cursed.

"How many?" asked another nearby.

"One hundred, two hundred, maybe," said Steding's aide, a young page named Johann von Twickel. But it was hard to tell, because the torches that the Anabaptists carried as they gathered across the cathedral square magnified and distorted everything.

"They seem to be clustered around the St. Margaret's Chapel, my lord," said von Twickel.

"Give them a volley," ordered Steding.

The mercenaries fired two cannon blasts against the Anabaptist position, but both balls struck glancing blows on the thick stone walls of the chapel and whined on aimlessly down the street. Almost immediately, from the chapel, came a counterblast. A muzzle flash, a deep sulphuric cough, and then the crashing mayhem of a direct hit on a small knot of mercenary soldiers. Cursing, and shouting, and cries of pain and dying.

"They're armed over there!"

"Do they have more guns?"

"We need to move," said Steding. "We can't allow ourselves to be trapped in here. They may have guns trained on us from every direction."

So Steding suddenly took his invading force out from the cathedral. With torches extinguished and feet still padded, they headed into the dark, away from St. Margaret's chapel, into the southern part of the city, carrying their wounded comrades on their shoulders. They still had not reestablished communication with von Dhaun's main army.

"WHERE DID THEY go?" shrieked Heinrich Krechting, the brightest military mind in Jan Bockelson's kingdom. He had around him now several hundred eager Anabaptist warriors, fairly well armed and angry, and he had been ready to launch an assault on the invaders in the cathedral when it became evident that they were not there any more. "Find them!"

Runners went out into the streets and alleys that radiated from the cathedral square.

Jan Bockelson, dressed half in night clothes and half in royal robes, and with the golden orb of the world pierced by two swords – the symbol of his messianic authority – dangling from his neck on its chain, thundered up to Krechting in a wagon pulled by six men. He jumped out.

"What is happening?"

"Your majesty, it seems that several hundred of the prince-bishop's mercenaries have entered the city. We are searching for them."

"You will find them, and kill them."

"Certainly, your majesty, certainly."

"And we will guard and arm the wagons," added Bockelson.

STEDING'S FORCE WOUND through the streets. Their location could hardly be kept a secret now, for along the streets the awakened residents heard them and began pelting them from above with bricks and stones and boards. Krechting and Bockelson and Dusentschuer and Knipperdolling, all together now with the pursuing Anabaptist defenders, found them along Margaretstrasse. Steding had really lost his way and found himself locked in an alley with no exit and threatened with annihilation. Almost the entire armed force of the Anabaptists, the eight hundred or so healthy males left in the city, now pressed upon them from the street, while maniacal women threw things on them from above. Steding cursed and cursed and cursed. Why couldn't von Dhaun hear the commotion and firing and simply storm the wall?

Still, he must be a soldier. If he were to die here in the dirt and the dark, he would die fighting.

"Musketeers, here!" he called. He placed his musketeers to the sides, and in the center, his pikemen. The defile was narrow. Most of his men were piled up behind, in the alley, waiting to replace the men in the front when they died. The Anabaptists, he could tell, were massing just out of sight, around a curve in the street.

In the very front of Bockelson's line was Jürgen Fromme, with Marga tethered to him like a dog. Anabaptist women, free and strong spirits that they were, moved in and among the male warriors as they pleased, and many even took up arms and fought. Fromme's large musket was loaded, and the fire in his firebox was hot, and his little pouch of powder was at the ready.

"Let me go," pleaded Marga.

"Never," he said.

"We're all going to die!" she insisted.

Fromme laughed. "We're going to win! We're going to slaughter these heathen, beginning right here, and march to Rome!"

"I have another husband!" she shouted, defying the din. "He's here, he's here, he's come for me. I must go to him!"

Krechting's command rang out: "Now with the Lord's help, we put our enemies to flight!" And the condensed line moved out at a run around the street-curve to face Steding's line. Marga tried to hide her body behind Fromme's. And she felt the large, lean muscles of his back and shoulders contract as he lifted the muzzle of his weapon.

ONLY A FEW YARDS away, Paulus stood massed with the other Anabaptist pikemen. He had been trained for this. On the command to attack, he was to march in lockstep with his fellows toward the enemy line, with his left hand forward on the spear and his right hand behind; upon contact, he was to thrust at the legs and feet of the enemy, while the man next to him would thrust at the faces. On the command to hold, he was to brace the butt of his pike on the ground and kneel.

How strange, that this killing drill was rolling through his mind. He had no intention of killing. What would he do when the time came? *Onkel, what should I do?* Had the angry brother in Wesel been right, that there was a time when every man would fight? What a hellish, unearthly scene it was! The women screamed, and the men roared, and the torches in the hands of moving men sent fractured planes of light back and forth across the heads and the rising houses along the street and the shining spear heads. Yet, in the middle of it all, there was a horrifying, calm rationality. Both sides were preparing to kill and to die. This, then, was war. This was the world's judge, and god, and scripture.

In the cacophony, Paulus heard a high, angry female voice. It sounded like Marga.

"Now with the Lord's help we put our enemies to flight!" cried Krechting, and Paulus was pulled along by the advance of his unit. Around the corner, dimly, brokenly, he saw the faces of the mercenary soldiers. *Was that Marga? Onkel, what do I do?*

At close, murderous range, the musketeers fired, and the sound of it in the confines of the street was like a thunderclap in an iron box. Balls slapped against walls, and the wounded cried out and fell and then moaned. The mercenaries, better trained and more desperate, sent their pikes out first, through the smoke.

Marga screamed at the noise. She felt a huge tug as Jürgen Fromme's body sank to the ground, and she saw with a mixture of horror and relief that he was dead. Part of his skull had been carried away by a musket ball, and Marga had been sprayed by his blood and tissue. Trembling, she sank to the ground to protect herself and pulled at the leash that still held her to him.

And she saw Steding's pikemen advancing through the smoke.

Paulus saw them too. He braced his spear against a cobblestone and put his right knee on the ground. Then he caught a glimpse of Marga, standing in the smoke and pulling convulsively on her tether *Get down, get down.*

He did not see the pike-point coming; it caught him on the left shoulder, with animal horselike strength behind it, and spun him sideways, carrying him away from his pike, tearing it out of his hands, and threw him back several yards before muscle and ligament tore and he fell. There was no pain, but his whole body simply went limp. And he fainted away.

Now, suddenly, the Anabaptists broke and ran. They lost their nerve because Steding had sent part of his force through the houses, and around behind the Anabaptists, and had attacked them from the rear as well at from the front. Steding had saved his force. He found a secure defensive position, and licked his wounds.

It was still dark, though the nights were short in late June. Jan Bockelson opened negotiations with Steding, offering freedom and pardon in exchange for a humble plea for forgiveness. Steding had no intention of asking for Jan Bockelson's forgiveness, but he needed time – time for the dawn to arrive, and time for his servant Johann von Twickel to get to the north gate and call in von Dhaun's army.

Von Twickel had navigated his way back to the Holy Cross Gate and had managed to scramble to the top of the wall. There, as dawn arrived, he called to the waiting army on the plain. At this signal, von Waldeck's three thousand soldiers stormed the walls, pried open the Holy Cross Gate, and were inside the city. The dam had broken. Faced with overwhelming enemies, exhausted, starving, and drained of faith, the Anabaptist army that had gathered in the night broke apart. A couple hundred stayed by Krechting and took refuge in the circled gun wagons in the cathedral square, but everywhere else the sack of the city began. Where Anabaptists fought at all, they fought alone, or by twos and threes.

The bishop's soldiers had been waiting many months for their chance to plunder a wealthy city. Now they found nothing but a ruin. Munster's king had already wrung all the wealth out of it. It made them angry, and they vented their anger on the impoverished citizens through murder, torture, and rape.

This futile plundering allowed the survivors of Jan Bockelson's kingdom to gather in the cathedral square. Here, in a concentrated mass, they huddled in their wagon fort, as Bockelson and Knipperdolling, by a titanic effort, brought some order to the frantic crowds. Again, furniture came tumbling out of the buildings, tables, cabinets, chests, full length mirrors, even the beds of the queens with the pastel bedclothes fluttering. Women herded the children to the center of the wagons and sat them on the ground.

Bernhard Rothmann stood on a crate and read martial psalms in his magnificent voice. Knipperdolling paced from place to place, shouting unnecessary orders; he had the look of a cornered animal. Bernt Krechting and his brother Heinrich sat together with their backs against the south side of the cathedral, out of the main path of activity; all the life and fire had gone out of them. Divora and the other wives of the king worked side by side with the other people building the barricade. Divora's dark hair fell uncombed about her shoulders and her dress was stained with sweat under the arms.

Bockelson's women served him faithfully, pathetically, to the end. These were the women who had been the heart and soul of the New Jerusalem from its rowdy origins and had brought Jan Matthys to power and had made a king of Jan

Bockelson with their cheers and love and had endured hunger and rationing with patience, women once nuns or girls or housewives and now saints in the city of God. They were starving and sick and moved like arthritic old women, but they did their best.

Jan Bockelson stood in the center of the square, near the children, royal looking, with his hands behind his back and the golden orb of the world hanging conspicuously from his neck. Still on stage, still performing, still having fun.

PAULUS AWOKE, AND raised himself on his elbows. Bodies lay around him. It was still dark. His left shoulder throbbed.

Where was Marga? He crawled to the large body on the street. There was still a cord attached to the dead man's belt, but Marga's end was loose. At least she had not died here in the hail of bullets.

Now Paulus brought his knees under him, like an animal. Now he stood.

He could not find her in the city; it was too large, and he was too weak. Nor could she find him. The only rational thing to do was to go to his house and hope that she came there.

Somehow, Paulus tottered through the back streets without being found and got home.

Paulus reached his house before the companies began their looting in earnest, or he would have been caught in the streets and killed. It was strange to find it completely empty, with the floor littered as always with clothes and blankets, but no human beings. He sat first in the place he usually slept, and looked at the wound in his shoulder. The pike-point had caught him in the hollow place just above the armpit, and stuck, and coming out had opened a gash upward. It was ugly, and it still oozed blood, but Paulus knew it was not serious. If Marga came, he would be alive to greet her.

But what in the world were the chances of her keeping

her appointment with him, with the whole city in an uproar? Would she survive? Would she remember?

He took the meatbone from his shirt and pried its fragments of meat loose with his teeth.

The plunderers were coming down the street, singing and shouting. He ran for the kitchen, climbed over its tangle of debris, pulled aside the piece of floor that they kept over the tunnel, and went in. He placed the floor carefully over the opening above him and waited in the dark. Men entered the house; he could hear their feet. He heard throwing, and clubbing, and breaking sounds. They came to the kitchen, and Paulus heard the whole pile of stuff that filled it being tugged and searched. Hard boots stood directly above him. One man spoke to another about how dirty this place was, and how its people lived like pigs, and how the place stank. Paulus was ashamed when he heard it.

They never detected that the floor had a trap door, and they left after venting their anger for another half minute on anything they could find, with much crashing noise. Paulus took a deep, deep breath. The wound stung and pulsated.

IT WAS ALMOST noon before Wirich von Dhaun reorganized his pillaging forces. The bands had combed the city block by block and house by house, finding little. Only when the two parts of the army, from the north and the south, had mingled and merged in a loose ring around the central marketplace did von Dhaun and his undercaptains begin to sort the companies and hoist the battle flags. Then the soldiers found their way to their units.

Wilkin Steding rushed up to the prince-bishop on his horse.

"They wish to surrender, my lord."

"Those among the wagons?"

"Yes."

"Is the king among them?"

"Reports differ. We don't know."

"Guard the perimeter! This pretender must not be allowed to escape. Allow those in the wagons to surrender. Take their arms."

The pitiful Anabaptist rabble came out, after so many months, to face the prince-bishop of Münster. He looked at them and was filled with wrath at their stupidity and stubbornness, and at the trouble and expense they had caused him.

"Wirich," he said to his commander. "Identify the leaders and hold them. Spare the women and children. Kill the rest."

So the slaughter began anew, with muskets cracking and swords flailing on the heads of the now defenseless Münsterites. They ran away, if they could, down the streets, or fell dead in their own blood in the cathedral square, while the women and children fell to their faces in horror and wept.

The king was not there. One mercenary found the golden orb on the pavement, and swung it above his head in triumph. The prince-bishop saw the glint of it and said to von Dhaun:

"I want that thing."

The mercenaries chased the Anabaptists up and down the streets, and into the houses where they fled for protection. Von Dhaun let them go; they had done their work well and deserved their fun. He called for food from his supply wagon and his servants spread a nice meal for him and von Waldeck, which they ate just outside the big west door of the cathedral, in glaring sunlight.

Some small cells of Münsterite fighting men, those who had not ended up in the wagon fort, survived and made ferocious, futile stands in alleys and dining rooms and street ends. Julius Fettbauch was with several others, still armed and free. All through these last hours he had fought his best, trying to recapture the profound ecstasy he had experienced on the wall in August. He knew it was the end, but he wanted to be noticed and praised by the king once more. He was now a tall, large-boned man; drill and a new identity had given him a swaggering way of walking, and starvation and the certainty of death had made him mean. Jan Bockelson's kingdom, at least for him, had kept its promise to make new men.

But they found themselves cornered against the bank of the Aa river in a place where it had been channeled between stone and mortar walls. Von Dhaun's greedy soldiers came at them from two sides. Julius Fettbauch looked frantically for the king. He would have to make his last stand before himself as the audience. It was a vicious defense they made, for they were well armed and skilled, and several of the mercenaries went limping away from the skirmish before it was over. At the last, only Julius was left fighting; the others were dead or wounded on the ground, and his lonely sword swung to and fro while he hummed in a sing-song to its rhythm. They stabbed him several times before he fell into the river.

"Tough fighter," said a mercenary to his fellow.

"Crazy fighters, all of them, it's not easy fighting with crazy men, they don't act the way they should."

"What was he saying . . . that one?" pointing to the corpse of Julius Fettbauch, middle class goldsmith, now floating in the river.

"Some kind of poem, I think . . . *Since you hurt and killed my wife, Come here let me take your life* . . . something like that."

"Crazy. But he fought like a real man."

THE WOMEN SIMPLY ran, and the soldiers had great fun chasing them down, slapping them around or raping them, and then herding them back to the center of the city. Paulus dared not venture too far from the hole. He had listened to the battle in the cathedral square, had heard it end, and surmised that people would again be coming up the street and possibly into the house. He hid in the kitchen and peered out, and scenes of death and bestiality played themselves out on the street, scenes which he was powerless to prevent and from which he averted his eyes. But he had to be there if Marga came.

CHAPTER 32: ALMOST
June, 1535. Münster.

Paulus, catlike, waiting. Three times, rampaging invaders enter his house, find nothing, smash things. Paulus slips into his hole, pulls the covering over it, waits. Outside, in the street, periods of silence alternate with eruptions of voices and screams.

Wait for Marga. Wait for Marga. You can't find her if you go out into the streets. Trust God.

Another spasm of violence coming up the street. Mercenary soldiers chasing women and children. Men's voices, laughing, yelling foul profanities. Women's shrieks. Then, above the other sounds, a high pitched, desperate call:

"Pa - a - u - u - lus!"

Paulus springs for the door. Several women, among them Marga, run before a line of the prince-bishop's black-armored riders. The riders overtake them. Bloody fists thrust deep into heads of hair, shaking, dragging, capturing. Paulus sees Marga. She sees him coming out from his house. Their eyes meet.

"Marga!" Paulus cries.

An armed man on horseback bears down on Marga, and he has her suddenly by her hair. Her feet drag along the street and she screams. Paulus runs to her and wraps his arms around her. He is already logically and lucidly aware that he has lost her. With his weight he slows the horseman. The horseman curses at him. But Paulus' arms are around Marga's body.

"Forgive me!" Marga is able to say.

"Yes, yes!" says Paulus.

"Forgive me!"

"Yes!"

A soldier on foot steps up behind Paulus and delivers a hammer blow of his fist to the side of Paulus' head. Paulus goes limp and slides to the street in a bony pile. With one arm, Marga's tormenter hoists her tiny body, by the hair, onto the saddle in front of him; he roars in victory, spurs his horse, and the animal is off in a splatter of hooves against cobblestones.

The storm passes over Paulus as the mercenaries chase down the remaining women.

On the street it is quiet again. A thin, waif-like woman goes to Paulus' outstretched body and begins to pull it by the feet towards the house. It is Ari. It is heavy work for a small, starving woman, and she pauses often to catch her breath. In, through the door. Across the floor, back to the kitchen. She opens the door to the tunnel. She puts Paulus' feet in first. She drops him into the tunnel and closes the floor over him.

"You were kind to me, Paulus," she says. She returns to the streets, to meet her fate along with her king.

NIGHT ON THE twenty-fifth of June fell but the searching and butchering and raping went on by torchlight; all that was forbidden to the companies was lighting the city on fire, which they wanted very much to do when it became obvious that there was nothing worth looting. They slaked their thirst on butts of beer and casks of wine brought into the city from the siege lines through gates that were now wide open. The cathedral square became crowded with wagons, horses, groups of soldiers eating and drinking, streams of captured women who had been ferreted from every corner of the town, and children. Wirich von Dhaun went home to his place outside the city, his work done; Franz von Waldeck sat on his horse long into the hours of darkness and circled the cathedral.

In the Market Square street, the mercenaries amused themselves killing some of the few Anabaptist men left alive in the city by tossing their trussed up bodies off the roof of the Town Hall onto the pikes of others below. There was great laughter at the results. Some of the victims were impaled on the pikes, others missed and hit the stone pavement and their bodies burst like melons. Told of this, the prince-bishop said:

"They're soldiers, let them have their fun. They've waited long enough."

Before the night was over they found Jan Bockelson, Bernhard Knipperdolling, and the king's treasure. The prince-bishop promptly took half of the hoard and sent it with his own retainers to his house. The next morning, in the presence of von Dhaun, he distributed the rest to the captains. The mercenaries grumbled and went home.

For a week the laborers, called in off the farms, buried the dead in two pits dug in the cathedral square, and in the hot sun a stench went up, from which von Waldeck protected himself with a perfume-soaked cloth over his mouth and nose.

And all the rulers of Europe breathed a sigh of relief, and were happy to return to their normal and Christian pursuits. For the bishop of Münster, it would be a year of reconstruction, interrogation, and retribution upon the men who had embarrassed him before the whole empire of the German nation.

CHAPTER 33: PROVIDENCE
July, 1535. Along the Rhine.

Paulus comes to consciousness. He is in darkness. He has landed in a heap at the bottom of the shaft of the tunnel. It is by the smell of the place that he finally knows where he is.

How did I get here? It will always be a mystery to him.

Marga is gone, I lost her in the streets. There is nothing I can do now. I did all that I could do. God, what are you doing?

He went to the end of the tunnel, where it reached up toward free ground outside the city wall. He picked at it and the earth and gravel fell past him. There was a gust of clean air. Above him, a small section of night sky appeared, speckled with stars. He crawled to freedom. Eight months in this impregnable prison with no logical hope of escape, and now he just walked out.

ONKEL, WHAT IS God doing?

As Paulus wandered among the farms and forests of Westphalia, he tried to understand the pattern of God's working. He tried to see it as Onkel Langshammer would see it.

He was able to feed himself along the way, with methods he had learned during his trek to Moravia. It was easy. In July, things were growing and it was warm at night, and he spent long hours sleeping. All the time, thinking.

When he came to the Rhine, he followed it, against the current, southward. It would take him toward Switzerland. Switzerland was where Onkel had first met God. Paulus was not superstitious about places, but he had no place now and Onkel's place seemed as good as any place.

Onkel, I spent eight months waiting for Marga, and learning from God to forgive Marga. What is the meaning in this?

Onkel would say that Paulus needed to learn about grace. Paulus was sure that Onkel would say that. And he would say that Marga needed to learn about peace, and Paulus hoped that she had. He would say that God had brought Marga into Paulus' life because he was not ready for celibacy. God knew: Paulus needed to be married. Not forever, but for a time.

And Onkel would no doubt say that God had put Marga there, even as Paulus' great love, to test his loyalty to Christ. She had battered his doctrine of peace with her arguments, her disdain, and finally with her adultery. And Paulus had remained faithful to Christ.

But Marga, apparently, was not something that Paulus could keep. God had his own plan for her. And for him. Now he was tested, and purged, and toughened, and ready for the life of single-minded dedication to the kingdom of Christ. He even felt like he might preach again, or lead a congregation. He certainly was not afraid of death, after his experience in Münster.

That is what Onkel would say. Paulus was sure of it. The shape and the weight of this interpretation of his marriage to Marga settled into his mind like a large building – resting entirely on the premise that Marga had died in Münster.

Onkel, I will devote my whole life to Christ now. I have finally learned what you wanted me to learn. I will be like you were.

But Marga did not die quietly. There were times when Paulus' cogitations and philosophizings gave way to a fierce and fiery longing for Marga that made him growl, and groan, and kick things, alone in his hiding places, like a crazy man. The longings became somewhat less painful as day followed day. God provided merciful relief through the summer rains, and the warm sun, and the cycle of day and night and sleep and waking.

CHAPTER 34: HISTORY
September, 1535. Switzerland.

Along the old road, which snaked its way over the hilly countryside toward Zürich, Paulus asked people where St. Matthew was, but no one had heard of it until he was almost there. An old farmer, whose face was brown and wrinkled from the sun and the Alpine winds, told him the way.

"St. Matthew. Not much of it left," said the farmer.

"What happened?" asked Paulus.

"Eight, maybe nine years ago, they all left, almost all."

"Why?"

"Anabaptists," the peasant said in a low, knowing voice.

"Ah, I understand."

Paulus followed the man's directions. He had to leave the beaten path to get to the top of the hill, but once there, he saw the wooden steeple of a church rising out of the trees below. The village was on the very edge of the valley, against the slope of the hill.

In St. Matthew, peasant huts clustered around the wooden church. *Onkel's church, where he muttered masses.* It all had the look of neglect and decay. Thatch roofs were broken through and doors hung open, and weeds grew everywhere, even in front of the double doors of the church. There were a few people, mostly old, who looked suspiciously at Paulus as he wandered among the cottages. After he had weathered their glares, and gone through the area several times, and by the church twice, he worked up the courage to speak to one of them.

"Good day."

The man looked up but kept on with his raking of hay. He was bald and tall.

Paulus said, "Have you ever heard of Heinrich Langshammer? I think he once lived here."

"Why?" the man asked.

"He was a friend of mine."

"And of us all. What's become of him?"

"He's dead."

The man tightened his lips. "You'll want to speak with Maria, won't you?"

"Maria?"

"She lives beyond the church, against the hill. She has a red door."

The place with the red door – a red the color of rust – was half house, half cave. A single pitched roof, covered with grass and moss, extended out from the side of the hill. An animal pen to its left was empty.

Paulus knocked on the door and there was no answer; some paint fell off when he knocked. He was tired and sat down with his back against the wall. As he waited, the memories of Onkel filled his mind; Onkel had been here and someone else remembered the man. Why he had been sent to this Maria, he did not know: maybe she had lived long and knew him well.

A woman came up a path, not from the direction of the church, but from the grassy low-lying ground in the opposite direction. She was a large woman, not fat, but heavy framed; her hair was silver gray, long, gathered in a big knot on the top of her head. She walked with firm, almost masculine strides. She carried a wicker basket full of blackberries and blackberry leaves.

"Good day, mein Herr," she said in a resonant alto voice. Then she smiled. Her mouth was large and her teeth white. Her face was tan from the sun, laced with fine wrinkles, especially around her eyes, and shapely. The skin under her chin was tight and smooth.

"Good morning, you must be Maria," said Paulus, and he returned the smile and stood, brushing the dust off his seat. "The bald man pointed me to you."

"Ah, yes, Giovanni. And you?"

"Paulus Ketterling is my name."

"Now then, Paulus Ketterling, I have a basket of what may be the very last blackberries. And you are hungry, if I know the look of a hungry man."

"I don't want to impose, I only want to talk."

"Nonsense, I can't eat all of them. Come in, young man."

He followed her into the place that was her home. It was warm and impeccably tidy. The outer wooden section was a kitchen. The walls were almost covered with needlework products – embroidered towels, pictures of trees, bushes, cows, sheep, framed cloth pieces with biblical proverbs, knotted cords with little brass bells and charms. There was a small stone oven, a table and stool, and a bench with knives and spoons and two tin pails on it. Maria put the berries on the top of the oven with a *humph* and wiped her forehead with her apron.

"I have fresh milk from Giovanni," she said, pointing.

"I noticed."

"Berries and milk?" She took a bucket of milk by its leather handle and lifted it with one strong arm. Paulus saw the muscles tighten near her elbow. A strong woman.

"That would be good," he said.

She filled two bowls with berries and then poured milk.

There was a relaxed deliberation about her that made Paulus feel quiet and comfortable.

"Now," she said, "you must let me sit on my own stool. You must let old people have their own way in the little habits, Paulus. And since I have no other place for you to sit, I will have to invent something." She cleared off the bench and pulled it next to the table.

The blackberries were ripe and sweet, and the milk was still warm. Paulus tried to eat slowly, like a gentleman, but haste and hunger must have shown anyway.

"I was right, you are a hungry man."

"Very hungry."

She folded her hands on the table. "So," she said, "why are you here to see Maria? St. Matthew is not exactly the crossroads of the world, and hardly anyone knows me. I can't tell you how curious I am."

"I've come to St. Matthew to ask about Heine Langshammer."

Her face changed. The eyes widened, the lips pinched a bit.

"Do you know him?" she finally asked.

"I knew him."

The past tense was an obvious correction of her question. She swallowed what was in her mouth.

"Is he dead?" she asked.

"Yes. I'm sorry. You were obviously close to him. I was too. He was like my father."

"Close to him," she mused, "You say that I was close to Heinrich. You don't know, do you?"

He shook his head no. "What?"

"I was his wife." Her chin puckered and quivered.

Paulus heard her words, but they struck him as if she had said that the sun was purple or that cows fly.

"His wife? I thought that he was celibate."

"He did too, later in life. But there is more to it than that."

"Then we need to talk."

Onkel and Marga and Münster were rising up out of the grave of the past, prematurely dug.

"Oh yes, we need to talk. I think we have things to tell each other about Heine Langshammer. But later. Finish your blackberries. Then there are a couple of things you can do for me. You understand, as long as I have a man around the place, I might as well take advantage of it, no? Then, then we will talk about Heinrich."

MARIA WAS CLEANING out her garden a short ways from the house, and there were some large rocks she could not move by herself. *Rocks, rocks,* she kept saying; she did not understand why anyone would want to farm in Switzerland; if God had wanted farms here he would not have placed so many rocks in the ground. And that was not the worst; you could clear a plot this year and next spring, after the frost had squeezed the ground, more rocks would rise up to the surface. But the two of them worked at it, dislodged the stones, and rolled them into a pile. The day was pure autumn and Paulus enjoyed the work. At the end of it, Maria filled his belly with bread and porridge and milk from the buckets.

Onkel, you had a wife. And this strong, noble woman is just the wife for you that I would have imagined, if you had let me. You still have some surprises for me, don't you.

"Now, you tell me about yourself," said Maria when they had finished their supper.

"Shall I begin with meeting Onkel? What should we call him?"

"He was Onkel to you, but Heinrich to me. Heine to other people. But no, begin with yourself. I won't understand what you say about him unless I know something about you."

"My family is from Württemburg . . ." Paulus began, and traced the story of his life in some detail. He held nothing back, and he watched for signs of boredom in her face but saw none. He described his months alone on the road; his bumping into the Montau community and his meeting with Onkel; his love for Marga. She nodded gently from time to time. She understood. He came finally to Onkel's arrest, and return, and death.

"And what had they done to him?" she asked.

"I left that out on purpose."

"He was my husband. I have a right to know."

"They had burned his feet."

She shook her head and clicked her tongue against the roof of her mouth and her eyes became wet. "Oh no, oh no," she said softly. "Poor Heinrich. You know, he never could bear any kind of pain. The pain of souls he could endure, in that he was a giant. He could wrap the arms of his heart around a hundred people and hold them all up, hold their pain and take it away from them. But the pain of the body he could not endure, or think about." She wiped her face. "But stop, Maria. I am rambling and it is your turn. And where is Heinrich, now?"

"I buried him somewhere in Saxony, on a hill above the Main river. I'm not sure I could find it now."

"And his soul is in the blessed presence of Christ. Go on."

Paulus went on, recounting the flight from Moravia in more detail, and the dwindling away of the church that he thought Onkel could have kept together.

"You feel guilty about this," she said.

"Yes."

"Did you ever think, maybe it was best for everyone that the church scatter?"

"No, I never thought that."

"That church was Heinrich's," she said. "More than that,

it *was* Heinrich, he was the soul, the church was his body. I think it was good that it ended."

He told her about the birth of the baby that had the name Heinrich. She smiled. He told her about the murder of Max Holzmann and their trip down the Rhine to Wesel, and the visit of the priest to take their son. "I looked high and low, Maria, everywhere. He's gone. They've probably given him a new name now, and he's changed so much that I wouldn't recognize him if I saw him."

"Have you given up looking?"

"I've just worn out. I don't know where else to look, what else to do."

"Don't give up. Keep trying. The day will come when you'll need him."

Then he told her of Marga's decision to go to Münster, and of his following her there. This took a long time because he left nothing out. He remembered it almost day by day.

"Are you so sure she is dead?" asked Maria when he had finished.

"I'm sure, yes. They were killing everyone, and she had been one of the king's wives. The rider had her by the hair and was lifting her off the ground. That's the last I saw of her."

"Tell me about her, I would like to know her."

"Beautiful, beautiful. The most beautiful woman in the world, really. So beautiful to me. White clear skin from her forehead to the bottoms of her feet, and dark hair, the thickest hair you ever saw, hanging to the middle of her back. Very small, and thin, but shapely. Large eyes."

"Brown?"

"Dark brown. And large teeth, with a gap between them, which she was embarrassed about but which I loved. Everything she did, she did intensely. But there was more than intensity. It was a kind of lust for the present. She lived, I think, totally in the present. When she was happy, it was an absolute happiness that consumed her and drew me into it and consumed me too. And when she was sad, or angry, it was overwhelming. I often wondered how she could live that way. I think I would grow old and die within a year if I felt things that sharply. But I would not have changed her, because the love she had for me was the same frightening kind of thing. I experienced it, and at the same time I stood back and observed it with wonder.

"She was never content with our doctrine . . . always obedient to it, but not content. I'm sure the brethren saw her as a faithful bishop's wife, but she chafed under it. She could never accept with her heart the doctrine of peace as we believed it. Her father had allowed himself to be arrested in the Tyrol and she held it against him, saw it as a lack of love for her; and I know she felt the same about me, when they came to take Heine. She was a fighter. She fought for what she loved. Because she lived so much in the present. And I think it all makes good sense. I think, to let yourself be hurt or killed goes against nature, and to go against nature you must have a greater stake in the future than you do in the present. Marga lived in the present and I lived in the future."

"That's the way it is, Paulus, for all of us. It's true that God has given to the woman a greater stake in the present. Because of children. Women bring children into the world and protect them from death. But a woman does not have to have children to be this way. God has built into woman the passion to live and see others live. You men, you're concerned about glory and reputation and how your descendants will remember you. For glory, you are willing to die, or to kill. You are always looking forward, forward. Now, Paulus, here's the thing: all that force you expend on the past and the future and the affairs of nations and kingdoms, the woman expends on life now, and on her children, if she has them."

Paulus was listening, and believing her. Maybe she had gotten her wisdom from Onkel. Maybe Onkel had gotten his wisdom from her.

"I want to tell you about Heinrich. But first, some tea, it's turning cool."

She had made a tea of blackberry leaves, and the tin pot had been warming on the stove. She poured them each a bowl.

"Now about myself," she said. "I'm Italian by birth. There are quite a few of us around here. My father was a municipal clerk in Milan when the Visconti were great. There was some sort of plot – I was three years old at the time – and we had to flee. I remember only riding in a lurching wagon for days and days, I know now that it was over the Alps. We stopped here, in St. Matthew. We lived in this very place, where we sit, six of us, if you can believe it! My father worked with his hands for the first time in his life, and the work and the humiliation killed him at a young age.

"When I was sixteen, Heinrich came here as the priest. He was in the prime of his life then, and brilliant; all the rumor had it that St. Matthew was only going to be a quick stepping stone to bigger things for him. But he never acted like we were just a stepping stone. He was not a handsome man, even then, but he had plenty of blonde hair and his eyes were good. And the smile! When he smiled his whole soul was revealed, and because it was a good soul, the smile was beautiful. And I was sixteen, and beautiful myself, if you can believe that. I was very proud of my own golden hair and well developed breasts, for a sixteen year old. Heinrich was not made of stone, of course. He noticed me, and I was clay in his hands because he was the priest and I loved his smile. There was a danger about the whole game that I loved. There is no delicate way to put it. He took me to bed and after that I became his concubine. There was some vicious gossip and complaining in the village about it, but neither of us cared. And Heinrich loved the people so much and cared for them so much that they quickly forgave him this sin, and they loved him back.

"Here, especially, is what you must know about Heinrich at that time: he loved me as if I were his wife, and he never touched another woman. I think that he was the most faithful man in St. Matthew, even though our relationship was illegal in the eyes of the church. There was a small house by the church, which is gone now. That's where we lived. I did his cooking for him – like a good concubine! But we also talked and talked. He was attracted to the new learning of the humanists and so we talked about morals, and language, and the education of women, which he said he believed in, and the reforming of the church. He read Erasmus to me, and even taught me the Greek alphabet, which I have long since forgotten. But he loved to talk. When you knew him, did he love to talk?"

"He loved to hear himself talk, but he was also a good listener."

"Yes, he was! Is it right to think back to that time and say that it was truly good? Even though we were living in fornication?"

"There are worse sins than fornication."

"Yes. We had a son. His name was Ernst. Heinrich lavished love and attention on him and wanted him to become a scholar, and perhaps a churchman. He was a beautiful boy. Some people said he looked like a Greek god, which pleased Heinrich. He became large and strong of body and handsome in the face, Heinrich's body and my face, they used to say!" She laughed. "But if he was a god, he was Mars." She was serious again. "For all he loved were the weapons of war. It was something hardly to be avoided in those days, with young Swiss men with pikes so much in demand everywhere. The boys talked about it constantly, and played war, and each one had his own pike, cut from the birch trees. And when the recruiters from the canton came through the village, I believe it was in 1518, when he was seventeen years old, they saw that he was proficient with the pike, and strong as a horse, and they promised him money and glory and the sights of Italy. He went with them, and it grieved me but it almost broke Heinrich's poor heart. I think that is when he began to hate war. From that time we never knew where he was, but we assumed that wherever the emperor's new wars led him, Ernst was there. More tea?"

"This is enough." Paulus held his hand over his bowl.

"In 1522 – the years become more distinct now – Heinrich began to read Luther. And he made several journeys to Zürich to meet with Ulrich Zwingli. I will never forget the long conversations we had in those months, especially when he would get back from Zürich, tired but excited. It seemed that the world was flooded with new things. He began to speak critically of the pope; he began to question the value of the sacraments of the Roman church. He preached sermons on the new things and the village was stirred. I will never forget when we drank the wine of the mass for the first time! Heinrich's right hand shook as he held the cup out to the people. But it was joy, not fear. Heinrich feared no man. And it was the greatest of joys for us to discover the truth together. I was younger then, Paulus, and whatever he did or thought was right. I think now I would question him more, but he would still probably convince me in the end.

"Then, inevitably, there came the day when we discussed marriage. Priests and monks and nuns were already marrying in parts of Germany, we heard. And we could no longer keep a clear conscience since it was not a necessity for us to live any more as we had. If we could marry, he said, we should. And that made me very happy. I had always wanted to call Heinrich my husband, oh, he had been all of a husband to me, but I wanted so much to call him *husband*! We married in a simple ceremony right here" – she pointed in the direction of the church – "and there was a feast in the village for us." Her mind wandered briefly. Paulus was remembering his own wedding, smelling the heavy August night, roasting meat, Marga's skin .

. . "Those were beautiful days, Paulus. Heinrich was so gentle to me. He was a lion in the church but a lamb with me. He spoke so kindly to me. He said to me, often, *I love you*. Often. And we were part of a movement of truth that seemed to be gaining the victory everywhere.

"The Bible became Heinrich's food and drink and sleep. His nose was always in it, and his eyes were getting bad. I will have this eternal image of Heinrich hunched over a table, under a burning candle or lamp, his eyes pressed almost to the very pages."

Paulus struck the table gently. "And I, the same image!"

"He would often whistle, or exclaim softly, and say, *Maria, dear, listen to this!* and read to me a new discovery or a new connection with something he had already known."

"His shoutings," said Paulus.

"Yes. Once he exclaimed, *Grebel is right!* and I could tell that from that time he was disturbed about something because he kept saying, *I must discuss this with Zwingli.* He was speaking, I know now, about infant baptism. He returned one time from Zürich in an agitated state. This was now . . .1524. And we had a long discussion of infant baptism. It was all new to me and very upsetting. We would argue and he would say, *Dear, I will not give up. If I cannot convince you of this then perhaps I am wrong.* See, I had not stood up to him enough; he thought he could convince me of anything. But as we talked, and as he showed me the parts of the scriptures that teach about baptism and reported Zwingli's arguments, I saw what he was saying. I really did this time, I was not just caving in to him. Then he began to preach against infant baptism, and soon after that against the use of the sword by Christians, and against oaths, and all the practices based only on the Old Testament. He put the village in an uproar once more, as if the reformation were beginning all over again. The village was much larger then. Some people were angry and left, or stayed and made life miserable for Heinrich. But others came in from the countryside to hear him preach. He was not baptizing infants any more.

"Then came the word from Zürich that Grebel, and Blaurock, and Manz and others had been rebaptized. He was off to Zürich again, and came back two days later with one of the brothers from the Grebel group, who baptized him in front of all the people. Not in the church, but by the village well. Then Heinrich called upon all true believers to receive baptism at his hand, and they crowded in toward the well and he baptized them from the same bucket."

"And you?"

"I was one of them."

"Did you believe it all?"

"Yes! With all my heart, and I still do believe it."

"Did you ever feel angry that he read so much from the Bible?"

"Not angry. Frightened, that every time he sat down with his Bible he would come to some new conclusion that would throw our lives into chaos again."

She stood and stretched. Paulus admired her dignified beauty. "I'm getting my shawl," she said. "It's cold." She wrapped a shawl of large wool yarn around her shoulders.

"Now I must tell you the sad part of the story. I may cry. Will that bother you?"

"Of course it will bother me. You can't imagine the weeping I've heard. I want to hear nothing but joy and laughter for the rest of my life."

"I'll try not to cry, then. The next two years were good years, despite the fact that we and almost the whole village were outlaws. Messages of warning came to us but nothing ever happened. We were too remote and too small. But the persecutions were beginning. Grebel and Manz were imprisoned again and again. Heinrich was worried constantly during these days. He was not himself. Then came the news of

Manz's execution in the Limmat river. When he heard about it, Heinrich went off by himself to the hills for a few days and came back with nothing but exhaustion in his face. It was then that he began to look old, Paulus. My heart broke for him.

"When he had just started to be himself again, the news came from Rottenburg that Michael Sattler had been killed. You know of Sattler's death? Do you know how they put him to death? They drew him through the streets of Rottenburg in a cart and at every corner, seven times, they tore his flesh with red hot tongs. And when they reached the stake they tore out his tongue with the tongs. Then they burned him."

They sat silently. Maria was crying and trying to stop.

"Can you imagine how that felt?" she said.

"No. Who can?" The screams of the burning man in the Place Maubert.

"That's what Heinrich said: *can you imagine how that felt*? He said it over and over, lost within himself. Then, one day, he said to me, *we can't be married any more*. I thought he was joking with me. I thought divorces were only for kings and princes who need heirs and alliances. And I was hurt that he had been thinking about this for some time and had never spoken to me about it, as we had done always. Of course I wept and asked him to explain himself. He said that he was an *anabaptist* now and a marked man, like Manz and Sattler, and that it was only a matter of time before he too would face torture and death. I said, *how can you know this for sure?*, and he wagged his stubborn bald head at me and said that he knew, he knew. And he said that he feared torture terribly and knew that when it came he would tell them anything they asked, even if it meant betraying me, or even Christ. He said that he knew that I too would suffer and die because I was his wife. He could not bear to think of it. And he had been meditating on St. Paul's words about celibacy in the Corinthian letter, how Paul said that he wished all Christians could be celibate like himself, and that the celibate person is free to serve the Lord. He was convinced this was what we should do, separate, and voluntarily end the marriage. He would, of course, never marry again or touch another woman. He would never love or desire another woman than me; he made that clear. Then I turned to the text and read him others parts of it, which he had passed by – where St. Paul commands that every Christian remain in the status in which he was called to salvation, which for us was marriage. But he shook his head at me because he had already made up his mind. And I felt then how it was to be on the opposite side of an argument with Heinrich Langshammer. We ended with shouting and crying, and I grasped his knees and he told me he loved me and would never love another woman in all creation. But that he must be celibate. From that day on he didn't touch my body again."

She sniffled again for a while, then continued. "A couple weeks after this, a message came from the Zürich council: we were either to conform to the established faith, or face the consequences. There were many who decided to conform to the Zürich church, but Heinrich organized the rest of the people to leave St. Matthew. He told me, *you will stay, you are a single woman now, with no children, and they will not bother you, you can live in peace.* I said, *let me come, I'm your wife.* He refused. I said, *promise me one thing – that if the day comes when we can live in peace with the world, you will return to me.* He said, *the day will never come, how can it, the church at peace with the world? But I will promise it.* Then they all left."

"The people I knew in Moravia, you knew too. It's hard to believe."

"And you might have known me too, before now."

"Why did you stay? Why didn't you just follow him?"

"Because he was my husband, and I was used to obeying him. Because I could see how frightened he was, and I really hoped that it would not be too long before he missed me and came back, or sent for me. But he didn't. That's the frightening thing about Heinrich, he always did what he said. He always meant what he said. Did he ever speak of me?"

"Not a word. He often spoke of celibacy."

"What a stubborn, stubborn man. Can you understand how angry that makes me?"

Paulus let her seethe for a few moments. Then he continued.

"I wanted at first to follow him in celibacy. But then he was taken away, and then Marga came. I went ahead and married her, even though I felt Onkel looking over my shoulder."

"Good for you! You went ahead and married this beautiful woman. Good for you." She wiped the tears from her eyes with the tip of her shawl. "And something else, Paulus. You know now, I hope, why he treated you as a son. Because he lost his own son. You look much like Ernst – not as tall or heavy, but you have the same nose and the same active eyes that Ernst had. I'm sure Heinrich took one look at you and said to himself, *now is my chance to be a father again and to have a scholar for a son*. I'm glad you came, Paulus. I'm glad you gave him some human joy in his old age. I'm still angry at him, but I would never wish him ill."

"We had joy together. He taught me the faith. He taught me how to think, and how to live as a Christian. But I don't understand how he could do what he did to you."

"You *should* understand. You're doing it to Marga. You're following him as a faithful little disciple."

She was through crying, and was now looking him in his furtive eyes. He felt afraid.

"Marga is dead," he said weakly.

"You don't know that, not until you put the flowers on her grave do you know that. Until then, she must be alive to you! If she is dead, it is only because you have pronounced her dead in your heart, and because you are following the same phantom as Heinrich did, trying to find a way to live the Christian life without bearing anyone else's load."

"Not bearing anyone else's – how can you say that? What I've borne with Marga, and for Marga, God knows." He held his head between his hands. "God just tore us apart, isn't that clear?"

"Not at all. It's a dangerous thing, this trying to read the plan of God through what happens to you, because you never have the end of the story. I think you just got tired of loving. But don't. Better to go by what is written."

The secure cocoon of Paulus' freedom was being shredded, and the powerful vision of Marga, whom he had indeed consigned to death, was rushing back within him. "Which is?" he asked meekly.

"That a man and a woman are married until death." He must have looked pitiful, for Maria reached out her firm warm hand and put it on his cheek like a mother would. "You have time to learn these things. Can you learn from Heinrich's mistakes, from his sins, as well as from his precepts?"

He could not answer aloud. For instead of a simple yes or no, the answer would have been the acknowledgment that until this minute the person and then the ghost of Onkel Langshammer had dominated his life, and he was too embarrassed to say so.

"He was a great man," she said. "One of the greatest. But he sinned with me. Face it. Let him be dead. Let Marga live, let poor Heinrich be dead."

Onkel Langshammer was almost dying in his mind.

"Would you like to know the piece of truth you missed?" she asked after a few minutes. She was going to tell him in any case. "It is true that we women live in the present. And it is true that you men live in the past, and the future. But it is also true that because we are human and not beasts, we are not bound to instincts, like the beasts. That is why marriage only exists among us. And I believe that a woman is capable of living her man's dream for the future, if her man is willing to love her in the present. It's a trade, yes. A compromise. Men like you and Heinrich have trouble making compromises, but you must. God calls you to it. Heinrich disobeyed that call. And Marga, if I understand her, felt that you were depriving her of her present. So she searched for it in Münster, and she sinned. But be thankful, Paulus, that she didn't seek it in the old world, and just give up the faith. She searched for it in her faith. She was still yearning for the kingdom of God. She learned from her sin. But that is past. She has learned. Have you?"

"Perhaps Münster has done something to me too, that I didn't see. I thought I had resisted it. Perhaps my supply of love ran out on that last day."

"It can be replenished."

CHAPTER 35: EXECUTION
Winter 1535-36. Switzerland.

Maria sent him back, first, to his father. She said that she would not be his hiding place from the people he should love. He made the short journey north to Württemberg in October, and he enjoyed greatly walking in the clean, chilly wind, hunkered down in the woven sheepswool coat that Maria had made for him.

Malbeck was the same as always, and the servant Sebastian was still answering the door, quiet and dignified. His father, however, was in failing health; terrible small stones passed out with his urine from time to time and almost killed him with pain. Sebastian said he had summoned an Italian physician from the University of Bologna, and that the physician had recommended that the count stop eating so much of the cheese that he loved with his red wine and meat, and that the count had refused to comply, and had paid the physician and sent him back home, cursing all physicians. When Paulus saw his father it was in the high ceilinged hall, and his father sat in his usual chair, but with a blanket over his legs.

Time had done nothing to diminish the distance between the two men; it was not a warm conversation they had, and there was no meeting of the hearts. But their conversation was civil. Paulus saw clearly, facing his father and remembering the last time he had done this, how much he had been through since that time and how much he had grown into a man. He related his experiences with cold factuality, which he knew his father would appreciate, and his father listened intently throughout. The count spoke briefly of his own problems, and of Franz, who was in the east, near Vienna, but did not seem to want to elaborate very much. He came back always to his sickness.

"It changes everything, the pain," he said. "Tiny little things, the stones, but they feel like cannonballs. Nothing else seems important any more. And one of them will kill me, eventually."

The count was most interested in Paulus' son, and promised to write some letters to his friends and connections in Westphalia. Paulus thanked him. Paulus did not think that these efforts would do any good. But the efforts would do his father good.

Before Paulus left, the count had Sebastian bring a bag of money and gave it to Paulus. Paulus accepted it. "Use it to find my grandson," said the count.

PAULUS WENT BACK to St. Matthew and spent the winter with Maria. He was deeply tired and his shoulder ached with the cold and damp. He slept long nights and napped during the afternoons, and spent the morning hours reading the battered, soiled Bible he had carried out of Münster.

One day Maria said to him, "You should get rid of that Bible."

"It's Onkel's," he said, surprised.

"I know. That's why you should get rid of it."

"I don't think so."

Now, for the first time, Paulus saw Maria roused to wrath.

"I insist!" she said. "This Bible of Heinrich's, it's more to you than a Bible. You can get another Bible, a new Bible. Your Bible. This is not a Bible to you. It's Heinrich himself. I've watched you hold it, turn its pages, smell it. It's not good this way, you remember him too much."

"He was my shepherd. He was the man who brought me to Jesus. It is right for me to remember him, and this is all that I have of him." Paulus, feeling desperate, looked down at the open pages, at the marginal notes, at the tears and folds, and he knew that Maria was right.

"Paulus, now you listen to me! I am older and wiser than you! This man, this great and terrible man, Heinrich Langshammer, is *dead* – "

"I know, I buried him with my own hands."

"You buried his body, maybe. But his soul, and his ideas, and his sinful, wicked, selfish, childish obsession with celibacy, you never buried them!"

"It is not wicked! Our Lord, and the apostle Paul were celibate!"

"But Heinrich Langshammer was not! He was married! He made a vow, and he broke it! What about you? Paulus, what about you?"

"What about me?"

"Will you keep your vow to your wife?"

"And what do you expect me to do?"

"Bury Heinrich. Let him die. Dig a hole and put this Bible in it and say farewell to Heinrich once and for all, and then go find your wife. Let Heinrich be dead. Let Marga be alive."

Maria put out her hand and took one side of Onkel's Bible, which was lying open on her table. She had only pulled it toward her a little bit when Paulus planted his hand hard in the middle of the book, right over the spine, and stopped its movement along the table.

"What are you doing?" he asked.

"We're going to bury it. Bury him." She tugged. He held on. "You came here all the way from Westphalia, Paulus. God brought you here, and this is why."

This made sense to Paulus. The furniture in his mind – Onkel, Marga, Münster, celibacy, marriage, kind speaking – began rearranging itself. She was right.

She went on. "This Bible is mine, anyway. It passed to me when Heinrich died. This is my Bible, and I insist that we bury it."

Maria pulled once more, and Paulus let go. When she had taken Onkel's Bible from him, she paged through it for a minute or two. Paulus could tell that she was not looking at the text, but at Onkel's notations along the margins. Then she closed it, fastened its metal clasp, and led him outside, taking with her, on the way out, a small pointed shovel.

They dug a hole in the ground near the tottering church of St. Matthew and buried the Bible in it, without the words but with all the solemnity and finality of a funeral.

Then, the next day, they made the trip to Zürich , and used some of Paulus' money to spend the night comfortably in an inn and to buy a newly printed German Bible at a bookseller's, as well as a good quality metal tipped pen and a bottle of ink. He would never be a doctor of theology in a university, but he would write his notes like one.

He wrote his own notes in the margins of the new Bible, beginning at the gospel of Matthew. Maria allowed him to be alone with his thoughts and his study. Paulus knew, of course, that Maria wanted him to search for Marga, but Paulus felt somehow that he must meet God again and strengthen his own soul first.

Then, in the spring, he became sick. The warm winds were melting the snow, and it was the season that made him smile and dream, but he was sick in bed. He could tell by the way Maria looked at him that she was worried. In the mornings he coughed up phlegm, and when the coughing was over he was too exhausted to do anything but lie down. He bore it with patience. After Münster he had patience. He kept reading, and thinking, and a yearning grew in him to go north and seek his son and his wife.

"We'll get you well, Paulus, and then you go find her," said Maria.

Maria applied poultices and stuck his face in ill-smelling steam and prayed, and from some or all of these causes he began to mend. It was May, and one year had passed since he had seen Marga in a hail of bullets, and held her body in the street, and it felt now to his rested, rejuvenated soul that Marga should be alive. He had strong hope. This May of 1536 he would return to the bishopric of Münster and find his family. Maria crushed him in a hug as he left. He had one more thing to tell her.

"Before Onkel died . . . he was babbling things right before he died, and I didn't understand any of it except one phrase . . . he said, *Speak to her kindly.*"

"It's from Hosea, isn't it," said Maria.

"Yes, Hosea and Gomer, God and me."

"You and Marga."

"Of course, that's how I've taken it. But I don't think Onkel was thinking about me at the time. I think he was thinking about you. I think he was somehow repenting, and missing you, and wishing that he had never left you at all."

Paulus hoped that this was the truth. In any case, it was a kind thing to say to Maria. Her eyes narrowed and moistened and she hugged him again, for a long time, before he turned away from her and walked to the north. He stopped several times and waved to her.

PAULUS TRIED TO locate his son in Wesel. He was not

afraid to identify himself, even here. He had left all his fear in Jan Bockelson's terrible city. Boldly he entered the monasteries and the convents and the other ecclesiastical establishments that might be harboring orphans. He told them exactly who he was and what he wanted, and they all knew nothing. It was really possible that they knew nothing, since Heine's trail was cold by now and he could be living almost anywhere, with a new name. And the child would not remember Paulus or Marga. But still Paulus combed the whole region, working outward from the city, until he was convinced that only a miraculous coincidence would bring him into contact again with his son. Now, he would be able to say to Marga, should he see her again, that he had done everything.

He devoted himself to this work with greater diligence, knowing that whenever he gave it up he would have to turn to Münster, and the thought moved him with strange, mottled feelings – dread, excitement, something even like joy. It was only there that the mystery of Marga could be solved.

WHILE PAULUS WAS reading and then burying Onkel's Bible, in January of 1536, Marga and several hundred of the captured women were herded into the Market Square one more time, under the steeple of St. Lambert's church, to behold the king they had served. These women, spared from the slaughter, had been held in custody since the conquest of the city, interrogated, neglected, and carted about from place to place with Bockelson, Knipperdolling, and Bernt Krechting, who went in cages like bears and were gawked at by crowds throughout northwest Germany. Everyone wanted to see what an Anabaptist looked like.

But the prince-bishop eventually tired of this sport, and the interrogations were finished. It was time for the execution, and for this purpose a wood platform had been built in front of

St. Lambert's church, on which rested, not a throne but a torture stake. It was the prince-bishop's final decree for these captive women that they be forced to watch the destruction of their messiah. After that they would be free to go.

Von Waldeck's servant Johann Wesseling read the sentence:

> *Inasmuch as Jan Bockelson, inspired by pride and the devil, has overturned the duly constituted authority of the bishopric of Münster, confiscated the property of its citizens, murdered innocent people who resisted his proud claims, spoken many words of swollen pride in which he claimed to be a prophet, an apostle, an angel, even the Christ, mocked the holy institution of marriage and the sacraments of the Holy Roman Church, and has thrown an entire principality of the empire into fear, poverty, and confusion, the prince bishop, Franz von Waldeck, decrees: he shall be publicly displayed, his body torn in seven places with hot tongs, and his heart pierced. This by the authority of the bishop and prince.*

An executioner carried out the sentence according to the decree, while Franz von Waldeck watched from the high window of a house across the street. Marga closed her eyes and shook while the carnage went on. Many of the women wailed and cried. At the end, the three torn bodies hung at the stake with bowed heads, and the smell of burnt flesh lingered near the platform.

"Wasn't the man an actor?" the prince-bishop asked his secretary.

"Yes, he confessed it several times."

"He died where he belonged, with the eyes of the people upon him. He would have been a very great man if he had not been a heretic."

The prince-bishop covered his nose with a handkerchief

to keep out the smell, and went away from the window in a glum mood.

They put the bodies in three iron cages and hoisted them up to the bell-tower of St. Lambert's church, where they were to remain perpetually as a reminder of the wrath of God on heretics, insurrectionists, and destroyers of good order.

WHEN PAULUS WALKED up the Market Square street in June of 1536, the execution platform had been long removed, and the citizens of Münster had already stopped noticing the three cages on St. Lambert's tower. There was a bustling, chaotic commerce again along the Market Square street, where Bockelson had preached and Matthys had marched. The white symbols and numbers had been washed off the houses. Bells rang from the churches. The sound of monks chanting wafted from the inner court of a familiar place; Paulus knew it as a food warehouse, but he recognized now that it was, and had always been, a monastery. The city was, again, just Münster. The men of the world were good at what they did: the prince-bishop had pacified the city.

The Aa was clean again, its water moving normally through the city. Vegetable gardens grew everywhere, as they were supposed to grow. Paulus could not resist a walk along the New Bridge street, past the house where he and Arndt and Julius had talked and slept and dug. The house was there, but if there were any inhabitants, they were not home.

He found his way through the prince-bishop's officialdom to the clerk who had the records of the captured Anabaptists.

"Marga Roth, Marga Roth . . . here it is."

"Her name is there?" She had not given his name, but her own.

"Marga Roth. She was released with the others earlier this year, after the execution."

"Where?"

"Wherever she wants to go. She's free."

Paulus put his hands to his head and rubbed his temples.

"You know her?" the man asked.

"My wife."

"Heavens, she came to Münster. That must have been horrible for you."

"Yes," said Paulus.

The man's words kept coming back to him: *wherever she wants to go.* Where would Marga *want* to go? He forced himself, against his exhaustion, to believe in her love. He wanted to believe that she would go back to Montau. And he wanted to go back to Montau. It was all the way across the empire, but it was what he was going to do.

"Can you find her?" the man asked.

"Probably."

"Where?"

"I believe that she will be in Moravia."

The clerk whistled and shook his head.

CHAPTER 36: COVENANT
August, 1536. Moravia.

The summer grass grows in barbarous profusion, laced with wild flowers; little fir saplings sprout everywhere; insects sing and whir. The sheep fence stands in broken ruin and most of the stick and wattle chimneys have washed away in the weather. There has been some decay and reversion to the forest, but the settlement of Montau still stands, and as Paulus views it from the encroaching edge of the woods it seems sad and lonely, as it had when he and the brotherhood had left it in the winter night.

Everything he sees produces a memory. Coming across the meadow through the tall grass, still wet with morning dew, he feels like the old dead Paulus sneaking out of the woods to steal. The clearing should be full of children playing, and the two babysitters, usually Hansi and Susanna, should be standing by the well, talking with mouths and eyes and hands and ignoring the children. Now he should catch the smell of the sheep pen as he passes by the storehouse. There, there is the woodpile. Extraordinarily, it is untouched. The split logs are weathered gray and are dry and perfect for burning. Around the chopping stump some pieces lie, still unstacked, and among them lies an axe, its head eaten and pitted by rust. His? Did he leave it lying there that day? The large kitchen-meeting room is still intact. There should be piney smelling smoke coming out of the chimney and the soft drone of the women's voices coming out of the open windows of the kitchen.

But it is a dead place, a relic, and the memories only accentuate the deadness. The people are gone now, blown south to Austria and west to Germany. Some are no longer Anabaptists, having come to the end of their endurance; some are dead, violently or quietly, still peaceable. A few remain, but they will never come back here. Montau is forfeit. It will keep on decaying.

In his own little compartment, the wall between Onkel's bed and their bed still stands. Their bed is crumpled, stripped of its blankets, and covered with a thick layer of dust and mouse dung. In the corner, the reading table stands with the stool pushed tidily under it, ready to use. Paulus should be there, carefully studying the scriptures, worrying about nothing but the solemn task of feeding God's sheep with the truth; and Marga should be asleep in the bed or brushing out her hair. No, Onkel should be at the table.

The wind has blown through the room for almost four years. No one has seen, or cared, or cleaned. The footprints of various little creatures trace paths in the dirt on the floor.

LATER IN THE day Paulus made the long walk to the manor of the Count von Abersicht, to see if the old man was still alive, and if he had seen Marga.

The count lay trundled up in his bed. Two middle aged female servants attended him. His legs were wrapped with yards of bandages and suspended in the air by ropes from the ceiling.

"Do you remember me . . . Paulus Ketterling?"

The old man scowled and thought.

"The Anabaptist."

"Yes, my lord. How are you?"

"Terrible, can't you see? These gouty old legs have finally won the victory. Gout is a terrible disease, I hope you never get it." He snapped his fingers and one of the women came to his side. "Hoist me up here, my dear, let me see this man. Look at this man, he's quite a man, you'll hardly see one like him, I'll bet. Now, let me see . . . the old man, Langshammer, whatever became of him?"

"He's dead, my lord."

"Yes, yes, yes, just as well, no?"

"I suppose."

"You loved him, didn't you."

Paulus nodded. "I am at the settlement, for the present. I request my lord's permission to stay there."

Von Abersicht began to laugh, and phlegm gurgled in his chest. "You people! I can't believe you people! You're so unbelievably proper. Nobody's been there since you left and I'd never know about it anyway. Yes, of course, it's fine. Stay there as long as you like. Times are bad here. Sometimes it seems like you and your people were a blessing to me. Since you left, everything has gotten worse. My gout, the weather, the fanatical king sticking his Hapsburg chin into everybody's business. I hope you'll stay, perhaps you'll bring me a blessing. Can you pray for my gout?"

"Of course, my lord."

"And where have you been all this time? Seen some of the world, I'd guess. How is the world these days?"

"Wicked. You know our belief. I have experienced nothing to change that belief."

"Ah yes, yes. Don't bore me. No, I'm sorry, I didn't mean to insult you, this gout makes me mean. As a matter of fact, if I could believe anything, I suppose it would be your doctrine. At least you people are not hypocrites, like the rest. Catholics, Hussites, Lutherans, Zwinglians, what does it all mean? What does it all matter? And if they spend their time killing each other, how will they ever find out who is right? They can't all be right, can they?"

"No, my lord. But they can all be wrong."

"But someone is right?" There was pathetic longing in the old warrior's voice.

"Yes, my lord. We are right. The people everyone else thinks are wrong . . . we are right."

"Could be . . . could be. The books, the debates, the armies marching, the princes negotiating, the executions in the name of Christ, it's all very . . . complex. Shouldn't it be simple, Herr Ketterling? Shouldn't you be able to find the true Jesus Christ with one simple question?

"What is that question, my lord?"

"Where are the people who really love their fellow men as themselves? Christ commanded that, I think."

"It's a good test, my lord."

The count shifted painfully. "So, Herr Ketterling, why are you here?"

"I lost my wife. I've looked for her in all the places that make any sense. I can't think of what else to do. So I'm going to wait for her here."

"You love her a lot. Maybe I can help. I know some people, highly placed."

Paulus bowed slightly, acknowledging his acceptance of the favor, though he was not hopeful that the count's help would matter much. The count winced as one of the women adjusted his leg.

"Wretched gout, wretched gout," he whispered. "No, I can't believe anything. I'm too old and bitter and I've cursed God too many times, and I guess he's shown how he feels about me. My wife died of consumption, bless her soul – that was long before you and your people came. She gave me two daughters, plain looking to put the best light on it, and one married into the Polish nobility and the other went into a convent, married Christ, as they say. And then this gout. Not much of a life, is it. God, if he is there, has not been good to me."

"My lord, may I be bold?"

"Certainly, what can I do to you if you are?"

"My lord . . . if God were to restore your wife from the dead, and heal your gout, and give you a houseful of sons, would you then believe in him? Can you say that?"

"It would be easier."

"Then why are the richest and most favored men of this world the most godless? I have, as you said, seen much of the world, and I have seen that faith does not flourish in prosperity."

Von Abersicht grunted and said, "Then I, of all people, should have lots of faith." He snapped his fingers again. "But you must go now. I have to relieve these miserable bowels. Getting into position to empty my stinking bowels is like a military operation. You stay here as long as you want. If you need anything, ask." Paulus was about to turn and leave. Von Abersicht suddenly growled, with something of young martial ferocity. "Herr Ketterling!"

"Yes, my lord." Paulus was startled.

"I won't let them drive you out again. You won't fight, but I will. I'll be down there with my horse and fight them. I'll swing my leg at them. I'll empty my bowels on them. I'm going to die soon, I'd enjoy one last tussle, even if I lose."

Paulus bowed. "Thank you, my lord. And I will pray for your gout, I promise."

He turned to leave as the servants began to lift the count from his bed.

"Herr Ketterling!" said the count. Paulus turned. "What is your wife's name?"

"Marga Roth. Or Marga Ketterling."

"And where might she be?"

"I saw her last in Westphalia. Münster."

"Münster, heavens, that was a mess! But I know some important people in Westphalia. I will look into it, make myself a nuisance to someone. Come and talk with me again, Herr Ketterling. Perhaps this rotten old soul can still be saved."

PAULUS WALKED THE old overgrown paths, and hunted for food. Some of the vegetables in the garden were growing up by themselves. There was still some grain in the storehouse that had not sprouted or molded, buried beneath the surface and protected from the air. He read his Bible at the table, and thought and thought about what he should do. He stayed awake late into the night, listening to the crickets, and slept until the sun heated the room and woke him. At times it seemed almost absurd for him to be here, in the wastes of the east, expecting to find Marga, and he felt like going back to Westphalia. But each day he decided to wait another day, to postpone the decision, and to enjoy being in Montau.

He went again to talk to the count, and the count told him war stories, and the history of the castle. The count had sent some letters of inquiry to noble relatives in Westphalia.

Paulus went again, several days later, and this time the count wanted to talk about God. He was, Paulus found out, a man with an acute sense of righteousness and a monumental disaffection with the lies, tricks, manipulations, and hypocrisies of his class, the ruling class, and the church. He had not been to mass for years. Paulus told the count about his expulsion from the University of Paris and his months of wandering across Germany and Austria. When the count heard this story, he exclaimed:

"That's just how I feel, alone in this tottering old castle. Like I'm the only one who sees the world the way I do."

Paulus told him about Marga. The count's eyes were bright and attentive. "I'll send more letters. I know a few more people."

PAULUS HAD BEEN back in Montau about three months when it happened. One afternoon a male servant from the count, a man Paulus had never seen before, rode into the settlement and summoned him to the count. The old man wanted to talk, he thought. He decided to take his Bible with him.

The count was waiting for Paulus in the main hall of his house this time.

"I have something nice for you," said the count, and lifted his hand. A person entered the room through a door; it was Marga.

She was stunning to Paulus in her beauty. She wore a deep green dress, formal and regal, which came fully to her neck and ended in tufts at her wrists. She held her hands clasped in front of her. Her hair was still long, and although two large swatches of it had been pulled from her temples and tied with a ribbon in back, it still looked as Paulus remembered it: wild and free. Everything was there. The milky skin, the dark lips, the almond shaped eyes, black and intense, the girlish body – how could such a thing survive what she had endured? It was a miracle of God.

He went to her, and they embraced. His arms were above, hers below. He felt the bones beneath her shoulders with his hands, and her little arms tight around his waist. Then they both sank somehow to their knees, weak with joy, and rocked gently back and forth, as if dancing to an inaudible music in their minds. He took deep breaths and filled his lungs with the smell of her hair. He felt her chest in his arms, inhaling, exhaling, alive. There was nothing of any particular form in Paulus' mind. No thoughts, no pictures, no reasonings, no sequences, no words or sentences or memories, just light, pure sunlight, not the illuminated things on which the sunlight falls, but just the sunlight itself seen straight on, blinding and immense. Marga's hands came up to his head from behind and he felt her fingers caressing his hair. How long it had been since he had been touched in love!

He felt the warmth of her breath directly on his ear even before he heard the words.

"I'm sorry," she said. "Forgive me."

"I forgive," said Paulus. They swayed gently back and forth.

"God has given you back to me, bless his holy name," said Paulus. He took her face in his hands, gently, and brushed his fingers over her forehead, eyebrows, cheeks, mouth, and the line of her chin that led down to her neck. These things had been with him only in his imagination for two years.

"It's all there," she said and smiled.

Von Abersicht watched them courteously, allowing them their joy. Once he thrust his knuckle toward his eye.

After many minutes, Paulus and Marga stood.

"Are you happy now, Herr Ketterling?" asked the count.

"Yes, my lord, very happy."

"Your happiness is my happiness. I pulled some strings, called in some favors. I still know a few people. And I got lucky."

"Thank you," said Paulus, and went to the count and took his right hand, his sword hand.

"I can still do a few things. It was my pleasure, believe me." The count ahemmed and said, "I have an invitation for you. Stay with me tonight. There is a clean bedroom, and an expensive bed, I really have some very fine linen that I never use, and I would be honored if you two would enjoy my hospitality. It would make me happy." When Paulus did not reply immediately, the count added: "I insist, I demand it."

The count served them dinner, and there was some quiet conversation. They drank red wine with him. The count dismissed himself to bed.

One of the female servants led Paulus and Marga up some stairs to the bedroom. It had stone walls and an oak floor, but the walls were painted white and the floor was covered with Turkish carpets. The bed in the center of the room was a massive piece of furniture with ornately carved legs that reached almost to the ceiling and supported the curtains and canopy. The room had obviously been cleaned and prepared for them.

"It was the count's bedroom, when his wife was alive," said the servant woman before she left. "He has me clean it once in the year, but this was special." As she left, she couldn't resist another comment. "And the dress, it was his wife's. I had to take it in a bit."

"Thank you," said Paulus as he closed the door. "It's beautiful."

"Heine," she said when they were alone.

"I searched for him," said Paulus. "Believe me, I searched. Marga, believe me that I searched for him. I'm so sorry that your son is lost."

"Paulus, he was your son too."

"Marga, we can't talk too much about Heine, not right now. It would be ungrateful of us to ruin this joy with a sadness we can't control. Let's be happy. It's been so long since I was really, really happy."

"I'm happy, Paulus. There was a time when I couldn't imagine ever being happy again."

"This is the happy time, love. It's real."

Marga pulled open the bed curtains with her two hands. They both looked in. Under the canopy, behind the curtains, it was a small soft world with dusty light and an old, but not unpleasant, aroma. There were puffy, upholstered pillows and embroidered quilts.

She looked at him. He knew what she was thinking; he was thinking the same thing.

"I'm not sure how it stands between us," he said. "I'm not sure we're married. Are we married?"

"I'm not sure," she said.

"We should be sure," said Paulus. "Before we act married. God is here. God is watching."

"I'm so tired, Paulus. Just let me sleep by your side."

Paulus entered the bed, and Marga slid in beside him and put her head in the crook of his armpit, and they pulled the quilts over them to capture the warmth of their bodies. Silently, in joy and peace, they fell asleep together.

PAULUS AND MARGA refrained from sexual intimacy while they reconstructed their friendship. When they returned to Montau, Paulus slept in his bed, and Marga slept in Onkel's, on the other side of the wall that Paulus had built. This restraint was surprisingly easy. The months in Münster had filled their souls with a lifetime of suffering, and waiting, and enduring, and being afraid, and this self-discipline seemed small by comparison. And there was genuine happiness in their merely being together, safe, alive, and whole.

But they had to find their way back to each other, completely.

"Should we even talk about Münster?" she said.

"We have to."

"We should be careful what we say."

"You're right, not everything needs to be said."

They were walking around the settlement of Montau, holding hands.

"I have something wonderful to tell you," he said.

"What?"

"Onkel had a wife."

They were walking on a warm day, and when Marga

heard this she stopped suddenly and grabbed his arm.

"Onkel had a wife?"

"Onkel had a wife. I saw her in Switzerland, where Onkel's congregation came from. She is a handsome woman and very kind, I felt like she should be my mother. She told me the whole story of his life. She was first his concubine, when he was still in the Roman church, and when he left it they married. After he became a believer, and the persecutions began, he developed the idea that they should just end their marriage and be celibate. He was afraid of torture. When the people of his village were chased out of Switzerland, he told her to stay behind, and never saw her again."

"You were wrong," she said. "Wrong about him, all the time."

"In a way, yes. He never lied to me about this, he just never told me the whole truth. He talked sometimes about his longing for a woman, and I thought it was the longing of a man who had never had a woman. But it was the longing of a man who had lost a woman."

"This is not a man I can resent any more," she said, shaking her head.

"Did you resent him?"

"Oh yes," Marga said slowly. "Not even so much before he died. I pitied him. But after he died, and you continued to think about him, then I resented him. It was as if we carried his ghost around with us, everywhere."

"He brought me to Christ, and Christ to me. That's important."

"I know. I know now how important that is."

"And he taught me how to live."

"I know. I'm thankful to him now. And I admire him somehow . . . he was trying, in a clumsy, stupid way, to spare his wife the pain he knew was coming. He was thinking of her feelings."

A strange thing, that the fact that had liberated Paulus from Onkel was now drawing Marga closer to the old man.

"And let me guess," said Marga, "he had a son that he somehow lost."

"Yes. How did you know this?"

"I guessed it. Am I right? It all makes perfect sense, Paulus. He had obviously treated you as a son. I shouldn't have said that I resented him, I'm sorry. But I was jealous."

"I love your jealousy. It irritates me, it's sinful, but I love it."

"So Onkel had a wife," she said, and smiled. "That changes everything, doesn't it."

"It changes a lot."

"I'm not sure completely for the better."

"What do you mean?" asked Paulus.

"I mean, that now you can love me and be my husband, and still be doing what Onkel did. I know I'm a possessive woman, Paulus, but I was looking forward to winning you *from* Onkel. I wanted you to choose me instead of him. Me *over* him. Now you can have us both."

Now Paulus was emphatic. "You're wrong. Onkel had a wife, but he chose not to keep her. I will not follow him in that. I choose against him."

"You were not sure, were you, the first time, when you married me. Sure that it was the right thing to do."

"Not completely. Oh, I loved you, and wanted you so much I couldn't help myself. I think that even if Onkel had been standing there saying, *Don't marry her! Don't marry her!*, I would still have married you."

"And you would have felt bad about it. I had your love, Paulus, but not your mind. You were willing to let the marriage crumble under the events. In your heart you were an Anabaptist monk with a concubine."

Those words stung. Marga could still sting. "We were

going to be careful what we said," he said.

"That was very carefully said. I felt it for four years."

"I am not an Anabaptist monk. Not any more. I've chosen you. But I *am* an Anabaptist. Are you?"

"What do you mean?"

"If I was an Anabaptist monk, you were an Anabaptist soldier with a sword behind your back all the time. I mean, do you believe in our doctrine of peace?"

She looked down, then up at him, but before she could speak, Paulus pushed on; he had to say this clearly.

"I believe in peace," he said. "It is what I believe, and it is what I am. It is how I am going to live, no matter what happens. And I am tired of wondering about what you think. I need to know that you are with me."

"Do you mean, can I live with a man who will not lift a finger to defend me?"

"Exactly. And can you live without lifting a finger to defend *me*? Can you let Jesus Christ do it?"

"I will try, Paulus. Because I *believe* this too, as you do. But I am not going to be a fool and say how I will behave in a crisis."

"The crisis comes and we have to trust God, Marga. I stood with a pike in my hands, and I really wondered what I was going to do, if I had not been hit first. But I am still a man of peace. I just want to know that you believe as I do, in your heart."

"I do."

"What changed your mind?"

"Nothing. I always believed it, since my baptism."

"Then why did we argue?"

"Because I didn't like it. Maybe I still don't. I was testing you, I guess. I'm a contentious person. But I know now, after Jan Bockelson, that I like the other way even less."

"I just want you to know that I have not changed my

doctrine."

She pondered. "Paulus, I'm a different person from the one that went to Münster, and so are you. I think what we need is a new covenant."

"Between us?" he said.

"Yes, a new marriage. Paulus, are we married? Can we be married when I've had two husbands since you?"

"You'll have to ask the venerable doctors of the Sorbonne about that. For me it's clearer. After Münster fell, I gave you up as dead. I didn't know if you were dead, but I gave you up as dead. Isn't that almost like a writ of divorce?"

"I don't know, was it?"

"Yes, I think so. I was sending you away. Maria said that I just got tired of loving."

"Paulus, we've tangled this whole thing up, haven't we. We need to get married, again. I think we need a new covenant."

"WILL YOU WITNESS our covenant, my lord?"

Paulus and Marga stood before the Count von Abersicht, in his great hall. Outside, it was raining heavily, and the sound of water splashing down the gutters could be heard through the open windows.

"I don't understand, I'm afraid," said the count.

"It's a wedding, between us," said Paulus. "We were married once, but too much sin has come in between, and we want to marry each other again. Will you be our witness?"

The count smiled in a silly way, then frowned, then smiled again. "It's heretical, you know, to marry without a priest. It won't be a real sacrament." He laughed. "You must promise never to tell anyone that I participated in this."

"We promise. But you must promise something too."

"What?" The count was not accustomed to demands being made upon him by commoners.

"You will hear our covenant with each other. At the

judgment day, you will bear witness against us if we break it."

"And must I follow you around like a chaperone?"

"God will do that."

"Then go ahead. Wait! Come!" He clapped his hands a couple of times and the servant women came to his side. "I want you to see this," he said to them. "These people really love each other. You don't see much of that, watch it closely."

Paulus had a piece of paper with him, on which both he and Marga had written their promises. "You read first," he said to her.

"This is my covenant with Paulus Ketterling: I will remain with him until I die, or he dies. I will not run from him, with my feet or with my heart. I will not desire another man, or give myself to another man. If I become unhappy, I will remember my sins and God's grace to me, and I will cling to Paulus Ketterling as the man God has given me." She took the pen that lay ready on the table and signed her name beneath her vow. Then Paulus read.

"This is my covenant with Marga Roth: I will remain with her until I die, or she dies. I will not consider her a burden or a hindrance to me, but a gift of God. I will be happy in her company, and bear her load, and do my best to fill her life with joy." He signed his name below hers.

"Do I need to say something here?" asked the count, fascinated.

"No, the promises make the marriage," said Paulus.

“Strange, strange people,” muttered the count.

They rolled the paper up and bound it with a string, and Paulus asked the count if he had a vault or a chest where it would be safe. He did; there they left their new covenant. They went back to Montau as husband and wife.

"HOW DID YOU feel when you went to Münster?"

"Free," said Marga.

"Free from me."

"Not free from – free to. I never really wanted to be free from you. It seemed to me that there must be something I could do . . . against evil. So much evil, evil everywhere, and we seemed so ineffectual against it."

"Free to fight," he said.

"Yes, free to fight, free to be good and right and not be ashamed of it. That's how I felt. And I looked forward to smiling and shouting together with other believers. Victory, I looked forward to victory. You know, I hoped that the prince-bishop would get together enough mercenaries for a real battle. I hoped that he would not run out of money. I wanted to see us win."

"Did you think about me?"

"At first, often. Then, for a long time, hardly at all. Then, towards the end, all the time. Usually, when I thought about you, I felt sorry for you."

"I don't want that, ever," he said, the pitch of his voice rising. "I don't ever want you to feel sorry for me. Whatever I am, I am because I want to be, and for such a person there is no need to feel sorry."

She stared at him, a little unnerved. "Don't get angry," she said.

"That's what I felt, more than anything else, your pity. Toward the end, before you left, I could feel your pity. Your disdain. I was not worth your arguing or persuading. You pitied me and left me that way."

"Be fair, Paulus. Could I have persuaded you to come to Münster?"

"No, but you didn't try."

"Others did. I heard them."

"But you were my wife."

"I'm sorry. I'm sorry."

"Your silence murdered me, again and again."

"I'm sorry."

Stop, Paulus, be careful what you say. You live in a new covenant with this woman. You murdered her, too.

"Maybe you shouldn't tell me how you felt," Paulus said.

"No, Paulus, we have to say these things. You're wondering about me, and I'm wondering about you. What happened to us wasn't one of the normal things that happens to people. We can't draw on some accumulated store of common human experience, there's nobody else to talk to."

"We just need to be careful, love. Not everything needs to be said."

"WHAT WAS HE like?"

"Bockelson?" Marga's eyes said that she did not really want to talk about this.

"Yes," Paulus insisted.

"Powerful. He had power over people. He had a style, a flair. It is said that when the prince-bishop finally saw him up close he said, *And you are a king*?" Marga used the German *du* for *you*, the form of address used for children and inferiors. "And Bockelson replied, also with *du*, *And you are a bishop?"*

"Did he have a demon?"

"Maybe, maybe, now that I see it all from a distance. At his execution he was in one of his trances. He went through the torture with scarcely a sound or a motion, as if he felt nothing. Only once did he cry out."

Paulus got the wave of sickness that the mere mention of torture gave him. *Just like poor Michael Sattler,* he thought. "They made you watch it?"

"Oh, yes. The prince-bishop brought us out and lined us up like cattle and ordered us to see what would happen to him. After that they let us go."

As the surge of nausea passed, his forehead became clammy. He closed his eyes to stop the sensation that the room was reeling. "I saw him many times and felt his power too, in spite of my loathing of the man. I could feel how the others felt. There was a time, at night, when I wanted to scream along with the whole city."

"I know it too. When I first came, I was confused, and frightened, and felt guilty about leaving you. If you could have reached me then, I might have listened. But all the new refugees, especially the women, were brought before the king. He looked them over like cattle at a sale. The men he interrogated, and felt the muscles of their arms, and even looked at their teeth. It's unbelievable, I know, I see that now, but the man could do it and it seemed right. He seemed right doing such things. That's what I mean by power over people. With the women, it was a different kind of scrutiny. He didn't touch us, at least at first. He just looked into our eyes. I think he could tell by looking into our eyes whether we really believed in him or not, so there was no theological questioning."

"You believe that – that he could tell your faith by looking into your eyes?"

"I think so. The day I came there were about ten or twelve other women with me. We passed by him one by one. It was the eye contact, with his eyes he could open up your soul and lay it bare and place into it whatever he wanted. When his eyes were on me, I thought, *Here is a man of God!* because he seemed almost physically full of the Spirit. I was tired of meek, gentle men, as I thought of you. I was tired of men that I pitied. I wanted a hero, a doer, a real man of God. Right then and there, he saw me and selected me."

"This business of manhood, it really bothers me."

"I love you, Paulus. You are my man. I shouldn't be telling you about Jan Bockelson. He was nothing compared to you."

"I want you to know how I think about it. No man can think about himself as a coward. When our Lord Jesus went to the cross, was he a man of lesser, or greater, courage for not lifting a finger to defend himself?" Paulus' voice was rising and thickening.

"Oh Paulus, you are my man."

"I believe it took more courage to do what Jesus did than to do what thousands, millions of other men would have done. I think it takes courage to live as I do."

"I see that now." Tears of remorse welled out of Marga's eyes and went down her cheeks. "Paulus, you have the courage of a lion. To do what you've done, to stand alone as you've stood alone, to chase me into that terrible city, to wait, to starve, to go before bishops and magistrates and ask for our son – it puts to shame the courage of the soldiers who merely kill. Next to you, the knights and the kings are boys with toys. You are my roaring lion."

Paulus felt his spirit soaring, and out of this flying fullness he took Marga's face in his hands and said, "You went into the city of destruction. I came after you to rescue you, and I rescued you!"

"You rescued me, Paulus!"

"I won you back from the king!"

"You won me! You won my heart! Your love was stronger than his spears and guns."

"I fought for you."

"My roaring lion."

THE EXTRAORDINARY COMPLEXITY of what had happened to them both in Münster produced many difficult questions. There was one that Paulus kept thinking about. He did not ask it until there had been much joy, and much love and healing.

"Did he love you, do you think?"

"Bockelson? He was incapable of love. He never received, or gave, a kind word. His dealings with all people were held together by power."

"Did you ever. . ."

"Love him? I knew you would ask that, I guess you have to. No, my love, I did not love him. He would not have allowed it. Love and power can't be together. To be loved is to be conquered."

He had been sitting right where he was now, on the end of his bed, where the wooden frame would hold his weight up, and Onkel had been sitting where Marga now was, when the old man had told Paulus that the love of a woman was power, like an army with banners.

"Onkel was right," said Paulus. "That's why he ran from Maria, because she really loved him."

"He had to have that one island of autonomy."

"Don't be too hard on him. Perhaps he saw it in a different way. . . perhaps he could not in good conscience allow his soul to be conquered by two people at once."

"Maria and Christ, you're thinking."

"Yes."

"Because you've had that thought yourself."

"Yes, I suppose."

"Can you imagine, Paulus, how it has been for me to have to compete with Jesus Christ? Of course, it can't be done, not with you. Let me down from his level. Let me love you, but never like Christ."

"If Jan Bockelson had loved you, would you have loved him too?"

"He loved only himself. He couldn't love anyone else."

IT WAS A SUNDAY, and they were alone in the ruins of Montau.

"We should have worship," said Marga.

"I've almost forgotten," said Paulus. "Thinking about sitting with the brotherhood, singing, praying, it makes me so lonely for the old days."

"We'll have it again some day, I believe. Will you preach to me?"

"Now?"

"Yes."

"I thought you never liked my preaching."

"It was your doctrine that upset me. Your preaching was good, I never knew how good until Münster. Oh, it was one sermon after another in that city, especially in the king's household, the public never heard one tenth of what we heard. It was a torrent of words, prophetic diarrhea. One after another they all said the same things. It was as if the whole kingdom were resting on their hot breath, and if they once let up it would come falling down. I thought, *Paulus wouldn't rant like this, Paulus would explain the scripture, Paulus' voice is not nearly so loud, and he keeps his hands behind his back, and he pauses to think about what he's saying. Paulus would explain the scripture.*"

"I want to do that again, some day, but not today. Let's just read some psalms."

"That's fine for now. But you need to preach again some day. You need to lead the church."

They sat outside, in the sunshine, and read psalms to each other.

AUTUMN CAME, AND with it the question, how would they eat and live? It was answered, unexpectedly, by Count von Abersicht. He sent for them, and when they met him at his table he was emaciated and pale and had trouble talking.

"Herr Ketterling, good day. Are you well?"

"Very well."

"Are you happy?"

"Very happy."

"I envy you, for your youth, and for your happiness. There's no hiding it, is there? I'm dying. You can see it in my face."

He was right, and Paulus said, "I'm sorry, my lord."

"It amazes me how little I care about the things that used to drive me crazy with anxiety. The harvest was poor, but do you think I've given it a thought? This good old castle has held off bandits and Turks, and now is capitulating to the worms and termites, and will certainly continue to do so if it depends on me to fix it. But it really doesn't bother me. I don't care what Kaiser Karl or King Ferdinand do, not even a little. I've been thinking of other things."

He paused to catch his breath, and it almost hurt Paulus physically to watch his labored breathing.

"I want to go to heaven when I die," he said slowly.

"Then you must repent and believe in Christ," said Paulus.

"Will you baptize me?" asked the count. "Baptize me as you people are baptized?"

"I will instruct you, my lord. And then, if you understand and believe, it will be my great joy to baptize you."

"A remarkable man," said the count. "Woman, this is a remarkable man you have here. Never let him go." He wheezed again and his chest rose and fell; his lungs sounded paper thin. "But then, why should it surprise me when you as much as tell me that I am an ignorant heathen? You are not much frightened of me, are you?"

"My lord, God has pressed all the fear from us, I think."

"You will tell me some day how this happened, I hope."

"If you want." Paulus came closer to the count, holding Marga's hand. "There is something else we ask you to do for us."

The count waited. "Well?"

"Our son was taken from us by the authorities. In Wesel. We've searched. You found my wife, and maybe you can find my son."

"I'll do what I can. This is what the Christian religion is

all about, is it not, Herr Ketterling? Love?"

The count was looking at Marga through his flesh-enveloped eyes. "Frau Ketterling, you have beautiful hair. May I touch it?" Marga came closer to him and leaned forward, and her hair fell toward him. He extended a hand with curled, pained fingers, and took some of her hair with the first finger. "Your cheek," he said, "may I touch it? Herr Ketterling, I am not a lecher, but your wife is so beautiful." The count touched her cheek lightly with the knuckles of the cramped hand, and his eyes drifted shut. Marga took his hand in both of her own and kissed it.

"You are a great man, my lord," she said with dignity. "We love you." And she bent and kissed him on his leathery, whiskered cheek. With her lips against his ear, she whispered: "Find me my baby."

Marga moved back to Paulus and the count put his hand back under the blanket that covered his legs.

"Do you understand what you have here?" the count asked Paulus, nodding as he did toward Marga.

"Yes, my lord," said Paulus. "Now I do."

"So, I am to be instructed again, like a child at catechism. Why not? What better thing can a man do with his life than get ready for death? I wish you people would stay here with me, brighten my last days a little, help me clean up my filthy old soul for the judgment day. Will you?"

Made in the USA
Charleston, SC
24 March 2010